31.99   6/1/15   31500243

THE GREAT ZOO
OF CHINA

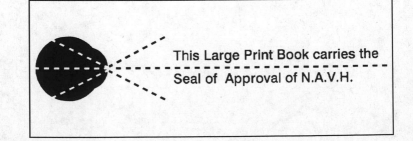

This Large Print Book carries the
Seal of Approval of N.A.V.H.

THE GREAT ZOO OF CHINA

A THRILLER

MATTHEW REILLY

THORNDIKE PRESS
A part of Gale, Cengage Learning

GALE
CENGAGE Learning·

Farmington Hills, Mich • San Francisco • New York • Waterville, Maine
Meriden, Conn • Mason, Ohio • Chicago

Copyright © 2014 by Karanadon Entertainment Pty Ltd.
Map design by Jeffrey Ward.
Thorndike Press, a part of Gale, Cengage Learning.

ALL RIGHTS RESERVED
This book is a work of fiction. Any references to historical events, real people, or real places are used fictitiously. Other names, characters, places, and events are products of the author's imagination, and any resemblance to actual events or places or persons, living or dead, is entirely coincidental.

Thorndike Press® Large Print Thriller.
The text of this Large Print edition is unabridged.
Other aspects of the book may vary from the original edition.
Set in 16 pt. Plantin.

LIBRARY OF CONGRESS CATALOGING-IN-PUBLICATION DATA

Reilly, Matthew.
    The great zoo of China : a thriller / by Matthew Reilly. — Large print edition.
        pages cm. — (Thorndike Press large print thriller)
        ISBN 978-1-4104-7838-2 (hardcover) — ISBN 1-4104-7838-6 (hardcover)
        1. Zoos—Fiction. 2. Dragons—Fiction. 3. China—Fiction. 4. Large type books. I. Title.
    PR9619.3.R445G74 2015b
    823'.914—dc23   2015001709

Published in 2015 by arrangement with Gallery Books, a division of Simon & Schuster, Inc.

Printed in Mexico
1 2 3 4 5 6 7 19 18 17 16 15

For Kate,
Lovely, loyal and brave, too

[American zoos] are visited each year by more than a hundred million people, a number that exceeds the combined attendance of all big league baseball, football and basketball games.

— National Geographic

Here, there be dragons.

— Warning written on ancient maps to define an unknown region

INTRODUCTION

From: Fischer, Adam
China vs the World
(Macmillan, New York, 2013)

CHAPTER 5:
CHINA AND THE POWER OF DISNEYLAND

It is difficult to describe just how dynamic modern China is.

It is setting records that no other country can match: it builds a new city every year, its economy is growing at rates the West can only dream about, and its burgeoning middle class grows wealthier by the month, demanding all of the products that China used to manufacture for Western consumers.

And at every opportunity the Communist Party proudly reports these achievements to the Chinese people through state-controlled media.

But there is a problem.

China desperately wants to be Number One, the preeminent nation on Earth. In the Communist Party this passionate desire even has a name: "the China Dream."

But to achieve that dream, China must seize the position currently occupied by the United States of America, and to do that it must first match America's twentieth-century achievements in war, in space and in industry: it must build a powerful military, it must land a man on the moon and it must create companies that are known worldwide.

And then — *then* — to truly replace America as the world's most dominant nation, it must do something even more difficult.

China must replace the United States as the cultural ruler of the planet.

How America came to dominate global culture is nothing short of astonishing.

After defeating the Axis powers in the Second World War with its military and industrial might, the United States then set about waging and winning a far more subtle war against the whole world: a war of cultural superiority.

This war was not fought with guns or

tanks. It was fought with movies and music, Coke and Pepsi, Fords and Cadillacs, and, of course, arguably America's greatest weapon in soft diplomacy: Disneyland.

Put simply, American culture became the world's culture — drive-in burger joints of the 50s, *Easy Rider* in the 60s, platform shoes in the 70s, Coca-Cola ads in the 80s.

Hollywood played a big part in this, helped along later by MTV. Thanks to hundreds of American movies, TV shows and music videos *set in America,* the names of American cities, towns, roads and products became known worldwide: New York, Vegas, Fargo, Key Largo; Route 66; Mickey Mouse, Donald Duck, Bugs Bunny; DeLorean, Nike, American Express.

Apart from Beijing, Shanghai and Hong Kong, can you name another Chinese city? Can you name a Chinese brand of sport shoe?

What, I ask you, apart from the panda bear and a very long wall, is singularly and uniquely Chinese?

And here lies China's biggest problem in the twenty-first century.

It has nothing truly its own.

It makes other people's stuff. Every Apple product is a slap in the face to China when it declares: *Designed by Apple in California. Assembled in China.* A limitless supply of cheap labor might build you a new city every year, but it ultimately just makes you the factory floor for other countries' companies.

China wants to rule the world. But without the soft diplomacy of *culture,* China will always play second fiddle to the United States.

Where is China's Ford?

Where is its Coca-Cola?

Where, I ask you, is China's Disneyland?

PROLOGUE

Guangdong Province, China
16 February

Breathless, bleeding and covered in sweat, Bill Lynch dropped into the mouth of the cave and crab-crawled further into it as quickly as he could.

He snatched his cell phone from his trouser pocket.

NO SIGNAL. SOS ONLY.

"Fuck," he said to no one. The bastards had jammed the entire valley.

Voices from outside made him spin. They spoke in Mandarin.

"— went this way —"

"— into that cave on the cliff-face —"

Lynch heard the safeties on their assault rifles click off.

Beyond the mouth of the cave, Bill Lynch saw a jaw-dropping view: a broad valley featuring lakes, rivers and waterfalls. In the middle of it all, shrouded by the hazy air common to southern China, was a huge central mountain that stabbed the sky.

Dramatic landscapes like these had rightfully made the nearby region of Guilin famous. Soon, Lynch thought, this copy of the Guilin landscape — and it *was* a copy; it was nearly all man-made — would be more famous than any other place on Earth.

And by the look of things, Dr. Bill Lynch — senior herpetologist from the University of Florida's Division of Herpetology — was not going to live to see it.

Right then, the smell of the cave struck him. Lynch screwed up his nose at the stench, the rank odor of rotting flesh.

The smell of the lair of a carnivore.

Alarmed, he spun to search his newfound hiding place for its owner.

But the cave was empty . . . except for the flesh-stripped skeletons of three large animals. They looked like the skeletons of horses — yes, horses, up in this cave three hundred feet above the valley floor. Their elongated skulls were tilted backwards in frozen shrieks of terror. Their bloody ribs pointed skyward.

Holy shit, Lynch thought.

He knew the creature that lived here.

14

The cave delved into the cliff, and although it looked like a naturally formed cavern, it was not natural. It had been constructed to look that way. Indeed, carved into the otherwise natural-looking floor was a brass plate with an ID code etched into it: E-39.

"Dr. Lynch!" a voice called from outside in English.

Lynch recognized the voice and its Chinese accent.

It belonged to Colonel Bao, the head of security at the zoo and a bona fide asshole.

"Dr. Lynch, we can make this quick and easy for you, or we can make it very painful. Please come out of there so we may do this the easy way."

"Fuck you!"

"Dr. Lynch. This facility cannot be allowed to fail just because of an unfortunate incident."

Lynch stepped deeper into the cave as he spoke: "Unfortunate incident?! Nineteen people are dead, Colonel!"

"Over twenty men died during the construction of the Brooklyn Bridge, Dr. Lynch. Does anyone regret that? No, all anyone sees is a marvel of its time, a great achievement in human ingenuity. So it will be here. This place will be beyond great. It will be the envy of the entire world."

Lynch strode further into the cave. After a dozen steps, he stopped abruptly.

It was a dead end.

There came a sudden *beep!* from his wrist and he looked down to see the green pilot light on his watch wink out.

Lynch's blood went cold. They'd deactivated his sonic shield. Now he had no protection from the animals. Lynch suddenly realized what Bao had meant when he'd said this could be done the easy way or the hard way.

"You can't kill every witness, Bao!" Lynch yelled.

"Yes, we can," replied the voice. "And yes, we will. Fear not, Dr. Lynch. Your death will be a noble one. We will announce it to the world as an awful accident, the result of a light plane crash. It will be such a shame to lose so many brilliant people in the one accident. Of course, our facility will need to find another reptile expert to do what you have failed to do. I was thinking of your protégée, the young Dr. Cameron."

Bill Lynch yelled, "You bastard! Let me give you some free advice. Don't mess with CJ Cameron. She's tougher than I ever was."

"I'll be sure to remember that."

16

"And another thing, Bao. You're a fucking psychopath."

There was no reply.

The Chinese soldiers were probably getting ready to storm the cave.

Lynch turned away, searching for something he could use as a weapon. As he did so, behind his back, a large reptilian head at the end of a long serpentine neck curved in through the entrance to the cave and stared directly at him.

It made no sound.

Lynch snapped a rib off one of the horse skeletons and turned —

The animal now stood in the mouth of the cave.

Its fearsome silhouette completely filled the cave's entrance, blocking out the light. It was a prince, Lynch saw, nine feet tall, wingspan twenty feet. A red-bellied black.

The great beast peered at him as if surprised to find an intruder in its lair.

Its stance was powerful. In the dim light, Lynch could make out its sinewy shoulders and razor-sharp claws. Its wings were folded behind its body. Its long barbed tail slunk back and forth with cool calculation.

But the head didn't move. It was eerily still. In silhouette, the creature's high pointed ears looked like demonic horns.

17

The giant reptile took a step forward. It bent its head low, sniffing the ground.

Then, very slowly, it opened its mouth, revealing two rows of long jagged teeth.

It growled. A deep angry sound.

Lynch felt his heart beat faster and in a deep analytical part of his brain, he realized that the animal could sense this.

He also now realized why Bao had stopped talking from outside. The Chinese colonel and his men had seen this thing coming and had wisely got out of the way.

Bill Lynch had no time for another thought for just then the massive thing roared and rushed at him, and within seconds Lynch was lying on the floor of the cavern, screaming desperately and spitting blood as he was foully eaten alive.

FIRST EVOLUTION

THE UNKNOWN DESTINATION

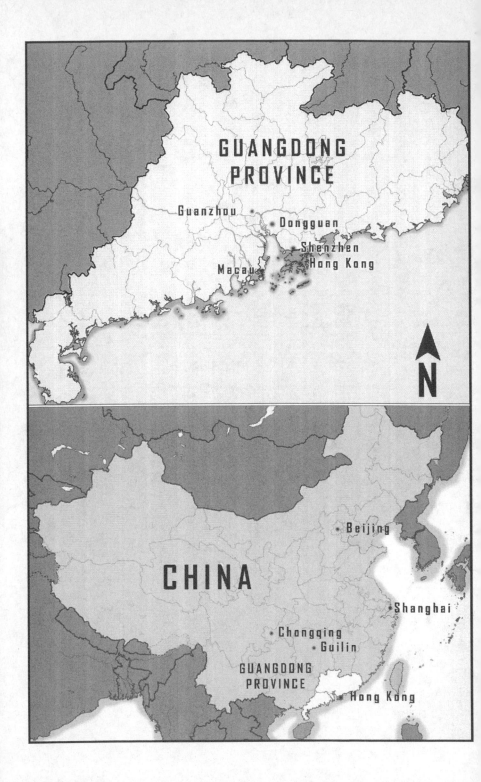

The myth of the dragon is a very peculiar one, precisely because it is a truly global myth.

Giant serpents appear in mythologies from all over the world: China, Scandinavia, Greece, Persia, Germany, Central America, the United Kingdom, even Africa.

There is no discernible reason for this. How could the myth of a large serpentine creature be so consistent across the ancient world?

From: *Dragons in History*
by Eleanor Lock
(Border Press, London, 1999)

Hong Kong, China
17 March
One month later

The sleek private jet shot through the sky above the South China Sea, carrying two passengers who had never flown in a private jet before: CJ Cameron and her brother, Hamish.

The plane was a Bombardier Global 8000, the most expensive private aircraft in the world, the jet of choice for Saudi princes and Russian billionaires. This Bombardier, however, did not belong to any individual. It belonged to the Chinese government.

Dr. Cassandra Jane "CJ" Cameron peered out her window as the plane landed at Hong Kong International Airport, an ultramodern facility that had been constructed on an enormous man-made island.

"Is there anything China can't build?" CJ said, gazing out her window.

"I heard they built some wholly fake Apple Stores," Hamish said. "Did you read about that? It wasn't just a few counterfeit iPhones, they were whole frigging *stores*. They even had Genius Bars. All the employees thought they really were working for Apple!"

CJ threw a sideways glance at her brother. "Wiseass."

A black Maybach limousine was waiting for them at the base of the jet's airstairs. Standing beside it was a pretty young Chinese woman dressed in a perfectly pressed navy skirt-suit. Not a hair on her head was out of place. She had a Bluetooth earpiece in her ear that looked to CJ like it lived there permanently. When she spoke, her English was flawless.

"Dr. Cameron, Mr. Cameron, welcome to China," she said. "My name is Na and I will be your escort during your stay here. Should you require anything — anything at all — please don't hesitate to ask. Nothing is too much trouble."

Na ushered them into the Maybach, which whisked them out a side gate. No Customs and Immigration. The limo then took them to the Four Seasons where they were put up in penthouse suites, all expenses paid. The next morning, they were told, they would be picked up at 9:00 a.m. sharp.

This was all very unusual for CJ Cameron.

Once a renowned herpetologist — a reptile expert — these days CJ worked as a vet at the San Francisco Zoo. At thirty-six, she was a petite five foot six, with piercing amber eyes and shoulder-length blonde hair.

CJ was fit, athletic, and pretty in a sporty kind of way. Men often approached her, only to turn away abruptly when they came close enough to see the grisly scars that dominated the left side of her face.

The scars stretched all the way from her left eye to the corner of her mouth, looking like a sequence of poorly aligned Xs. The ophthalmic surgeon had saved her eyesight. And the plastic surgeon, one of the best in America, had managed to reconstruct her jaw, but the slashing wounds to her left cheek had proven to be too much even for him.

CJ didn't care. For vapid men or for herpetology, not after the incident. All her life she had been something of a tomboy anyway. She didn't bother with makeup and she didn't mind getting her hands dirty. She lived outdoors: hiking, camping, horse riding. A keen horsewoman, she sometimes preferred the company of horses to people.

Once upon a time, she'd been a star

lecturer at the University of Florida's Division of Herpetology, widely regarded as the best reptile faculty in America. Specializing in alligator research, she'd worked mainly at the university's field site in the Everglades.

But not anymore.

In addition to her doctorate in herpetology, she was also a trained veterinarian, and now she worked as far from alligators as possible, tending to sick and injured animals in the clinic at the San Francisco Zoo.

Which was why she'd been surprised when her old boss from *National Geographic,* Don Grover, had called and asked if she'd go to China to write a piece on some big new zoo.

"No thanks," CJ had said.

"It's all expenses paid. Private jet. Swanky hotel."

"That sort of thing doesn't impress me, Don."

"The Chinese asked specifically for you."

That stopped her.

"Really?"

"They've read your stuff. Done their homework. They mentioned the pieces you did for *Nature* on the hunting behavior of saltwater crocodiles and the *Nat Geo* documentary you did with Bill Lynch on alligator vocalizations. The Chinese asked for

26

Lynch to go over there and write a piece on this zoo, but then he died in that plane crash. Now they want you."

CJ had been saddened by the news of Bill's death. He had taught her everything she knew and had begged her not to leave the university after the incident.

"They also know you speak Mandarin," Grover said. "Which is a big plus."

That had been CJ's father's idea. When she and Hamish had been little, their father, a humble insurance salesman with an insatiable curiosity and a penchant for dragging his two children away on unbearable camping trips, had insisted on them taking Mandarin lessons: "The future of the world is China, kids," he'd said, "so you should learn their language." It had been good advice. Their dad wasn't rich or famous, but he'd been ahead of his time on that one. As for the camping trips, he would always dismiss their whining complaints with the cheerful phrase, "Hey, it's character building."

"Photos, too?" CJ had asked Grover.

"It's a full-feature spread, kid. Come on, do it for me. The Chinese government is gonna pay me a king's ransom for this. It'll cover my bills for five years, and your fee will pay yours for ten."

"I want to bring my own photographer," CJ said flatly.

"Who?"

"Hamish."

"Goddamn it, CJ. So long as I don't have to bail him out of jail for deflowering some senior minister's daughter —"

"Deal breaker, Don."

"Okay, okay. You can take your stupid brother. Can I call the Chinese back and say you're in?"

"All right. I'm in."

And so, a week later, CJ and her brother had boarded the private jet bound for China.

At nine o'clock the next morning, CJ and Hamish arrived in the lobby of the hotel to find Na and the Maybach waiting for them in the turnaround. Na was again dressed in her perfect navy skirt-suit and wearing the Bluetooth earpiece in her ear.

CJ wore her standard field clothes: hiking boots, tan cargo pants, black San Francisco Giants T-shirt and a battered brown leather jacket. Around her neck she wore a leather strap, hanging from which was a three-inch-long saltwater crocodile tooth: a gift from Bill Lynch. She wore her hair tied back in a careless ponytail. After all, they were just visiting a zoo.

She and Hamish slid into the backseat of the Maybach, their destination a military airbase twenty miles inland.

While CJ was immune to the charms of expensive hospitality, Hamish wasn't. Sitting in the back of the limo, he munched on not one but two packets of potato chips.

"How cool is this, Chipmunk?" he grinned. "Free mini bar."

"There's no such thing as a free lunch, Hamish."

"But there *are* such things as free plane rides, free penthouse suites in six-star hotels and" — a surreptitious glance at Na up in the front of the limo — "free bathroom products."

CJ rolled her eyes. "You didn't steal the hotel shampoo?"

"And the conditioner." Hamish wore his tattered multi-pocketed photojournalist's vest over a Bob Dylan T-shirt. He lifted the flap on one pocket to reveal four hotel-sized shampoo and conditioner bottles. "It's Molton Brown. That's top-shelf."

"Why do you need shampoo? You hardly bathe anyway."

"I bathe." Hamish sniffed his underarms.

"You're an idiot."

"No. I'm *awesome.*" Hamish settled into

29

the seat beside her and resumed munching his chips.

They couldn't have been more different, CJ and Hamish, in size and in personality. The Bear and the Chipmunk, that's what their mother had called them.

It suited.

Four years younger than CJ and a towering six foot three inches tall, Hamish was large in every way: a photographer and videographer who had done tours in Afghanistan and Iraq, he lived large, partied hard, drank a bit too much and was always getting into trouble. He even had oversized features: a big face, square jaw, huge blue eyes and a great booming voice. He rarely shaved. He wore a red rubber Wrist-Strong bracelet on his right wrist intertwined with a couple of hemp surfer wristbands.

CJ, on the other hand, had always been the good girl: quiet, mature, unobtrusive and very academic. Having a near-photographic, or eidetic, memory helped with that.

While Hamish went to war zones and parties, she'd worked away at the university, penning papers on her specialty, reptilian behavior, specifically that of crocodiles and alligators. Among other things, it was CJ who had quantified the intelligence of big crocodilians, proving they were as smart as or even smarter than chimpanzees.

Other intelligent animals — like chimps, wolves and hyenas — might set simple traps. Crocodiles often set traps *several days* in advance. If an eighteen-foot saltwater crocodile saw you coming down to a riverbank at 7:30 a.m. for four days in a row to check your lobster cages, on the *fifth* day it would wait at the water's edge, just below the surface, and pounce when you arrived. Crocodiles had extraordinary patience and amazing memories. Their ability to spot routine was incredible: sometimes they would set up ambushes based on the weekly, even monthly routines of their prey.

CJ's considerable professional success had not been reflected in her personal life. While Hamish had gone through a swathe of girlfriends over the years, CJ had not had many serious boyfriends, just the one in fact, Troy, and that had ended badly: immediately after the incident that had destroyed her face. Only Hamish had stayed by her side, her ever-loyal brother.

"Is everything okay back there?" Na said from the passenger seat up front.

"We're fine," CJ said, glancing at her brother's stolen hair care products.

"Remember, nothing is too much

trouble," Na said as the limo turned off the main road and zoomed through the gates of the airbase without stopping. Clearly, Na had called ahead. "If you need anything, just ask."

The Maybach drove out onto the runway, where CJ saw the Bombardier from the previous day waiting for them, its airstairs folded open. Only today, CJ noticed, there was something different about the private jet.

All its windows had been blacked out.

CJ stepped warily up the airstairs.

"Why black out the windows?" she whispered to Hamish.

"I have no idea," Hamish said, equally concerned. He carried his Canon EOS 5D digital SLR camera slung over his shoulder.

Arriving in the plush main cabin of the jet, CJ stopped, surprised.

Already seated there were two Americans, both men, one of whom was in the process of being interviewed by a Chinese television crew.

CJ paused in the doorway, not wanting to interrupt.

She had always been a good observer, a close watcher of things. It came, she guessed, from observing predators in the wild — you didn't settle in to watch a croc or a gator without first assessing the surrounding area for other predators. Whether she was in a shopping mall, a meeting or here in a private jet, CJ's eyes always swept the area for important details — and with her memory, she remembered everything.

She saw many details here.

A sticker on the television camera read CCTV: that was the Chinese state television network. The cameraman's jacket was a cheap Lacoste rip-off, common in China. The female TV reporter looked like a stewardess on an airplane: crisp brown skirt-suit with the same CCTV logo on the breast pocket.

The American being interviewed — and he seemed quite comfortable being the center of attention — was a big-bellied man of about fifty with a carefully trimmed gray beard that had clearly been grown in an attempt to conceal his wobbly jowls, the jowls of a man who had enjoyed many long lunches.

"That's Seymour Wolfe," Na whispered reverently to CJ, "from *The New York Times.*"

Na needn't have singled him out. CJ knew who he was. Everyone knew who Seymour Wolfe was.

He was not just a columnist at the *Times,* he was *the* columnist, the paper's most well-known and influential op-ed writer. After a few successful books on twenty-first-century global affairs, he was regarded as the man who informed America about the world.

He also, CJ saw, appeared entirely untroubled to be travelling in a jet with blacked-out windows.

CJ heard snippets of what Wolfe was saying:

"— I was here for the Beijing Olympics in 2008. What a spectacle! Things move so fast here. If the government wants a new high-speed train built, it is built. If it wants a new city, then a new city is built. It is just so *dynamic* —"

"— China is the future and the rest of the world had better get used to it. One in five people on this planet is Chinese —"

The CCTV reporter smiled broadly, almost fawning as she asked, "Are you excited about what you are going to see today?"

Wolfe leaned back and smiled. "I'm not sure what to think, as I don't yet know exactly what I am going to see. If China has reimagined the concept of the zoo, then I am curious to see what she has done. I cannot imagine it will be small. I am . . . how shall I put this . . . officially intrigued."

The interview concluded and CJ and Hamish were ushered inside the jet.

Na introduced them to Wolfe, before

indicating the other, much younger man travelling with him. "And this is Mr. Aaron Perry, also from *The New York Times,* from their e-news division."

Aaron Perry was about thirty and he had spiky black hair that had been carefully molded into position with large amounts of gel. He wore serious thick-framed glasses, a designer suit and the attitude of someone who knew more than you did. He slouched in his seat. CJ hadn't heard of him, but evidently Hamish had.

"You're the Twitter guy!" Hamish boomed. "I love your shit, dude. Forget the paper, I get all my news from your Twitter feed."

"Thank you." Perry smiled wanly, apparently too cool to accept praise. He held up a small Samsung phone. "My office. Although not today."

"Why not?" CJ asked.

Na answered. "Our destination is a secure facility. It is covered by an electronic scrambling system. No cell phone signals in or out."

"And the blacked-out windows?" Hamish asked. "You don't want us to see where we're going?"

"Please forgive us, but the location of our zoo is a closely guarded secret, at least for

36

now," Na said. "Not only must cell phone tracking systems be disabled, but even visual references. You will understand why when we get there. I am very sorry."

The blacked-out Bombardier didn't take off immediately. Apparently, it was still waiting for two final passengers.

As the plane waited, the Chinese TV reporter approached CJ.

"Dr. Cameron?" she asked. "Dr. Cassandra Cameron from the San Francisco Zoo? I am Xin Xili, China Central Television. Would you mind if I interviewed you?"

"Sure," CJ said.

The reporter gave CJ a quick up-and-down, her gaze pausing for the briefest of moments on the scars on CJ's left cheek. It was not exactly a pleasant evaluation.

When the interview began, the fawning smiles of her interview with Wolfe vanished.

"You are an expert in reptiles, are you not, Dr. Cameron?" Xin asked quickly.

"I am."

"One of the world's leading experts in large reptiles: the Nile crocodile, the Australian saltwater crocodile, the American and Chinese alligators."

"That's correct," CJ replied.

"Not for much longer," Xin said curtly.

She then signalled for the cameraman to stop recording, smiled tightly at CJ and turned away.

CJ watched her go, perplexed.

Just then, another private jet pulled up alongside the Bombardier, a smaller and much older Gulfstream.

Looking out the open door, CJ saw that it had an American flag painted on its side plus the words UNITED STATES DIPLOMATIC SERVICE.

Two men in suits emerged from the Gulfstream and walked over to the Bombardier.

The taller and older of the two — he wore a perfect gray suit, had perfect silver hair, a perfect tennis tan and perfect teeth — swept into the jet as if he owned it. He smiled broadly at everyone, the practiced smile of a professional politician.

"So sorry to keep you waitin', folks," he said with a distinctly Texan drawl. CJ noticed he was wearing expensive cowboy boots. "I'm Kirk Syme, U.S. Ambassador to China. Just flew down from Beijing. Got caught on the phone to the President. You know how it is when the boss is on the line. You gotta take the call." He indicated his offsider. "This is Greg Johnson, my chief aide from the embassy in Beijing."

Johnson was a younger and more compact version of Syme: about forty, with close-cropped salt-and-pepper hair and sharp dark eyes. He carried himself in an odd way, CJ thought, tensed, hunched, like an athlete who seemed uncomfortable wearing a suit. He did not, she saw, wear cowboy boots like his boss, just regular brogues.

With everyone present and accounted for, the Bombardier's airstairs folded up and the plane taxied down the runway.

CJ still felt a little unnerved sitting inside the blacked-out plane. It was claustrophobic and, well, kind of weird. It was a very trusting thing to do, to allow yourself to be flown to an unknown destination. But then, she told herself, she *was* travelling with some serious VIPs — the U.S. Ambassador to China and two high-profile *New York Times* journalists — and they seemed perfectly fine with the arrangement.

The Bombardier took off, heading to God-only-knew-where.

The Bombardier flew for about two hours.

We could be anywhere in southeast Asia, CJ thought. Thanks to the blacked-out windows, she didn't know if they had flown in a straight line or in circles.

The Chinese were very keen to keep the location of their new zoo secret.

When it finally landed, the Bombardier taxied for a few minutes before coming to a halt at an airbridge. The six American guests disembarked to find themselves standing inside a brand-new airport terminal. The walls and floors gleamed. None of the many shops were open but they looked ready to go. The entire terminal, built to handle the movement of thousands of people, was eerily empty.

High floor-to-ceiling windows revealed the landscape outside: spectacular mountains and moss-covered limestone buttes.

"Ah-ha, we are still in southern China,"

Seymour Wolfe said. "If I were to hazard a guess, I'd say we are in the north of Guangdong province."

Na nodded and smiled.

As she guided them all through the empty airport, Wolfe said, "This area is famous for these incredible landforms. Towering pinnacles and mossy buttes. There's a well-known crater out here not unlike Meteor Crater in Arizona: it's not as big as Meteor Crater, but it's beautiful, perfectly circular, and over the eons it has filled with water, so it's called Crater Lake."

Na said, "That is correct, Mr. Wolfe. Crater Lake was created by a nickel meteorite that hit here about three hundred million years ago."

Wolfe said, "Make no mistake, people, with its natural wonders and its industrial centers, southern China is a commercial juggernaut, the engine room of the entire country. The two megacities of this area, Guangzhou and Dongguan, are home to sixty million people. But fly a short way inland and the cities vanish and you essentially travel back in time to landscapes like this. Out here, you'll find only small communities of rice farmers."

Three Chinese officials were waiting for them near the exit.

They were all men.

The first was dressed in a bright red blazer with a yellow tie. He had slicked-down hair and a pencil moustache and Na introduced him as Zhang, the deputy director of the zoo. CJ noted that he had a peculiar nervous tic: he kept smoothing his tie, as if it had a crease he couldn't flatten out.

The second man wore a military uniform. The stars on his shoulders indicated that he was a colonel. He had no nervous tics. He stood with the firm, feet-apart stance of a commander who was used to being obeyed.

Na introduced him as Colonel Bao, and when he shook CJ's hand, he said in English, "Dr. Cassandra Cameron? You are Dr. Bill Lynch's protégée, are you not? He actually visited our zoo. I was most saddened by his death."

"So was I," CJ said.

The last Chinese man was easily the youngest. He was a lean, handsome fellow of about forty-five. He wore a stylish navy suit and a dark tie: the standard attire of a Communist Party member. He also had one singular physical feature: just above his right eye, he had a sharply defined patch of pure white hair on his otherwise black-haired head, a condition known as poliosis. CJ had known a few people in her life who'd had poliosis and they'd dyed the offending patch of snow-white hair, making it disappear. This man had not done that: in an otherwise entirely black-haired country, his white forelock made him distinctive and he was evidently quite happy about that.

"Why, hello!" he said brightly to them all in English. "I am Hu Tang."

As Hu moved down the line of visitors, Seymour Wolfe whispered to CJ: "Don't be fooled by his age. Mr. Hu Tang is the most senior man here. Youngest ever member of the Politburo. He's what they call a 'princeling' of the Communist Party, a member of the Red Aristocracy, those party members who trace their ancestry to great revolutionaries like Mao. Educated at Harvard, Hu Tang is part of the new wave. He supervised the construction of the Great Firewall of China, the system that censors the Internet here. Now he's the head of the Department of Propaganda and a member of the all-powerful Standing Committee of the Politburo."

"They have a department of propaganda?" Hamish said in disbelief.

CJ ignored him. "The U.S. Ambassador *and* a Chinese heavy hitter? What kind of zoo is this?"

"I'm wondering the same thing," Wolfe replied.

Hu Tang spread his hands wide. "Ladies and gentlemen, welcome. Welcome to the most incredible place on Earth."

A short walk to a beautiful — and also brand-new — glass-enclosed train station followed. It was a gigantic space with a curved glass-and-steel roof.

Four state-of-the-art maglev trains were parked at parallel platforms underneath the high soaring roof. The bullet-shaped trains looked very fast and very, very powerful.

A huge red sign above the space blazed in English and Mandarin:

Welcome to the
Great Zoo of China!

Within a minute, CJ and her VIP party were aboard one of the trains and zooming through a tunnel at four hundred miles per hour, heading for the mysterious zoo.

As the train shot through the tunnel, Hu Tang and Deputy Director Zhang spoke with the U.S. Ambassador and his aide.

Even in a group such as this, CJ saw, a subtle hierarchy still existed, and a good host always spoke to his most important guests first.

CJ and Hamish sat with the two *New York Times* journalists further down the carriage. The lights of the tunnel outside whizzed by like laser bolts in a science-fiction movie.

Wolfe said: "This region of China is the perfect place for a new tourist attraction. The weather is better than in the north and the region is already buzzing with business and tourist activity.

"Hong Kong is the party town, all glitz and glamor. Macau is Vegas, keeping the casino crowd entertained. Mission Hills golf resort isn't far from here — *eighteen* golf courses designed by the likes of Jack Nicklaus, Greg Norman, Nick Faldo and Annika Sorenstam. Biggest golf complex in the world. But then, that's what China does better than anyone else."

"What's that?" Hamish asked.

"Big," Wolfe said. "China does *big* better than any other country, including America. Mission Hills is the perfect example. How do you build eighteen golf courses — *courses* — in the rainforests of Guangdong? Easy. You pay the best golf-course designers in the world whatever price they ask and then you bring in an army of laborers and a whole lot of dynamite and you shape the landscape to your needs. Then you build hotels adjoining those golf courses and provide a superfast ferry to convey golfers there from Hong Kong and — *voilà!* — your mega-resort is ready to go."

"Do you think that's what they've done here with this zoo?" CJ asked.

Wolfe shrugged. "There have been whispers of a major project in these parts for a long time. There are rumors that a special no-fly zone has been imposed on this region for some time and since all the local airlines are government-owned, it's easy to enforce."

"Sounds expensive," Hamish said.

"In a world of debt, young man, China is a net *creditor,*" Wolfe said. "They have the

46

largest cash reserves in the world: $3.7 trillion at last count. And that's not including the $1.4 trillion that America owes them!

"When they built the Three Gorges Dam — the biggest dam in history — they didn't have to issue a single bond. They paid for it out of national savings. In the last ten years, China has built over two thousand miles of maglev bullet-train tracks like the ones we are travelling on now, without borrowing a cent.

"Cost is no issue. China has a limitless supply of cheap human labor to build this kind of infrastructure. The world has not seen such a concerted effort in national infrastructure-building like this since Britain built its railways in the nineteenth century."

The Twitter guy, Aaron Perry, looked over at that, emerging from his splendid isolation. He had been writing notes on his otherwise useless phone till then. "And as far as the Chinese *people* are concerned, led by the ever-fabulous Communist Party, China leaps from one great achievement to the next. The state news agency, Xinhua, is a mouthpiece for the party and would never question any announcement from it. Take the great media fraud that is China's GDP figures."

"Aren't they supposed to be amazing?" CJ said.

"They *are* amazing," Perry said. "A little too amazing. It takes Western nations about *three months* to ascertain their Gross Domestic Product figures. In China, it takes one week. One week. It's as if the central government is telling each region what numbers to present.

"And no one in the Chinese media questions it. But, then, who would dare? Never forget, the Communist Party of China is perhaps the most successful authoritarian regime in history. It is ruthlessly repressive. China smiles and plays nice for the world, but it is still a very dangerous place to be a dissenter.

"Take Tiananmen Square. The massacre that took place there in 1989 has been effectively erased from Chinese history. During the recent 25th anniversary of the massacre, prominent activists, artists, journalists and students were rounded up and placed in 'detention centers' for fifteen days, so they couldn't talk about it. Hell, if you Google 'Tiananmen Square' on a computer inside China, you only get tourist information about the square. Tourist information! You get nothing about the massacre. The Chinese government will not tolerate any kind of dissent and it will move quickly and decisively to crush anyone suggesting change."

Hamish nodded. "Yeah. Like with Bob Dylan."

Perry paused at that, not understanding. Wolfe did, too. "Huh?"

Hamish said, "Bob Dylan. The singer. You know: 'Blowin' in the Wind,' 'All Along the Watchtower.' "

"We are aware of who Bob Dylan is," Wolfe said flatly.

"Dylan did a concert in China a few years back," Hamish said. "But the Chinese Culture Ministry insisted on approving the set-list that he would sing. And Dylan *didn't* sing 'The Times They Are a-Changin'.' I mean, it's his most famous song. A song all about change. The Chinese government was afraid of a *song.* Don't you guys follow the music scene?"

Wolfe coughed. "Well, no, not really."

Hamish indicated the Bob Dylan T-shirt underneath his vest. "You didn't think I wore this shirt by accident, did you?"

CJ smiled at her brother.

"Still, China faces a problem," Wolfe said, resuming his role as information giver.

"What's that?" CJ asked.

"The construction of the Three Gorges

Dam was supervised by an American company, Harza Engineering. The new Hong Kong International Airport was designed by Norman Foster, the British architect. This maglev train could only have been built by one of two German companies, Siemens or ThyssenKrupp.

"China's problem is that it builds nothing of its own. Whatever we are about to see, take note of the nationality of the designers and experts who built it. Few will be Chinese. That said," Wolfe shrugged, "I must confess that I really am rather intrigued. Bringing a cohort of international journalists to see some new zoo is not exactly earth-shattering. It's a standard marketing tool. Nor is bringing the U.S. Ambassador, for that matter — he might have helped a U.S. company get an important contract on the project or something like that. But the presence of Hu Tang lifts this mysterious trip to a whole new lofty height. Politburo princelings do not act as tour guides. Something is going on here. Something big. And it looks like we are about to get a front-row seat to see exactly what that is."

He nodded over CJ's shoulder. She turned.

Hu Tang and Deputy Director Zhang — followed and filmed by the CCTV crew —

were coming down the aisle toward them.

Hu stopped in front of the group.

He threw a quick glance at the deputy director, who checked his watch and then nodded.

CJ saw it. It was as if they were timing this speech to coincide with something.

"Ladies and gentlemen," Hu began, "thank you for joining us on this most auspicious day. Today you will see a project that will be like nothing you have ever witnessed before, a $244 billion project that has been forty years in the making. It is a zoo that was built in absolute secrecy because when it is revealed to the world it will cause a sensation.

"Now, I know what you are thinking." Hu Tang paused. "You are thinking that there are hundreds of zoos, why does the world need another one? Indeed, what can China do with a zoo that has not already been done before? Ladies and gentlemen . . . *this* is what we can do."

At that moment, the speeding bullet train burst out into brilliant sunshine and CJ found herself staring at an awesome sight.

The train zoomed out across a vast trestle bridge that spanned a gorge four hundred feet wide and five hundred feet deep. While spectacular, however, the gorge was not the sight that seized her attention.

On the far side of the gorge sat an absolutely colossal landform that resembled a volcano, with high slanted walls that appeared to enclose an immense valley. It appeared to be rectangular in shape, its sides stretching away into the distance for many miles.

A towering mountain peak poked up out of the center of the rectangular crater, a storybook pinnacle.

And flying around that peak, gliding lazily, their wings outstretched, were seven massive animals, animals that were far larger than any flying creature CJ knew.

Even from this distance — and the train was still at least a few miles from the crater — CJ could clearly make out their shapes: sleek serpentine bodies, long slender necks and, most striking of all, enormous batlike wings.

Five of the creatures must have been the size of buses, while two were bigger still: they each must have been the size of a small airliner.

"Good lord . . ." Wolfe said, mouth agape.

"Holy Toledo . . ." Hamish gasped.

CJ couldn't believe it either, but there they were, lifted from myth and flying around in front of her.

She was looking at dragons.

"Ladies and gentlemen," Hu grinned. "Welcome to our zoo. Welcome to the Great *Dragon* Zoo of China."

■ ■ ■ ■

SECOND EVOLUTION

THE LEGEND OF THE DRAGON

■ ■ ■ ■

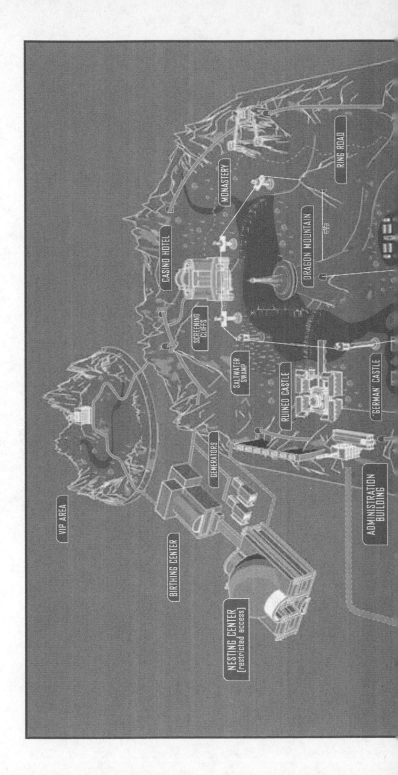

VIP AREA

MONASTERY

RING ROAD

CASINO HOTEL

DRAGON MOUNTAIN

SCREENING CLIFFS

SALTWATER SWAMP

RUINED CASTLE

GERMAN CASTLE

GENERATORS

BIRTHING CENTER

ADMINISTRATION BUILDING

NESTING CENTER [restricted access]

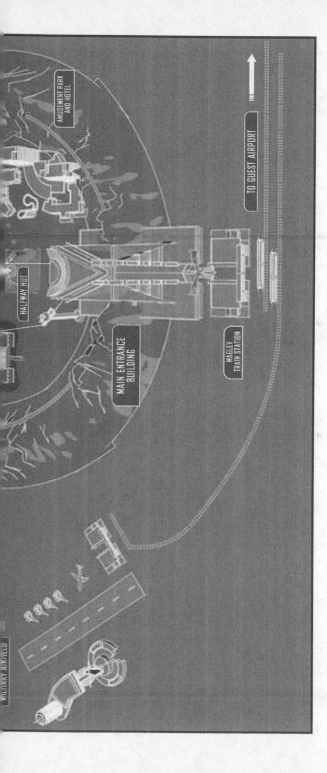

Fairytales cleanse and sanitise what were once true stories.

In fairytales, knights are chivalrous, clean-shaven and wear shining armour — when in truth they were swarthy, filthy rapists and thugs. Castles are bright and gay when in truth they were grim fortresses.

If dragons were real, then in all likelihood they were not graceful, high-chested, noble creatures; rather they would have been dirty, ugly, reptilian and mean.

From: *The Power of Myth*
by Craig Ferguson
(Momentum, Sydney, 2013)

As the train rushed toward the crater, Deputy Director Zhang quickly put on a new blazer.

It was bright red in color, just like his old one, but it bore a different logo on the breast pocket: a gold dragon inside a gold circle, with the Chinese flag filling the background. Ringing the circumference were the words *The Mightiest and Most Magnificent Place on Earth.*

Red information folders emblazoned with the same logo were handed out.

CJ felt both intrigued and misled. A carefully prepared switch had just been executed by her hosts right in front of her eyes.

She also felt a twinge of anger when she saw the smug CCTV reporter, Xin Xili, and her crew filming CJ's surprised reaction. Xin's snide remark about CJ not being one of the world's leading experts on large reptiles for much longer echoed in her mind.

Hu Tang affixed a Great Dragon Zoo of China lapel pin to his jacket and said, "I must apologize for all the fake branding at our train station and on our people's uniforms, but it has been necessary to keep our zoo a secret for so long. As you will see, it is worth it."

About five minutes later, the bullet train pulled into a station in front of the main entrance to the Great Dragon Zoo of China.

The entrance building was magnificent.

Jutting out from the front face of the immense crater, it was a glorious white building that looked like a cross between a castle and a spaceship. It must have been forty storeys tall. Two high-spired towers shot skyward from its roof, framing the central edifice.

The structure's marble walls were glittering white and perfectly smooth. They shone in the sunlight. And there wasn't a sharp corner to be seen on the thing: it was all sweeping curves of marble, glass and steel. It was a postmodern masterpiece.

A long silver drawbridge spanning a moat led to an eighty-foot-high silver door that gave access to the incredible structure. Right now, the drawbridge lay open.

The entire building rose all the way up the southern face of the mighty crater, reaching right up to its rim.

A vast piazza lay before the glistening white building. Standing proudly in the middle of it was a gigantic crystal statue of a dragon rearing up on its hind legs, wings outstretched, jaws bared. It must have been seventy feet tall.

"Our main entrance building was designed by Goethe + Loche, the prestigious German architectural firm," Zhang said as he guided the group out of the train station and across the piazza to the drawbridge. "And our crystal dragon was designed by the French sculptor Christial. It is rather striking, is it not?"

"Magnificent . . ." Wolfe said.

"Superb . . ." Perry said.

CJ said nothing as she walked underneath the statue.

Everything about the scene — the marble square, the crystal dragon statue, the moat and drawbridge, the postmodern castle — it all just sparkled.

It was, she had to admit, impressive. More than that, it was *distinctive,* as distinctive as Disneyland.

But as she considered this, CJ also realized that Seymour Wolfe had been correct: the Chinese hadn't designed any of what she'd seen so far; it had been the work of European architects and artists.

Countless bollards and rope fences had been erected around the square, creating aisles that switched back and forth in anticipation of the enormous crowds the Chinese expected to come here.

There were no queues today, but CJ could imagine them. If the Chinese had really created a zoo with dragons in it, the crowds would be monstrous.

With those thoughts in her mind, she followed her hosts across the drawbridge and through the superhigh silver doorway into the Great Dragon Zoo of China.

Entering the main building, CJ stepped into the loftiest atrium she had ever seen in her life. The ceiling of the vast space hovered an astounding thirty-five storeys above her, as if it had been designed to house a space shuttle.

CJ saw a tangle of white-painted girders up there, suspended from which was a collection of enormous — and very lifelike — dragon sculptures that appeared to be made of fiberglass.

Some had their wings outstretched while others dived toward the ground, hawklike, talons pointed forward. Others still stood on massive pedestals in coiled, crouched stances, as if ready to pounce. All had their fearsome jaws open, fangs bared.

The dragons, CJ noted, came in several sizes. Their colors also varied: some were brilliant and vibrant, with splashes of red-on-black or yellow-on-black, while others were more earthy: rocky grays and olive greens.

Eight glass elevators ran up the side wall of the giant atrium and CJ and her party rode up in one of them, rising past the suspended dragons, all the while filmed by the CCTV crew.

"This," Wolfe said, gazing at one of the more aggressive dragon statues outside the elevator's glass walls, "is simply amazing. This is what it would be like to fly with dragons."

Hu Tang smiled. "My dear Mr. Wolfe. You have not seen anything yet."

The elevator opened onto an entertaining suite. Food and drinks had been laid out.

A fifty-yard-wide bank of floor-to-ceiling windows and glass doors faced north and CJ found herself drawn to them. The glass was tinted to keep out the glare, so she could only just make out the vista beyond the windows.

It looked like a primordial valley, with forests and rock formations, lakes and waterfalls, all of it veiled in the ever-present mist of southern China.

With Hamish behind her, CJ pushed open one of the tinted doors and stepped outside. Sunlight struck her face and she squinted.

When her eyes recovered, CJ saw that she was standing on an enormous, *enormous* balcony. It stretched away from her until it stopped at a vertiginous edge more than four hundred feet off the ground.

CJ stopped dead in her tracks at the view that met her.

"Goddamn," Hamish breathed.

What lay before them was more than just a primordial landscape.

It was a colossal valley, roughly rectangular in shape, encased by high raised rims like those of a meteor crater or volcano. But it was far larger than any meteor crater or volcano that CJ knew of. By her reckoning, this megavalley was at least ten miles wide and twenty miles long.

And it was breathtaking.

The central mountain dominated it, and now CJ noticed a man-made circular structure near its summit. Ringing the central mountain were several lakes and some smaller limestone peaks. The gray soupy mist that overlaid the scene gave it a mythical quality.

CJ could make out some modern multi-storeyed buildings dotting the valley, a couple of medieval-style castles, and an elevated freeway-like ring road that swept around the inner circumference of the crater, disappearing at times into tunnels bored into its rocky walls.

Even more impressive, however, was the network of superlong and superhigh cables from which hung slow-moving cable cars that worked their way around the mega-valley.

And soaring above all of this were the most astonishing things of all: the massive dragons, wings flapping languidly as they banked and soared.

"We're definitely not in Kansas anymore, Chipmunk," Hamish said. "This is even better than when Stephen Colbert took over from David Letterman."

"How do you build something like this?" CJ asked.

Wolfe appeared beside her, also staring slack-jawed at the view. "And without anyone knowing about it?"

Hamish lifted his camera and took a bunch of shots. When he was done, he nodded skyward. "This crater's completely open to the sky. Why don't the dragons — or whatever they are — just fly out of here?"

CJ turned to find their two hosts, Deputy Director Zhang and the politician, Hu Tang, watching them with broad smiles on their faces. They had expected this reaction.

Hu said, "I am sure you all have many

questions. My team and I will be more than happy to answer them. Please, come this way."

They were guided to a wide semicircular pit sunk into the floor of the great balcony, a large amphitheater. It was about the same size as a tennis stadium, with raked seats angled down toward a central podium-like stage.

Looking down on it, CJ noticed that its northward side had been removed entirely, giving spectators seated in the amphitheater an unobstructed view of the glorious mega-valley.

As she and her party waited at the top of the amphitheater, they were each handed a small gift pack branded with the Great Dragon Zoo of China logo.

"Cool! Free stuff!" Hamish exclaimed.

"In boys' and girls' colors," CJ said drily. Her pack was pink, while Hamish's was black. And they were —

"Oh my God, fanny packs," Aaron Perry said. "Hello, 1982."

CJ smiled. They were indeed fanny packs; the kind you wore clipped around your waist and which screamed "tourist."

And, CJ had to admit, Perry was right. They were a bit naff. That was the funny thing about China: it desperately tried to mimic the West but it often seemed to get it wrong in small, clumsy ways.

Hamish — the hotel shampoo thief — burrowed into his fanny pack enthusiastically. "Okay . . . Audemars Piguet watch with Great Dragon Zoo logo: nice. Weird sunglasses with Great Dragon Zoo logo: okay. Thirty-two-megapixel Samsung digital camera with Great Dragon Zoo logo: very nice for the eager amateur. Oh, hey!"

He extracted a Zippo lighter from his pouch, plus two Cuban cigars, all branded with the circular golden logo.

"Now *that's* sweet!" He grinned at CJ. "Check yours out."

CJ looked in her pink pouch. It contained a dainty white Chanel watch with a Great Dragon Zoo logo, plus some odd-looking sunglasses and a digital camera.

"No cigars in the ladies' pack, it seems. But wait . . ." She pulled out a hairbrush, some cosmetics including moisturizer, cleanser and even a small travel-sized can of hairspray, all bearing the Great Dragon Zoo of China logo.

"Nice to know what China expects of a woman," she said flatly. "They forgot to include a Great Dragon Zoo apron."

Na came over. "Please, put on your watches. Audemars Piguet for the gentlemen. Chanel for the ladies. They are very expensive."

CJ could see that. She could also see that despite the packs' oddities — who gave out cigars anymore? — Na was clearly very proud of them. Despite herself, CJ put on the watch *and* the fanny pack.

She felt a tug at her jacket and looked down.

A Chinese girl of perhaps eight was looking up at her and smiling.

"Hello, miss! Are you American? May I practice my English with you?"

CJ smiled. The kid was cute as a button. She held a teddy bear close to her chest and wore an adorable Minnie Mouse cap, complete with mouse ears.

"Certainly," CJ said. "What's your name?"

"My name is Min, but Mama calls me Minnie. What is your name?"

"I'm Cassandra, but my mom calls me CJ."

Minnie, it appeared, had been at the head of another group of visitors leaving the

70

amphitheater. They emerged from it now behind her.

This group comprised four Chinese men, all in their fifties and all dressed in outdoorsman gear: cargo pants, khaki vests, hiking boots, slouch hats. They emerged from the amphitheater chatting excitedly, oohing and aahing. All four wore their black fanny packs clipped to their waists.

One of the men said to CJ in English: "I hope my granddaughter is not bothering you, miss."

"Not at all," CJ said, smiling. "She wanted to try out her English and it's excellent."

Behind the men came three Chinese women in their mid to late forties. All three wore expensive designer clothing — Dior, Gucci, Louis Vuitton — with matching handbags and sparkling jewelry. Their hair was perfect, their shoes high.

The group was escorted by a female tour guide — a clone of Na — and by a very pleased-looking gray-haired, gray-moustached Chinese fellow wearing a red Great Dragon Zoo of China blazer just like Zhang's.

Once again, CJ zeroed in on the details: all of the men's outdoorsy clothes were brand-new, right down to their hiking boots.

More than that, these guys looked like

men not accustomed to *ever* wearing rugged clothing. They were all potbellied, well fed, which in China meant they were probably party officials. And judging by their age, CJ thought, senior ones.

She also noted that there were four men and four female companions: the three women and the girl. She guessed that each party man had brought one guest along: a wife or, in the case of Minnie, a granddaughter.

Her group, CJ realized suddenly, were not the only VIPs being shown around the zoo today. And perhaps hers was not the most important one either.

The gray-moustached man in the Great Dragon Zoo blazer stopped at the sight of Hu Tang and smiled broadly. He spoke in Mandarin, so CJ silently translated in her head.

"Comrade Hu! How delightful to see you!" he said. "What a glorious day to show off our wonderful zoo!"

Hu nodded. "Director Chow. How is your tour going?"

"Marvelously," the man named Chow said. "Just marvelously."

Hu Tang turned to his American guests and switched to English. "Ladies and gentlemen, this is the director of our zoo, Mr.

Chow Wei. Director Chow, these are some very influential members of the Western media, so please do not say anything impolitic! Messrs. Wolfe and Perry from *The New York Times,* and CJ and Hamish Cameron representing *National Geographic.*"

Director Chow bowed. "Welcome to our zoo," he said in English. "As I am sure you will have realized by now, there is nothing in the world like it. Enjoy. I believe I will be seeing you all later this evening for a banquet. Please excuse me, I must attend to my guests."

He guided his party away.

"Goodbye, CJ," Minnie said as she was led away. "It was very nice to meet you."

"It was very nice to meet you, too, Minnie," CJ said.

Standing beside CJ, Wolfe watched the other group go. "Do you know who those men were?" he said softly.

"Communist Party bigwigs?" CJ said.

"Communist Party *super* bigwigs. Two Politburo members, one state governor and one casino billionaire from Macau. Plus their companions."

"Why were the men wearing brand-new hiking outfits?" CJ asked.

Wolfe shrugged. "Must be doing a different tour from us."

"Ladies and gentlemen." Hu Tang ushered them down into the amphitheater. "This way, please."

CJ and the others settled into the front row of the amphitheater while Hu Tang and Deputy Director Zhang ascended the stage and stood behind a lectern.

It was a curious sensation, CJ thought, to be sitting in a stadium that was built so high up. They were four hundred feet above the ground, up near the rim of the crater.

Xin Xili and her CCTV cameraman continued filming them from the side.

Hu Tang stood on the stage, framed by the glorious megavalley. With its high central mountain, moss-covered buttes, castles and dragons, it looked fantastical, otherworldly.

Hu pressed a button on the lectern and a large plasma screen rose up out of the stage beside him. On it was the question:

WHAT IS A DRAGON?

Oh, great, CJ thought, *a PowerPoint lecture.*

"I imagine you have many questions," Hu began, "which Deputy Director Zhang and I shall endeavor to answer now. For instance, what exactly is a dragon and how

74

did China manage to find and raise them, when no other nation on Earth has ever done so before? To help me answer these questions for you, I might call on a friend to help me."

Hu pressed a button on his lectern theatrically.

Bang! Flames rushed into the air from vents arrayed around the stage — a pyrotechnic effect often used at rock concerts — and a cloud of smoke engulfed the stage.

With a sudden *whoosh,* something large rushed low over CJ's head, making her hair flutter, before landing on the stage right beside Hu.

The smoke cleared . . .

. . . and there, beside Hu, stood a dragon.

CJ stared at it in awe.

She had actually wondered if the dragons she had seen from afar might have been somehow fake — perhaps sophisticated animatronic robots — but now that she saw this one up close, she was under no illusions. This was a living, breathing beast.

It was the size of a large horse, like a Clydesdale, about nine feet tall, but it was skinnier than a horse, more skeletal. That said, it probably still weighed close to a ton.

The animal's head — at the end of a long,

slender neck — stood a few feet above Hu Tang's right shoulder. It was brightly colored. Vivid yellow-and-black stripes ran down its body, from the shoulders to the tip of its tail.

As it had landed beside Hu, the creature's wings had folded quickly and efficiently to its sides, all but disappearing from view. The wings were batlike, huge spans of translucent hide stretched taut between elongated vestigial finger bones. Where they met the dragon's body, the joints and fascia were thick and strong, as one would expect of musculature that had to lift such a substantial weight.

The skin on its back and legs was armored with what appeared to be thick plating. That plating was shot through with striated patterns and osteoderms like those found on a crocodile's back and tail. Its underbelly appeared softer and CJ could see its rib cage pressing against its dark leathery skin as it breathed powerfully in and out.

It had four legs on which it walked. They were thin and bony yet well muscled, and the forelimbs had long fingerlike claws that looked capable of gripping things.

The whole animal seemed built for light and fast movement. It had not an ounce of excess weight on it. It stood like a jungle cat, low and coiled, with perfect balance.

CJ noticed a small and obviously unnatural marking on the dragon's left hind leg: a black stencilled letter plus some numbers. The marking on this dragon read Y-18. An identifier of some sort, like a brand on a cow.

And then there was its head.

It was bright yellow on top, jet black on the bottom, and rather than the long donkey-like skull shape that people were accustomed to seeing in movies, it was snub-nosed and reptilian, more like a lizard or a dinosaur. It had high sharply pointed ears and running along the top of its head and down its long neck was a crest of spiky bristles.

It had a menacing cluster of exposed teeth in its snout: the fourth tooth of the lower jaw protruded, fitting perfectly into a matching fold in the upper lip.

Its eyes held CJ absolutely captivated. Narrow and slitlike with a nictitating membrane that occasionally flitted down over them, they gleamed with intelligence.

The animal peered closely at the group, as interested in them as they were in it, passing over every member of the party. When its eyes fell on CJ, she could have sworn it paused for an extra moment.

It felt like it wasn't just looking at her, it was looking *through* her, into her. And then the creature's gaze moved on and the spell was broken.

CJ blinked back to her senses, and as the animal turned its attention to Wolfe beside her, she glimpsed something on the side of its head that was not natural.

It looked like a small metallic box, with wiring that disappeared into the animal's skull. The box was attached to the side of the dragon's head but painted to match the skin color, to camouflage it. But then the animal turned again and CJ lost sight of the box.

"Fuck me," Hamish gasped beside her.

"You can say that again," CJ said.

"Fuck me." He began firing away with his camera.

CJ couldn't take her eyes off it.

It had a dangerous beauty to it. Its proportions were simply perfect. Even the way it stood had a dignity and majesty to it. It was proud. It was magnificent.

It was quite possibly the most beautiful thing CJ had ever seen in her life.

Hu Tang smiled.

He had seen this response before and would no doubt see it many times again.

Newcomers were always struck dumb at their first sight of a dragon. It had been the same with him.

He felt a rush of profound satisfaction. He had staked his reputation on this zoo; more than that, his entire career. In high-level meetings of the Politburo, he had countered the arguments of the older party men by saying that China *needed* a place like this — a place of wonder, joy and happiness — if it was to overtake the United States as the preeminent nation on Earth.

And he had delivered. The Great Dragon Zoo of China would be the making of Hu Tang. Specifically, it would make him the next President of China.

Now, news of this place was about to spread. Today, it was *The New York Times* and *National Geographic.* They had been chosen very specifically to see the zoo first because of their reputations for reliability and integrity. Next week, it would be the American and British tabloid press, plus of course, TMZ, along with some influential movie and music stars — Brad and Angelina, or maybe Beyoncé and Jay-Z. The zoo's "image consultants" from New York had been very clear about this: establish your believability first, then go tabloid.

Judging by the looks on the faces of these

79

guests, Hu Tang thought, it was all going exactly according to plan.

"Ladies and gentlemen," he said, "meet your first dragon. Meet Lucky."

A Chinese woman joined Hu on the stage.

She wore a futuristic-looking outfit: a figure-hugging black bodysuit and a fitted black-and-yellow leather jacket that matched the dragon's colors. She had also streaked her otherwise black hair with electric yellow highlights, so that it too matched the dragon. CJ noticed that the woman's jacket was more than just decorative. It bore the functional features of a motorcycle jacket: pads on the elbows and Kevlar armor on the spine.

The woman also wore an earpiece in her left ear with a tiny microphone in it. When she spoke, her voice was amplified by speakers around the amphitheater.

"Hello, everyone," she said. "My name is Yim and I am the head dragon handler here at the zoo. Even though she is female, Lucky here is what we call a yellowjacket prince."

Yim blew an odd-shaped whistle.

81

Instantly, four more dragons flew out of the sky and landed on the stage around her. Each landed with a heavy *whump.*

They were the same size as Lucky, but different in color. These four animals all had jet-black backs and bright red bellies. Their crests were a fierce scarlet, but each had a unique mottling of red on their otherwise black heads. They snorted as they breathed, braying like horses, and they shifted on their feet. Their tails slunk back and forth behind their thin muscular bodies and they also had armor plating with striated patterns. CJ saw that they too had brands on their left hind legs: R-22, R-23, R-24 and R-25.

As the visitors gasped at these new arrivals, Yim threw each dragon a treat of some sort: they looked like dead rats to CJ. The dragons caught the morsels in their mouths and gulped them down like — CJ winced — like performing seals.

Oh, God, she thought. *They've trained them . . .*

CJ turned to check how her fellow visitors were taking this.

Wolfe and Perry were staring in open-mouthed awe. Hamish was digging it. The American ambassador seemed delighted by the show he was seeing. His aide, Greg Johnson — whose presence CJ had almost forgotten; he seemed very good at melting into the background — was gazing at the dragons with narrowed eyes, assessing them very closely.

Yim keyed her headset mike again, just like a seal trainer at a regular zoo.

"And these four strapping young males are red-bellied black princes. You will see dragons of three sizes here at the Great Zoo. The largest we call *emperors*. They are approximately the size of an airliner. Next are the *kings:* they are about the size of a public bus. And then there are these ones, the *princes*. As you can see, they are roughly the size of a horse.

"The prince class of dragons weigh approximately one ton."

At those words, Lucky hopped lightly on the spot, landing with a resounding boom.

The audience laughed.

"They have a top flying speed of one hundred and sixty miles an hour —"

Lucky took to the air, her wings spreading wide with surprising speed. She beat them powerfully and did a quick, tight loop.

"But given the considerable exertion it takes to stay aloft, dragons can only maintain flight for short distances, a few miles at best. They are mainly gliders. As such, they cannot cross oceans; indeed, we have found that one of the few things they cannot stand is salt water. They hate it."

Lucky landed again beside Yim, who flung her a fresh treat. The yellow dragon caught and swallowed it happily.

Yim said, "Skeptics who have doubted the existence of dragons have always questioned how something so large could possibly fly. Now we know.

"Firstly, as you can see, dragons are not lumbering, fat-bellied beasts — they are lean and light. Secondly, like pterodactyls, they possess a peculiar kind of bone structure: their bones are hollow but with a crisscrossing matrix of high-density, low-weight keratin. This makes their bones extremely strong yet remarkably light. And lastly, their shoulder muscles and fascia — the ligaments and tendons connecting their wings to their bodies — are *incredibly* powerful. All of this creates an animal that can —"

"Wait. I'm sorry. What about sight?" CJ asked. She couldn't help herself. "What sort of visual acuity do they have?"

Yim seemed momentarily vexed by the interruption, but she shifted gears smoothly. "Dragons nest in deep underground caves, so their eyes are well adapted to night vision. They have slit irises, like those found in cats, and a *tapetum lucidum,* also found in cats and other nocturnal animals. That is a reflective layer behind the retina that reuses light.

"Now, light is measured in *lux.* One lux is roughly the amount of light you get at twilight. Pure moonlight is 0.3 lux. 10^{-9} lux is what we would call absolute pitch darkness. Our dragons can see perfectly in 10^{-9} lux. Does that answer your question?"

CJ nodded.

Yim went on, clearly glad to be resuming her script. "Now —"

"Can they also detect electricity?" CJ asked quickly. This question drew odd glances from her American companions.

Yim frowned. She threw a look at Hu, who nodded.

"Yes. Yes, they can detect electrical impulses," Yim said. "How did you know this?"

CJ nodded at the dragon. "See those dimples on its snout? They're called ampullae: ampullae of Lorenzini. Sharks have them. They are a very handy evolutionary trait for a predator, a kind of sixth sense. All animals, including us, emit small electrical fields by virtue of the beating of our hearts. A *wounded* animal's heart beats faster, distorting that field. A predator with ampullae, like a shark — or one of your dragons

— can detect that distortion and home in on the wounded animal. It's like being able to smell electrical energy."

"They are remarkable in many ways," Yim said diplomatically. "In fact," she added, sliding smoothly back into her patter, "one of the most remarkable things about them is their bite."

Yim stepped aside, revealing a cloth-covered object on the stage behind her. She removed the cloth to reveal a brand-new bicycle.

"No way," Hamish whispered. "Not the bike. This is *so* cool."

Yim said, "A large dog has a bite pressure of about 330 pounds per square inch. A saltwater crocodile has a bite pressure of a whopping 5,000 pounds per square inch. A prince dragon has a bite pressure of *15,000* pounds per square inch. Allow me to demonstrate."

One of the red-bellied blacks strode lazily forward. This dragon had large dollops of red on its head and snout. Indeed, it looked like its otherwise black head had been dipped in a bucket of red paint.

It stared at Yim with what could only be described as insolence . . . and didn't do anything.

It just stood there.

And then something happened that only CJ saw: by virtue of the angle of her seat, she saw Yim produce a small yellow remote control from her belt and subtly hold it out for the dragon to see.

Seeing the yellow remote, the dragon promptly turned and, with a loud crunch, casually bit down on the bicycle. Like a soda can being crushed, the bike crumpled within its massive jaws.

The audience gasped.

"Whoa, mama," Aaron Perry said aloud.

The red-faced dragon spat out the bicycle and stomped back to its place, its forked tail slinking behind it.

But all CJ could think about was the yellow remote that had prompted the creature into action. Trained animals reacted to stimuli: rewards and treats or, in the less enlightened places of the world, pain. She wondered what kind of stimulus that remote triggered and suspected that the answer was pain.

Yim bowed. "Thank you, ladies and gentlemen. I will hand you back to the deputy director now."

Zhang stepped forward. "Let me ask you this: *what precisely is a dragon?* Myths of gigantic winged serpents have existed for thousands of years. As with many other things, they originally appeared in China. The first Chinese dragon myth dates back to the year 4700 BC, to a statue of a dragon attributed to the Yangshao culture of that time."

On the plasma screen behind him, a time-line appeared. The words 4700 BC CHINA popped up at the left-hand end of it.

"The Babylonian king, Gilgamesh, fought a fierce dragon named Humbaba in the epic tale that bears his name. He lived around 2700 BC."

2700 BC BABYLON/PERSIA appeared on the timeline.

"The ancient Greeks spoke of Hercules fighting a dragon in order to steal the apples of the Hesperides, the eleventh of his twelve labors. Hercules is generally thought to have lived around the year 1250 BC."

1250 BC GREECE popped up on the time-line.

"From about 100 BC and for the next 1500 years, several Mesoamerican cultures, including the Aztecs and the Mayans, vener-ated a flying serpent named Quetzalcoatl.

"And, of course, the United Kingdom has long lauded the bravery of St. George, who slayed a dragon not in England but in Libya around the year 300 AD.

"In the eighth century, the Scandinavians

wrote of Beowulf fighting a fire-breathing dragon and in the thirteenth century, the Vikings sang of Fafnir."

At each mention of a historical period, the appropriate date sprang up on the timeline on the plasma screen, until it looked like this:

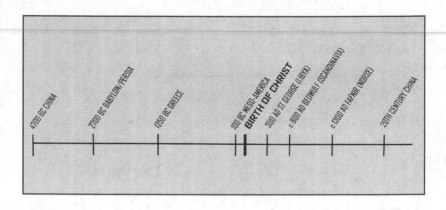

Hu took over. "There is something very curious, however, about all of these mythologies. In every single one of these myths found across the ancient world, *the dragons are the same.* Their features are consistent *around the globe.*

"Mythical dragons are almost universally large hexapods with four walking limbs and two wings."

At that moment, all five of the dragons on the stage opened their wings while remaining standing on their four legs.

Yim rewarded them with more treats.

At which point, CJ glimpsed another detail that caused her some concern.

While the yellowjacket accepted her treat happily, one of the four red-bellied black dragons took its treat with what could only be described as a long, lingering glare at its handler. Its tail began to twitch, a bit like an alligator did when it —

Entirely ignorant of this, Hu went on: "Dragons of lore were serpentine creatures with scaly reptilian skin."

The yellowjacket turned on the spot, showing off its leathery hide like a model doing a turn at a fashion show.

The others laughed. CJ didn't. The dragon, she saw, got another treat.

Hu added, "And, of course, most famously, some dragons . . ." he paused dramatically, ". . . breathed fire . . ."

The five dragons suddenly opened their jaws wide, crouched low and aimed their open mouths at the audience.

Seymour Wolfe sat bolt upright. Aaron Perry gripped his seat. Hamish tensed. Ambassador Syme made to shield his eyes with his forearm. His aide, Johnson, half sprang to his feet.

CJ was already out of her chair by the time the dragons had opened their mouths. She had seen their body language change —

seen them crouch and lower their heads —
and had immediately dived clear, her re-
flexes honed from years of working with
crocs. She was on the stairs and out of the
line of fire and about to sprint away when
the laughing started.

She looked up.

Hu and Zhang were chuckling.

"I'm very sorry," Hu said. "Alas, the ability of a dragon to breathe fire *is* the stuff of
legend. None of the animals at the Great
Dragon Zoo of China is able to breathe
fire."

The audience visibly relaxed, smiled
nervously at each other. CJ resumed her
seat, nonplussed. The dragons got more
treats.

Zhang continued. "But the question remains: how could this happen? How could
the fundamental characteristics of this
mythical creature be so consistent across an
ancient world without mass communication
or intercontinental travel? The answer is
obvious: *there were dragons everywhere
around the world.* And they became the stuff
of myth and legend because they only appeared irregularly."

Wolfe threw up his hand. "What do you
mean by that? 'Irregularly'?"

"I am glad you asked," Zhang said, "because this brings us back to our original question: what precisely is a dragon? The answer is actually quite simple. The animal we know as a dragon is a dinosaur, a most unique kind of dinosaur that survived the meteor impact that condemned the rest of its species to extinction."

CJ leaned forward, intrigued.

Zhang explained. "After much study by paleontologists from the Universities of Shanghai and Beijing, it has been determined that our 'dragons' are part of a hitherto unknown line of dinosaurs belonging to the family or 'clade' of creatures known as *archosauria.*

"The archosaurs ruled the Earth after the Permian-Triassic extinction event, a mass extinction event that occurred 250 million years ago, not unlike the famous Alvarez Meteor that struck the Earth 65 million years ago causing the extinction of the dinosaurs. Archosaurs were the dominant land animals during the Triassic Age and they are the ancient ancestors of crocodilians and, importantly, the branch of flying reptiles known as pterosaurs."

"Ah, pterosaurs," Wolfe said, getting it. Beside him, Ambassador Syme nodded, too.

CJ cocked her head. It probably wasn't quite as simple as that, but she could see what the Chinese were doing. Convincing someone to believe something that was inherently unbelievable often meant getting that person to make a quick and easy comparison to something they already knew. By linking dragons to a dinosaur with similar features — the pterodactyl — the Chinese could get the paying public to accept their logic quickly and readily. They had just done exactly that with Wolfe and the U.S. Ambassador.

But as a herpetologist, CJ knew that the pterodactyl's lineage was famously uncertain: it was neither a dinosaur nor a bird. It didn't fit at all into the so-called Great Tree of Life. It was the same with the archosaurs — they were a catch-all category for any ancient creature whose origins couldn't be easily explained.

Zhang said, "Scientists here at the Great Dragon Zoo believe that our dragons — our archosaurs — survived the Alvarez Meteor 65 million years ago by hibernating deep beneath the surface of the Earth underneath dense nickel and zinc deposits. Their hibernation techniques are very advanced and really rather fascinating; they also explain the consistent worldwide myth of the dragon."

"How so?" CJ asked.

"Many animals hibernate," Zhang said, "although usually the term *hibernate* is limited to warm-blooded creatures. For reptiles, the technical term is *brumate,* and fish experience what is called *dormancy,* but for now, for simplicity's sake, let us just use the term *hibernate* for all animals. Rodents and bears do it, so do alligators and snakes. As a general rule, hibernation involves a creature slowing down its metabolism to an incredibly low level, sometimes only a single heartbeat per minute. The animal gorges itself before entering hibernation and slowly, over a long period of time, its body consumes that fuel.

"Mammalian hibernation usually occurs over the winter — rodents will hibernate for up to six months until the next feeding season. Classic rodent hibernation also involves a decrease in body temperature. Bears, on the other hand, employ a special variety of hibernation called *torpor* that involves the remarkable recycling of both urine and proteins.

"Reptiles exhibit other qualities in their hibernatory states: when it gets very cold, an alligator can float to the surface of a pond, allowing its nostrils to sit above the waterline; as the water freezes, the alligator will be frozen *into* the very surface of the pond yet it is still able to breathe. Alligators can slow their heart rates down to unbelievably low levels, far lower than any mammal. When the ice melts, the gator simply swims away."

This was true, CJ thought. The remarkable abilities of members of the animal kingdom never failed to impress her. Indeed, it was one of the reasons she enjoyed being a vet.

Zhang continued: "And then there are the 'group hibernators,' like dormice. These animals hibernate in packs and have a rather unusual waking routine: they select one of their number to emerge from the den and see if the season has changed. If it has, the lead animal wakes the others and they emerge. If it has not, the lead animal returns to the den and resumes its slumber.

"Our archosaurs here at the Great Dragon Zoo of China exhibit many of these hibernation techniques but their genius is they exhibit them on an incredible timescale.

"First, our archosaurs are warm-blooded, not cold-blooded, so while they may look like reptiles, they are not. They exist somewhere in between mammals and reptiles, so they exhibit the capabilities of both when it comes to hibernation.

"They also have one other advantage: their hibernation is done in an egg state. Since the animal is not yet fully formed but rather is still in a fetal state in albumenic fluids it is capable of considerably longer hibernatory periods.

"Our animals went into hibernation a long, long time ago, at a time when dinosaurs ruled the Earth and when the Earth was much, much warmer. And like the dormouse, they have been periodically sending forth one of their number ever since that epoch: a lone egg will hatch and a young dragon will emerge to check if the climate has warmed enough for the rest of their group to emerge.

"Let me direct you to our timeline from before." Zhang indicated the plasma screen. "Now let's overlay the average ambient land temperature from each era to that timeline."

A wavy red line appeared below the timeline.

CJ saw the match instantly. "I'll be damned," she said.

Zhang said, "The appearance of dragons in human mythology *perfectly* matches every rise in average land temperature on this planet, from the rise in temperature that occurred around the building of the pyra-

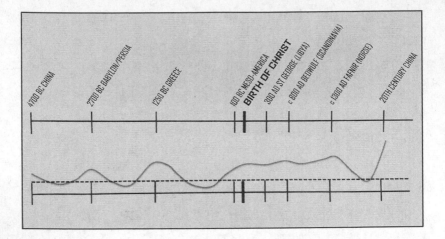

mids in 2700 BC to the Medieval Warm Period.

"Why does the dragon legend persist around the world so consistently? Because all around the world, for thousands of years, *lone dragons* have been emerging from hibernation to test the atmosphere, checking on behalf of their clans to see if the ambient temperature has risen enough and the time to emerge has arrived.

"Myths arise from actual events, remarkable events that get talked about precisely because they are remarkable and which then get embellished in the retelling. This does not change the fact that the original event actually happened. We believe that all of those ancient dragon myths, from Gilgamesh to Hercules to Beowulf, have their genesis in real events, real events that occurred at times when the Earth was warmer.

"And now the world warms again — more than it ever has in recorded history — and about forty years ago, a lone dragon emerged. We here at the Great Dragon Zoo of China were waiting when it did, for by chance we had found its nest. Come, let me show you how it happened."

He clicked his fingers and right on cue — clearly as rehearsed — the five dragons took flight, leaping into the air with a great beating of wings.

CJ was surprised to see that the woman, Yim, now sat on Lucky's back in a custom-made saddle. While Hu and Zhang had been speaking, she must have slipped it onto the dragon. Yim was *riding* the flying yellow-jacket and with considerable skill, too. Handler and animal glided away over the view, flanked by the red-bellied black princes.

"What a fucking show," Wolfe whispered to Perry.

CJ had to agree with him.

Leaving the amphitheater, Hu and Zhang led the group back to the glass elevators. They boarded an elevator and it descended briefly.

As the elevator eased downward, CJ whispered to Hamish, "What do you think, Bear?"

Hamish shrugged. "It's all pretty cool and impressive . . . if you never saw fucking *Jurassic Park.* Did you see the fangs on those things? How do we know they're not gonna go all medieval on our asses and start munchin' on the juicy little humans? I like old-fashioned zoos where they keep the animals in cages."

After travelling only a few floors, the elevator stopped. The group was then led around a catwalk suspended high above the entry atrium, and into a room that looked like mission control at NASA.

Three broad descending levels containing

perhaps thirty shirt-and-tie-wearing Chinese computer operators looked out over the megavalley through a perfectly circular three-storey-high window. Plasma screens and monitors were everywhere, displaying all kinds of graphs, charts and digital images. It was a kaleidoscope of blinking lights and data: the nerve center of the Great Dragon Zoo.

"This is our Master Control Room," Zhang said proudly.

CJ's gaze was drawn to the biggest and most central monitor. On it was a huge white-on-black map of the zoo.

It was an animated map: scattered all over it were colored icons — red crosses, yellow triangles, gray circles, and purple diamonds — many of them moving.

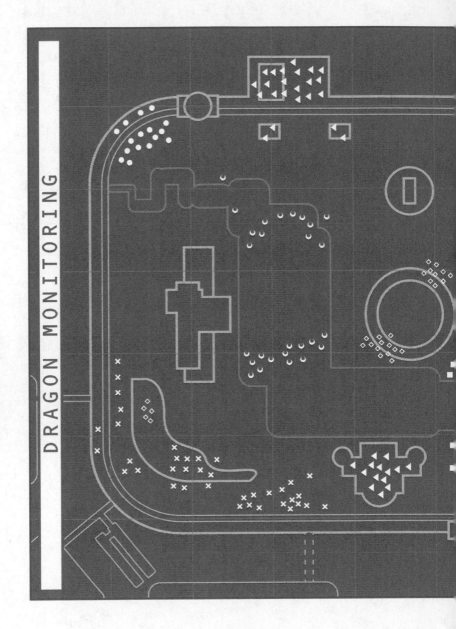

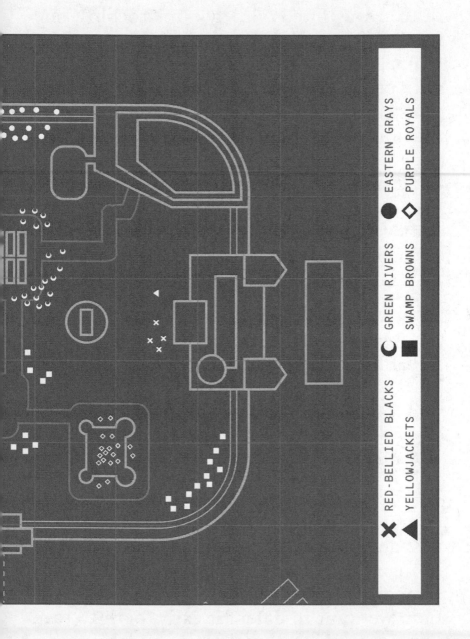

RED-BELLIED BLACKS   GREEN RIVERS   EASTERN GRAYS

YELLOWJACKETS   SWAMP BROWNS   PURPLE ROYALS

"Every icon is a dragon?" CJ asked Zhang.

"Yes," he said. "In their infancy, each dragon was fitted with two microchips: one in the brain, the other grafted onto the animal's heart. Those chips give us real-time data on the dragons' heart rates, respiration rates, brain activity and other health information. The microchips are also GPS-capable, so we know where each dragon is at all times."

Zhang grabbed a mouse and ran the cursor over one of the red icons. Instantly, a text box appeared beside the cross. It read:

DRAGON ID:	R-09
HEART RATE:	67 bpm
RESPIRATION RATE:	13.6 min^{-1}
O_2 CONSUMPTION:	0.06 ml g^{-1} h^{-1}

The numbers changed constantly, giving data in real time. Impressive.

"You can see the heart rate of every dragon in the zoo?" CJ asked.

Zhang smoothed his tie again. "We want to maintain a close eye on the health of our animals. If any of them catches an infection, we want to detect it early, both to save the animal in question and prevent an epidemic spreading to the other dragons."

Below the main map screen was a legend, which allocated the colored icons to names written in both Chinese and English:

RED-BELLIED BLACKS
YELLOWJACKETS
PURPLE ROYALS
EASTERN GRAYS
GREEN RIVERS
SWAMP BROWNS

"Nice names," Ambassador Syme said. "Catchy."

"Thank you," Hu said. "We hired a brand-consultancy firm in Los Angeles to come up with them. Of course, we have given the dragons formal Latin names — *Draconis Imperator, Draconis Rex* and the like — but this facility is built for tourists, not academics."

CJ scanned the rest of the map.

She immediately noticed how icons of the same color mostly appeared to cluster together.

The dragons stuck to their clans: red with red, yellow with yellow, and so on. It even looked like they had claimed their own territories: the purple ones dominated the central mountain, the red-bellied blacks the northwestern corner, the gray dragons the eastern slopes, while the yellowjackets appeared to live in two tight clusters on either side of the valley. The green and brown dragons lived almost exclusively in the rivers and the lakes.

CJ looked out through the giant circular window.

Like an enormous eye, it offered a commanding view of the zoo: the forests and lakes, the high central mountain. Once again, off to the left, she saw the two castles. The nearer one was beautiful, white and clean, with many fluttering banners, while the more distant one, erected on the western side of a curving waterfall, was in ruins.

The beautiful white castle seemed to be populated by purple royal dragons. They lounged on its walls and curled lazily on its rooftops.

The second castle was more utilitarian: squat and defensive; all bricks, crenellations and arrow slits.

And it looked like a bomb had hit it.

Its battlements were crumbled. Its watchtowers had literally been torn apart. Lying in the maw of its gate, underneath its grim portcullis, like a cat with its head between its paws, was a huge yellowjacket emperor. Two prince-sized yellow dragons sat atop the castle's two watchtowers like dutiful sentinels.

CJ nodded at the castles. "I like the castles. Nice touch."

Zhang said, "Like any zoo, we try to give our animals places to nest, sleep, hide and hunt in. Some of our structures resemble naturally occurring landscapes — caves, dens, glens — while others, like the castles, well," he shrugged bashfully, "they are more theatrical and designed with our human guests in mind."

Off to CJ's right was a many-storeyed hotel with an adjoining amusement park. A roller coaster twisted and turned all around it, starting at the top of the hotel and sweeping down into the amusement park. It looked like it had been lifted straight out of Vegas and dropped here.

"Hours of fun for the whole family," Hamish said as he took more shots with his camera.

"Yes," Zhang said enthusiastically, not sensing the sarcasm.

CJ's eyes ran over some of the other monitors in the master control room. She saw one that looked like an overhead map of the crater and its surroundings, and another that looked like a seismograph:

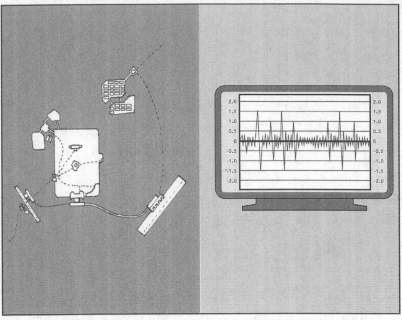

MAIN POWER STATUS   LOW FREQ AUDIOSCAN

She was about to ask about them, when Hamish said to Hu, "Hey, dude, I don't want to be the jerk who asks the obvious question, but what's keeping your pet lizards inside this crater? There's no roof or cage above this valley. Why don't they just fly out of here?"

Hu smiled kindly. "That is a very good question and this is the best place to answer it. Ladies and gentlemen, if I may draw your attention to this console over here . . ." He stepped behind a Chinese technician at a computer.

On it was a side-on view of the zoo:

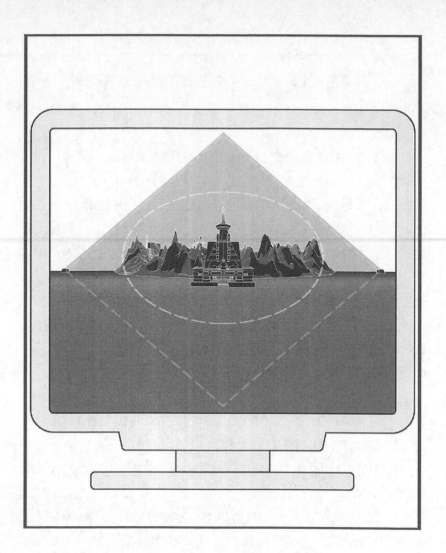

"Mr. Cameron's question," Hu said, "is a very astute one. When we conceived the Great Dragon Zoo, we didn't want it to look like a prison. We wanted visitors to see our dragons as they were meant to be seen: soaring against the wide-open sky."

He held up a finger. "Having said that,

our dragons are still very much our prisoners. As you will see on this display, there are two barriers — invisible to the human eye — keeping our dragons captive here inside the zoo.

"They are electromagnetic fields. The first and innermost field is in the shape of a dome, the second is in the shape of a pyramid. The first covers only this valley, the second covers a much larger area *around* the valley. The two domes are essentially invisible walls of ultra-high-voltage electromagnetic energy. They also, I should add, extend underground, just in case our dragons attempt to tunnel their way out.

"Now, as Deputy Director Zhang mentioned earlier, each dragon has a microchip grafted onto its brain."

He indicated another nearby screen, on which was an X-ray image of a dragon skull seen from the front and from the side. CJ saw the chip situated immediately behind the left eye of the skull:

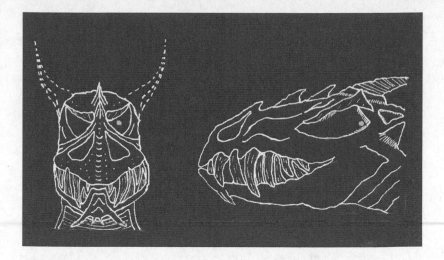

"That chip," Hu said, "is actually fitted to the limbic or pain center of the dragon's brain and it is capable of emitting a powerful electric shock in certain circumstances. One of those circumstances is when a dragon comes into contact with either of the electromagnetic domes."

CJ recalled the yellow remote from the trick show and wondered if that was another such "circumstance."

Hu said, "If a dragon touches one of our domes, it will experience a shock sent directly into the pain center of its brain. This, I can assure you, is an exceedingly painful experience."

"How painful?" Wolfe asked.

"If a dragon hits that dome," Hu said, "it will black out instantly and drop from the sky. The dragons learned very quickly not to touch the inner dome." He rounded on Hamish. "And, as a matter of fact, Mr. Cameron, we did see *Jurassic Park.* From a very early stage in the development of this facility, we were cognizant of the dragons' dangerous potential.

"Make no mistake, my dear guests, these are dangerous animals and we know it. But then this is why people go to zoos in the first place: to see the dangerous animals. The tigers, the bears, the alligators. But we must also recognize that these are important animals, the likes of which the modern world has never seen. As such, we have endeavored to develop systems that *contain* our dragons without unnecessarily damaging them. Wire fences, steel walls, even visible lasers were all no good. We want to alter our animals' behavior without harming them and we want our visitors to see our animals without the crude intervention of bars. The electromagnetic domes have worked perfectly in containing them."

"What about protecting your visitors?" Perry said.

Hu smiled again and CJ had the distinct feeling that Aaron Perry had been the sucker who asked the question Hu had been waiting for.

"Have a look in your gift pack," Hu said, "and please take from it the rather unusual pair of sunglasses that came with it."

CJ and the others all pulled from their fanny packs the strange-looking oversized sunglasses.

"Put them on," Hu invited.

CJ put on her sunglasses and looked out the bank of windows.

"Whoa," she breathed.

Whereas before she had seen the wide valley surmounted by empty sky, now she saw a grid of iridescent green laser-lines forming a perfect geodesic dome above it. The dome stretched from wall to wall, rising up and over the central mountain, completely and perfectly containing the massive space. All the dragons flew and wheeled within it.

Above the green dome, she glimpsed another laser-like lattice: this one was reddish in color and it looked more flat-sided than dome-shaped.

"What you are seeing now," Hu said, "is what a dragon sees. Your odd-looking sunglasses depict the ultraviolet spectrum of light. This is how dragons view the world. Incidentally, modern birds also see this way. Every shield at the zoo is shot through with ultraviolet beams so the dragons can see them."

113

CJ was more enthralled than impressed. She found it fascinating to see the world through an animal's eyes. Being able to see ultraviolet light gave a predator several advantages, including the ability to spot the urine trails of prey. In the ultraviolet spectrum, urine glowed like neon. That was how hawks and falcons spotted their prey on the ground.

As she scanned the megavalley, taking in the environment as a dragon would see it, she saw many tiny ultraviolet spheres of a *third* color: light blue.

The glowing blue spheres — invisible to the naked eye, but visible through the glasses — enveloped all the cable cars, every building in the valley, and even all the worker trucks she could see moving along the roads of the zoo.

There were dozens of the shields, but if you weren't wearing the glasses you'd never know they existed.

"What are the *blue* shiel—" she asked, turning to look back at her fellow travelers.

She cut herself off.

Each of *them,* including herself, had a small pale blue shield around their body.

"Ah-ha . . ." she said.

Hu noticed. "As Dr. Cameron has just discovered, if you look through your glasses at each other, you will see why our dragons do not touch any of our guests.

"The designer wristwatch that each of you was given on your arrival here at the zoo emits a small but very powerful ultrasonic field around your body — it is essentially a sphere of high-wavelength sonic energy beyond the range of human hearing. But a dragon has exceptional hearing. They can hear on wavelengths undetectable to the human ear. This is great for hunting but our clever engineers at the Great Dragon Zoo have used this talent against them. To a dragon, the sound emitted by your watch is absolutely ear-piercing — it would be like someone sounding an air horn right next to your ear."

Zhang added, "You will notice small antennas on every vehicle and structure in the valley. These emit similar ultrasonic shields. Dragons are not exactly small animals. If one brushed against a cable car, even by accident, it would do significant damage."

At that moment, CJ saw a cable car emerge from within the main building directly beneath the control room. The cable car did indeed have a small plastic snub antenna on its roof, similar to the ones you saw on expensive cars. Through her glasses, she saw the pale blue sphere around the vehicle.

"So it's the same sort of thing as the domes above the valley?" Wolfe asked.

"No," Zhang said. "The domes are electromagnetic. The personal shields are ultrasonic. Since our dragons come into contact with our cars and buildings far more regularly than they do the electromagnetic domes, the smaller sonic shields give them a jolt that is not as devastating as the one they would receive from the domes. The sonic shields will shoo a dragon away; the electromagnetic domes will knock them out."

The group nodded.

"Come now," Hu said, smiling. "Enough of these lectures. It's time to get on board one of our state-of-the-art cable cars and see the Great Dragon Zoo!"

Leaving the master control room, the group took a glass elevator down a few more floors, arriving at a high-ceilinged hall that looked like a train station. Only this was no train station.

First, it opened onto thin air. It had no northern wall. The platform at that end just dropped away, a full three hundred feet to the floor of the megavalley.

And second, the "carriage" parked beside the platform didn't stand on rails. Instead, the huge double-decker carriage hung suspended from a thick overhead cable. It was a cable car, at least thirty yards long, with wide viewing windows that curved up and over its roof. And it looked very modern, all sleek and silver, with the obligatory Great Dragon Zoo of China logo on its flank.

The sturdy cable from which the cable car hung stretched out from the station, lancing across the valley in a dead-straight line, passing through a watchtower-like way station before disappearing into a tunnel bored into the front face of the central mountain out in the middle of the megavalley, several miles away.

The group boarded the cable car and it eased out of the station and suddenly they were all moving high above the valley.

The ambience inside the cable car was like that of a drawing room: soft music played and, except for the loudest of sounds, outside noise barely crept in. There was a bar at the rear, manned by a Chinese bartender in a bow tie and vest.

Seen from the cable car, the valley took on a whole new level of splendor.

Lucky — with Yim on her back — swooped and glided theatrically around the moving cable car. Yim waved happily. The four red-bellied black dragons from the show banked and flew in wider circles around the car.

Hamish's camera now sounded like a machine gun, he was taking so many photos.

The dragons flew like alligators swam, CJ saw. Alligators swam with their four limbs tucked close by their bodies while their tails drove them forward. These animals flew with their four walking limbs held tightly against their sides, making them incredibly streamlined, while their wings — many times larger than their bodies — flapped powerfully.

As they made their way along the cable, CJ saw other dragons: gigantic purple royal emperors gliding around the central mountain; olive-green kings lounging on the banks of a river village. They looked like supersized lizards, basking in the sun.

Some king-sized purple royals sat perched atop high rocky crags that lined the cable car's route. They sat upright, tall and noble, as they watched the cable car slide by. When the cable car passed close enough to one of the dragons, CJ would spot the branded number on the animal's hind leg.

As the car approached and passed them, the various dragons barked and shrieked at each other, ear-piercing squeals and screams.

"Not exactly pleasing to the ear, are they?" Wolfe snorted.

"Their vocalizations may not be pleasant," Zhang said, "but they do have meaning. Our dragons employ several different methods to communicate with each other: complex subsonic grunting, for one thing, and body vibrations not unlike those employed by modern alligators. Dr. Cameron will be aware of these forms of communication."

CJ nodded.

Alligators did indeed communicate in this way. Their barks and grunts were both complex and very specific, a kind of guttural language. One of her old colleagues from the University of Florida, Dr. Benjamin Patrick, had pioneered the study of alligator vocalizations, going so far as to compile a database of over sixty distinct sounds made by alligators. He had run those vocalizations through a purpose-built supercomputer in an attempt to find similarities and commonalities among them; in effect, to translate their language.

Similar studies had been done with dolphins and chimpanzees. Dolphins were known to vocalize their names when they jumped out of water and packs of chimps had specific grunts that meant "leopard" or "hyena." Patrick's work with gators had been an attempt to take this to the next level.

Six years older than CJ, Ben Patrick had also been the most handsome guy in the faculty and every woman there had had a crush on him. When he'd asked CJ — fresh out of graduate school and before her disfigurement — on a date, she'd jumped at it. But there had been no second date, because during that single dinner, CJ discovered quite clearly that Ben Patrick loved only one thing: Ben Patrick. He had talked only about himself. It pained her, even now, to recall that one disastrous date.

Arrogant and self-absorbed as he was, CJ had to admit that Patrick was brilliant. His analysis of alligator vocalizations was simply extraordinary. But then about eight years ago, when his research seemed to be hitting a peak, he had suddenly left the university for a much higher paying job at the University of Shanghai. CJ hadn't seen or heard from him since.

"A colleague of mine named Ben Patrick once did some excellent work in the field of alligator vocalizations," CJ said.

"He did indeed," Hu said, "which is why he is working here, right now, at our zoo. His discoveries here have far outstripped the ones he made with alligators. He works in our Birthing Center. When we stop by there later, hopefully we will run into Dr. Patr—"

Suddenly, with a great *whoosh-whoosh,* two purple emperor dragons swept past the cable car. They were indeed the size of airliners and their fly-by caused the cable car to rock gently and the trees on a nearby crag to bend and flutter.

Everybody grabbed a handhold.

Hu chuckled. "It's okay. These cable cars are the best in the world. Swiss designed. Our emperors don't realize the wake they make when they fly past."

CJ whipped around, following with wide eyes the two purple emperors that had swept by.

Their heads alone were simply monstrous in size, as big as a four-wheel drive. Their long teeth, protruding menacingly from their lips, were almost as big as she was.

"Good God," she breathed. "Good God."

The cable car passed through the watchtower-like way station halfway between the main entrance building and the central mountain.

"We call this the Halfway Hut," Na said. "There is a café-restaurant above us that offers excellent views and affordable meals. Also, hikers walking along the valley trails can access a cable car here if they run out of breath."

As his guests watched the dragons, Hu Tang watched them. They seemed to be enjoying the cable car ride. Hu was particularly pleased to see the two *New York Times* men nod approvingly when Na mentioned the affordable meals at the Halfway Hut.

122

The consultants had said American visitors would like that: having differently priced restaurants to suit people of different levels of wealth.

The cable car pushed on.

Rising up directly in front of it, dominating the valley, was the central mountain. A silver disc-shaped structure sat atop its summit.

"What do you think that is?" CJ asked Hamish. "A revolving restaurant?"

Hamish shrugged. "Or a captured flying saucer."

Hu stepped forward, resuming his presentation: "We think it was the thick layer of nickel in the earth here that saved these animals from the meteor strike that wiped out the dinosaurs 65 million years ago. Two miles of solid nickel insulated them from the impact and since the dragons were buried so deep and their hibernation skills so advanced, they were able to keep hibernating through the thousand-year winter that followed the meteor impact. Our zoo is built on top of the second-largest nickel deposit in these parts; the largest is over at Crater Lake about fifteen miles to the northwest."

Wolfe said, "It's a pity you couldn't build your zoo around Crater Lake. Now *that* would have been a sight."

"Indeed," Hu said. "In any case, in November 1979, miners in a nickel mine near here broke through to a most unusual underground passageway. It was unusual because it was not natural; it had been *dug* out of the nickel — which is no mean feat given how hard nickel is — and then refilled with soil that had settled into it over the centuries. We dug out that soil to discover that the tunnel led to a cavern two miles underground, a cavern that was *filled* with eggs, eighty-eight of them to be precise, large leathery eggs that were bigger than any egg ever seen on this planet.

"Now, for over two thousand years, this area has fostered dragon myths and legends, usually involving a lone dragon tormenting the locals for a short period. We believe those legends related to this nest: that every now and then, a lone juvenile dragon would leave the nest to test the atmosphere and see if it was suitable for the rest of the clan to resurface."

Wolfe said, "November 1979. That was when the Iranian hostage crisis was going on."

"Correct," Hu said. "While it was a most unpleasant event for America, it was quite fortuitous for us, for it occupied the world's attention for well over the next year, allowing our experts to examine the cavern in absolute secrecy. Deputy Director Zhang can provide the technical history of what happened next."

Hu stepped aside and Zhang took over smoothly: "We brought in reptile experts to examine the eggs. They determined that they were not fossils but rather living ova containing animals in deep hibernation. X-rays and ultrasound scans revealed that the eggs contained lizard-like fetuses curled into tight balls.

"We closed the nickel mine and dispatched all the workers. We then lined the walls of the cavern with cameras and sensors of every kind — temperature, humidity, sound, ultrasound — so that we might learn all we could about this astonishing discovery.

"But we did not seal the cavern. Instead we sealed the land *above* it. We built a massive steel dome — it still stands over the Nesting Center to the west of this valley, the oldest structure here at the Great Zoo. And then we waited. Waited and waited.

"And then in July 1981 one of the eggs hatched.

"A dragon emerged, covered in birth matter. It was a baby prince, a red-bellied black, and the size of a dog. The whole event was filmed. It is amazing footage. The prince ate two of its brethren, consuming the albumen and vitellus of those eggs, giving it strength, and then it went to the tunnel leading to the surface. It emerged inside our steel dome, sniffed the air, tested the water . . . and then it went back down to its cavern and began awakening the other eggs.

"When the other eggs began to hatch, we had already prepared our facility up on the surface. When they emerged, we caught them one by one."

"But you didn't tell anyone?" Wolfe said.

"This was the greatest zoological discovery *in history,*" Zhang said. "We wanted to make sure of what we had. We wanted to make sure the dragons would survive. If we showed the world a single specimen and it died, we would become an international laughingstock."

Hu stepped forward and interjected: "It was also felt by some senior party officials that this discovery could be the making of modern China, so it was decided that it should be kept secret until we could show it off to the world. It was thus determined that a zoo would be built *on top of* our discovery. And so it was. This zoo has been a project nearly forty years in the making."

Hamish gave a low whistle. "Now *that's*

what I call patience."

"In any event," Zhang went on, "as the world warmed, more dragons hatched and our Nesting Center began to overflow, so we built a second 'Birthing Center' beside it. And we fashioned this valley to suit our needs — it required twenty thousand workers, working over twenty years, and through sheer force of Chinese resolve, we bent the landscape to our will."

"You bent the landscape to your will?" Aaron Perry asked. "What do you mean by that? Are you saying this valley *isn't* natural?"

Hu decided to answer that one. He gestured toward the towering mountain ahead of them. "Oh, no, this valley is not natural at all. Our glorious central peak — Dragon Mountain — is natural, as are a few sections of the wall encircling this valley. But otherwise, this land only *became* a valley when our army of workers connected some rocky mounts by building the wall out of introduced limestone and concrete, turning it into a crater."

Hu saw his guests turn and reappraise the colossal wall of the valley, now aware that it was not a naturally occurring landform. "The wall containing our main entrance building, for instance, is entirely artificial.

127

All the lakes, waterfalls and other waterways in this zoo are entirely our creation. The smaller peaks are artificial, as are most of the cliffs — they were designed from the outset to accommodate the dragons."

Hamish whistled again. "You have got to be kidding me . . ."

Zhang said, "Throughout the whole time the crater was being constructed, not one of the ordinary workers saw a single dragon. They thought they were building the world's greatest zoo, which in a sense they were. They just didn't know what the animals would be.

"And all the while, we studied these creatures, watched them grow, watched them feed, observed their habits, even trained some of them, as you have seen."

The cable car continued its slow glide over the megavalley, moving toward the central mountain. Dragons soared around it.

Hu said, "Thank you, Deputy Director." He turned to the group of visitors. "Now, do you have any questions?"

The questions came rushing at him:

"How did you build this place for twenty years without anyone in the world finding out?" Perry asked.

"How many dragons do you have here?" Seymour Wolfe asked.

128

Hamish asked, "What do they eat? How do they interact? Do they fight each other?"

Ambassador Syme asked, "Apart from salt water, do they fear anything else?"

Hu held up his hands, laughing. "Okay! Okay! These are all very good questions and I will take them in turn."

Still smiling, he noticed that CJ was standing silently off to the side, staring out at a king dragon gliding in a slow circle. She had not asked a question, let alone an excited one. In fact, at his call for questions, she had actually turned away to look out at the view.

Hu frowned. "Dr. Cameron? What about you? Do you have any questions about our dragons?"

CJ didn't turn when she spoke. She kept staring at the flying leviathan outside.

"Yes," she said. "I have one. But I'm not going to ask it now."

Hu frowned, confused — and even a little offended — but he regathered himself and turned to the others.

"Ah, look, we're arriving at Dragon Mountain," he said.

The cable car had indeed arrived at the tunnel that bored into the mighty central mountain. The great peak loomed above them.

"Let us go inside and I shall answer all of your questions over lunch."

The cable car disappeared inside the mountain.

Inside the mountain, the cable car stopped at a station cut into the very heart of the peak.

The station's walls were natural rock, gunmetal gray in color, and they had been sculpted into enormous dragon shapes — it looked as if the dragons were emerging from the walls in frightening attack poses, jaws open, claws bared.

Since the cable cars were double-deckers, the platform of the station had two levels, too. A modern grated catwalk led from the upper deck of the cable car to the upper doors of a huge double-leveled elevator.

A group of Chinese workers was there, standing near the elevator. Seeing the arrival of the cable car with its VIP guests, they stopped their labors and stood to attention in a line, waiting for the visitors to pass.

CJ figured they were electricians, judging

by their work belts, coveralls and the clusters of naked wires protruding from the walls.

The youngest of the workmen had clearly gathered his tools together in a hurry, for he held them awkwardly against his chest, and as CJ's group passed him by, the poor fellow dropped his bundle with a loud clatter. A screwdriver, some pliers and about thirty metal clips scattered all over the floor.

The group walked on, but as they did, CJ turned and she saw the foreman strike the young electrician across the face, hissing in Mandarin, "Idiot! Not in front of the guests!"

CJ flinched. Such a thing would never happen back home, but in China it was still common for low-level workers to be beaten. She went back and, crouching beside the young electrician, began helping him pick up the many metal clips.

"I am sorry," he whispered in English, bowing his head repeatedly. "So sorry. So sorry."

"It's okay," CJ said, picking up clips. "What's your name?"

"My name is Li, ma'am."

"Take it easy, Li. It's all right. It was an accident. You haven't offended anyone or made the zoo look bad."

Sweating, Li nodded in thanks, but a fearful glance at the foreman suggested that things wouldn't be good for him after CJ and the others left. CJ picked up the last clip and the floor was clean.

She headed off, but as she walked past the foreman, she whispered casually in Mandarin: "You touch that man again and I'll have you fired. You understand?"

The foreman blanched in shock.

CJ rejoined the group at the elevator just as Hu was saying, "To answer Mr. Wolfe's question: we have 232 dragons here at the zoo: 31 emperors, 81 kings and 120 princes. They range in age from thirty-five years to infants that are only a few months old, but don't let that fool you. Dragons grow fast. A month-old prince is the size of a lion. At six months, it is as tall as a man. It is full-sized at a year, but immature, so it will defer to its seniors."

They entered the elevator and CJ felt it zoom smoothly upward. The manufacturer's plate by the doors showed it was German made. It hardly made a sound.

Zhang said, "To answer Mr. Cameron's question from before regarding their eating habits: our dragons are omnivorous; they eat both meat and vegetable matter. The emperors are mostly herbivorous, like their large dinosaur forebears, while the kings and princes are predominantly carnivorous."

"What do you feed them?" Wolfe asked.

"Sheep and cows mainly," Zhang said simply. "We have a farming facility adjoining this valley, where we breed the dietary requirements for our dragons. As you can imagine, they require substantial amounts of meat, so our farming system works around the clock."

Hu said, "Mr. Cameron also asked if they fight each other. They most certainly do, but in a very unusual and rather ritualistic way that we have termed 'jousting.' Two dragons will face off and fly directly at each other. As they pass, claws are extended and one dragon usually comes away the better. We have found that such battles usually occur over —"

"Territory," CJ said.

"Yes. Yes, that's right," Hu said. 'Territorial disputes. We considered attempting to segregate the dragons in order to stop the practice, but they eventually established their own territories and the jousting largely stopped."

Perry asked, "And how did you manage to build this place without anyone knowing?"

Hu said, "Simple. We told the truth. You saw the sign at the maglev station reading

'Welcome to the Great Zoo of China.' There have been *many* others like it. In addition to telling every worker who worked on this project that they were building an enormous zoo, we created a whole set of logos and letterheads which featured on every sign, every truck, and on every invoice with every contractor who worked on this place. We gave them T-shirts and caps emblazoned with the fake logo of the Great Zoo of China. While they toiled, the dragons were sequestered underground in the Birthing and Nesting centers, so no worker ever saw a dragon.

"Only the most trusted contractors were shown the dragons: those who were working on security features like the electromagnetic domes and the sonic shields, and of course the experts who helped us analyze the dragons' behavior."

"What about satellites?" Wolfe asked, turning to the American ambassador, Syme. "What did America think was going on here?"

Syme turned to Hu and a look passed between them, the look of two men who knew the realities of international politics.

Syme said evenly, "In November 1979, all this land and the air above it was designated restricted military airspace. This whole valley is technically a military site subject to military laws."

Syme gave Hu another look and the Chinese Politburo member nodded in return. Their two nations, vying to be the world's dominant power, knew all of each other's secrets, or at least most of them.

Syme said, "Until today, the United States government didn't know the significance of that date. We knew of the sonic shields — but we use them ourselves at air force bases for cellular jamming, so we figured the Chinese were just doing the same thing. And since no major aircraft or missile technology was tested here, it wasn't seen as a particularly special base. We processed the visas of the animal experts they brought in but then we saw the Great Zoo of China paraphernalia and I guess, well, we fell for it, too."

The elevator pinged and the doors opened onto an elegant room high above the valley. The room was perfectly circular, with curved and slanted floor-to-ceiling windows that offered unobstructed views of the megavalley.

It was, CJ realized, the interior of the disc-shaped structure at the summit of the central mountain, or Dragon Mountain, as Hu had called it.

And it was indeed a revolving restaurant. Well-appointed tables and chairs had been arranged on four broad descending tiers so that every table had a view over the valley. Only the central section of the structure stood still; the tiers all revolved at a slow pace around it.

"There is a second identical restaurant on the level below us," Hu said. "Guests who ride up in the lower half of this elevator get out there."

Outside, dragons swooped and banked. It was like dining at the top of the Eiffel Tower, high in the sky, with only the clouds and the dragons for company.

It was stunning.

Lunch was served.

Hu said, "The menu is by Gordon Ramsay. He is very popular in China. The Chinese people consider him to be a — what is the phrase — a lovable rogue."

While the more important guests — Ambassador Syme, Seymour Wolfe and Aaron Perry — sat with Hu Tang and Zhang at one end of the table, CJ found herself eating alongside the ambassador's aide, Greg Johnson. She'd almost forgotten Johnson was even there, he'd been so silent on the cable car ride. It was like he had professionally blended into the background.

"What do you think so far?" Johnson asked as they ate.

CJ said, "I think this place is going to make China *the* tourist destination of the world. In one hit, it blows Disneyland, Disney World and the Grand Canyon out of the water. What about you?"

Johnson shrugged. "It's pretty awesome. Although, having said that, I must admit I'm curious."

"About what?" CJ said, popping some buttered broccoli into her mouth.

"About what your single question is," Johnson said.

CJ stopped chewing and eyed the ambassador's aide closely. Johnson stared straight back at her, his dark eyes narrowed, focused, evaluating, and she wondered what kind of aide he really was.

Johnson let the moment pass and smiled. "How about this view, huh?"

With a final glance at Johnson, CJ looked out at the view. It *was* incredible. What the Chinese had done was remarkable — not only had they bred ancient animals, they had sculpted the very landscape to accommodate them.

As she turned away from the view, she saw two people get up from another table. It was the only other table in the restaurant that was occupied — by a Chinese man and a younger Chinese woman — and now they were in the process of leaving.

The woman, in her early twenties, wore a skirt-suit and looked very nervous. The man was short and a little on the plump side. He wore a red Great Dragon Zoo of China polo shirt and, unusually for a Chinese man, he had a long ponytail.

"No way," CJ breathed. "It couldn't be. Go-Go?" she called.

The man turned at the name. He saw CJ and his face broke out in a delighted grin.

"Why, if it isn't the lovely and talented Cassandra Jane Cameron!" he exclaimed in a twee voice as he rushed over.

CJ stood and they embraced warmly. He didn't so much as glance at the scarring on her face.

"So? What do you think of this place?" he said. "Is it not . . . *is it not* . . . the biggest *mind-fuck* in history?"

CJ laughed. Go Guan had always been like this: short, loud and flamboyant. A huge fan of Shanghai nightclubs, his nickname, Go-Go, had come naturally.

"It's certainly blowing my mind," CJ said.

Go-Go stepped back from her. "God, look at you, girl! You are *smoking* hot! How do you get your butt so perfect? I do these squat classes at the gym, but look at my ass — look at it — it's still the sad, sagging derriere of a fat little Chinaman. Urgh! What are you doing here?"

"Doing a piece for *Nat Geo.* What about you? I haven't seen you since you were working for me, stealing eggs from alligator nests on the Yangtze River and running from their angry mothers."

"I've moved up in the world, honey babe," Go-Go said. "Working for Ben Patrick in the Birthing Center. This place needs every expert and grad student it can get." He indicated the young woman standing discreetly nearby. "I'm doing lunches all week with the successful candidates. Goodness me, no one's called me Go-Go in years. It's so great to see you. Listen, I have to run. Maybe we can grab a sneaky chardonnay after your tour's done."

"Sure," CJ said.

Go-Go and the young woman left and CJ returned to the table as Seymour Wolfe said, "It must have taken a small army of laborers to build this place. How did you feed them and house them while they built it?"

Hu gestured to the northeast: "If you look out that way, you will just make out the rooftops of some buildings."

CJ and the others looked in that direction and, sure enough, over the top of the northeastern corner of the valley, they could just see the roofs of what looked like a dozen tall apartment buildings.

"That was our worker city," Hu Tang said. "It was a complete small-scale city, with residential buildings, gymnasiums, food markets, parks, even sporting grounds. Our workers lived there while they fashioned this valley out of the natural landscape."

"Was?" Perry asked.

"Now the city is largely empty — our animal keepers live there in just one building — but we maintain all the empty neighborhoods because the city's usefulness is not exhausted. When our wonderful zoo opens to the world, it is going to need another small army to operate it: tour guides, hotel staff, cleaning and custodial staff, and they will need somewhere to live."

While the others marveled at the ready-made city outside the valley, CJ gazed out at a nearby, smaller pinnacle to the east.

A gigantic gray emperor dragon lounged on a ledge high up on the peak. Flanked by a few gray princes, it turned suddenly and looked right at CJ, right into her eyes.

Hu Tang caught her looking.

"Dr. Cameron," he said gently. "Are you

141

all right? Is there something worrying you?" He seemed genuinely concerned. "Are you perhaps ready to ask your question?"

CJ turned to find the whole table looking at her expectantly. It seemed as if everyone was interested in hearing her question. She made eye contact with Greg Johnson: he seemed especially attentive.

"Okay," she said. "But you might not like it."

"Please," Hu encouraged. "We are happy to answer any query you might have."

"All right," CJ said, turning fully in her chair. "Mr. Hu, exactly how many people have your dragons killed so far?"

Hu looked like he had been slapped in the face. "How many — what? How many people have they *killed*? Why would you ask that?"

"Because from everything you've told us so far, this animal is perhaps the greatest predator this world has ever seen," CJ said. "Everything about it indicates that it is a killing machine with no equal on this planet except for perhaps the Great White Shark."

She counted off on her fingers: "Deep broad nostrils for sniffing out prey. Those ampullae on its snout, they don't just sniff out electricity, they are designed to detect the bioelectrical *distress* emitted by the rapid beating of a wounded animal's heart. Those wings are for chasing prey, those claws are for grabbing prey and those fangs are for eating prey.

"Evolution is a master craftsman, Mr. Hu. Over millions of years, it has designed this

143

creature for one purpose and one purpose only: to be an apex predator. Given their size, these dragons could be more than that: they could be *the ultimate* apex predator. They are built to do three things: hunt, kill and eat. Like crocodiles and alligators, that is *what they do.* That is *why they exist.* And these animals are smart: hell, you've managed to *train* a few of them. Hence my question. How many people have they killed already?"

Hu Tang did not say anything at first. He pursed his lips.

"None," he said stiffly. "There has not been a single injury or fatality at this zoo caused by a dragon. And we intend to keep it that way."

"Really?" CJ said, cocking her head. "Mr. Hu, putting a couple of electromagnetic domes over this valley is a very sensible idea. But putting little sonic shields on all the vehicles, buildings and people makes me think that your dragons have attacked the vehicles, buildings and people before. In fact, if these animals respect those domes and shields then *by definition* it means they have been stung by them in the past. Animals don't fear electromagnetic domes and sonic shields because they can see them. They fear them because they've been hurt by them. Are you seriously telling me that your dragons have only taken the odd snap at a truck or building and not a human being?"

"Yes, that is what I am telling you," Hu said with a straight face.

CJ stared back at him. "Right. So it's like Chinese GDP figures, then."

"I beg your pardon?"

"Never mind."

After dessert was served, the group returned to the cable car and resumed their aerial circuit of the zoo.

Departing Dragon Mountain, the cable car ventured eastward, passing through the smaller pinnacle that CJ had seen earlier, before turning north again.

Hamish nudged CJ and pointed off to the right. There, nestled atop a chasm cut into the eastern wall of the crater, was an enormous monastery built in the style of the old Taoist monasteries found in central China.

This one had three levels, all with pointed roofs and wide balconies overlooking the high chasm. A pack of yellowjacket dragons had taken up residence in it: an emperor, two kings and one prince lay on its broad balconies.

Zhang said, "Our monastery is obviously

a homage to the famous Purple Cloud Temple in the Wudang mountains of Hubei province."

"Obviously," Hamish said, raising his camera to take a few shots.

Moving away from the side-chasm, the cable car began a gradual descent that brought it low over a long straight waterfall.

Several large rocks protruded from the waterfall's lip, while some flat-topped rock ledges jutted out from the face of the falling curtain of water. On these rocks and ledges sat a dozen olive-green prince-sized dragons.

"Green River dragons," Zhang said. "They love the water. We can't keep them out of it."

Voices in the master control room, speaking into radios:

"North waterfall team, stand by. Guests are en route."

"North waterfall team, ready."

"Prepare for fish release. In three, two, one . . ."

The cable car passed across the face of the waterfall, level with its lip, within twenty feet of the olive-green river dragons on the ledges — when suddenly the dragons saw

146

something in the water and they leapt into it with whip cracks of their tails.

"Look how fast they go!" Perry exclaimed.

CJ was thinking the same thing. They had moved with astonishing speed, far faster than any crocodilian she had seen.

The cable car moved past the waterfall, now rising higher again, and CJ glimpsed the freeway-like ring road that ran around the circumference of the valley. It was artfully concealed, disappearing every now and then into tunnels cut into the rock wall.

Shortly after passing the waterfall, the cable car arrived at an open-air station that serviced a hotel-like building at the northern end of the valley. Flashing lights blared *Welcome to the Dragon's Tail Casino!*

It reminded CJ of the Bellagio in Las Vegas: it had beige walls, immense columns and Italian-style windows.

The cable car, however, did not stop at the casino. It only slowed as it passed through the station before continuing on, gliding around the northern edge of the lake, moving past a second broad waterfall which also had river dragons perched on rock ledges jutting out from its lip and face.

As their cable car moved away from the second waterfall, CJ saw four silver Range Rovers emerge from a garage at the base of the casino building and speed along a gravel road that ran parallel to their cable car.

Hamish saw them, too. "Nice wheels. Range Rover Sport."

They could just make out the occupants of the cars: the four Chinese party men in their freshly bought outdoorsman outfits.

"The big kahunas," Hamish observed.

The four silver Range Rovers zoomed alongside the cable car for a short time, kicking up dust clouds behind them, before their road curved northward and they peeled away. Their gravel road, CJ saw, wrapped around some dramatic cliffs — covered with dragons — that formed a kind of natural screen in front of the northwestern corner of the crater.

CJ stopped herself.

It wasn't a *natural* screen at all. This entire valley had been sculpted by thousands of Chinese workers for the specific purpose of building a tourist playground. Those cliffs — and the screen they formed — were there for a reason.

"Looks like the big shots are on a very different tour from us," she said.

Hamish turned to Zhang. "Yo, Zhangman. Where are those dudes going?"

Zhang smiled. "Our esteemed party officials are about to enjoy a very special section of our zoo, which you will see later. Forgive me if I don't tell you what it is now. I don't want to ruin the surprise."

"Oh, okay. Cool," Hamish said.

Everyone else in the cable car was focused on the dragons on the dramatic cliffs. The cliffs, CJ thought, had been well designed: the dragons lay on high ledges or sat perched on striking peaks. It seized the attention. It was a postcard shot and Hamish duly took many photos of it.

While all this was happening, the cable car travelled over a broad swamp filled with reeds and, it appeared, many large crocodiles.

"Why the crocodiles?" CJ asked Zhang.

Zhang said, "Crocodiles are the only surviving members of the archosaur line in the modern world. Large crocs lived back in the Triassic Period. We thought having some of them around would be good for the dragons: a reminder of the world they used to live in."

"Those are saltwater crocs," CJ said, "which means that's a saltwater swamp. I thought you said your dragons don't like salt water."

"They don't."

"But that swamp adjoins the lake and

there are dragons in the lake. How does that work?"

"Well spotted, Dr. Cameron," Zhang said. "We cheated a little. You can't see it, but just below the waterline is a Perspex barrier that separates the saltwater swamp from the freshwater lake."

"Do the crocs ever venture out into the lake?" Perry asked.

"The larger ones do, but not the smaller ones," Zhang said. "The dragons, on the other hand, *always* avoid the swamp. They hate it. When it comes to salt water, they're like cats: precious and fussy."

When it was about halfway across the swamp, the cable car turned southward and soared grandly out over the lake, travelling twenty feet above the surface.

It was now heading back down the western side of the valley. CJ saw the enormous main building way off in the distance ahead of them, dominating the southern end of the valley, perhaps ten miles away.

On the nearby western wall of the crater, she saw about twenty dragons of various sizes — but all clustered in small groups of the same color — alternately sitting on or moving around the crater's rocky wall.

The voices from the master control room

came through a tiny earpiece in Hu Tang's ear:

"Western wall team, stand by. Guests are en route."

"Western wall team, ready."

"Prepare for horse release, in five, four, three . . ."

Hu Tang knew that his zoo was a wonder beyond compare. But these were influential American journalists and he didn't want them reporting that his dragons just lazed around, doing nothing.

Sometimes you had to make the animals perform.

Gliding along in the cable car, CJ again saw the ring road, disappearing into and re-appearing from tunnels in the mountain-side.

Then she saw something that made her start.

It was so well camouflaged, she almost missed it.

On the sheer black cliff above the ring road, CJ saw a lone dragon, a large red-bellied black king, crouched in a very unusual position. The dragon clung to the cliff on its belly, perfectly vertical but upside down: its head pointed downward while its barbed tail was pointed upward.

The animal was the size of a subway carriage and it did not move. It just lay there, eerily still.

CJ frowned. She was about to ask Zhang about it, when sudden movement caught her eye.

Four yellowjacket princes burst out of some trees below the ring road, chasing a group of six wild horses across the hillside. The horses galloped hard, blasting between the trees, fleeing for their lives. The dragons ran swiftly and easily, with the cool agility of big cats. With their tails raised, their heads bent low and their muscular limbs bouncing over the uneven landscape with ease, they looked like oversized leopards.

Then suddenly two of the dragons took flight, flanking the horses, herding them to the right where —

— two more princes sprang from a cave and crash-tackled the first two horses with crunching, side-on hits.

"Ow!" Hamish yelled.

The two horses — who themselves must have weighed more than 1700 pounds each — shrieked as they went down, hoofs flailing, heads turning from side to side, eyes bulging with fear.

The two ambushing dragons were on them in seconds, wrapping their oversized jaws around the horses' necks, crushing their windpipes. The horses stopped struggling, went still.

At this point, the other four yellowjackets arrived. But they did not engage in a feeding frenzy on the carcasses of the horses. Instead, the four chasers waited a short distance away as the two ambushers took the first bites out of the fallen victims.

CJ watched, entranced.

"They're like wolves," she said. "Wolves observe a strict hierarchy, both in the hunt and in the feeding that follows. The junior pack members drive the prey into the ambush, where the senior members wait. The senior members — an alpha male and an alpha female — carry out the kill. They always eat first. Then the juniors take their turn."

CJ saw one of the senior dragons bite down on the carcass of one of the horses. It tore off the dead animal's head with one mighty rip.

Ambassador Syme stepped up beside CJ, staring in awe at the bloody scene.

"You don't see that on the *National Geographic* channel," he said in a whisper.

The cable car continued on its journey over the western lake.

Up ahead of it was the ruined castle. The castle stood beside a third and final waterfall which curved in a wide U-shape. From where she stood, CJ could only see the lip of the waterfall dropping away like the rim of an infinity pool.

Above and behind the castle, however, was a far more modern structure: a fifteen-storey glass-faced building that sat half-embedded in the sloping wall of the crater.

Just below the point where the building's lowest floor met the hill, CJ saw a tunnel that allowed the ring road to burrow into the slope. She guessed that there was some kind of internal entry to the building inside the tunnel.

At the top of the glass building was a sleek white tower that looked like an air traffic control tower. It had many large radio antennas sticking up from it.

"What's that building?" CJ asked Zhang.

"That is our administration building," Zhang said. "Running a zoo of this size is like running a small city. The administration building houses all of our admin and support staff. Its lower floors contain loading docks that receive all the building materials that come into the zoo as well as coordinating waste management and disposal."

"And the tower at the top?"

"Dragon monitoring and observation," Zhang replied, a little too quickly and casually.

CJ noticed.

"Does it have anything to do with the electromagnetic domes?" she asked. "I mean, you wouldn't want one of the bigger dragons to accidentally crash into it and knock out your dome."

"Oh, no," Zhang said. "The inner dome emanates from twenty-four concrete emplacements built into the rim of the crater. You can see them up there, beside the tower. Each is heavily reinforced; the concrete is nine feet thick. The dragons couldn't damage them if they tried."

CJ put on her oversized sunglasses and looked up at the rim.

Through the glasses, she saw the curving luminescent green rays of the inner dome lancing skyward from a series of emplacements on the crater's upper rim. They looked like World War II pillboxes: supersolid concrete blockhouses with slitlike apertures from which the dome's beams sprang upward.

She shrugged and took off the glasses and was turning back to look at the administration building, when she spied a group of vehicles speeding out from the ring road tunnel at its base.

It was a convoy of five gasoline tanker trucks: eighteen-wheelers with long silver tanks on their backs. The tankers rumbled north along the ring road before disappearing into another tunnel.

"Deputy Director, what is that?" CJ heard Hu whisper harshly to Zhang in Mandarin.

"It's the two o'clock fuel run," Zhang said. "They're taking diesel to the cable car stations and the generators."

Hu hissed, "The drivers should have been informed that we had visitors today. Remember what the Disney consultants said: visitors should never see the backroom machinery at work. *Never.* Make sure those drivers and their supervisors are disciplined."

CJ didn't outwardly acknowledge their words. They must have forgotten she spoke Mandarin.

A deafening roar made her and everyone else in the cable car spin.

CJ's eyes went wide.

An emperor dragon was hovering *right alongside* the cable car!

It kept itself aloft with the occasional flap of its vast wings and it peered curiously into the cable car.

CJ hadn't even heard it approach. She couldn't believe the sheer size of it. It defied the senses to see something so big hovering in the air. And it thrilled her to be able to see it so close.

The great beast roared again, an ear-piercing shriek that seemed to shake the whole valley.

It was a red-bellied black dragon. Its underbelly blazed scarlet. Its black plated armor looked strong beyond belief. When it roared, its teeth flashed.

CJ noticed that it was looking closely at her and her companions, as if evaluating them.

CJ found herself admiring it. Curiosity in an animal was a sign of intelligence and it was rare. You found it only in a few members of the animal kingdom: chimpanzees, gorillas, dolphins.

Her eyes swept up the curve of the great beast's neck and she gazed at its fearsome head. Its eyes were a pitiless black. The sinews of its jaws were stretched taut. Its crest was sleek and sinister, while the rest of its massive head was covered in ugly scars and gashes, presumably from fights with other dragons —

CJ frowned.

Wait a second . . .

Something about this dragon's head didn't look right, but she couldn't quite put her finger on it.

Suddenly, with a final hideous screech, the massive creature beat its wings and banked away, flying off to the north, and everyone in the cable car started murmuring with wonder.

Shortly after, the cable car came to the great ruined castle. When she'd seen it before from the main building, CJ thought it hadn't looked so big, but now she realized that that had been a trick of the distance.

Seen from up close, it was absolutely enormous; dark, grim and imposing.

"We got the production designer from *The Lord of the Rings* movies to design this castle," Hu said to Wolfe. Hu seemed a little standoffish toward CJ now.

"It's awesome," Hamish said.

CJ had to admit that it did look pretty impressive. Indeed, it looked as if the fictitious inhabitants of the castle had done battle with invading dragons and lost badly. The brick battlements had crumbled. Whole towers lay askew on the ground. Some staircases ran nowhere, ending abruptly at ragged ends.

The whole thing was covered in black char-marks, causing CJ to remark, "I thought you said there were no fire-breathing dragons here."

Zhang offered a bashful smile. "We took some liberties with the design of this castle, for the sake of theatricality."

"I like it," Hamish said.

About a dozen dragons moved in and around the ruins, all yellowjackets.

At the base of the castle, at the point where it sat at the same height as the waterfall, an elongated wooden platform stretched out from the front gate.

It resembled a drawbridge, only it led nowhere. It just extended out over the curving waterfall directly in front of the castle, looking like a bridge that had been stopped halfway through its construction. It took CJ a moment to realize what it was.

"It's a landing platform for the dragons,"

she said.

"And a cable car stop for us," Zhang said, smiling. It was only a hundred yards ahead of them.

"I have another question," CJ said suddenly.

"Yes?" Deputy Director Zhang cast a worried glance at Hu, no doubt fearful of another awkward question from the *National Geographic* woman.

"You said you found 88 eggs in that cavern," CJ said. "But then you said that you have 232 dragons in this zoo. How does that work? I would have thought one egg means one dragon, so 88 eggs means 88 dragons, unless they've laid more eggs."

Zhang visibly relaxed. This was apparently a question he could answer easily.

He smiled. "You are correct, Dr. Cameron. One egg equals one dragon. And no, they have not laid any more eggs since they emerged from their nest. But we have been working and studying these animals at this facility for nearly forty years now. In that time, we have introduced some *augmented* breeding methods to bolster our stock of — What is that?"

He was looking out over CJ's shoulder, peering northward, his smile fading.

CJ turned, following his gaze.

What she saw made the blood in her veins freeze.

She saw a gang of five red-bellied black dragons of various sizes coming right for the cable car, led by the emperor that had checked them out only a few minutes earlier.

And as she beheld the gang of dragons coming toward her, CJ realized what had been wrong with the emperor's head.

It had no ears.

The scars and gashes on this dragon's head weren't injuries from battles with other dragons.

This emperor dragon *had scratched off its own ears* — deeply, too, tearing out the entire auditory canal, leaving two foul bloody sockets — which meant that the sonic dome protecting the cable car *would not have any effect on it at all.*

"Deputy Director, what is going on?" Hu asked ominously.

"Sir, I've never seen them do anything like this before," Zhang said.

"Hang on to something," CJ said to Hamish. *"Right now."*

The dragons rushed at the cable car and when they reached it, they did not stop.

The lead earless emperor smashed into the cable car with all its might, leading with

161

its upraised claws. Glass exploded everywhere and the cable car rocked violently
and in the space of a few terrible seconds
CJ Cameron's tour of the Great Dragon
Zoo of China went to hell.

■ ■ ■ ■

THIRD EVOLUTION

THE UNDISCOVERED PREDATOR

■ ■ ■ ■

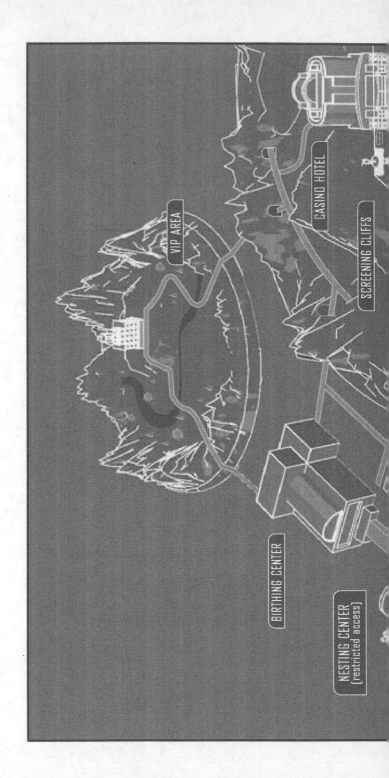

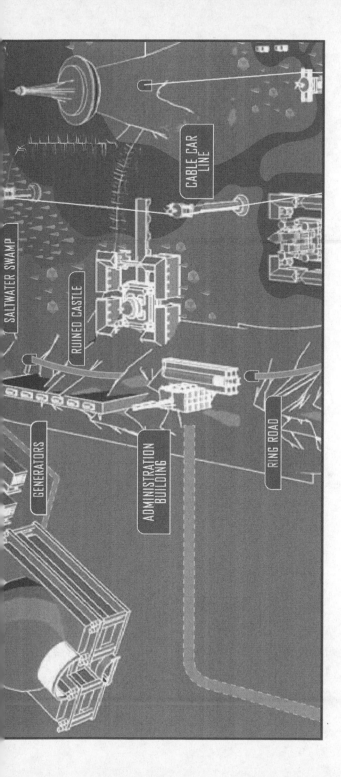

At a zoo or conservation park, you do not confront a photograph or a video. You confront the living, breathing animal.

— Bill Conway
President of the
New York Zoological Society
National Geographic, July 1993

The cable car swayed wildly, swinging through almost ninety degrees, such was the force of the emperor's blow.

CJ and Hamish grabbed hold of a railing as the world around them rocked crazily.

Beside them, Greg Johnson managed to get a grip as well and he held on to Ambassador Syme.

The others were less lucky.

The CCTV reporter, Xin, screamed as she was hurled sideways. Her cameraman went flying across the car and slammed against a window — a split second before the window shattered under the weight of an incoming red-bellied black dragon, this one a prince.

Like the lead emperor before it, this prince had no ears, so it was unaffected by the sonic shields enveloping the cable car and the individuals inside it. The prince exploded through the window with its jaws bared and before anyone knew what was happening, it grabbed the cameraman with its claws and swept him out of the cable car with a stifled yell.

"Holy fucking shit!" Hamish shouted as wind rushed into the cable car.

The whole car continued to rock dramatically on its cable, like a child's swing out of control.

Xin and Wolfe tumbled past CJ and Hamish, sliding toward the smashed-open window. CJ and Hamish reacted in exactly the same way: they both reached out, CJ snatching Xin's outstretched wrist while Hamish caught Wolfe's hand a moment before he fell out of the cable car.

The *New York Times* columnist came to a sudden halt a few feet short of the open window and gasped with relief just as the gigantic head of the emperor appeared right below his feet.

The dragon roared. It sounded like a jet engine, it was so loud.

The animal tried to stick its snout inside the window but the opening was too small and only its flaring nostrils got inside.

CJ's eyes went wide.

Then suddenly the emperor's jaws chomped, biting off a whole section of the cable car, in doing so, catching hold of Xin's right leg! The giant creature yanked her out of CJ's grip.

Xin screamed as she was pulled into the creature's gaping jaws.

The dragon bit down on her stomach.

Blood and organs shot out of Xin's mouth, expelled by the sheer force of the bite. CJ felt sick at the sight of it. Then the dragon extracted its snout from the window, taking the TV reporter with it.

Hamish was speechless.

CJ wasn't.

"Get away from the window!" she yelled, scrambling over the bar. "Before it comes back!"

It came back a few seconds later, jamming its huge teeth in through the shattered windows. But everyone had taken CJ's advice and they were out of range. When it came up with nothing, the emperor roared and pulled its snout from the cable car.

Silence.

The cable car's swinging slowed until it was almost still again.

Everyone waited, tense, expectant, not daring to move.

Nothing happened.

"What *the fuck* was that?" Ambassador Syme said, glaring at Hu.

Hu made to reply, but he never got a word out, for at that moment the entire car was wrenched from its cable and thrown through the air.

If CJ and the other occupants of the cable car could have seen their cable car from the outside, what they would have seen was the emperor dragon hovering above it, its vast wings outstretched, gripping the cable car with its massive talons, wrenching it from its cable and hurling it into the waters of the lake.

The cable car rolled as it flew and it landed in the water roof-first.

It now bobbed upside down in the water, fifty yards from the waterfall in front of the ruined castle.

And then it started to move, carried by the current toward the surging lip of the fall.

Inside the cable car, the world had gone totally crazy.

Everything was upside down. The bar stools bolted to the floor now hung from the ceiling. Every bottle behind the bar had been smashed. Water was gushing in through the cable car's smashed and cracked windows.

CJ and the other occupants came down hard beside the ceiling lights.

CJ was on her feet first. Crouched in the ankle-deep water, she took in the scene quickly.

"We're moving and we're sinking," she said.

With a roar, an eighteen-foot-long crocodile suddenly burst through one of the windows in an explosion of glass and water.

CJ dived away from it and the reptile's slashing jaws missed her by inches. The croc hit the floor — or rather, the ceiling — of the cable car, landing on all fours, searching for the nearest prey. It found it in Hamish, lying flat on his chest in the water right in front of it.

CJ saw the equation instantly and it didn't look good.

A memory flashed in her mind.

Another place, another time.

A swampy enclosure in the Everglades. Alligators in a pen. Schoolchildren laughing and eating lunch, having just watched a presentation. CJ is eating her own lunch nearby. She has nothing to do with the school group. She is here doing research.

The teachers know nothing about alligators. They do not know that alligators will always take an opportunity to snatch the young of another animal. They turn their backs . . .

. . . as a little boy climbs up onto the fence of the alligator pen.

CJ sees him too late.

The boy is skylarking on top of the fence, showing off for the other kids. He never sees the bull alligator launch itself from the water.

The gator snatches the boy's leg, hauls him off the fence and takes him under.

CJ is over the fence like lightning, diving into the water after the kid.

Splashing and slashing.

Her world is a blur of muddy water, flailing limbs, the boy's cries and the alligator's tooth-filled mouth. And then in a sudden shining instant, she is looking right into one of the alligator's eyes.

It is terrible and cold, unnerving. It is without mercy or remorse.

CJ stabs the fucker in the eye with the fingernail of her thumb. It jerks and releases the boy and she throws the kid clear, onto the muddy shore, where a teacher grabs him. She clambers out after him on all fours, spent and exhausted, but clear of the —

The bull explodes from the water and grabs her head in its mouth.

CJ is yanked hideously backwards. The pain is excruciating. The gator's teeth tear apart her left cheek. Her fingers leave claw marks in the mud of the shore as she is pulled back into the water, her head bent at a terrible angle.

And no one does a thing.

She goes under with the bull.

CJ blinked out of the memory, came back to the present.

The croc had Hamish dead to rights. Her brother had nowhere to go and CJ was too far away to be of any help.

The croc lunged —

— just as a red-bellied black prince swooped in through the window behind the crocodile, grabbed the reptile in its fore-claws and bit down on its neck. The crunching sound that followed was sickening. The dragon had broken the crocodile's neck with one bite. The croc went limp.

CJ was gobsmacked.

An eighteen-foot-long saltwater crocodile. The biggest croc in the world. An animal without predators. And the dragon had killed it in an instant.

The dragon spat the remains of the crocodile onto the floor. CJ saw that this one also had no ears.

The cable car around her continued to flood. The water was now up to her knees.

"We have to get to the other level!" she yelled to the others as she sloshed through the water toward one of the two stairwells that connected the cable car's upper and lower levels.

The others followed suit, racing for the stairwells.

The prince roared, swinging its gaze back and forth, not sure which way to go. It eventually snapped at Hamish as he dived, last of all, into the small stairwell at the aft end of the cable car.

Running on pure adrenaline, CJ arrived at the upper, formerly lower, level of the overturned cable car and peered forward.

"Oh, you have got to be kidding me . . ." she gasped.

The waterfall dropped away mere yards before her, a surging cascade of water shooting out over the lip.

She searched for options.

Maybe there was a rock on the lip that

they could jump over to: no, nothing.

Maybe they could jump across to the landing platform jutting out from the ruined castle: she saw it off to the right, just outside the still-intact windows on that side of the cable car, but that wasn't an option either because it was too late.

The cable car was already at the edge of the waterfall, and with a sudden sickening tilt, it went over.

CJ's world tilted wildly yet again and for a moment everything went vertical . . .

. . . and then the cable car fell.

It plummeted through the air, nose-first.

But then after only a short fall, it stopped with a loud crunching noise and everyone was thrown downwards.

The forward windows of the car smashed inward, spraying glass.

The cable car had slammed down into one of the rock ledges that jutted out from the face of the waterfall.

From the outside, the cable car looked totally bizarre.

It was perched vertically on the face of the curving waterfall, its forward end smashed against the wide rock ledge, its aft end pointing skyward with the gushing water of the falls pouring down over it while two red-bellied black prince dragons clung to its outer walls.

Inside the vertical cable car, CJ was doing her best not to freak out. Too much was happening, too much to take in.

Stay calm, she told herself. *Gotta think clearly . . .*

She looked up and saw an escape route: the landing platform leading to the ruined castle. It was right above the upper end of the upturned cable car, only a few feet away from it. If they could climb up to the top end of the perched cable car, maybe they could —

"Everyone!" she called. "Climb! Get to the top and then jump across to that platform!"

No one was in a state to argue: Seymour Wolfe was whipping his head this way and that in a panic; Aaron Perry was clinging desperately to a seat; Greg Johnson was holding up his boss, the ambassador. Hu Tang kept stammering "Oh God, oh God" in Mandarin while Deputy Director Zhang wore the blank despairing expression of a man who had just seen his entire future go up in flames. Hamish seemed okay, but then, he'd been in war zones before.

They all followed CJ, using the bolted-down seats as a kind of ladder, and soon they were up at the sliding doors at the top end of the cable car.

Hamish and Johnson yanked them open — and immediately a torrent of water came rushing in, slamming into their faces, almost knocking them back down the car. The waterfall was now gushing directly into the upturned cable car.

"Go!" CJ yelled. "Hurry!"

Hamish went first, then Johnson. They stood on top of the car and began helping the others out.

One by one, the group climbed through the column of water streaming down into the cable car, with Johnson and Hamish pulling them up from above: Wolfe, Perry, then Ambassador Syme, Hu Tang and Zhang. They all emerged from the cable car before jumping tentatively across to the landing platform.

Only CJ, Na and the bartender remained inside the cable car. Water rushed into the car through the upper doorway in a thick unbroken gush. Smaller cascades tumbled over the seats.

Climbing up beside CJ, Na was sobbing, shivering.

Then CJ heard a groan.

It wasn't an animal or human groan, however, but the sound of rending metal.

Filling with water, the cable car was literally bursting at the seams.

Abruptly, a window exploded under the weight of water and the whole car jolted . . . and began to tilt slowly away from the waterfall.

"CJ! The car's about to fall off the ledge!" Hamish yelled through the pouring water. "Come on!"

CJ hauled ass, clambering up the last few seatbacks, with Na and the bartender moving desperately beside her.

"Move it, people!" Hamish called from the doorway.

CJ, Na and the bartender reached the doorway just as something large and black came rushing in through it, borne on the water, and collided full-on with the poor bartender, who was hurled down the length of the vertical cable car.

The impact with the bartender had halted the dragon's fall and suddenly there it was in his place, right in front of CJ and Na!

It was a prince-sized red-bellied black dragon.

It hissed at them, right in their faces, and CJ saw the deep bloody wounds where its ears should have been.

It was a creature of another time, a terrible serpent-like thing. It was everything that human beings — soft and clawless — feared. Its fangs were long, its talons scythe-like, its hide armored. No human could fight such a thing. And you couldn't reason with it either.

This red-bellied black prince, CJ saw, had an almost entirely red head and a small camouflaged box grafted to the left side of its skull . . . and suddenly she realized that she had seen it before: it was one of the dragons from the amphitheater, the sullen prince that had reluctantly performed for the female trainer —

The dragon moved before CJ could react. It snatched Na's throat in one powerful claw and bit her head off with a shocking tearing bite. Blood sprayed all over CJ's face.

CJ was horrified — not just by the savageness of the act but by the speed of it. It had happened so fast!

The red-faced dragon dropped Na's headless body and turned its gaze on CJ.

Others might have been stunned motionless in such circumstances but CJ had fought nasty things before. Instinct kicked in and she lashed out at the creature with her right boot.

The kick connected and she caught the dragon square in the mouth.

The dragon recoiled at the kick and in doing so fell back into the column of water gushing into the cable car and was swept away, down to where the bartender was.

The red-bellied black prince landed with a splash at the base of the cable car. The dragon squealed and thrashed beside the hapless bartender.

CJ looked down at them, at first too stunned to move.

The red-faced dragon shrieked again, looking directly up at her.

There came another metallic groan and suddenly someone — Hamish — was grabbing her by the collar, calling, "You can't help him!" and CJ was yanked up through the column of pouring water and all of a sudden she was standing in daylight beside her brother and Zhang on the top end of the upturned cable car, on the face of the curving waterfall, in front of the elongated landing platform that led to the ruined medieval castle.

Bizarre.

The cable car was still tilting slowly away from the waterfall. CJ saw the landing platform only a short jump away, but then she caught sight of a shadow moving behind the curtain of water just a few feet away from her.

A second black prince, also earless.

At first CJ couldn't figure out what it was doing there. Its head was bent over something. Then she saw it wrench something off the roof of the cable car with its jaws and with horror CJ realized what that something was.

It was the cable car's snub antenna.

The device that generated the cable car's sonic shield.

"CJ! Come on!" Hamish yelled.

Just then, the dragon pushed its head through the curtain of water.

It took a step forward, moving like a tiger, emerging from the wall of water one claw at a time, its head bent low.

The cable car groaned again. It was leaning ever further, about to topple off the ledge on which it was so precariously balanced.

Zhang leapt away to safety.

"Jump!" Hamish yelled.

And they jumped, together . . .

. . . just as the second dragon lunged at them, but it missed, and as they dived off the cable car at the very last moment — grabbing on to the end of the landing platform with their fingertips, their legs flailing behind them — the cable car toppled off the face of the waterfall, taking the two black princes and the unfortunate bartender with it.

The big double-decker car fell a full eighty

feet down the face of the waterfall before it landed with a great splash in the roiling whitewater at the base and went under.

CJ and Hamish dangled from the end of the landing platform, high above the dizzying drop.

Greg Johnson reached down and hauled CJ up.

"We can't stay here!" he shouted over the din of the falls, showing more coolness under pressure than CJ would've given him credit for.

Within moments, she and Hamish were on their feet and running with the group along the length of the landing platform as dragons wheeled and shrieked and shot by overhead. They dashed into the ruined castle just as the red-bellied black emperor that had started the whole thing rushed by in a hurricane of wind and fury.

Hamish slammed the doors of the castle shut behind them.

Silence, save for the muffled sound of the

waterfall outside.

Wolfe and Perry both fell to the floor, breathless. Hu and Zhang just looked shell-shocked. Greg Johnson checked on the U.S. Ambassador, who leaned against the wall, soaking wet.

CJ peered up at the interior of the castle around them.

They were in a high-ceilinged entry atrium. It was the size of an airplane hangar and it looked old and decrepit, with gaping holes in the ceiling and charred walls. Torn tapestries hung from crossbeams. Two sweeping staircases ran in matching semi-circles on either side of the hall, leading to a chamber of some sort. But one of the staircases was useless: it had a ragged void in its middle, presumably created by an angry dragon.

There were no dragons in sight.

There was, however, one out-of-place feature: high up near the ceiling, a modern black catwalk ran around the wall.

There was no ladder to it. It entered the hall from the north and exited to the south. At first CJ couldn't figure out what it was. Then she realized: it was for guests to walk on and observe the dragons in their castle home.

"Well, this isn't going to look good in *The*

New York Times," she said. "Okay, what do we do now? Where can we go?"

No one replied.

She jerked her chin at Hu. "I said, *what the hell* do we do now and *where the hell* can we go!"

Hu was still in shock. His jaw quivered. He couldn't speak.

"The administration building," Zhang said quietly. "It's on the western wall, right behind this castle —"

Boom!

The big door behind them shook, struck from outside.

Boom!

Again.

An enraged roar assaulted their ears.

The emperor.

"We gotta move, people," CJ said, running for the intact sweeping staircase. "We gotta move now . . ."

More shrieks rang out from outside. Two shadows whipped by overhead, shooting past one of the holes in the ceiling: red-bellied black princes.

The group hurried up the curving staircase.

They were almost at the top of the stairs when the main doors to the atrium blasted inwards in an explosion of splinters.

The red-bellied black emperor stood in the doorway, giant and menacing. It bellowed, its jet-engine roar shaking the walls of the castle.

"Hurry!" CJ called as the emperor thundered through the doorway, stomping into the atrium with great, whomping strides.

They dashed up the last few steps just as two red-bellied black princes smashed through a pair of stained-glass windows on the other side of the hall and landed at the top of the other, broken staircase.

"This way! Into the throne room!" Zhang called, leading them into the chamber directly behind the atrium.

They all hurried into it . . . only to stop dead in their tracks.

An absolutely gigantic yellowjacket emperor dragon lay before them, curled in a ball in the throne room of the castle.

Velvet curtains and torn tapestries hung around it. CJ saw some black steel spiral steps nearby that led up to another guest catwalk running around the ceiling of this room.

The massive yellowjacket was the picture of calm repose. Its coloring was magnificent, brighter than the coloring of the little female CJ had seen earlier, the one named Lucky. This one's yellow stripes were the most vivid yellow; its black stripes, the deepest black.

It raised its gigantic head and stared at the group curiously. Its slit eyes were huge and unblinking. And it still had ears, CJ noticed immediately.

Then, suddenly, two yellowjacket princes popped up from within the emperor's embrace. They had been sleeping inside its massive limbs and although they themselves were nine feet tall, they looked positively tiny beside the emperor.

Ever the loyal lieutenants, they leapt to their emperor's defense, placing themselves between it and this group of intruders.

One of the princes hissed at CJ and approached —

— only to recoil with a piercing squeal.

It had struck the sonic shield emitted by her watch and CJ saw that the princes also still had their ears. The shield generated by her watch still worked.

And then the yellowjacket emperor growled.

It was a sound of the most intense malevolence and it came from deep within the giant creature. The ultimate animal warning. The walls of the throne room quivered, so great was the sound.

CJ held her breath.

They had stepped into its lair, its territory, and it wasn't happy about it.

CJ found herself wondering: could their little sonic shields really withstand an emperor's charge? It didn't seem to her that they could.

Then, with surprising speed, the giant yellowjacket sprang from its position and leapt at them!

There was nothing CJ could do. Nothing any of them could do. It was too fast.

But the yellowjacket thundered *over* them and with a mighty thwack of flesh against flesh, it slammed into the red-bellied black emperor that had appeared in the doorway behind CJ's group.

Territorial behavior, CJ recalled. That some puny little humans might have encroached upon the yellowjacket's territory was one thing. But another emperor dragon, well, that could not be tolerated.

The entire castle trembled as the two airliner-sized dragons went rolling back into the enormous entry atrium. For a few moments, the two beasts were a single entity, a mass of yellow-and-black limbs intertwined with red-and-black ones with two flailing tails added to the mix.

The ground rumbled as they fought, jaws snapping, claws tearing.

The two yellowjacket princes leapt to the aid of their emperor and joined the fight with the earless red-bellied black emperor — at the same time as the two red-bellied princes from the atrium charged in to defend *their* massive brother.

CJ didn't need to be offered another chance. "Come on!" she called. "Get up onto that catwalk and follow it out of this place!"

The group obeyed.

Within moments they were up on the catwalk, running south. Sure enough, it led out of the castle, to a long pedestrian bridge that stretched over to a vehicle turnaround attached to the ring road.

It was all designed, CJ figured, so that guests could be dropped off here, walk through the ruined castle on the elevated catwalks, and then be picked up later at another turnaround.

Right then, she didn't care. She hoped by now that some kind of security force or rescue team had been dispatched to come and get them. If she couldn't get her group to the administration building, then at least she had to get them out in the open where they could be spotted by a closed-circuit camera or a rescue chopper.

Running out in front of the others, she

dashed across the pedestrian bridge and arrived at the turnaround. About two hundred yards to the south, down the black bitumen ring road, was a tunnel that bored into a sloping section of the western crater wall. At the moment, the mouth of the tunnel was sealed by a thick-barred gate. Towering above the tunnel, built into the sloping hillside, was the administration building.

Zhang saw it, too. "There is an internal entrance to the admin building inside that tunnel! Go!"

The eight desperate humans — six Americans and two Chinese — bolted down the roadway, running as fast as they could toward the gated tunnel.

As he ran, Hu Tang's mind swirled with a mix of incomprehension, fear and outright fury. He could hardly think. This was a disaster. *A disaster.* How had it happened? How had it been *allowed* to happen? Some of the dragons had ripped out their own ears from the roots to outwit the sonic shields. How had no one seen this coming? When they regained control, he swore, heads would fucking roll.

He looked about himself. He was running alongside CJ and Zhang and the two *New York Times* men. Behind them, Greg Johnson ran with the ambassador.

They were about a hundred yards from the tunnel when the grilled gate sealing it began to open.

It slid upward and three armored vehicles came speeding out of it: two Shorland four-by-four armored personnel carriers and a white-painted six-wheeled Hotspur field ambulance.

The Shorlands were painted olive-green like army vehicles while the white Hotspur looked like the UN peacekeeping vehicle that it usually was.

The thick-barred gate guarding the mouth of the tunnel slid closed behind the three vehicles.

Relief flooded through Hu when he saw them. "An Emergency Response Team! They're coming for us!"

The three armored vehicles boomed down the ring road, coming toward the group . . .

. . . and sped right past them.

Hu's jaw dropped. "What the — ?"

The cars zoomed away down the ring road, racing off into the distance before entering another tunnel about a mile to the north. That was just a regular tunnel, with no gate sealing it.

"We're not the most important VIPs here today," CJ said wryly. "They're going to save those other guys. We gotta do this ourselves, on foot."

Hu was beyond furious. "This is outrageous!" he fumed.

194

"Wait, look!" Hamish yelled.

He was pointing up the ring road in the direction the rescue team had gone.

Two hardtop jeeps were coming *back* down the road, coming toward them at considerable speed.

"That's our ride!" CJ called. "Wave them down!"

The group stepped out into the middle of the road, waving at the jeeps.

The oncoming jeeps showed no sign of stopping. They just kept speeding wildly down the road.

Hu Tang could make out two men in each of the cars: workmen of some kind, no doubt fleeing the dragons. He stepped out in front of the others, raising one arm, palm outward. He knew with his distinctive patch of white hair, the workmen would recognize him and render assistance.

The two jeeps didn't stop. Like the rescue team before them, they just swerved wildly around the group and kept on going.

Hu was stunned. "What —"

"You cowardly motherfuc—" Aaron Perry shouted, but he was cut off by a loud crash as two red-bellied black princes shot out of the sky and slammed into the two jeeps from the side.

The two jeeps were lifted fully off the road

195

by the stunning impacts, and they flipped and tumbled as their inertia carried them a further twenty yards down the ring road. One jeep ended up upside down, on its roof, while the other landed with an awkward thump back on its wheels, seventy yards from the barred tunnel but now facing the wrong way.

As the dust settled around them, Hu saw no movement within the two crumpled cars.

But the two dragons weren't done. They wrenched open the jeeps' doors and reached in with their claws to extract the bloodied but live occupants: four Chinese zoo workers in overalls.

These two princes, Hu noticed, were also earless, so the cars' sonic shields were useless against them.

"Quickly!" CJ hissed, grabbing Hu by the sleeve. "Get off the road!"

They hurdled the low guardrail at the edge of the ring road and dived in among the shrubs on the slope below it. The others hurriedly followed.

From the cover of the bushes beside the roadway, CJ stared at the two crashed jeeps, the two prince dragons and the four Chinese workmen.

The princes were fearsome-looking things:

nine feet tall, with high crests and blazing red bellies. With brutal efficiency, the first dragon pinned a workman under one of its forelimbs and proceeded to bite down on the man's left arm, wrenching it off in a fountain of blood.

The man screamed in agony.

The second dragon promptly did the same to a second and then a third workman, while the first black prince ripped the left arm off the last worker. This last worker tried to flee but the dragon just knocked him to the ground casually and held him down with one of its hind legs.

"What are they doing?" Hamish whispered.

"They're biting off the workers' watches . . ." CJ said, ". . . to remove their shields. Quick, move," she hissed. "We don't want to be here in the next few seconds —"

With a bloodcurdling shriek, a much larger red-bellied black dragon arrived on the scene, landing on the ring road with a weighty *whump.*

If the princes looked fierce, and the emperor had been simply gigantic, the king looked absolutely terrifying. Terrifying, cruel and yet somehow *regal.* Its long neck was arched, rearing back before it curved forward, giving the creature a real sense of majesty.

It was as long as a city bus and each spike of its magnificent crest was taller than a man. Its tail appeared to have a mind of its own: it swept up behind the massive beast, slithering back and forth, a sinister barb at its tip.

Crucially, CJ noted, it *had* ears. Hence the need for the removal of the workmen's watches.

"The princes are giving the king a food offering," she said.

"A what?" Johnson said.

"It's a feeding ritual, a hierarchical feeding ritual. The lesser pack members catch the food and give it to the pack leader to eat first. They only eat after he does."

One of the princes pushed two of the workers toward the king. The workers, clutching their recently amputated arms and screaming in terror, could hardly stand. One dropped to his knees, wailing.

The king dragon peered down at the workers imperiously.

Then it lunged forward and CJ heard a hideous crunch and then the dragon lifted its head again and suddenly one of the workmen was only half as tall as he had been.

CJ's eyes widened in horror.

It had bitten the man in two with a single bite!

The dead workman's legs toppled to the roadway.

The king then tilted its head sideways, scooped the legs up and gulped them down, too. Then it turned its gaze on the second, kneeling workman.

Its huge mouth opened at the edges as it glared down at the man, revealing its fearsome fangs. It looked like a smile, the cruel smile of the ultimate predator toying with its prey.

The kneeling workman held up his remaining hand pathetically, as if that would do him any good.

It didn't.

He simply exploded in a spray of blood as the king's jaws clamped down on him like a bear trap.

"Holy Mary, Mother of God . . ." Syme breathed.

Hamish came up beside CJ. "Sis, excuse my language, but what the fuck do we do now?"

CJ was wondering the same thing.

She turned to look at the nearby tunnel, the one giving access to the administration building, currently resealed by the thick-barred gate.

"Those workmen were trying to get to the admin building," she said. "Which means they could open that gate . . ."

Hamish said, "You think —"

"Yep. There's a remote control in one or both of those jeeps. A remote that opens the gate."

Hu heard them. "You want one of us to go out there and get into one of those cars?"

"Yes," CJ said, "while the rest of us run down to the tunnel, to be there when the gate opens."

Wolfe said, "And how exactly are we going to choose who goes on this suicide mission?"

CJ ignored him, turned to Hamish. "We have to do this *now,* while they're feeding. I was always quicker than you. Just be ready to close the gate behind me when I get there, okay?"

"You got it," Hamish said.

CJ made to move, but then she remembered something. She tore off her Great Dragon Zoo watch and thrust it into Hamish's hand. "Here, take this. I don't want any of those dragons spotting me out of the corner of their eye with a big blue sphere of light around me."

Hamish took the watch, frowning. "Then you won't be protected —"

But CJ was already off, leaping over the low guardrail and crouch-running across the road while the three dragons looked the other way, consumed by their meal.

Hamish pushed the others through the scrub that ran along the edge of the road, heading for the tunnel, every now and then turning back to check on CJ.

He had gone thirty yards when he saw her — unseen by the dragons — slip through the open door of the upright jeep.

The hardtop jeep was facing away from the tunnel, having flipped that way when it had crashed, and through its rear window, Hamish saw CJ search for the remote until she found it up near the rearview mirror. She turned and gave Hamish a thumbs-up.

Huddled in the jeep, CJ didn't hit the remote straightaway. She was waiting for the others to get to the gate. She slouched below the dashboard, staying low, trying to remain unseen by the dragons only ten yards away.

The king dragon ate the third workman while his two lieutenants looked on.

She saw Hamish and the others reach some bushes next to the tunnel just as the king stepped back and allowed the two princes to have the last sobbing workman.

201

They tore him apart, one taking his upper body, the other his lower half.

At which point, CJ hit OPEN on the remote.

With a dull mechanical clunking, the gate sealing the mouth of the tunnel slid upward, opening.

Hamish and the others didn't need any prompting. They hurdled the guardrail and dashed inside the tunnel.

The three dragons spun at the movement.

Hamish found a panel on the wall, hit CLOSE and the gate slid back down, closing with a soft *whump*.

Inside the jeep, CJ exhaled with relief. They were safe.

Now she had to get herself to the tunnel. She figured if she lay low in the jeep, the dragons would eventually take off and then she could just sneak down to the tunn—

Beep-beep . . . beep-beep.

A soft electronic beeping sound made CJ turn to see the huge head of one of the princes on the other side of the driver's window, staring right at her!

CJ sprang back. "Ah!"

She turned the other way — to see the *second* prince peering at her through the passenger side window!

"Ooh, shit . . ."

The first dragon roared, loudly and furiously, and CJ saw it more clearly: it was the one with the red face and the box-shaped implant grafted onto the side of its head. Now, however, it had a Bluetooth earpiece wedged between two of its bloody teeth. To her horror, CJ recognized it as Na's ear-piece.

The Bluetooth earpiece was making the beeping sound as it searched for a device to pair with.

This was the same red-faced dragon CJ had kicked in the mouth inside the cable car and which had last been seen falling to the bottom of the waterfall inside the car.

It must have got out.

Red Face bellowed again and, glaring malevolently at CJ, punched the driver's door with its foreclaw. The door dented inward. The car rocked.

The second prince roared as well and with nothing else to call on, CJ turned the key in the ignition and miraculously the battered jeep started.

The two dragons withdrew at the revving of the engine.

CJ jammed the jeep into reverse and floored it.

With a squeal of tires, the jeep took off, shooting back toward the gated tunnel.

The king dragon turned idly at this sudden movement, seemingly more intrigued than disturbed. It didn't move.

But its two earless princes did.

They bounded after the jeep and as CJ

sped backwards in reverse, Red Face launched itself onto the hood of the car and roared fiercely at CJ through the windshield.

The second dragon landed on the roof of the backward-speeding jeep and the roof bent inwards under the animal's weight, almost crushing CJ.

Leaning low, CJ kept her foot on the gas and the jeep raced down the ring road in reverse.

Riding on the hood, Red Face punched through the windshield and CJ ducked as glass exploded all around her and suddenly a massive black forearm with razor-sharp claws was *right there* in the jeep's cabin with her, trying to get at her.

One claw slashed across CJ's left shoulder, slicing through her leather jacket, drawing blood.

CJ screamed in pain.

Then she yanked left on the steering wheel and the car swerved crazily, forcing Red Face to withdraw his claw to keep himself from falling off the speeding jeep.

Her shoulder burning with pain, CJ turned to look through the rear window of the jeep: the tunnel was now only thirty yards away.

Then the entire rear door of the jeep was wrenched clean off and the second dragon swung in through the opening and snarled at CJ from point-blank range.

At the same time, on the hood, instead of reaching in with his claw, Red Face jammed his head through the shattered windshield and suddenly CJ found herself staring into the open jaws of that dragon, too.

CJ gritted her teeth in determination.

"You guys wanna go for a drive? All right, then . . ."

She jammed the gas pedal all the way down, yanked the steering wheel hard right, causing the reversing jeep to swing that way and then she dived out the driver's side door just as the speeding jeep crashed through the guardrail separating the ring road from the hillside.

The jeep shot off the road, with the two black princes on it, and it bounced and jounced for fifteen yards before it slammed into a tree, sending the two dragons flying off it. Red Face slammed into a thick tree trunk, wrapping around it. The second dragon tumbled further down the hill, end over end over end.

Up on the road, CJ rolled to a halt, grazed but alive, only ten yards from the gate.

"CJ!" She saw Hamish on the other side of the barred gate. "Move your butt!"

He hit an unseen button and the thick-grilled gate slid up a couple of feet. CJ scrambled forward on her hands and knees, rolled under it, and the gate came down and she exhaled with relief, safe.

Smack!

Red Face slammed against the bars of the gate, inches away from her, and she fell back onto her butt. The enraged dragon reached through the bars — frenzied and furious — desperate to grab her, but CJ scuttled backwards, away from its grasping claws.

The dragon hissed.

But it couldn't get past the gate, and as she sat on the floor of the tunnel, her chest heaving, tears welling in her eyes, CJ looked up at Hamish.

"Now *that's* character building," she said.

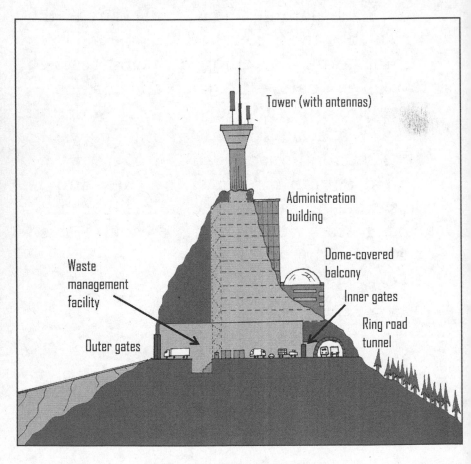

Tower (with antennas)

Administration
building

Dome-covered
balcony

Waste
management
facility

Inner gates

Ring road
tunnel

Outer gates

THE ADMINISTRATION BUILDING
AND TOWER
(PLUS WASTE MANAGEMENT FACILITY)

Safely behind the grilled gate, CJ wiped her eyes clean and stood. "All right, folks. Let's go find someone who can get us out of here."

"Aye, aye to that." Hamish handed her back her Great Dragon Zoo watch. "Here, you better put this back on."

The group headed down the tunnel. It was modern and well lit, with a high curving ceiling that spanned a two-lane bitumen road. Two full-sized semitrailer rigs could pass through it side by side. It stretched ahead for about five hundred yards where it met another barred gate through which daylight shone.

Seymour Wolfe's lower lip was quivering. He was, CJ could tell, visibly coming to terms with what they had just endured. "This is just . . . just *unbelievable.*"

Aaron Perry had already progressed to anger. "It's FUBAR, is what it is: Fucked

209

Up Beyond All Recognition."

CJ noticed that Hu Tang was saying nothing. He just walked along with his head bent, lips pursed, deep in thought. Deputy Director Zhang walked beside him, desperately avoiding eye contact.

Glancing behind her, CJ saw the grim silhouette of Red Face at the northern gate. He had been joined by the other black prince and the two dragons paced back and forth on the other side of the bars.

It's only the red-bellied black dragons that are attacking, she thought. She wondered why. Was there something about them that was different from the other dragons?

Then, abruptly, the two dragons stopped, turning to face something that had caught their attention, and took to the air.

CJ was happy to see them go.

About a hundred yards down the tunnel, her group came to a set of oversized garage doors embedded in the wall.

"This is our waste management facility," Zhang said.

As the group arrived at the doors, one of them rumbled open and three Chinese men in suits came running out. They raced straight to Hu Tang, babbling with concern, but he brushed them off with a few sharp words.

CJ entered the waste management facility.

A fleet of twenty-four brand-new garbage trucks were parked in perfect rows. They were big Isuzu trucks, with large hydraulic compacter units at their rears and THE GREAT ZOO OF CHINA painted on their white sides.

Clearly the Chinese hadn't got around to changing the logos on them yet, CJ thought. After today's attack, she wondered if they ever would.

Beyond the fleet of garbage trucks was a gigantic concrete pit — sixty yards by fifteen yards — that was partially filled with refuse. Along one of its long walls were several huge piston-driven compacters, designed to compress the waste against the opposite wall. Overhead cranes then lifted the compacted waste into dump trucks that were parked in loading docks on the opposite side of the great pit, facing some more oversized garage doors that led westward, out of the crater.

On the left-hand side of the space, parked by some diesel pumps, was a collection of fire trucks. Painted bright red and glistening with newness, there were four mid-sized water pumpers and two superlong ladder trucks.

It was an impressive facility, even if the

whole massive place did stink of garbage.

There was one other thing about the hall that struck CJ.

There was a dragon here.

But it wasn't on the loose or on a rampage. Indeed, quite the opposite.

It was the yellowjacket prince that CJ and the others had seen do tricks in the amphitheater: the one named Lucky.

Right now, Lucky sat obediently, if a little nervously, inside a caged trailer that was coupled to a Great Dragon Zoo pickup truck. The dragon still wore the saddle on its back.

Its female handler, the young woman with yellow-streaked hair — CJ recalled her name was Yim — stood beside the cage, stroking Lucky through the bars. Yim was still wearing her black bodysuit and her radio earpiece but not her armored black-and-yellow leather jacket.

"What's happening, sir?" Yim called to Hu in Mandarin.

"Some of the dragons have become . . . aggressive," Zhang replied as he kept walking. "What are you doing here?"

"Lucky is hurt. After we did our fly-by past the cable cars, she landed on a loose rock and rolled her ankle. I hope it isn't broken. Our truck was here getting refueled. I was about to take her to the Birthing Center when all the alarms sounded."

"Just stay here," Zhang said, not stopping.

Looking very confused, the handler stayed with her caged yellow dragon.

CJ didn't care. She just followed Zhang and Hu, who were drawing a crowd as they strode toward a pair of elevators in the right-hand wall.

"Where to, Chipmunk?" Hamish asked.

"I need to find a suture kit," CJ said. The entire left shoulder of her brown leather jacket was now stained with blood. "Then I want to get on a plane, go back to the hotel in Hong Kong and take a long hot fucking bath."

She jerked her chin at one of the suits fawning around Hu Tang and said curtly in Mandarin: "Where is the infirmary?"

The suit nodded quickly. "Level three," he said in English. He then spoke into a radio in Mandarin.

An elevator arrived. CJ got in. The others followed.

Greg Johnson stood close beside CJ.

Amid the noise of all the others talking, he said softly: "Dr. Cameron, in your professional opinion, what just happened here?"

CJ glanced sideways at Johnson. "You move well . . . for an embassy aide. You're

213

not just an ambassador's assistant, are you?"

He raised an eyebrow. "That's not relevant right now. What *is* relevant are our chances of survival. What just happened?"

CJ said, "These animals are clearly smarter than our Chinese friends have given them credit for. The Chinese came up with what they thought was an ingenious system to protect their cable cars — the sonic shields — but the dragons scratched off their own ears so they could attack the cars. They also know about our watches. They're problem-solvers, Mr. Johnson, and that's what I find most worrying."

"Why?"

"Because intelligence in the animal kingdom is directly proportional to brain size. As a percentage of body size, humans have the biggest brains of any creature on this planet, hence we are the dominant species. Chimps and apes and whales and dolphins come next, and *all* of them exhibit problem-solving skills: the ability to use X to achieve Y.

"Crocodiles have medium-sized brains, but the reptilian brain doesn't waste space with notions of empathy or conscience. When a crocodile looks at something, all it is thinking about is how it will go about hunting it and eating it. Crocodiles also exhibit problem-solving skills both in their trap-setting and in their evasion techniques: it is well known that you will never capture a crocodile with the same technique twice.

"What worries me is these dragons have really big brains. The sonic shields on that cable car and on our watches were preventing the dragons from getting to us. So they solved the problem: they tore off their own ears or wrenched off those workmen's arms, removing their watches."

Johnson looked at her for a long moment. Then he spoke in a low voice. "There could be other problems for us here as well."

"What do you mean?" CJ said, wincing. Her shoulder burned.

"I mean —"

Just then the elevator doors opened onto the third floor of the administration building. After the artificial underground light of the tunnel and the waste facility, CJ was assaulted by brilliant daylight.

A wide bank of floor-to-ceiling windows met her, windows that opened onto a glass-domed balcony overlooking the valley. CJ could see the rear of the ruined castle and beyond it, Dragon Mountain.

A female Chinese secretary hurried up to CJ and, bowing, handed her a shrink-wrapped first-aid kit.

215

CJ took the kit and walked out onto the glass-domed balcony, followed by Hamish.

Seymour Wolfe's traumatic reaction had progressed to anger. He yelled at one of the Chinese suits: "You are gonna get me on *the first fucking flight* out of here! You cannot *imagine* what I am going to write about this in the *Times* when I get back! Go! Make it happen!"

Aaron Perry was also shouting, "Get me out of here *right now* so I can get on the fucking Internet!"

Hu Tang was speaking animatedly to the other suits, giving orders and directions, pointing at Ambassador Syme and the two journalists.

"Bring my plane here from Hong Kong," Syme said to Hu. "We'll fly direct to Beijing from here."

Hu nodded in reply and began walking off with his people. "Stay here. I'll take care of everything."

While all this was happening, CJ sat down on a bench on the broad balcony and opened the first-aid kit. She slipped off her jacket and hiked up the sleeve of her T-shirt. Her shoulder was a bloody mess. She was reaching for an antiseptic swab in the kit when Greg Johnson sat down beside her.

"Here, let me help you with that," he said,

taking the swab from her.

CJ eyed him closely. "You have experience field-dressing wounds, Mr. Johnson?"

"Maybe." He dabbed the gash on her shoulder, cleaning away the blood.

"Bullet wounds?" Hamish asked.

"Maybe." Johnson tossed away the swab and picked up a needle and thread. "You might want to bite down on something. This is gonna hurt."

CJ grabbed her leather jacket and bit down on its collar. She grunted sharply as Johnson pierced her skin with the needle and started sewing up the wound.

While Johnson worked, CJ gazed out over the valley.

The dragons, she saw, were flying with extra speed now. It wasn't the lazy gliding she'd seen before. It had *purpose.* Gangs of red-bellied black dragons flew in coordinated packs, while the other types of dragons clustered together defensively.

After a couple of minutes, Johnson tied off the last stitch. "You're done. All patched up."

"Thanks," CJ said. The needlework was good. The scar would be small.

"What are you thinking?" Johnson asked.

CJ nodded at the red-bellied black dragons flying around the valley in their groups. "I'm wondering what *they're* thinking. I'm wondering why they attacked *our* cable car? Why today? Why now? Wait a second . . ."

She pulled her oversized UV glasses from her fanny pack. Amazingly, they were unbroken. She put them on. The electromagnetic dome still glowed green above the crater, lancing up from its emplacements on the rim. Beyond it, much higher up, the second red dome remained in place, while a pale-blue sonic shield pulsed around the admin building.

"Patterns," she said to no one. "What pattern were they exploiting?"

"Huh?" Hamish said. "What do you mean?"

CJ turned to face Hamish and Johnson, still wearing the glasses. Their sky-blue sonic shields pulsed around them. Gazing around her, CJ noticed that many of the Chinese workers inside the admin building bore no such spherical shields. Given that the building had its own shield, they probably saw no need to wear individual ones.

She took off the glasses and chewed on one of the earframes, thinking.

Then she blinked.

"The two o'clock fuel run," she said.

"The what?" Johnson said.

CJ's head snapped left, scanning the valley and the sky above it.

"Reptilian predators like crocodiles and alligators love patterns, repetition. If you do something every day at the same time, they'll notice it. And if it helps them hunt you, they'll use that pattern against you. Just before the attack on our cable car occurred, I saw some fuel tankers doing a standard refueling run at two o'clock. The dragons were waiting for those tankers to appear at the usual time —"

CJ cut herself off and turned to Hamish. "This isn't over yet."

Almost in response, a terrifyingly loud shriek could be heard from across the valley.

All three of them turned.

And their mouths opened.

"Oh, you have *got* to be kidding me . . ." Hamish gasped.

Three red-bellied black emperors were flying through the air, banking toward the administration building. Each dragon carried something large in its massive claws.

Hamish said, "Are those — ?"

"Yes," CJ said.

"Holy shit . . ." Johnson said.

The two lead dragons carried *fuel tankers* in their clutches. The long silver tanks of the semitrailer rigs glistened in the sun while the cabs dangled limply from them.

The third emperor dragon carried a different cargo.

It held a dripping-wet cable car that was covered with reeds. It was their old cable car, resurrected from the base of the waterfall. All its windows were smashed, and inside it CJ could make out shapes, moving shapes, lots of them.

Red-bellied black princes.

"We took refuge in the wrong building," she said flatly. "Brace yourselves."

But by the time she said it, it was too late.

The two lead emperor dragons swooped in toward the administration building — with its airport-like control tower at its summit — and like dive-bombers in World War II, released the tankers.

The first fuel-filled tanker slammed into the control tower with tremendous force. Something must have sparked because then the fuel inside the tanker ignited and the whole tower exploded in a gigantic billowing fireball.

Then it fell.

CJ looked up in horror as the great tower toppled like a slow-falling tree off the summit of the admin building and fell down the face of the structure!

For a moment she thought it was going to fall right on top of their glass-domed balcony, but it tumbled and bounced southward. Parts of it broke off as the flaming tower crashed down the slope until, with a

221

colossal noise, it slammed down onto the ring road to the south of the admin building, right in front of the tunnel there.

"Fuck a duck," Hamish said.

The second tanker was hurled into the top floor of the administration building, right underneath an array of antennas situated on the corner of the roof.

That tanker exploded, too, and the whole top corner of the building simply fell away in one massive chunk. It freefell down the face of the building, heading right for the glass-domed balcony on which CJ and the others stood.

"Run!" CJ called, the quickest to react.

They dashed inside, followed by the others, running for all they were worth, as behind them the corner chunk of the building smashed down onto the glass dome. The dome shattered as the chunk of building blasted down through it and the balcony was suddenly open to the elements.

CJ dived to the floor as shards of glass landed all around her. They'd got clear, just.

She rolled, facing upward, held her UV glasses to her eyes . . .

. . . and saw that the blue sonic shield around the admin building *was no longer there.*

By destroying the antenna array, the

dragons had knocked it out.

She was on her feet in seconds.

"Move! Move!" She raced for the elevator.

"What? Why!" Wolfe called, still taking cover on the floor.

CJ kept running. "They just brought down the sonic shield protecting this building! Now they're bringing in the attack troops!"

Wolfe turned and saw what CJ had foreseen.

For right then, in came the third red-bellied emperor dragon, carrying in its claws the wrecked cable car filled with princes.

The emperor swooped in low and released the cable car directly at the smashed-open dome of the admin building's balcony.

With a deafening crash, the huge double-decker cable car came flying in through the broken dome and slid for a full thirty yards before it ground to a halt *inside* the building, right near the spot where CJ and the others had been standing only moments before.

Dragons burst out from it.

There were maybe fifteen of them, all prince-sized red-bellied blacks. The five leading dragons had no ears while the rest did.

They sprang out of the cable car like a

rampaging army, heads low, tails high, fore-claws spread wide, searching for prey.

CJ didn't bother waiting for the elevator. It wouldn't get there in time.

Instead, she just threw open a heavy door beside the elevators labelled FIRE STAIRS in both Mandarin and English.

Closely followed by the five other American guests plus Zhang, she bolted down the stairs three at a time, swinging round the corners.

Loud booms echoed out above her: the dragons were ramming the fire door.

Then there came a sharp cracking noise and suddenly a furious roar rang out in the stairwell.

"They're in!" CJ called.

She came to the base of the stairwell, hurled open the door there, and found herself once again inside the vast waste management hall.

She glanced to her right and saw the massive external garage doors — and she realized why the dragons had stormed this building: *those huge doors led outside.*

Her group really had taken refuge in the wrong place.

This was what the dragons had wanted all along. They hadn't been after the *people*

224

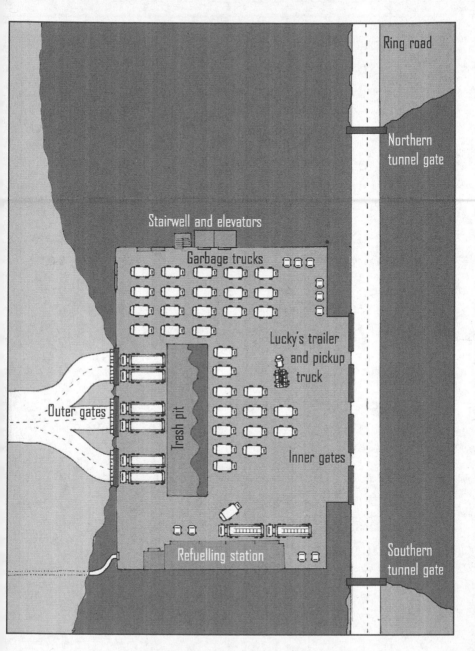

Ring road

Northern
tunnel gate

Stairwell and elevators

Garbage trucks

Lucky's trailer
and pickup
truck

Outer gates

Trash pit

Inner gates

Refuelling station

Southern
tunnel gate

THE WASTE MANAGEMENT FACILITY

inside her cable car. They had just wanted the cable car.

For this.

For this assault on the administration building: one of the few places in the Great Dragon Zoo of China with an exit.

In an academic corner of her mind, CJ found herself marveling at the ingenuity of the dragons. This wasn't just problem-solving behavior. This was complex *combination* planning.

Misguided though their plan was — even if they got out of the valley via the loading dock, there was still the *second* electromagnetic dome outside the first one, and how could they possibly bring that down? — it was still a plan.

These creatures, CJ realized, were more intelligent than any animal she'd ever encountered.

"They're coming!" Johnson called from the rear of the group.

"Hamish, block the door!" CJ yelled.

Hamish climbed up into the cab of a nearby garbage truck, started it up, jammed it into reverse and backed it up against the stairwell door —

— just as the first prince arrived there with a shrill squeal and poked its head through.

Hamish rammed the big garbage truck against the door, slamming it, and the dragon's head, sticking out from between the door and its frame, was sliced off, guillotined. Then the door slammed shut, held closed by the weight of the garbage truck.

There came a series of loud bangs from the other side as more dragons arrived there and started ramming it. But they couldn't get it open — yet.

Bang!

The garbage truck jolted slightly.

Bang!

Again.

As the banging continued, CJ spun to check her options.

The waste facility was just as she had left it: the wide refuse pit, the external doors leading outside, the inner doors leading back to the ring road tunnel, a couple of dozen garbage trucks and the pickup truck with the yellowjacket dragon inside its trailer.

At that moment, one of the elevators arrived with a *ping* and fifteen Chinese office workers in shirtsleeves and slacks hurried out of it, panic-stricken.

A dozen Chinese workmen in blue waste facility coveralls raced to a locked steel cabinet on the northern wall of the hall.

Their leader fumbled with a set of keys before managing to open the cabinet's padlock and fling its thick doors wide.

It was a gun cabinet.

CJ saw guns on racks inside it — handguns and a few assault rifles that looked like AK-47s. The Chinese workmen started handing them out.

CJ turned again and saw the external doors. "Seems to me that the safest place to be right now is outside those doors and outside this valley. How do we open them?"

"That control panel over by the elevators," Zhang said, pointing. "But immediately outside those doors are heavy safety gates. We'd have to open them, too."

Two of the Chinese workmen evidently had a similar idea about the external doors. They were already running for the control panel beside the elevators that Zhang had indicated.

They were ten steps short of the panel when CJ realized.

It was quiet.

The banging had stopped.

The dragons weren't trying to get through the stairwell door anymore.

She turned slowly.

"Where will they — ?" she said as it happened.

The two elevator doors suddenly burst open from within and red-bellied black dragons poured out of them!

They'd come down the elevator shaft.

First there were two dragons, then eight, then twelve. They fanned out rapidly. Some were earless though most still had their ears — but then CJ recalled that most of the Chinese workers in the admin building weren't wearing their protective watches. There was plenty of prey for all of the dragons, earless or not.

The two workmen who had been running toward the control panel beside the elevators were attacked first.

Two earless dragons tackled them, hurling the men to the ground before leaping on top of them and tearing out their windpipes, almost ripping off their heads in the process.

CJ's face fell.

"We're not going that way now," Hamish said.

"Got any other ideas?" Perry asked.

It was at that moment that the Chinese workmen opened fire with their guns.

Within seconds, there was mayhem all over the waste management hall.

Dragons shrieked. Gunfire clattered. Sparks bounced off the walls.

The Chinese workmen took cover and

fired their guns at the oncoming dragons, but just as a man hid behind a garbage truck and opened fire, a dragon would fly over the truck and fall on him from above and it ended in screams and blood.

CJ saw one dragon ruthlessly slash one of its foreclaws across the front of a workman's body. Four lines of blood exploded from his chest and the man fell.

She saw another dragon rip a man in two with its foreclaws. Blood and intestines poured out from the corpse.

A third dragon flew past and bit the head off another man. His headless body kept standing for a few seconds — the gun in its hand still firing — before the decapitated body finally collapsed to the ground.

The Chinese workers' gunfire seemed to have little effect on the dragons. Sparks pinged off their armored hides and foreheads. Occasionally, CJ saw a gout of blood spray out from an *un*armored section of one of the dragons' bodies and the animal would shriek, more in annoyance than pain. Then it would just continue its forward charge.

The Chinese office workers were jumping into any kind of car or truck they could find.

CJ saw three office workers dive into a Great Zoo of China hatchback, only for two dragons to grab the car from either side and fling it against the wall. The little car slammed into the wall roof-first, crumpling instantly, its occupants crushed.

"Get into the garbage trucks!" CJ called. "They're heavier! They'll give better protection!"

The group split up, hurrying for the nearest garbage trucks.

Zhang climbed into one truck, while CJ clambered into the cabin of another with Hamish and Ambassador Syme. Johnson joined them but not before risking a dash to grab a pistol that had been dropped by one of the Chinese workmen. CJ glimpsed Wolfe and Perry disappearing inside the thick-doored gun cabinet and slamming the door shut behind them.

"You know, we're lucky it's just the little ones," Syme gasped. "The princes."

There came an almighty muffled roar and suddenly the brickwork above the elevators broke out into a spiderweb of cracks. A moment later, the entire wall above the elevators was smashed open from within and an enormous — *earless* — red-bellied king dragon burst out from it, bellowing furiously.

"Mother of God," Hamish said.

The bus-sized animal reared up on its hind legs. It absolutely dominated the space.

It bounded forward, sweeping garbage trucks out of its path with its forelimbs.

Six-ton garbage trucks were flung away like children's toys.

One skidded down the length of the hall before slamming into the concrete wall. Another two bounced end over end before disappearing into the refuse pit.

The king roared and with its every booming stride, the floor shook.

There was movement everywhere now. Workmen ran for their lives. Office workers in about seven Great Zoo–emblazoned hatchbacks sped out of the hall into the ring road tunnel, fleeing. Prince dragons hunted between the upturned vehicles.

CJ turned to face the imposing external doors. While she was sure they could contain the prince dragons, she wasn't certain they could withstand an assault by a king or an emperor.

The king wanted to know as well.

With a deafening bellow, it wrenched away one oversized garage door, revealing a thick-barred gate beyond it.

The dragon hurled its shoulder against the gate . . .

. . . but it held.

The dragon roared with fury, tried again,

but again the gate withstood the mighty impact.

"They can't get out this way," Syme said with relief.

"And neither can we," CJ said. "Not without letting them out with us."

As she said this, she thought she glimpsed two prince dragons stealing away to the left toward a small red door over in the far corner of the hall; it looked like an electrical booster room of some sort.

But it was only a fleeting glimpse, because it was cut off a second later when the king dragon stepped right in front of CJ's windshield and stared into her eyes.

Then the great animal lunged forward and grabbed hold of her garbage truck and CJ's world spun crazily again as the truck was flung through the air.

The garbage truck sailed through the air for a full three seconds before it landed on its side with a bone-rattling thud.

Then it slid for twenty feet across the slick concrete floor, stopping right on the edge of the refuse pit. It finished with its cabin protruding out over the pit, twenty feet above the base. There was only a modest pile of garbage in the pit, since the zoo was not yet fully operational.

Its occupants all now lay awkwardly on top of the driver's door. Hamish lay squished on the bottom with Greg Johnson on top of him and CJ and Syme on him.

"Is everyone oka—" CJ began to say just as the upper door to the cabin was wrenched away from the outside and a red-bellied black prince peered inside, hissing.

"Hamish!" CJ called. "Open your door!"

"But then we'll —"

"Now, Hamish!"

Hamish did so, just as the dragon reached down to grab CJ. As the driver's door swung open, Hamish, then Johnson, then Syme and CJ fell down through it, dropping into the refuse pit, landing on the small pile of rubbish there.

The dragon came a moment later.

As she hit the pile of garbage, CJ rolled, a split second before the dragon's claws landed right where she'd been. Now, CJ was lying on her back and the dragon was standing over her, roaring into her face —

Blam!

The dragon's chest was hit by a bullet. The dragon recoiled, but was unhurt.

Blam! Blam! Blam! Blam! Blam!

More gunfire. More rounds hit the beast, in the chest, in the snout, even in one eye.

Now the animal wailed in pain and a final shot — from Greg Johnson, levelling the pistol he'd found — went up into the dragon's mouth, through its brain, and the big beast flopped backwards, squealing and convulsing before finally it lay still on the stinking trash heap, dead.

"Nice shooting," CJ said.

"Thanks." Johnson checked his clip. "Don't expect much more, because I only have one round left."

Just then, CJ caught sight of something in

235

her peripheral vision, something big and red flying through the air.

"Duck!" she called as a fire truck went soaring overhead in a high arc. It was one of the huge ladder trucks. It sailed down into the pit, presumably flung by the king, and slammed into the opposite wall.

"Jesus!" Syme yelled.

"We can't stay here," Johnson urged.

"I know — wait a second." CJ sniffed. "Do you smell that?"

"We *are* in a trash heap," Hamish said flatly.

"No. It's not trash. It's gasoline . . ."

Her eyes fell on the newly arrived fire truck. It lay at the edge of the hill of rubbish, crumpled and broken.

And a small fountain of gasoline was spraying from its tanks. The tanks must have ruptured as the big fire truck had smashed into the pit. The leaking fuel was forming a pool around the big red truck.

With a shriek another black prince landed on top of the fire truck, its wings spread wide.

CJ snatched the pistol from Johnson, but instead of firing it at the dragon, she fired its final bullet downward, at the pool of fuel.

A spark ignited . . . and the pool around the fire truck came alight and a wall of fire

236

sprang up around the dragon!

The dragon was engulfed in flames and it squealed before flying off.

"Not bad," Johnson said.

"Yeah," Hamish said, "only now our pit is *on fire.*"

He was right. Choking black smoke began to fill the pit.

"Okay, boys, here's the plan," CJ said, climbing up the trash heap, heading for the rim. "We find ourselves a garbage truck and we run the blockade out of here."

"Aye, aye to that," Hamish said, taking off after her.

They arrived at the rim of the pit to find that the waste management facility now looked like a battlefield.

Where once all the garbage trucks had been parked in neat rows, now they lay crumpled against the walls or upside down, wheels pointed skyward. Red-bellied black princes variously crouched on top of the upturned trucks or prowled around them. Low afternoon sunlight lanced in through the thick bars of one external gate. The king dragon stood over by the southwest corner, roaring.

There was no gunfire anymore and less movement. The dragons had taken care of the gun-wielding Chinese workmen and all the office workers were either dead or had fled onto the ring road in the hatchback cars.

"That truck over there!" CJ pointed at a garbage truck over by the inner doors. It was even aimed at the open doors of the ring road tunnel, ready to go.

The four of them made a break for it, running fast, keeping low, dashing from garbage truck to garbage truck.

Johnson scooped up an AK-47 from beside a dead Chinese workman's body and threw CJ a Glock pistol.

As they hurried past an overturned garbage truck, they heard a groan.

CJ ducked to see Zhang huddled inside it. Hu Tang, she recalled, had stayed up in the building earlier.

"Come on, Zhangman," Hamish said as he leaned in and dragged the zoo's deputy director out.

CJ, Hamish, Johnson, Syme and now Zhang hastened toward the garbage truck by the inner doors.

At one point, Hamish and the other three ducked left around an overturned truck while CJ went right, and suddenly stopped.

Beep-beep . . . beep-beep.

She knew that sound.

Slowly, very slowly, CJ peered around the corner of her upturned truck.

She saw the yellowjacket dragon — Lucky — inside its caged trailer behind the pickup truck, looking extremely agitated.

CJ came further around and she saw why.

Lucky's handler, Yim, in her black body-suit and with her yellow-streaked hair, stood in front of Lucky's cage, facing four red-bellied black princes arrayed in a threatening semicircle around her.

"Get back!" she yelled in Mandarin, waving a broom at the four dragons. "Back, I tell you! Stay away from her!"

The lead black prince lowered its head, extending its long neck, and hissed at her, a deep low hiss of anger.

It was Red Face. He still had Na's beeping earpiece lodged between his teeth.

Beep-beep . . . beep-beep.

But there was more to this scene than just a confrontation between rival dragons, CJ realized.

She saw small camouflaged boxes attached to *all four* of the red-bellied black princes' heads, and she realized that these four dragons, including Red Face, were the *same* four dragons that had performed alongside Lucky earlier, up in the amphitheater.

It appeared that they didn't like their fel-

239

low performer.

They circled Lucky's cage like hungry wolves.

"Stay back!" Yim yelled. CJ saw that she still wore her earpiece with its inbuilt microphone —

Suddenly Yim moved, reaching for the yellow remote on her belt but, quick as a whip, Red Face launched himself at her and suddenly Yim was on the ground and the dragon was astride her and her hand holding the yellow remote was pinned to the floor.

With a sharp stomp, Red Face smashed the remote to pieces.

Then he hissed into his trainer's face, drooling into her eyes.

Yim screamed and Lucky shook the bars of her cage — straining to open them, crying out — as Red Face's claw came rushing down again, this time at the handler's head.

There was a foul burst of blood and brains as the dragon's claw came down and the trainer's head exploded and a pool of blood fanned out beneath Red Face's claw. Yim's body went limp.

Lucky roared with helpless rage and then, to CJ's surprise, began to whimper, a soft keening that seemed like genuine grief.

It's pining, CJ thought in amazement. *Pin-*

ing for its handler.

But then the four red-bellied black princes turned their attention to Lucky and the yellowjacket stopped whimpering and took a wary step back, even though it was still inside its cage.

The yellow dragon, with the saddle on its back and with its bright yellow coloring, suddenly looked very different from the other dragons: it looked tamed, civilized; a collaborator who had been caught.

Red Face swatted at the cage, his razor-sharp claws clattering across the bars. The other three male princes hissed, surrounding the cage.

CJ watched, horrified and captivated.

The red-bellied black dragons, she noticed, didn't just hiss and snarl: they made distinct burring sounds plus long exhalations. It sounded to CJ like —

Jesus, she realized. *They're communicating with each other.*

CJ also had to admit that she felt sorry for the yellowjacket. The lone female dragon had just lost her human companion and now, outnumbered and surrounded, she was about to be slaughtered.

"CJ . . . !" Hamish whispered urgently. "Come on . . . !"

She turned. Hamish and the others had

241

reached the garbage truck by the inner doors.

CJ frowned, looking back at the four red-bellied black princes surrounding the yellowjacket. One of them punched the cage, making it rock. They were toying with Lucky.

Surprising herself, CJ waved Hamish away.

"Go!" she whispered. "I'll catch up!"

Hamish frowned, not quite understanding. But then he must have seen something in her eyes — a stubborn conviction that he'd seen before — because he just said "Okay," and keyed the ignition on his garbage truck.

At the vibration of the garbage truck firing up, the four dragons surrounding Lucky whipped around. But after deciding that it was of no concern to them, they turned back to face Lucky.

Only when they did so, they found someone standing between them and the yellowjacket.

CJ.

She stood between the four dragons and Lucky, Glock pistol held in one hand and something that looked like a thick plastic suitcase in the other.

It must have made for a strange sight, she

thought: her — five foot six inches tall and armed with a single handgun — facing off against four red-bellied black princes, each of them nine feet tall, huge and menacing.

The imprisoned Lucky seemed the most surprised of all. She appeared to watch this unexpected development in shock.

Red Face glared at CJ, lowered his head and growled.

Beep-beep . . . beep-beep.

The dragon stepped forward —

Blam!

CJ fired her pistol into the concrete floor at the dragon's feet. The round sparked as it pinged away.

The dragon paused in mid-stride.

CJ was standing beside the pool of blood that had been Yim's head, and, glancing downward, she saw something: the dragon handler's earpiece. It must have been expelled from Yim's ear when Red Face had stomped on her skull.

Still aiming her gun at the dragons, CJ put down the suitcase-like object and scooped up the earpiece with her spare hand. If she got out of here alive, she might need to get in radio contact with Hamish and the others.

She put it in her ear — and immediately heard a garbled electronic voice come through it, a man's voice speaking in Mandarin.

CJ translated: "— *black dragons attack* —"

The rest of the zoo must be under attack. Jesus.

Red Face growled again, a sound laced with menace.

Then, without warning, one of the other dragons lunged at CJ from her left. But she was ready for it and she swung around, scooping up the suitcase-like object and flinging it at the incoming prince.

That object was a jerry can, half-filled with gasoline.

The jerry can hit the dragon in the snout just as CJ pivoted with the gun and fired, hitting the fuel can, and the container exploded into flames.

Liquid fire flew in every direction. All four of the dragons were hit and they recoiled, while some of the flames hit CJ herself and the sleeve of her jacket caught fire.

But the biggest victim had been the incoming dragon. That dragon squealed as flames engulfed its head and the animal immediately began rolling around on the floor, trying to extinguish the gasoline-fueled fire raging on its face.

CJ flung off her flaming jacket and took the opportunity to fire at a fuel tank mounted on an overturned garbage truck behind the dragons.

Her shot hit its intended target and the fuel tank exploded, issuing a massive fireball that billowed out all around her foes.

The dragons leapt away from the flames as CJ bolted, dashing down the side of the caged trailer and diving into the cab of its pickup truck.

She keyed the ignition and floored the gas pedal and the truck-and-trailer shot off the mark.

The pickup blasted out of the waste management facility, racing into the ring road tunnel with CJ at the wheel, driving hard and not daring to look back.

The pickup swept into the tunnel.

CJ wanted to go right — to the south, to get to the main entrance building and out of this fucked-up zoo — but no sooner was she in the tunnel than she realized that that wasn't an option.

The remains of the fallen control tower filled the road in that direction. It looked impossibly huge, out of scale with the two-lane road: the multilevel tower lay crumpled across the roadway, completely blocking it.

Tires squealing, CJ swung left — north — accelerating quickly to eighty, then ninety miles per hour, the caged trailer behind her bouncing wildly. Inside it, Lucky was tossed against its barred walls like a rag doll.

One hundred yards ahead of her, CJ saw Hamish's garbage truck arriving at the tunnel's northern entrance. The gate there was still closed, but Hamish must have had a remote in his truck, because as the truck arrived at it, the big gate began to rise.

CJ needed to get in contact with him. She touched her earpiece. Like a cell phone earpiece, it contained a microphone as well.

She went to press the TALK button on the earpiece, but as she did so, a garbled woman's voice came through it, speaking in Mandarin.

CJ translated. *"— Run . . . White head . . . Run —"*

She didn't know what the hell that meant. Busy channel. Clearly, the dragons were running amok all over the zoo.

The fluorescent lights of the tunnel flashed by outside.

She keyed the mike: "Zhang! Hamish! Anyone! Can you hear me?"

No reply.

She stole a glance in her rearview mirror and to her relief saw that the tunnel behind her was empty.

She scanned the cab for weapons or

anything else she could use. On the seat beside her, she saw Yim's black-and-yellow leather jacket, with its armored spine and neck.

That can only help, CJ thought, so she wriggled into it as she drove.

The truck-and-trailer sped through the tunnel.

Still no dragons behind it.

CJ came to the tunnel's mouth and burst out into bright sunshine. She immediately brought the pickup to a skidding halt.

Then she leapt out of the cab and ran to the back of the trailer, glancing down the tunnel —

— when, like bats out of Hell, the four red-bellied black princes came banking out of the waste management facility, flying low and fast.

CJ ignored them.

With Lucky looking on curiously from the other side of the bars, she fumbled with the bolt securing the dragon's cage.

She flung open the gate.

"Go on! *Out!* Get out of there!" CJ yelled at the yellow dragon. "Do you understand me? *Out!*"

The dragon just stared at her in what appeared to be amazement.

Then, glancing at the dragons roaring

down the tunnel behind them, it clambered out of the cage.

The yellowjacket — still wearing its saddle — slunk up onto the roof of the cage and with a final look at CJ, took to the air.

Then CJ was moving again, sliding back into the pickup's cab and jamming down on the gas pedal. The truck shoomed off down the ring road as the four black princes burst out of the tunnel a bare second later.

They immediately looked skyward — to see Lucky soaring away toward Dragon Mountain, out of reach.

But CJ wasn't out of reach.

They took off after her.

CJ drove fast. Faster than she had ever driven in her life.

Her truck-and-trailer combo shot down the ring road, gaining on Hamish's heavier garbage truck.

Ahead of the garbage truck, she could see one of the Great Zoo of China hatchbacks that the Chinese office workers had sped off in, fleeing from the waste management hall.

That was strange, she thought. She could have sworn she had seen six or seven of the little white hatchbacks speed out of the —

Wham!

A white hatchback landed on the road right in front of her pickup!

CJ swerved instinctively, avoiding the falling car by inches. The car had come flying out of the sky from the right and it went bouncing away to her left where it slammed against the rock wall on the outer side of the ring road.

CJ peered upward to see a pair of red-bellied black princes soaring away, having dropped the car at her.

She saw a second pair of princes coming in toward her, carrying another hatchback in their talons. They swooped in low and released the little car.

This car flew across CJ's hood in a flash of white, missing by inches. Then it was gone, smashing into the rock wall and exploding.

CJ's pickup was rocked by the blast, but she managed to keep it going down the ring road.

Holy shit, she thought. *The dragons are throwing cars at me!*

There came a sudden shuddering *whump* and her speeding truck was lifted momentarily off the ground. CJ turned to see that one of the four red-bellied black princes from the waste management hall had landed on the roof of her trailer.

CJ saw its head and she gasped.

Its black-and-red face was horrifically melted and blistered, exposing its jaw muscles and tendons. Some of the spikes of its crest had also melted, causing them to bend over. It was the black prince who had been closest to the jerry can when CJ had shot it, the one whose face had been engulfed in the fuel fire.

It roared at CJ, a shriek of unadulterated rage. Then, one claw at a time, it made its way forward along the top of the empty trailer, coming for her.

As it shrieked at her, CJ could have sworn she heard a garbled electronic voice coming again through her earpiece. It said in a stilted male voice in Mandarin: *"— Fear . . . me —"*

It was almost as if . . . no . . . CJ shook the thought away. *That was crazy.*

Ahead of her, she saw Hamish's garbage truck swerve around something, which she quickly realized was an overturned hatchback lying on the road, and suddenly she was almost on it herself, with Melted Face on the trailer behind her.

CJ hit the brakes, causing her pickup to fishtail past the overturned hatchback, at the same time causing her trailer — with Melted Face on it — to slide *right into* the overturned hatchback.

The trailer hit the upturned car with a mighty bang and the impact stopped it dead in its tracks, separating it from CJ's pickup and sending Melted Face flying forward onto the roadway, tumbling and rolling in a squealing mass of wings, tail and claws.

Never stopping, CJ hit the gas again, right-ing her pickup from its dry skid, and now free of the weight of the trailer she zoomed off at greater speed. Within seconds, she was right behind Hamish's garbage truck.

She pulled up alongside its driver's door and waved at Hamish, indicating her earpiece.

"What channel?" she called.

Hamish pulled Zhang over and asked him, and the deputy director — still wearing his own earpiece — looked over at CJ and held up four fingers.

CJ grabbed her earpiece and flicked it from 22 to 4.

"Zhang! Can you hear me?"

"Yes, Dr. Cameron." His voice came through loud and clear.

"Where can we go to that's safe?"

"About three miles up this road is the Nesting Center, the site of the original dragon nest. It's secure. We can take shelter there."

"Good enough for m—"

CJ's truck jolted violently and she turned to see Red Face land in the tray of her pickup, right behind her!

The dragon punched through the cab's rear window and CJ was showered with glass and suddenly a giant claw was clutching around the cabin trying to get at her.

CJ ducked low, lying flat on the seat of

the cab. She couldn't stay here.

"Zhang!" she yelled into her mike. "Tell Hamish I'm coming over!"

"What?"

"Just do it!"

CJ reached up and hit the pickup's cruise control. It now sped along beside the garbage truck as dragons wheeled and banked overhead.

She wriggled across the cab, underneath Red Face's scrabbling claw, and pushed open the passenger-side door.

Wind rushed into the cabin. CJ saw the garbage truck's running board only a couple of feet away, the road rushing by beneath it.

Do it now, before you think about what you are doing! her mind screamed.

Then Red Face rammed his head through the rear window of the cabin. His splotchy red head all but filled the little space, and the Bluetooth earpiece in his mouth was still bizarrely beeping, but by the time his head was inside the cabin, CJ was jumping out of it, diving out its right-side door, hands outstretched, hoping to catch hold of —

— her fingers latched onto the garbage truck's running board and they clung on tightly as her boots hit the roadway and bounced wildly.

The now driverless pickup truck — with Red Face half inside it, half outside it — peeled away toward the rock wall on the left-hand side of the road. The dragon yanked its head out of the cabin and took to the air an instant before the pickup hit the wall at speed and exploded in a ball of flames.

With CJ dangling from its left-hand side, the garbage truck thundered down the ring road.

"CJ! You still with us?" Hamish's voice came through CJ's earpiece. He must have appropriated Zhang's.

"Just!" CJ called over the rushing wind.

Whump!

A dragon landed on the garbage truck right above her.

It was another red-bellied black prince. Its hind legs gripped the roof of the garbage truck while it hung upside down *on* the side of the big truck, glaring at CJ. It opened its saliva-filled jaws in what could only be described as a broad, self-satisfied grin.

"CJ! I see it!" Hamish's voice called. *"Go under! Now!"*

CJ didn't bother to discuss her brother's plan. She grabbed a pipe underneath the running board and swung herself *under* the speeding garbage truck, the Kevlar back-plate of her jacket skimming against the roadway as —

— the garbage truck swept into another tunnel and —

— *whack!* Hamish swung the truck in close to the tunnel's mouth, so close that the truck's left flank hit the mouth of the tunnel, taking the dragon clean off it while the garbage truck continued on into the tunnel, with CJ safely underneath it!

The dragon fell to the roadway, bruised and confused, as the garbage truck sped away.

Then it shook its head, got back to its feet and took off, heading back into the fray.

■ ■ ■ ■

In the garbage truck's cabin, Hamish peered at his side mirror.

The creature was gone. But he couldn't see CJ.

"You still with us, Chipmunk?"

"I'm still here," CJ's voice replied. *"Thanks, little brother."*

"Can you get to the cab?"

"I'll try."

Hamish said, "You know, this is some seriously crazy shit —"

The windshield in front of him exploded inwards. The black-fisted foreclaw of a dragon appeared immediately afterward, quickly followed by the upside-down head of a fourth red-bellied black prince.

"Jesus Christ!" Hamish yanked his head back, involuntarily pulling on the steering wheel as he did so, causing the speeding garbage truck to slam against the side wall of the tunnel and kick up sparks.

On the underside of the running board, CJ swung wildly with the unexpected swerve and a blaze of sparks flew up all around her.

"Hamish! What are you doing!?" she called.

256

"I got a dragon problem of my own up here!" Hamish yelled.

The dragon in front of him was trying — in a furious frenzy — to tear away the windshield and get inside.

Beside Hamish, Greg Johnson levelled his AK-47 at the dragon and fired a short burst.

The bullets pinged off the animal's armored forehead. The dragon barely noticed.

It roared and lashed out, knocking the assault rifle from Johnson's hand.

As the garbage truck sped on, CJ used all her strength to haul herself out from under it and swing up onto its running board.

The running board — on which the zoo's garbagemen would stand as they went about their work — ran down the rear half of the truck.

CJ saw a steel ladder at the rear. If she could get to it, then she could climb up onto the roof and work her way forward to the cab.

As the garbage truck raced through the tunnel, swerving and weaving, she edged down the running board toward the ladder.

The fluorescent lights of the tunnel

whizzed by beside her as she made her way down the side of the speeding truck.

CJ arrived at the ladder, grabbed a rung and hauled herself quickly up it.

She poked her head up over the roof — to find herself staring into the sinister smile of the dragon that had been knocked off the side of the truck earlier!

It was perched on the roof of the garbage truck, tail slinking behind it, its chin pressed against the roof so that its huge head was perfectly level with CJ's face. It had been waiting for her. It was again grinning its smug, self-satisfied smile.

The dragon sprang forward, snapping, but CJ was quicker. She slid back down her ladder, dropping as the dragon's jaws came together with a chomp, catching nothing but air.

CJ gasped as she hit the bottom of the ladder.

But she couldn't stay here. The dragon on the roof would come over the side at any moment.

She turned to look forward just as — *whack!* — another dragon landed on the *side* of the speeding garbage truck, its claws piercing the steel wall like can openers, blocking her path that way.

It was Melted Face.

This is insane, she thought. There were now three dragons on the speeding garbage truck.

And she herself literally had nowhere to go.

Nowhere, except —

"Hamish!" she yelled into her earpiece. "Open the rear loader!"

"What?!"

"Just do it or I'm toast!"

"Okay!"

CJ edged back along the running board, just as the smiling dragon slunk down the same ladder she had used to escape it. Only two feet ahead of it, CJ swung around the rear of the garbage truck, hurling herself into its rear loader.

The rear tray stank. A hydraulically operated steel plate — the truck's compactor — lay before her. Right now it was closed, sealing off the truck's internal hopper.

Smiley poked his head around the side of the truck, grinning malevolently.

"Hamish . . . !"

Up in the cabin, Hamish was leaning as far back as he could in his seat. An inch in front of his nose, his dragon's claw snatched and clutched, trying to get at him.

He scanned the controls of the cabin,

looking for the switch that operated the rear compactor.

He saw it — a red button — and ducking under the snatching claw, quickly hit it.

With a mechanical clanking, the compactor began to open, creating a narrow opening at its base.

CJ dived for the gap as Smiley leapt around into the rear tray. CJ rolled through the small opening, through the remains of some stinking garbage. The gap was big enough for her but not for the dragon. She was clear.

"Okay, Hamish! Now close it again!"

The dragon attacking the cabin rammed its head through the smashed windshield and roared loudly at Hamish.

Zhang recoiled. Syme ducked. Greg Johnson was frantically trying to regather his AK-47 from the floor. And with the dragon now right in his face, Hamish couldn't reach the button that operated the rear compactor.

At the back of the garbage truck, to CJ's horror, the compactor's steel plate continued to open.

CJ was sitting inside the dark steel box that was the truck's hopper, pressed up against some compacted rubbish, powerless to do anything about the door that was opening further every second.

The dark silhouette of the dragon outside grew larger.

If Hamish reversed the door now, the dragon wouldn't be able to get in, but in a few seconds, the gap would be big enough for it to enter and then CJ would be trapped in here with it.

"Hamish! I need you to close the compacter door *right now*!"

With CJ's cries ringing in his ears, Hamish twisted in his seat, narrowly avoiding the snapping jaws of the dragon hanging off the front of the speeding garbage truck.

Then suddenly it managed to thrust its snout through the cracked hole in the windshield and it lunged for his face —

Blam!

Blood exploded from the back of the dragon's head and the animal snapped backwards.

Hamish turned to see Greg Johnson with his assault rifle levelled in one outstretched arm. He'd fired it into the dragon's left eye from point-blank range.

The dragon toppled backwards and fell off the speeding truck, dropping to the road beneath it.

The garbage truck bumped as it ran over the corpse.

"Hamish . . . !" CJ's voice came in over the radio.

"Oh, no, CJ . . ." Hamish gasped as he hit the red button again, closing the rear compactor.

But he did it too late.

At the exact moment that Hamish hit the switch, the compactor's door had come fully open, and CJ — her back pressed against the wall of compacted garbage — found herself facing the dragon she had christened Smiley, standing in the rear loading tray of the truck. Smiley had her.

Clenching her teeth, CJ yanked out her Glock pistol, levelled it and —

Click.

"No!"

Click.

Out of ammo.

Smiley grinned.

And then — thanks to Hamish — the door began to close again.

Smiley saw it lowering, so he just stepped inside the hopper, now only a few feet away from CJ.

CJ couldn't believe it. Out of bullets and

out of options, she was now stuck in here with the dragon.

"Oh, this is *not* fair," she muttered. "Not fucking fair . . ."

And then she saw it.

A small plastic bottle lying on the heap of compacted trash, one that had somehow avoided being completely crushed in the compacting process. A bottle of turpentine-based solvent.

The door was halfway closed, the gap at its base only four feet high and getting smaller by the second.

CJ grabbed the solvent bottle, unscrewed its cap and threw it at the advancing dragon.

Turpentine sprayed all over Smiley's face, splattering the dragon's eyes.

Smiley shrieked, clutching at its eyes.

CJ dashed forward, running low, and scuttled around the reeling dragon before dive-sliding on her belly under the slowly closing compactor door.

She slid back out into the artificial light of the tunnel — back out into the rear tray — just as the thick compactor door closed with a resounding boom and the squeals of the dragon became muffled.

"CJ!" Hamish's voice came through her earpiece. *"Are you inside the truck?"*

"No," she replied. "But one of our dragon

263

friends is. Crush it!"

"Sure thing!"

A moment later, the compactor door shifted slightly, beginning a powerful pushing motion — a compacting motion that was designed to compress its load of trash against the front wall of the hopper.

The squeals of the dragon inside became high-pitched wails as it realized what was happening.

Those wails reached a crescendo as the compactor closed in on the hapless beast. And then CJ heard a hideous crunching sound as Smiley was crushed to nothing by the compactor.

CJ exhaled a deep sigh of relief. "Goddamn."

It was time to get to the driver's cabin and rejoin the others. But after her previous experiences on the side of the truck, there was only one way she wanted to go: over the top.

"Hamish, I'm coming to you via the roof!" she said into her earpiece mike.

"Roger that. We're about to come out of the tunnel. There's another one up ahead. Zhang says there's a side tunnel inside it that leads to the Nesting Center. He says if we can get to that, we're golden."

CJ didn't waste any time. She climbed out of the rear tray and hoisted herself up so she could see the roof of the speeding garbage truck.

The roof was clear of dragons. It lay before her flat and empty. The ceiling of the tunnel whooshed by overhead.

CJ leapt onto the roof and, lying on her belly, edged forward along it. The steel roof of the truck was slightly corrugated, allow-

265

ing her to gain fingerholds.

Then, with a great *whoosh,* the speeding truck blasted out into brilliant sunshine — and CJ looked up in time to see Red Face swoop in toward her like a dive-bomber and release a hatchback car from its talons!

The little car shot downward through the air and CJ dived forward an instant before the hatchback slammed down *onto the roof of the garbage truck* and bounced off it, hitting the rock wall on the outer side of the ring road with terrible force.

CJ looked forward: the second tunnel that Hamish had mentioned was still about five hundred yards away.

"Hamish! Get us to that tunnel before I get pulverized!"

CJ was looking at the approaching tunnel when suddenly the disgusting blistered head of Melted Face appeared right beside her. He was still on the garbage truck, clinging to its left-side wall.

Melted Face rose up from the side of the truck, forelimbs tensed, eyes deadly.

"CJ, hang on!" Hamish's voice called through her earpiece.

The truck swerved wildly, avoiding a smashed hatchback on the road ahead.

Gripping the roof with her fingertips, CJ's legs were thrown sideways.

266

The dragon beside her never lost his balance.

"Hamish! Hit the brakes!" CJ called.

In the cabin, Hamish slammed his feet down on the brakes.

The garbage truck skidded.

On the roof, CJ grabbed a nearby strut as the inertia of their sudden stop flung her forward.

Melted Face wasn't so fortunate.

He was flung forward, clear off the side of the truck, and went tumbling end over end onto the roadway.

Hamish saw a sudden blur of black and red fly off his truck and hit the road in front of him. He jammed down on the accelerator pedal.

The garbage truck took off again, burning rubber.

Melted Face — grazed and skinned from the ungainly fall — looked up in time to see the truck's headlights rushing toward him and he leapt to the side at the last moment as the truck's front bumper clipped his wing. The dragon was knocked to the ground, flailing but alive.

Now finally free of dragons, the truck sped

into the next tunnel.

A hundred yards inside this new tunnel, the garbage truck skidded to a halt in front of a barred gate buried in the outer wall.

This gate's black iron bars were, if it were possible, thicker than the bars they had seen on any gate so far.

CJ leapt down from the roof and joined Hamish, Johnson, Syme and Zhang at the gateway.

Hamish looked CJ up and down. "Got all your fingers and toes?"

"Haven't had time to check," CJ said. "I think so."

Zhang raced to the barred gate and spoke to two soldiers on the other side. They were dressed in Chinese Army attire, carried modern Steyr assault rifles and their faces were entirely blank.

"Let us in!" Zhang said in Mandarin.

The two soldiers said nothing — and did nothing — in reply.

"I said, let us in!" Zhang cried.

One of the soldiers said in an emotionless tone: "You know they can't come in here, Deputy Director. The Nesting Center is off-limits to all unauthorized personnel."

"Unauthorized personnel!" Zhang repeated in astonishment. "Are you joking? We're in the middle of an emergency here —"

"Not even you can come in here, Deputy Director. You are not authorized." The soldier jerked his chin at CJ, Hamish, Syme and Johnson. "And we certainly will not allow *them* in. We have orders from Colonel Bao himself on this matter."

"Have you no decency!" Zhang shouted. "We're going to *die* out here —"

"Forget it," CJ said, pulling Zhang by the arm and glancing back down the tunnel.

It stretched away, empty and bare.

The dragons hadn't entered it yet.

She swapped a glance with Johnson before saying to Zhang: "If we can't get in here, where else can we go?"

Zhang was shaking with fury, but he regathered himself. "The Birthing Center, maybe." He threw the guards a withering look. "If it is not guarded by lowly dogs!"

"Er, Cassandra . . ." Hamish said flatly. He only ever called her that when it was serious.

CJ spun and saw what he was looking at.

The enormous shadow of a king-sized dragon stood in the tunnel entrance behind them, blocking out the light.

The dragon roared, the terrible noise echoing down the tunnel.

"Come on!" CJ called. "We try for the Birthing Center."

269

They all jumped back into the garbage truck and, once again driven by Hamish, it zoomed down the second tunnel. A few seconds later it burst out into daylight.

The road ahead bent to the right, following the curve of the crater wall. They were now at the northwestern corner of the valley. In fact, CJ realized, they were on the section of the ring road hidden *behind* the screen of cliffs near the casino. She wondered what was back here, what those artificial cliffs concealed.

She scanned the road ahead: there were no tunnels here; the freeway-like road was open to the sky. Two reinforced steel gates, however, bored into the outer wall.

The first of those gates was about three hundred yards ahead of them and it was open.

Zhang pointed at it. "That's the entrance to the Birthing Center!"

The garbage truck raced toward it.

As it did so, CJ leaned out the passenger-side window to look at the valley behind them, or at least the western half of it.

She saw a red-bellied black emperor perched atop the wreckage of the administration building, bellowing triumphantly. The building was almost completely destroyed: its tower was gone, its front windows were shattered and its domed balcony was in ruins.

Three kings circled the air in front of it, as if guarding the building.

They now consider it their territory, CJ thought.

Right then, however, four Z-10 attack helicopters shoomed over the top of the crater wall, blazing away with tracer fire at the emperor, causing it to take flight.

The Z-10 is the Chinese equivalent of the AH-64 Apache, a gunship with a stepped cockpit, a nose-mounted 30mm cannon, and stub-wings from which hang a variety of antitank and air-to-air missiles.

The three dragons surrounding the emperor sprang to his defense and zeroed in on the Z-10s. But the attack choppers unleashed their missiles and suddenly the dragons were exploding.

Two of the choppers hounded the emperor, chasing him across the zoo, their tracers sizzling across the valley like lasers, until one of the choppers loosed an air-to-air missile that banked and swerved after the fleeing emperor, hit it and detonated.

The airliner-sized dragon blew apart in a monumental spray of blood and pulp. Great chunks of flesh the size of boulders rained down from the sky.

"The empire is striking back," Ambassador Syme observed, peering out the window beside her.

CJ nodded. "This is now a fight between two territorial animals: dragons and humans."

And human technology, she thought, unleashed in brutal fashion by the Chinese, would ultimately win this battle.

At that moment, the garbage truck skidded to a stop in front of the open gates to the Birthing Center.

"Quick! Inside!" Greg Johnson called, jumping out and ushering them all through the entrance.

They hurried inside. Johnson slid the thick barred gate shut behind them just as another red-bellied black dragon smacked against the bars, screeching wildly.

As the dragon raged at the gate, the group dashed down the darkened tunnel.

CJ ran out in front.

For some reason, the ceiling lights here were out. The tunnel was almost completely dark: the only illumination came from the daylight behind them and from some dim artificial light coming from the other end of the tunnel. The dragon at the gate behind them continued to fume.

About twenty yards down the tunnel, CJ saw a thick steel door sunk into the left-hand wall. It was open. A warning sign on it read DIESEL GENERATORS — NO NAKED FLAMES in English and Mandarin. Inky darkness lay beyond it.

"I don't think we're going in there," CJ said. She preferred the dimly lit space at the far end of the tunnel. When it came to fleeing from creatures that could see in pitch darkness, even a small amount of light was better than total blackness.

They kept running and eventually came to a pair of wide security doors, also open.

They passed through them and emerged inside the Birthing Center. They all stopped dead in their tracks.

CJ swallowed. "We shouldn't have come here."

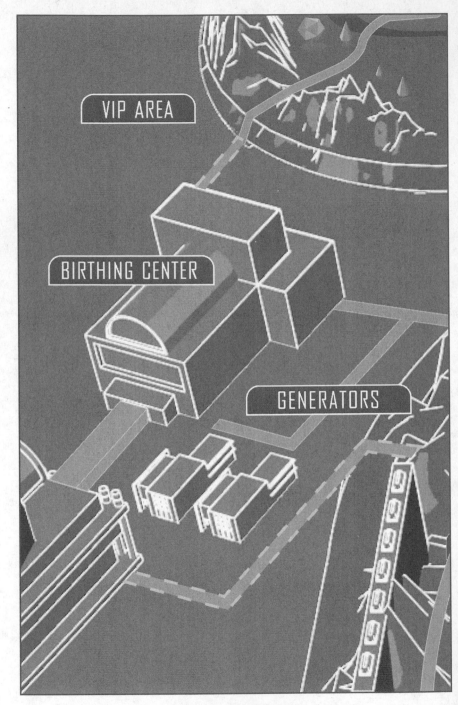

THE BIRTHING CENTER

CJ stared in horror at the Birthing Center — at what it was and at what had clearly happened in it over the last hour or so.

The center itself was a broad two-storey-high hall with glistening white-tiled walls and floors. The whole place had a feeling of antiseptic cleanliness.

But it wasn't clean anymore.

The Birthing Center was bathed in blood and gore. Dead bodies dressed in lab coats littered the floor; Chinese technicians who had been torn apart by rampaging dragons. Equipment had been smashed. Wires hung everywhere. Lights hung askew from the ceiling, giving off sparks.

The whole space — no doubt usually brightly lit — was cloaked in grim semidarkness.

In the middle of the hall was a broad rectangular pit, about the size of two Olympic swimming pools. A series of catwalk bridges spanned the pit while rung-ladders led down into it.

Two levels of glass-walled offices ringed the perimeter of the hall. They were variously filled with computer servers, microscope labs and centrifuges. There were even a few cages and some rooms fitted with surgical tables and medical equipment.

CJ stopped at the edge of the huge pit and peered down into it.

At its base, about seven feet below CJ, were dozens of rectangular cages packed tightly together in long rows, all half-submerged in a couple of feet of water.

CJ winced at what she saw inside the cages.

Saltwater crocodiles.

Big ones. Huge. And there were a *lot* of them, maybe seventy all up.

The usually fearsome reptiles, however, didn't look fearsome at all. Rather, they looked pathetic and miserable, for not only were they being held captive in the tiny cages, but their limbs were manacled to the cages' walls, immobilizing them. At the rear of their cages were flaps that appeared to allow any eggs the crocodiles laid to fall into catching trays. The trays were then taken away on conveyor belts.

The crocs bellowed plaintively.

CJ recognized the vocalizations. She had heard them many times before. They were female calls, the kind a mother croc made to gather her offspring to her. But these calls got no reply.

As she gazed at the wretched crocodiles, CJ thought: *They look like battery hens.*

The saltwater crocodile was one of the deadliest predators in the world, cunning and intelligent, cold and ruthless. It was hard to feel sorry for one, but CJ found herself feeling sorry for these crocs now.

She saw a smartboard nearby, a kind of high-tech whiteboard. It featured a map of the zoo and some handwritten notes which, curiously, were written in English:

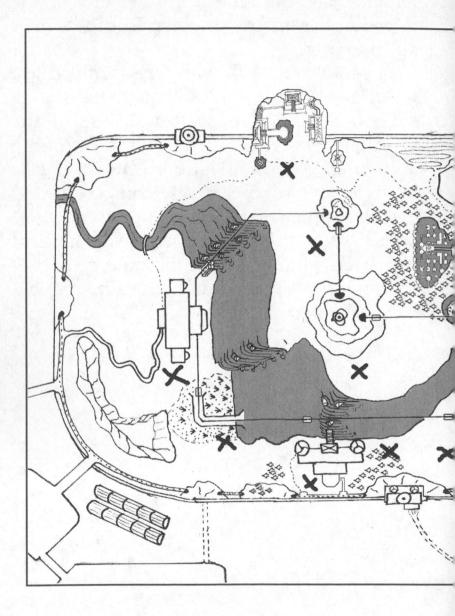

BRAIN DEFECTS
IN CROC-BORN
VARIANTS —
WHY ARE THEY
SO AGGRESSIVE?

RIVALS???

RED-BELLIES } RIVALS???
&
YELLOWJACKETS } RIVAL CLANS???

WHY ARE THEY
DIGGING?

RED-BELLIES
= HIGHER
STATUS?

THEY ARE STARTING
TO FIGURE US OUT.

CJ read the handwritten notes. It seemed that the dragons at the Great Dragon Zoo had been doing unpredictable things.

One note asked: *Why are they digging?*

An arrow beside it pointed at the map, and at a series of randomly arranged Xs marked on it.

The dragons were digging and their keepers didn't know why.

Other notes referred to the red-bellied black dragons — questioning whether they were of higher status than the other dragons and that perhaps they and the yellowjacket dragons were rival clans. CJ recalled noticing earlier that all of the dragons involved in the initial attacks had been red-bellied blacks.

A rather ominous notation at the bottom of the smartboard read *They are starting to figure us out.*

One note, however, captured CJ's attention: *Brain defects in croc-born variants — why are they so aggressive?*

"The croc-born variants . . ." she said aloud.

And suddenly the full horrific meaning of the name "Birthing Center" became clear.

These crocs *were* battery hens.

CJ now also understood the answer to one of her previous questions: how the zoo could have 232 dragons when the Chinese had at first only found 88 eggs.

The answer was right here in front of her: to breed more dragons for their zoo, the Chinese had been using the ova of saltwater crocodiles — the archosaur's closest living relative — as hosts for dragon embryos. All the high-tech equipment around the perimeter of the Birthing Center — the microscopes, computers and centrifuges — was for the purpose of nuclei insemination and fertilization.

But one needed lots of ova to get just a few viable embryos, hence the water pit filled with female crocodiles.

The scientists of the Great Dragon Zoo had created a donor egg–making *factory*.

But the smartboard revealed that all had not been well with the Great Dragon Zoo even before the events of today.

"CJ? CJ, we need you." Hamish's voice snapped her out of her thoughts and she returned to the present.

Hamish said, "Which exit do we take?"

CJ saw two possible exits from the Birthing Center: security doors at each of the far corners of the lab. The one off to her right was closed. The one to her left, open.

She stared at the open door. She wasn't certain but she thought she could hear a muffled whumping sound coming from the tunnel beyond it.

"Which one, Chipmunk?" Hamish asked.

"We could go back —" Johnson said, glancing down the tunnel behind them.

They could see the dragon still scratching at the barred entrance, seventy yards away, but then Johnson cut himself off as a new shadow slunk out of the side door halfway along the tunnel and snarled at them. It was another red-bellied black prince with no ears and it was *inside* the tunnel!

"Whoa, shit . . ." Hamish breathed.

"Hey! CJ!" a voice called. "Don't stay out in the open! Get to one of the cages *now!*"

CJ spun, surprised to hear someone shouting her name in English, and she saw three people cowering inside a cage recessed in the right-hand wall.

The speaker was Go-Go, the pony-tailed Chinese guy she'd seen in the revolving restaurant on Dragon Mountain. With him in the cage was the twentysomething female Chinese grad student he'd been dining with.

The third person in the cage was a handsome Caucasian man wearing horn-rimmed glasses and a lab coat.

They must have sought refuge inside the cage when the dragons had stormed this place and now they were all waving frantically at CJ and her newly arrived group.

CJ peered at the Caucasian man and for the second time that day, found herself recognizing someone here at the zoo.

"Ben?" she said. "Ben Patrick?"

"Go!" the man in the lab coat yelled urgently. "Before they smell you! There are two of them in the tunnel leading to the Nesting Center and if they catch your scent —"

A long low hiss made them all turn.

Two red-bellied black princes stood in the open doorway on the far left-hand side of the pit.

They were earless.

Their snouts were smeared with blood. Rags of human flesh dangled from their teeth.

They sprang forward, moving with astonishing speed around the rim of the croc-filled water pit. They ran like jungle cats, with fluidity and balance, their heads held low, their tails held high, their wings folded onto their backs.

CJ calculated her best move in a nanosecond.

She was at the front edge of the water pit. The nearest escape was the heavy door in the right-hand corner on the other side of the pit, if she could get it open.

"That door!" she called to the others. "Go!"

She broke into a run across the nearest catwalk spanning the pit. Hamish followed. Johnson, Syme and Zhang dashed around the pit.

As she ran, CJ called, "Go-Go! What's the code for that door?"

"6161!" Go-Go yelled back.

One of the black princes veered toward CJ and Hamish, bounding onto the catwalk bridge after them.

But the bridge wasn't designed to carry its weight and as it leapt onto the narrow span, the whole catwalk dropped into the water pit, taking the dragon, CJ and Hamish down with it.

CJ landed flat on her chest on top of a cage containing a very angry female saltwater crocodile.

Only inches away from her face, the croc bellowed and bucked. But there was a thin mesh of steel between them, plus the crocodile's limbs were shackled.

Hamish landed on the cage next to CJ's. Being heavier, he created a dent in his and the crocodile inside it roared.

CJ rolled off her cage and leapt to her feet, and standing in the knee-deep salt water, searched for a ladder leading out —

The red-bellied black dragon rose up before her.

Nine feet tall, with its long swooping neck, spikelike crests and fangs protruding from its snout, it towered over her, blocking the way to a rung-ladder on the wall of the pit.

There was nowhere for CJ to go.

The dragon was crouching to lunge when a greenish-brown blur slammed into it from the side and the dragon went flying into the water.

There was a great thrashing and splashing and at first CJ didn't know what was going on. Then amid all the spraying water, she saw that there were not one but *two* dragons in it: the red-bellied black prince and another prince, a greenish-brown one.

The greenish-brown dragon was quite possibly the ugliest thing she had ever seen in her life. Where the black prince had a majesty to it, this animal was something else entirely. It was mud-colored and looked like a cross between a crocodile and a giant salamander.

But it was equal in size to the black prince and a match for it, and the two dragons fought with terrible violence, exchanging blows and slashing at each other with their teeth as they rolled around in the water.

"Come on!" Hamish hauled CJ toward the rung-ladder and within seconds they were out of the pit and running for the door in the right-hand corner.

Johnson and Syme were already there. Johnson, ever cool under pressure, was punching in the code and the door unlocked, popping open with a gaseous hiss. They both slid inside it.

Zhang, slower than Johnson and Syme, was still running around the edge of the pit, with the second red-bellied black prince closing in on him. It flew fast and low across the broad hall.

CJ and Hamish hurried for the same door.

They bolted side by side, stride for stride. The dragon saw them, switching its gaze back and forth between them and Zhang, as if trying to choose which prey to go for.

And suddenly Zhang slipped on a puddle of blood and he went sliding clumsily onto his butt across the tiled floor.

It sealed his fate.

The dragon made its choice and descended on him. It all but enveloped Deputy Director Zhang as it came down on him with its claws raised. Zhang screamed as the dragon mauled him, raising his arms in defense, but the dragon just tore his chest apart before biting his throat out.

CJ and Hamish squeezed through the open doorway and Johnson slammed the door shut behind them. The lock clicked. They were safe.

Fifteen feet away from them, through a small window in the heavy door, they saw the dragon feast on Zhang's body, his still-warm blood dripping from its jaws.

CJ turned away from the grisly sight.

Still breathing hard, she took in the dark tunnel in which she now found herself.

The door they'd all just slid through was actually a seriously secure door: it was big and solid — even the glass in its little window was thick — and it had a rubber lining at its edges that created an airtight seal.

As the dragon feasted on the other side of it, cracking Zhang's bones, CJ could barely hear it. The door was almost soundproof.

"Everybody all right?" she asked.

"Only just," Hamish said.

CJ looked down the tunnel on her side of the door.

All the lights were out. The grim passageway ran for about a hundred yards or so, ending at a doorway that stood rather ominously open.

The glare of daylight came through that

distant doorway.

CJ started walking down the tunnel toward it.

"Where are you going?" Syme asked.

"Down there."

"Why not just stay here where it's safe?"

"Because we don't know it's safe." CJ peered down the tunnel. "And we won't know that till we know what's on the other side of that door down there."

She kept striding down the long, dark tunnel. The others took off after her.

The door at the other end of the tunnel was just like the one at the Birthing Center — thick and rimmed with air-sealing rubber — only it lay wide open.

CJ peered through it cautiously and found herself looking at a compact room with black-painted floors and black-painted walls. A lone door on the opposite wall stood open, allowing daylight to come in.

The black floor and walls left CJ with an odd sensation: she felt like she was backstage at a theater. Two black-painted side-tunnels branched away to the left and the right, disappearing into darkness.

"I don't like this . . ." Johnson said, looking around the empty space.

"What is this place?" Hamish asked. "I'm

guessing it isn't on the regular tour."

CJ wanted to know the same thing.

She stepped out from the tunnel, heading for the open outer door.

"Dr. Cameron," Johnson said. "I think you should come back inside the tunnel and get behind this door."

CJ arrived at the outer door and looked out through it.

She saw a small yet very beautiful valley enclosed by high rocky walls. It had lush savannah grass, a river and a forest. In the exact center of the little valley was a grass-covered hill on the summit of which was an opulent-looking wooden building. It oozed wealth and privilege. It looked like a golf clubhouse or a hunting lodge.

CJ's eyes narrowed.

Stepping out through the door, she looked back — and saw that the entrance to the small room was superbly camouflaged. Its doorway was sunken into a rocky cliff and the door — still open — had rock-camouflage material on its outer side, camouflage that made it blend in perfectly with the cliff.

Hamish came alongside CJ and he saw the camouflage, too.

"I repeat," he said. "What is this place?"

CJ was thinking quickly. "It's like a —"

With a squeal, a gray prince-sized dragon came charging out of some nearby bushes, bounding directly for CJ and Hamish.

It spread its wings and swooped at them, doubling its speed in an instant, and CJ glimpsed that it had no ears.

She and Hamish ducked back inside the doorway and slammed the camouflaged door shut and, through a little window in it, saw the dragon pull up short, foiled. It screeched at them, furious.

CJ and Hamish caught their breath, looking out at the raging dragon.

Then the gray dragon's head exploded, spraying blood all over the little window, and CJ and Hamish yanked their heads back in shock.

"Dr. Cameron," Johnson whispered from the doorway to the tunnel, "come back here *right now.*"

CJ turned at his tone and as she did so she saw a shadow emerge from the left-hand side-tunnel: another gray prince, head bent low.

It shrieked as it broke into a run and suddenly CJ and Hamish were sprinting, racing back to the tunnel door. They dived, sliding across the last few feet of floor as Johnson slammed the airtight tunnel door shut behind them and the dragon skidded to a halt outside it, bellowing —

Blam!

The dragon's head burst apart and dropped from view and suddenly CJ saw soldiers in Chinese Army uniforms fanning out into the black-painted room, guns up and shouting.

"Clear! Clear!" they yelled in Mandarin before one of the soldiers came up to the door and peered in at CJ and the others.

"Ni hao?" He saw CJ and switched to English. "Hello? Please. Open the door. The area is secure. The zoo is secure. You are safe now."

CJ slumped to the floor, relieved.

■ ■ ■ ■

FOURTH EVOLUTION

THE KNOWN PREDATOR

■ ■ ■ ■

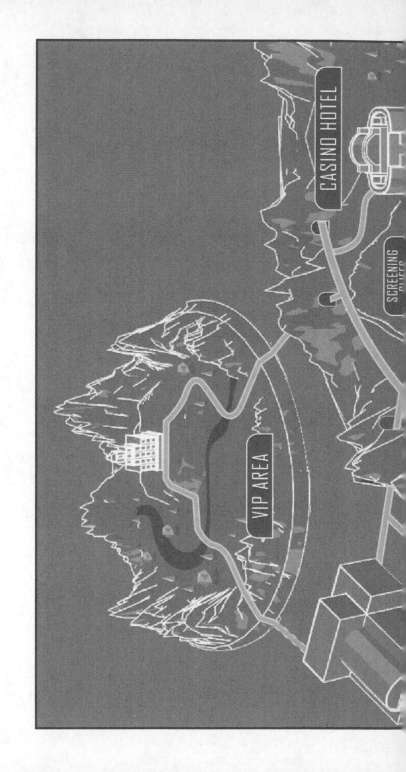

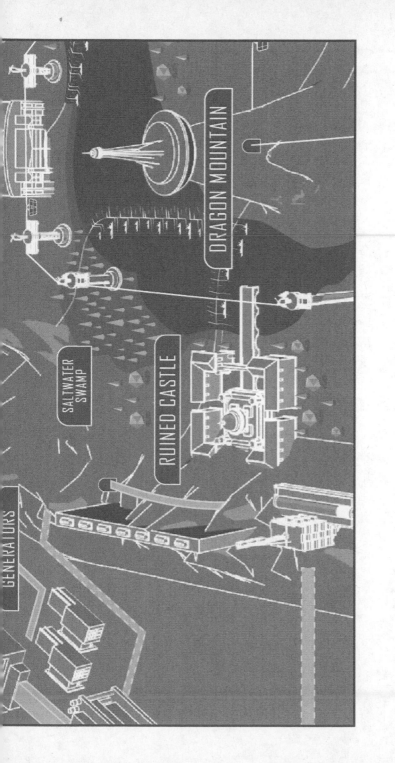

The man who fights too long against dragons becomes a dragon himself.

— Friedrich Nietzsche

Things happened very quickly after that.

CJ, Hamish and the two American diplomats were ushered out of the black-painted room and into the beautiful little valley, where they quickly found themselves surrounded by anxious zoo staff, much movement and lots of noise. About a dozen Chinese Army jeeps and a few troop trucks were parked nearby while overhead, three Z-10 helicopters hovered. Concerned paramedics attended to their scratches and scrapes.

Radios squawked. Junior officers barked into telephones. In the middle of it all, coordinating everything, was the gray-haired uniformed colonel CJ had met briefly when she had arrived at the zoo: Colonel Bao.

CJ picked up the odd phrase amid the cacophony of voices speaking in Mandarin:

"— we counted twenty-six dragons with their ears severed —"

"— forty-seven people dead in the administration building. Twenty-six in the Birthing Center —"

"— by ripping out their own ears, they made the sonic shields useless —"

"— backup generators are offline —"

"— what about the domes? —"

"— both electromagnetic domes are fine. They are still in place and working perfectly —"

A short distance away, CJ saw two of the four visiting Communist Party officials she had seen earlier. Their new hiking outfits were now torn and covered in dirt and grime. They looked furious. Director Chow bowed and scraped before them, trying to placate them, but they appeared to be having none of it.

With the two party men was a woman — whose Gucci dress was smeared with blood and mud — and the little girl named Minnie, whose clothes were also dirty.

They were all quickly ushered into a silver Range Rover which zoomed away, kicking up gravel.

CJ wondered what had happened to the other Communist Party VIPs and their lady friends. She feared the worst.

A captain came up to Colonel Bao.

"Sir, we have located and killed eighteen

of the dragons that had severed their ears. Fourteen were red-bellied blacks, four were eastern grays."

He held up a small tablet computer. It looked like an iPad mini, only one that was encased in a shockproof and waterproof rubber casing.

CJ caught a fleeting glimpse of its screen. It depicted a digitized map of the zoo similar to the one she had seen in the master control room earlier, complete with moving colored icons:

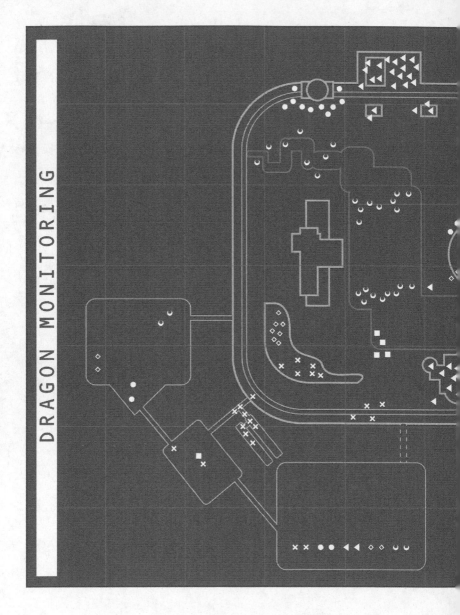

DRAGON MONITORING

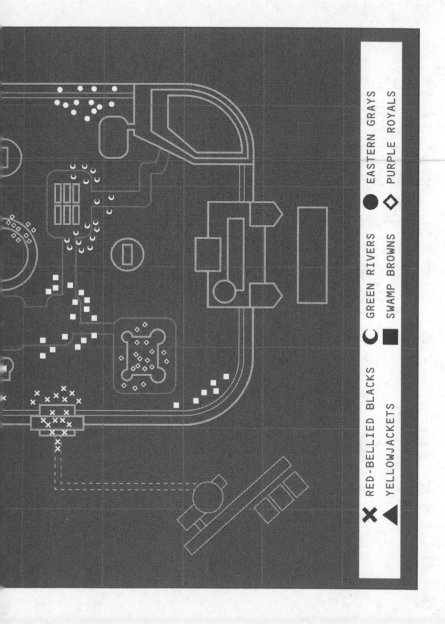

RED-BELLIED BLACKS

YELLOWJACKETS

GREEN RIVERS

SWAMP BROWNS

EASTERN GRAYS

PURPLE ROYALS

Even though her view of the digital map was brief, CJ could see that the clusters of the dragons around the zoo had moved: the red crosses, for instance, now swarmed over the administration building. She also saw a very odd arrangement of dragons inside the Nesting Center: ten dragons, two of each color, all in a strangely neat row, totally separated from the other dragons in the zoo. She wondered what that was.

The captain continued: "Eight earless dragons remain unaccounted for. Six are red-bellied black princes, two are red-bellied black kings. We are searching the valley for them now —"

"There are some in the generators and the others are probably underground somewhere, digging," a man's voice said in English and everyone, including CJ, turned to see the bespectacled, lab coat–wearing man from the Birthing Center.

"What makes you say that, Dr. Patrick?" Colonel Bao said.

"Because digging is what they do, Colonel," the bespectacled man, Ben Patrick, replied. "Digging into the Earth is how they managed to survive the meteor impact that killed the dinosaurs. They can see in pitch darkness, so they are perfectly comfortable underground. And they've been digging all over this zoo for months."

"If you are so knowledgeable about their behavior, Dr. Patrick," Bao snorted, "why didn't you predict this attack?"

"We are dealing with a species of creature never before seen in this age of the world," Patrick replied calmly. "They are intelligent in a way we have never known. Indeed, theirs is an intelligence that is far more ancient than ours."

"They are *animals,*" the colonel said.

"Their intelligence is just different," Patrick said. "We underestimate it at our peril."

"I repeat, they are animals."

"They may well be, Colonel. But which species is mopping up the blood now?"

"How do you know they're in the generators?" the colonel asked.

"Because I saw them break in there. The access door to the generators is halfway down the entry tunnel to the Birthing Center. I didn't follow them because at that point, two more attacked the Birthing Center. I also didn't follow them in there because, quite frankly, I do not wish to die. Those dragons are probably the reason why your backup generators are offline: I imagine they thought it was an exit and inadvertently dug through some key cables trying to get out."

Colonel Bao snorted again as another captain rushed up to him and said, "Sir. The two American journalists have been found in the waste management facility. They are alive. They are being brought here right now."

Bao waved his hand. "There is no need to bring them here. I doubt our guests want to stay any longer. Their little publicity tour is finished. Have Wolfe and Perry taken to the emergency departure area."

While this was being said, the man named Patrick came over to CJ and her group.

"CJ Cameron," he said.

"Ben Patrick," she replied neutrally. "They told me you were here."

Dr. Benjamin Patrick smiled. He was still amazingly handsome, with matinee-idol good looks: blue eyes, high cheekbones, square jaw. His glasses made him look even sexier.

His eyes scanned her scars. He hadn't seen CJ since the incident. "I heard about your face," he said. "Shame."

That was classic Ben: CJ couldn't tell if he meant it was a shame that she'd been hurt or a shame that her prettiness had been lost.

"How's the vocalization research going?"

she asked, changing the topic.

"It's amazing stuff," he said. "The opportunity of a lifetime. I've been here for six years now and the research is off the charts. I have a database of over three hundred separate and identifiable vocalizations. These animals are like nothing I have ever seen. They communicate. Every squawk and screech you hear has meaning. They live in strictly hierarchical packs, they have rivalries with other dragons. It is absolutely amazing."

"Until today," CJ said.

Patrick grimaced. "Yes. Until today. But our Chinese friends are a determined lot. To them this will just be seen as a setback, a necessary loss in their march toward their dream of a Great Dragon Zoo."

CJ shook her head. "You don't just *get over* something like this. Sixty-plus people are dead and *The New York Times* was here to see it. When Wolfe and Perry get back to Hong Kong, this'll be the biggest news story in the world."

"Hell, yeah," Hamish said.

Just then, a second silver Range Rover pulled up nearby.

Out of it stepped Hu Tang. Colonel Bao went directly over to him with Patrick and a pair of captains. A quick discussion was had.

305

CJ watched them. As she did so, Greg Johnson sidled up beside her. "Wonder what they're talking about?" he said quietly.

"Yeah," CJ said.

She kept watching Bao, Hu Tang and Patrick as she said, "I'm also wondering about you, Mr. Johnson. You're a cool customer under pressure and a pretty awesome shot for an 'embassy aide.' Tell me who you really are."

Johnson cracked a wry half-smile. "You're not bad under pressure yourself, Dr. Cameron."

"I've had practice with crocodiles that wanted to bite my head off. What about you?"

"I might also have had some practice," Johnson said. "Although my threats were more . . . human . . . in nature."

CJ turned to face him to find him staring evenly back at her, the half-smile still there, his eyes inscrutable.

Then abruptly Hu was marching toward them.

"Mr. Ambassador! Mr. Johnson, Dr. Cameron and Mr. Cameron," he said formally. "You are all okay, I hope. You are not hurt?"

"We're okay," CJ said.

"Honestly, words escape me," Hu said. "This is just terrible. I am both embarrassed

306

and distressed at this awful loss of life. I am so sorry you had to witness it. I do hope you will forgive us. As you will no doubt understand, I have much to do, especially over at the administration building where many lives have been lost. If you will accompany Captain Wong here, he will reunite you with Mr. Wolfe and Mr. Perry and take you all back to Hong Kong. Once again, I am terribly sorry. Our tour, sadly, is over."

It was getting dark as CJ's group was led to a white Great Dragon Zoo of China guest van to be taken home.

As the others got in the van, CJ went over to Ben Patrick.

"Ben, before I go, I just want to know: what is this little valley for?"

Patrick snuffed a laugh. "It's for VIPs only, and by that I mean *very* high net worth and *very* high-powered Chinese."

"So what is it?"

"It's a hunting area," Patrick said. "For a small fortune, the lucky customer can *hunt* dragons. It's targeted at the high-roller set from Macau and wealthy hunters from America. When the weekend warriors are done, they get to sip Hennessy cognac in the lodge and swap stories."

"Oh," CJ said, and suddenly she understood the party men in their new hiking gear.

It hadn't been hiking gear at all.

It had been hunting gear.

She also now understood the black room she had come through earlier, the one that had made her feel like being backstage at a theater — precisely because it *was* like being backstage at a theater. That must have been where the dragons were released into the hunting area. They would be led to the black room from the Birthing Center and released through the camouflaged door or, she guessed, through other doors that branched off the side-tunnels.

Unbelievable.

"See you, Ben," CJ said.

"Goodbye to you, too, CJ," Patrick said coolly.

CJ joined the others at the van. It was a brand-new Volkswagen model, nicely appointed, with leather seats and air-conditioning.

She climbed inside and, exhausted and sweaty, sank back into a cool leather seat.

The van pulled out and drove down the winding road that led out of the little valley.

The van emerged from the hunting area and turned left onto the ring road.

It was almost completely dark now and the ring road was lit by amber streetlights.

Storm clouds flitted across the face of the full moon, blotting it out.

CJ saw the taillights of the silver VIP Range Rover up ahead, heading along the northern border of the megavalley and about to enter a tunnel.

She wondered why the dragons had chosen today to stage their attack. What made this day special?

The visitors, she thought. *The two groups of VIP visitors.* The dragons could detect the elevated heartbeat of an anxious animal and today the staff at the zoo would most certainly have been extra anxious. Sensing the heightened levels of nervousness and anxiety in their jailers, the dragons must have seen their opportunity and taken it.

CJ let it go. What did it matter now anyway?

She closed her eyes. She was completely drained and now, safe at last, she allowed herself to relax and rock with the gentle motion of the van.

Then the van swayed unexpectedly and CJ felt herself lean left.

She opened her eyes.

They had taken a right turn, off the ring road. The taillights of the Range Rover disappeared into the tunnel, continuing on down the ring road.

That's odd, CJ thought.

She knew they couldn't go back to the main entrance building via the western side of the valley — the tower of the admin building was blocking the ring road there. Which was why, she figured, they were going around the long way, across the northern side of the valley and then down the eastern flank.

The van began to bounce. Its headlights showed the way ahead: the unlit gravel road that led to the casino hotel.

"I saw a helipad on the casino earlier," Ambassador Syme said. "Must be taking us there."

The van followed the bends of the uneven gravel road before it abruptly turned off onto an even rougher dirt track and suddenly CJ found herself moving in amongst eight-foot-high reeds and mangroves.

A distinct feeling of unease shot through her.

"We're in trouble," she whispered to Hamish.

"What do you mean?"

"This isn't the way back."

She called to the Chinese captain, Wong, sitting up front with the driver. "Excuse me, Captain? Where are we going?"

"Shortcut" was the curt reply.

311

CJ exchanged a meaningful look with Hamish.

"Stay sharp," she said.

"Understood," Hamish said.

It was now totally dark outside, the only light the bouncing beams of the van's headlights.

The van came to a sharp halt and everyone was thrown slightly forward.

Then the side door was flung open from the outside and CJ found herself staring down the barrel of an assault rifle held by a blank-eyed Chinese Army soldier. A second soldier, similarly armed, covered the others.

"Get out of the vehicle with your hands up," Captain Wong spat. "Your tour is officially at an end."

Naturally, the U.S. Ambassador to China wasn't impressed to find a gun pointed at his face.

"What in God's name do you people think you're doing!" Ambassador Syme snapped.

"Just get out of the van," the captain said.

Syme and Johnson stepped out of the van with their hands raised. CJ and Hamish followed, also with their hands held high. One of the soldiers snatched Hamish's camera from him.

CJ took in her surroundings.

A high wall of reeds surrounded the group. The foul stench of the swamp pervaded the air. The gentle lapping of water could be heard in the darkness, as well as grunting sounds that CJ knew: the vocalizations of saltwater crocodiles.

They were in the swamp to the west of the casino hotel, the saltwater swamp that adjoined the freshwater lake.

A wooden walkway disappeared into the wall of reeds ahead of her. It was elevated about two feet above the waterline. It was a tourist boardwalk, designed to allow visitors to have a pleasant stroll above the swamp.

The only light came from the van's headlights. Above the wall of reeds, CJ could see the top of Dragon Mountain. Floodlights illuminated it and the revolving restaurant at its peak glowed softly.

Syme and Johnson were pushed down the walkway; CJ was shoved after them, Hamish by her side. They were all covered by the three Chinese Army men: the captain and the two infantrymen. The two infantrymen brandished Type 56 rifles — the Chinese clone of the AK-47 — and wore gun belts across their chests with extra ammo clips and grenades on them.

As she walked, CJ noticed one, then two, then three saltwater crocodiles stalking them in the brackish water beside the elevated walkway, moving parallel to them.

The crocs know what's about to happen, she thought.

The Chinese have done this before.

Then suddenly she heard a voice up ahead, a voice she knew: that of Aaron Perry.

"Now, wait, wait, please, just wait a second, I'm sure we can —" Perry was saying

314

quickly, desperately.

CJ rounded a corner and saw Perry and Seymour Wolfe kneeling further down the walkway. A Chinese soldier stood with a pistol aimed directly at Perry's face while another soldier covered Wolfe.

Blam!

The first soldier fired, blowing Perry's brains out, and the young blogger's body collapsed, flopping to the walkway before toppling off the edge and splashing into the swampwater.

Almost immediately, a big crocodile rushed in, snatched the corpse and took it roughly away.

CJ swallowed hard, horrified. This was what Colonel Bao had meant when he'd said that Wolfe and Perry should be taken to the "emergency departure area." It was code for this place of execution.

"Oh, this is *fucked up*," Hamish said loudly. "I do *not* want to die this way."

The Chinese infantryman behind him jabbed Hamish with his rifle and he kept walking.

"We've seen too much," CJ said. "We can't be allowed to leave this place alive. And there can't be any evidence that we were ever here, either."

Walking last of all, the Chinese captain

must have heard her. "Dr. Cameron is correct. This zoo is the future of China. Its existence cannot be tarnished by negative reports in the Western media. No one can know what has happened here today and no one will. All witnesses must be eliminated. Minister Hu was very specific. He ordered me to reunite you with Mr. Wolfe and Mr. Perry, and that is exactly what I will do."

CJ recalled Ben Patrick's words from before: *"To them this will just be seen as a setback, a necessary loss in their march toward their dream of a Great Dragon Zoo."*

"Now, listen here!" Syme still seemed to think he had some influence. He turned as he walked. "I am the Ambassador to China from the United States of America! You cannot simply explain away my disappearance."

"But of course we can," Captain Wong said calmly. "Accidents happen all the time, Mr. Ambassador. Car accidents, small plane crashes, hotel room drug overdoses."

CJ turned. "Bill Lynch. He died in a light aircraft crash in China. It was you —"

Wong smiled. "Sadly, Mr. Lynch witnessed a similar incident. Fewer deaths but ugly ones nonetheless."

There came a scuffling sound from behind them, followed by a shrill male voice saying,

"Don't touch me, you fucking ignorant brute!"

Go-Go was pushed into view by a lone Chinese private.

"Go-Go," CJ said as their eyes met.

"CJ!" Go-Go said, "Some dickwad told Colonel Bao that you and I knew each other, so the good colonel said I had to die with you. Couldn't trust me to stay quiet. And you know what" — Go-Go spat at his guard — "the dirty motherfucker was right! I *so* would've told."

"Thanks, Go-Go," CJ said.

But her mind was racing. The Chinese were about to kill them all and feed their bodies to the crocs. She had to do something fast.

She and Hamish were still walking side by side, CJ on the right, Hamish on the left, with the two rifle-bearing Chinese infantrymen behind them. Johnson and Syme were a few yards ahead of them.

"Hamish," she whispered. "You still got your fanny pack?"

"Yeah? Why?"

"On the count of three, I want you to pull out your lighter, light it, and hold it out in your right hand at chest height."

"Why —"

"Just do it and be ready to duck, okay?

On three. One . . . two . . . three . . . Go!"

Hamish did as he was told, even though he didn't know why. Quick as a flash, he dipped his hand into his fanny pack, extracted his Great Dragon Zoo of China Zippo lighter and held it out at chest height to the right of his body, flicking the cartwheel, sparking it —

— at exactly the same time as CJ spun on the spot and, moving like a Wild West gunslinger, drew a small can from her own fanny pack, aimed it at the two Chinese infantrymen behind her and fired it.

It was her complimentary can of hairspray.

But when fired through the flame of Hamish's lighter it became a miniature flamethrower.

A horizontal column of fire lanced out from the hairspray can, lighting up the area as it engulfed the two Chinese soldiers. Their faces and chests were enveloped in flames . . .

. . . as were the grenades clipped to their weapons belts.

The two flaming infantrymen exploded in identical grenade blasts. They simply disappeared. One second they were there, the next they were gone.

By this time, CJ had hit the deck, pulling Hamish down with her. Blood and body parts went flying over their heads.

But then something that CJ had not intended occurred.

Damaged by the force of the blast, the section of the wooden boardwalk beneath them collapsed, and everyone on it dropped as one into the swampwater below, where the crocodiles were waiting.

CJ plunged into the foul-smelling swamp and for a brief moment her world went silent.

Then a line of fearsome teeth rushed past her, followed by a long pebbled body, webbed claws and a powerful tail. A flashing memory of a similar scene sent a wave of adrenaline coursing through her and she kicked out with her feet and they made contact with the bottom.

CJ stood, her head breaking the surface. The water was only chest deep.

As she resurfaced, she saw that the boardwalk was shattered in the middle, with spot fires burning at its edges. The burning flesh of the two exploded Chinese infantrymen had splattered the surrounding reeds.

Her companions — Hamish, Johnson, Syme, Go-Go and Wolfe — all surfaced nearby, equally horrified. Also in the water were the four remaining Chinese troops:

Captain Wong, the two soldiers who had been about to kill Wolfe, and the private who had brought Go-Go.

CJ saw a look of panic on Wolfe's face and she knew that he was about to bolt.

"Wolfe! Don't! Stay where you are! They go for the ones that flee!" she barked.

Despite his obvious terror, Wolfe somehow obeyed. He stayed still while the two Chinese soldiers near him sloshed desperately through the water, trying to get back to the boardwalk.

Two crocs zeroed in on them immediately.

They were much faster in the water than any person could hope to be and they overwhelmed the hapless infantrymen, dragging them under with screams of horror.

CJ gasped at the speed of it.

Usually solitary animals, crocs sometimes hunted in a manner known as "mobbing": at the sign of a lot of food — like, for instance, a herd of zebras crossing a river — they banded together. But they almost always went for the outliers of the herd, usually the slower or younger ones, or the ones that panicked and bolted.

Gunfire made CJ spin and she saw the private who had been guarding Go-Go firing his pistol at an oncoming croc. That croc veered away as the bullets hit the reeds around it but then the Chinese soldier was abruptly yanked under the surface. He disappeared in a spray of water, emitting a surprised shriek that was cut off when his mouth went under.

CJ snapped around — in time to see Captain Wong wading through the water right beside her, his face twisted in fury, his 9mm pistol coming level with her face. At the exact same time, she felt a surge of water and in an instant CJ knew that the captain's sudden movement had captured a croc's attention.

She grabbed Wong's gun hand in her own and hip-tossed him, jujitsu-style, right into the path of an inrushing crocodile.

The big croc — and it was indeed a big one — clamped its mighty jaws around Wong's head. Then, with incredible ferocity, it yanked the captain away from CJ and she fell back into the water, to find his 9mm pistol now held dumbly in her own hand.

CJ spun to see the croc rolling over and over in the water, still gripping Wong by the head, flinging his body like a rag doll: this was the death roll. A crocodile didn't suffocate you with a bite to the jugular like a lion did. No, it rolled you until you drowned. Then it ate you at its leisure.

CJ stepped slowly away from the death

roll taking place right in front of her. She saw the others over by the semi-destroyed boardwalk.

"Everybody, move slowly and together back to the boardwalk. We *must* stay together. No running and no breaking away from the group."

And so that was how they moved — slowly and tightly together — back toward the boardwalk.

By now at least five crocs were feasting on the four Chinese soldiers with perhaps six more watching from the reeds.

Gliding through the chest-deep water, CJ whispered, "Head for that side." She indicated the end of the exploded boardwalk farthest from the van that had brought them here. "There could be more Chinese troops on the way to make sure we're dead."

The group reached the end of the damaged boardwalk.

"One at a time," CJ said. "Keep it slow. No sudden movements. No splashing."

Syme went first, followed by Wolfe, Johnson, Go-Go and Hamish. Hamish and Johnson then scooped CJ out of the water together with a single powerful lift.

They all now stood on the boardwalk, gasping and soaked. The spot fires were beginning to peter out.

"What now?" Hamish asked.

CJ said, "I can't say I've been in a situation like this before but I don't think it'll be long before someone comes to see why these assholes haven't come back. We gotta move and we gotta move now."

She glanced at Greg Johnson, seeking the opinion of the only person there who she thought might actually have been in such a situation before.

Johnson nodded. "They'll come checking soon."

"But where do we *go*?" Wolfe asked.

CJ bit her lip, looked out into the darkness.

Across the lake Dragon Mountain loomed large, a black shadow against the cloud-filled sky. Around it was the megavalley, dotted with hills, forests and waterfalls, and infested with dragons.

She tossed the dead captain's 9mm pistol to Johnson. "Here, you can use this better than I can." Then, to the others: "We go into the zoo. And if we can stay alive long enough, we figure out a way to get out of it."

FIFTH EVOLUTION

INTO THE ZOO

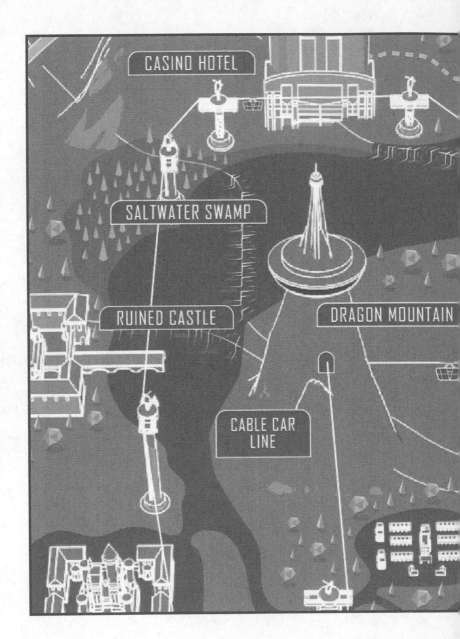

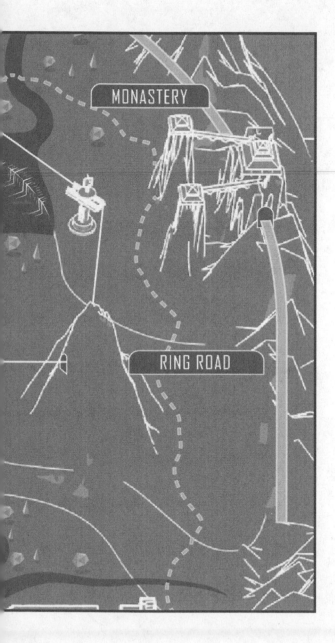

MONASTERY

RING ROAD

The most dangerous animal in a zoo is Man.

— Yann Martel, *Life of Pi*
(Knopf, Canada, 2001)

CJ ran quickly but quietly down the wooden boardwalk. The floorboards creaked. The waters of the swamp sloshed with the movements of crocodiles.

Hamish and the others ran behind her, also trying to move with minimal noise.

By now, night had fallen over the zoo, but it was relatively easy to see thanks to the many floodlights mounted on the rim of the crater. The full moon was hidden behind a dense layer of storm clouds.

Then the first drops of rain began to fall, spattering the boardwalk.

As she ran, CJ kept an ear out for another sound: the sound of realization. When the Chinese discovered that the American witnesses to the bloodshed had not been eliminated, there would be uproar. So far, she had heard no such sounds.

"CJ Cameron," Go-Go whispered as he jogged, "can I just say that you are Xena the fucking Warrior Princess! Nice moves back there, Honeypie."

"Thanks, Go-Go," CJ said.

"It *was* pretty impressive," Greg Johnson said as he came up alongside her. "Where'd you learn to build a flamethrower?"

"High school science class," CJ said. "Honestly, I was just trying to set them alight, create a distraction of some sort. The grenades were . . . well . . ." She let the sentence trail off. She didn't mention that her hands had been shaking ever since. She'd never killed anyone before.

"They got what they deserved," Johnson said, looking her in the eye. "They were going to kill you and all of us. Right now, the question is: now what?"

CJ regathered herself. "Now, we get as far away from this swamp as possible. When the Chinese find out we're not dead, they'll send more troops, maybe choppers, too."

"Concur." Johnson turned to Go-Go. "Hey, you. How many helicopters have your army guys got here?"

"Yo. Salt-and-Pepper. The name is Go-Go or Mr. Go-Go, okay? To answer your question, they have seven choppers in total: four of the little Z-10 attack birds, two big Mi-17 gunships, and one of those really big doublerotored transport choppers —"

"A Chinook," Johnson said.

"Yeah, that's it. It's also loaded with fucking guns. The dragons hate the choppers. Hate 'em. I've seen a few civilian helicopters here as well, but they come and go and they don't have any weapons on them that I know of."

Johnson turned back to CJ as they jogged. "So we evade and avoid capture. What then?"

"The first thing we need to do is find something that can put us in touch with the outside world: a working phone or a computer. We need to call for help and then find a place to hide till someone can come and get us," CJ said. "I figure the best place to hide is outside this crater, so after we find a telephone, we find a way out. Go-Go, where's the nearest phone?"

"The casino hotel." Go-Go pointed out over the reeds. "Lots of offices and rooms there with heaps of phones and computers."

"Where else?" CJ asked. "Give me options."

Go-Go nodded across the valley to the south, to where Dragon Mountain towered in the rain. "The mountain. There's a maintenance office inside the cable car station. There's also a manager's office up in the restaurant."

CJ looked up at the disc-shaped revolving restaurant at the summit of the peak.

"All right," she said. "Closer is better, so the casino it is. We stay out of sight, find a phone, call for help, then we get the hell out of Dodge. Everybody okay with that?"

There were no objections.

"Getting out is going to be next to impossible in daylight," Johnson said. "We need to do it tonight, under cover of darkness."

CJ turned as she jogged, appraised Johnson. With his salt-and-pepper hair and clean-cut features, he was kind of handsome, but there was something more to him, something in his sharp gray eyes.

"Okay, you," she said. "Since we're on the run from the Chinese Army in a valley filled with dragons, it's time to come clean. You're not just an aide to the U.S. Ambassador, are you?"

Johnson nodded. "I'm the deputy station chief for the Central Intelligence Agency at the United States embassy in Beijing. I was a field agent for nine years before I was shot in the line of duty and got sent to Beijing to drive a desk. It was supposed to be a nice cushy office posting. Look at me now."

"Why send a CIA agent to a new zoo?" CJ asked. "Did the Agency know about the dragons?"

"No," Johnson said firmly. "We didn't know a thing about the dragons. We knew about the zoo, we knew that it had been planned for years and that it was supersized. But the Chinese outflanked us on the dragons. They kept that very close to their chests. We were totally blind-sided."

"Then why were you sent here with the ambassador?" CJ glanced at Syme running along behind them.

"I specialize in observing China's strategic nuclear arsenal and other exotic weapon systems," Johnson said. "One of the ways the Chinese kept this place a secret is that it is built entirely on military land. I got intel a few weeks back that the Second Artillery Corps of the People's Liberation Army — the division of the Chinese military that controls its nuclear weapons and high-yield conventional devices — had sent three 6.5-ton thermobaric bombs to the military airfield adjoining this zoo. My job was to find out why."

"There's an airfield down here?" Hamish said.

"A few miles to the southwest of the main valley," Johnson said. "It's a mirror image of the civilian airport that you arrived at on the eastern side."

"What's a thermobaric bomb?" CJ asked.

"It's the most powerful conventional weapon short of a nuke," Johnson said. "It has a blast yield of approximately forty kilotons. A thermobaric device is often called a vacuum bomb. The initial blast will vaporize everything within a three-hundred-yard radius while the ensuing shock wave is far more devastating: it creates a vacuum that literally sucks the oxygen out of the air for a radius of ten miles. Any living thing in that ten-mile radius will be asphyxiated and quite gruesomely, too. Some reports say that the vacuum will suck your lungs right up out of your throat."

"What a charming image," Hamish said.

"So it's a big-ass bomb," CJ said.

"The biggest you can get without going nuclear, yes," Johnson said.

"And you say the Chinese have three of them here?" CJ said.

"Yes," Johnson said. "I've been tracking those three thermobaric bombs since the Chinese bought them off the Russians in a very shady deal. I know their serial numbers, their firing codes, even their override codes."

CJ said, "So why would the Chinese bring three of them to a zoo, even if it is a dragon one?"

Johnson shrugged. "Now that I know what's here at this zoo, my guess is that the thermobaric bombs are a fail-safe, a last resort in case the Chinese lose control of the zoo and the dragons get out.

"You blow one of them and you lose a small amount of real estate but you bring down every living animal for miles. It'd fix a dragon problem. Whatever the reason, three of those bombs are here . . . somewhere."

They had been running for about ten minutes in the slow-falling rain when they rounded a bend in the boardwalk and the wall of reeds to their right fell away to reveal a striking view.

A long high waterfall stretched away from them to the south. The lake beneath it glistened in the glare of the zoo's floodlights, the whole vista veiled by drizzling rain. At the other end of the waterfall, about half a mile away, rose Dragon Mountain.

In other circumstances, it would have been a beautiful sight, but not tonight.

CJ didn't like it here. The waterfall was so

loud, they couldn't hear anything coming, a dragon or a chopper. The boardwalk looped away to the left, heading off in the direction of the casino hotel —

Blinding white light blazed to life all around her, coming from above. An enormous Chinese Mi-17 helicopter thundered by overhead, banking low. It pulled up into a hover, its searchlights casting twin beams through the air, beams that centered on CJ and her group on the boardwalk at the edge of the swamp.

Muzzle flashes erupted from the left side of the gunship and the boardwalk was strafed by bullets.

"Into the water!" CJ yelled as she dived off the walkway a second before it was shredded by heavy-caliber gunfire.

CJ splashed into the brackish swampwater, right at the point where the reeds met the lake. Her feet found the bottom and she stood once again in the water. She flung her wet hair out of her eyes —

— to find herself staring right into the jaws of a huge saltwater crocodile. The crocodile's tail slunk back and forth behind it, catlike. It was a monster of a croc, easily seventeen feet long.

There was nothing CJ could do. The croc had her. She knew it. It knew it.

With a powerful lash of its tail, the crocodile lunged.

CJ threw out her right arm in defense and the croc clamped down on it.

She screamed in pain as the croc's fore-teeth slammed down on her shoulder. It felt like being pinned in a giant vise. CJ had expected to feel the hot searing pain of the animal's teeth piercing her skin, but her yellow-and-black leather jacket — taken from the dead trainer, Yim — had Kevlar plates sewn into its shoulders and the plates had thankfully spared her from that.

Still, the croc had her entire right arm in its mouth and a second later, the big reptile yanked her under.

Another flashing memory of the attack in the Everglades.

The bull alligator has dragged her under, her head in its jaws. Its teeth grate across her cheek. Bubbles and brown water fill her vision.

She has a pocket knife in a pouch on her belt. It is small but sharp.

As the gator swings her into a death roll, almost snapping her neck, she manages to extract the knife.

Everyone has heard that if you stab a gator or a croc in the eye, it will release you — but when your head is in its jaws, that's all but impossible.

So CJ thrusts her knife into the only place within reach: the alligator's soft underbelly.

The knife goes in. The alligator grunts in surprise but keeps hold of her, keeps rolling. So CJ just stabs away at its belly, shredding it, tearing the skin apart.

The opening in the beast's underbelly widens. CJ keeps stabbing. Blood pours from the wound. She keeps stabbing. Guts start falling out.

Finally the rolling slows. The bull is weakening. CJ keeps stabbing. She is fighting for her fucking life and she *will not relent.* As the roll slows, she jams the knife deep into the animal's heart.

It exhales loudly . . . and releases her head.

She falls away from it, staggers onto the muddy shore, her face unrecognizable, her clothes rags.

She collapses in the mud as some employees come running, firing rifles into the air to scatter the other alligators.

CJ blacks out.

She will wake up in the hospital two weeks later. When Troy, her fiancé, sees her destroyed face, he leaves her.

This time it was different: this croc had her by the arm.

Her whole arm, from shoulder to hand, was within its mouth. While her jacket had saved her shoulder from being punctured by the crocodile's teeth, the pressure of its bite was still incredible, the most powerful bite-pressure in the world — well, short of a dragon's.

In the previous attack, CJ had been all panic and adrenaline.

That wasn't the case now. Now she was calm, her mind sharp, and it was her mind that was going to get her out of this.

CJ braced herself for the death roll that was about to come. She had a plan, but she couldn't afford to break her shoulder in the execution of it.

With a powerful spinning movement, the crocodile rolled and CJ was yanked into the roll.

That's it, you bastard. Do what you do. But I've got a bigger brain than you.

It was trying to drown her, but as it did,

CJ did a strange thing: she stretched out with her right hand — the hand that was *inside* the croc's mouth — and grabbed hold of a fleshy flap of tissue at the back of the reptile's tongue and yanked on it hard.

That flap of tissue was the palatal valve and it was incredibly important to a crocodile, since it covered the croc's tracheal opening when it was underwater, preventing water from going into its lungs.

So when CJ lifted this crocodile's palatal valve, water began gushing down its trachea.

Now *she* was drowning *it*.

The croc didn't know what was going on. This had clearly never happened to it before: prey fighting back. It began to cough and gag, before . . .

. . . it released CJ and swam away, tail lashing.

Free of the croc's grip, CJ surfaced and sucked in gulps of air. She checked her shoulder. Thanks to the Kevlar plates in her jacket, it was fine, just a little bruised.

She rose into a kaleidoscope of light and sound.

The roar of the waterfall and the *thump-thump-thump* of the Chinese helicopter filled her ears; the glare of its floodlights created spots in her eyes; and from somewhere she heard Hamish's voice calling: "CJ! Behind you!"

CJ spun. The croc had returned. It had regathered itself for a second attack and was now five feet away.

CJ tensed for round two. She was standing at the edge of the swamp, where the high reeds met the glistening expanse of the lake, her back to the lake.

And then the crocodile stopped.

It didn't attack. It just stayed where it was, staring at her from a distance of five feet.

Then it did something even more unusual.

It edged backwards.

CJ cocked her head. That just didn't happen.

She frowned, her mind racing —

Uh-oh . . .

Slowly, very slowly, CJ turned to face the lake behind her.

There, five feet away from her in the *other* direction, staring up at her with only its eyes, ears and snout protruding above the waterline of the lake, was the only animal in the world that could scare off a seventeen-foot-long saltwater crocodile.

A two-hundred-foot-long olive-colored emperor dragon.

The thing was simply immense and it stared

at CJ with almost unnatural stillness.

More olive-colored dragons rose up out of the lake beside it, princes. Three, then five, then seven. A whole pack of them.

Rain pattered down on the water around them. Their slitlike eyes, horned ears and spiky backs were all that could be seen.

"Swamp dragons . . ." she heard Go-Go gasp.

It was then that CJ bumped against something under the surface. She looked down to see a chest-high Perspex retaining wall separating the saltwater swamp from the freshwater lake: the borderline between crocodile and dragon territory.

The gigantic emperor watched her.

But it didn't attack.

And in a moment of realization, CJ deduced why.

It still had ears and she was still wearing her wristwatch with its protective sonic shield.

She saw Hamish, Johnson, Wolfe, Go-Go and Syme nearby, also at the edge of the lake.

"Get closer to the dragons!" she yelled.

"Are you *insane*!" Wolfe said.

"CJ!" Go-Go shouted back. "They're swamp dragons! They're very agg—"

"They can't attack us with our shields!

But the crocs can!"

"Halt! Stay where you are!" a voice called from a loudspeaker on the chopper overhead. A line of bullet-impacts sprayed across the water's surface around CJ.

The dragons growled and hissed at the chopper. They'd clearly had bad experiences with gunships before.

CJ saw Johnson raise his newly acquired 9mm pistol up at the helicopter and she wondered what he was doing. A pistol would be useless against a gunship.

Johnson fired three quick shots.

Sparks flared on the side of the chopper, near the top of its cockpit windows.

Johnson grimaced. He'd obviously missed what he was aiming for.

He fired again and this time CJ understood.

A small explosion flared out from the chopper's fuselage, just above its cockpit windows, and CJ glimpsed something go flying off it.

The chopper's sonic shield–generating antenna.

The big gunship wasn't protected anymore.

The response from the swamp dragons was instantaneous.

The emperor swamp dragon rose out of

the lake with a mighty roar that drowned out both the sound of the chopper and the gushing of the waterfall.

Rising to its full height, it was impossibly huge. Gargantuan.

The great animal dwarfed the Mi-17 — one of the biggest helicopters in the world — its immense body making the chopper look like a toy. It spread its batlike wings wide as it rose and torrents of water rolled off them. With its pointed ears, skeletal body and immense wings, it looked like an angry demon rising out of Hell itself. The wave of water it displaced as it came out of the lake threw CJ back into Johnson.

The emperor reached out and snatched the chopper with its foreclaws and then dropped back underwater *with the ten-ton helicopter in its grip*!

The massive chopper went under tail-first, its searchlights tilting upward, sending beams of light lancing into the sky before the whole helicopter simply vanished beneath the waves of the lake, its rotors slapping the surface on the way down. The beams from the spotlights became eerie green glows as the chopper disappeared into the murky depths of the lake. Soon they vanished, too, and the lake became dark again.

"Holy fucking shit . . ." Hamish said.

"Come on," Johnson said, taking CJ by the arm. "This way."

He pulled her through the chest-deep water toward the waterfall.

As she allowed herself to be hauled along, CJ glanced back at the boardwalk and saw what Johnson must have already seen: the bouncing lights of cars and other vehicles coming from the direction of the casino hotel.

"The casino is no longer an option," Johnson said. "We go for the mountain. If we cross the lake behind that waterfall, maybe they won't be able to see us."

Pulling CJ with him, he plunged through the veil of falling water.

CJ emerged on the inside of the waterfall. It was somehow quieter here, the only noise the steady rush of water. A long rock wall stretched away to the south, hidden behind the cascade. The water here was shallower, only waist-deep.

"Come on, everyone," Johnson called, moving purposefully, gun up. "We can't stop moving."

The group waded down the length of the waterfall, hidden behind its veil of falling water.

Hamish walked up front behind CJ and Johnson. Hamish had been in Afghanistan and Iraq, and he'd seen some seriously weird shit in those hellholes, but here, now, in this zoo, he was still trying to process everything that had happened.

The whole time the group sloshed along behind the waterfall, they were shadowed by the pack of swamp dragons. The dragons followed close behind them and occasionally — startlingly — poked their heads through the curtain of falling water.

But they didn't attack. The sonic shields on the watches were still effective.

The swamp dragons, Hamish thought, were easily the ugliest of all the dragons he had seen so far. Perhaps it was simply a color thing. The yellowjackets, purple royals and red-bellied blacks, with their vibrant colorations, had a kind of style. These olive-green dragons, with their flatter snouts and spotted skin, looked like hideous monsters. The way they lurked in the water didn't help either, all hunched and craven.

Hamish recalled the ugly olive-colored dragon that had appeared out of nowhere in the Birthing Center and attacked the red-bellied black prince.

"These dragons look different to the others," he said to Go-Go as they pushed through the water.

"That's because they are," Go-Go said. "The swamp dragons were the first dragons at the zoo to come out of the bioengineering program."

"The what?" Wolfe asked. He hadn't gone through the Birthing Center before.

"The crocodile breeding program," CJ said.

Go-Go said, "The bosses wanted more dragons, so they utilized female saltwater crocodiles as hosts for dragon insemination. The program eventually managed to produce a lot of 'pure' dragons — mainly redbellies, yellowjackets and eastern grays — but at the start, as the engineers tried to figure out the right gene matrix, it produced an unexpected type of dragon, this species that we call the brown swamp dragon."

Hamish said, "So the swamp dragons didn't come from any eggs inside the original nest?"

"That's right, they are a totally new, entirely man-made, bioengineered dragon — essentially nine parts dragon, one part crocodile — bred right here at the Great Dragon Zoo."

"Which is why they look so different to the others," Hamish said.

"Precisely," Go-Go said.

"We saw your Birthing Center," CJ said flatly. "Not exactly the nicest place I've ever seen."

"It isn't nice. As you would imagine, dragon eggs are a lot bigger than crocodile eggs. Giving birth to a dragon kills the host croc."

"What!" Hamish said. "You *kill* the mother crocodile to get a new dragon egg?"

"A female crocodile's birth canal isn't wide enough to expel a dragon egg, so a caesarean section is made. This, unfortunately, is fatal for the host mother. I know, I know, it's callous and cruel," Go-Go said, "but for my bosses this is an acceptable sacrifice in the pursuit of building an amazing zoo."

"Just like *we* are an acceptable sacrifice," Ambassador Syme said.

"Yes," Go-Go said quietly. "Just like we are."

After about fifteen minutes of wading, they reached the end of the waterfall, where they were confronted by a small rocky cliff.

"I'll go first," Hamish volunteered.

He began climbing. The gushing of the waterfall filled his ears. If there was another Chinese helicopter waiting for them outside, he wouldn't know it until he poked his head above the top of the rock wall.

After a short climb, he tentatively raised his head above the little cliff . . . and was immediately assaulted by the harsh glare of a spotlight that came blazing to life.

There waiting for him and the others, its rotors stopped, its spotlight flaring, was a second Chinese Mi-17 helicopter gunship, with a dozen soldiers arrayed in a semicircle in front of it, their rifles pointed right at Hamish.

CJ's ragtag group — Hamish, Wolfe, Johnson, Syme, Go-Go and CJ herself — stepped out from the waterfall with their hands raised.

It was raining more heavily now.

The chopper stood about twenty feet above them, on a stone viewing platform overlooking the waterfall.

Dragon Mountain rose behind it, a steep slope of uneven black rock. A set of stone stairs led up from the waterfall to the viewing platform and then from the platform up the mountain: a hiking path of some sort.

CJ frowned.

The first time the Chinese had found them in the swamp could have been predicted. But this was different. It was as if the Chinese *knew* where her group had been going. She wondered how —

And then, with her hands raised, she saw the Great Dragon Zoo watch on her wrist, with its little pilot light glowing.

It didn't just create a sonic shield, she realized unhappily. It probably also had a GPS transmitter in it, so the Chinese could keep track of all their guests.

They've known where we were all along.

Looking at her raised hands, she also wondered why she bothered putting them up. These Chinese troops were probably going to execute her and the others right now —

The Chinese captain in charge of this unit — he held a battlefield display unit in one hand and a pistol in the other — barked an order and his men cocked their rifles.

They *were* going to shoot them, then and there.

"Aw, heck . . ." CJ scowled.

Then something very large flashed between her and the chopper and suddenly the twelve soldiers were only six. The large object was followed by a second one and the next moment, the six soldiers were only one: the captain was left standing there, alone and confused.

CJ snapped to look sideways and saw two earless red-bellied black kings flying away, gripping the Chinese soldiers in their claws, biting down on a couple of them.

The chopper's pilots reacted instantly.

They fired up the Mi-17's engines and its rotors began to spin.

The captain on the ground ran for the chopper just as, with a hideous shriek, two red-bellied black princes — also earless — came roaring out of the rain-filled sky and knocked him to the ground.

One held him down while the other gripped the captain's head in its claws and ripped it clean off.

Then the two princes sprang toward the helicopter. Its rotors were beginning to blur with speed and through its canopy, CJ could see its pilots looking out frantically at this new threat.

The two princes hurled themselves *right through* the Mi-17's windshield and soon all CJ could see of them were their tails, lashing back and forth as they mauled the pilots, spraying blood all over the side windows of the cockpit.

CJ stared at the attack. The sheer ruthlessness of it was astonishing.

But then she cocked her head to the side. There was something odd about it, something she couldn't quite put her finger on —

"Run!" Johnson yelled. "We're not gonna get many chances like this!"

"The stairs!" Go-Go called, pointing at the hiking stairs carved into the mountainside above and behind the chopper. "They go past a fire exit in the side of the mountain!"

"Roger that!" CJ was already moving, bolting across the viewing platform and passing the chopper, when the two kings returned.

As she dashed past the decapitated body of the Chinese captain, she spied his battlefield display unit on the ground beside his outstretched hand.

She scooped it up and jammed it in the thigh pocket of her cargo pants just as one of the kings swooped over her, low and fast, the wind gust almost bowling her over — before the big beast slammed hard into its real target, the chopper.

The Mi-17 rocked wildly and the king hit it again and this time, the chopper rolled onto its side, right behind CJ and her group.

CJ and the others dived forward as the huge Mi-17 slammed down onto the ground behind them. Its rotors, now tilted dramatically, fizzed like buzz saws, dangerously close. Weapons and crates went tumbling out of the helicopter's open side doors, scattering to the ground.

"Grab a gun!" Johnson called and CJ snatched up a pistol that had landed near her. Johnson grabbed something bigger, a long rectangular case.

"Up the stairs!" CJ yelled, leading the way. Go-Go ran behind her, then Johnson, Hamish, Wolfe and Syme.

CJ bounded up the stairs two at a time, rising above the smashed helicopter just as one of the earless red-bellied black kings landed like a gigantic eagle right next to her and roared at her face! It was classic apex predator behavior, designed to frighten its prey into a petrified, frozen stance.

But CJ Cameron was no ordinary prey.

She whipped up her pistol and pumped two rounds right into the beast's left eye.

The dragon screamed and, losing its balance, fell from its perch, dropping away from the stairs and — *squelch!* — its long neck landed astride the spinning rotor blades of the chopper and the dragon was instantly beheaded, its head falling from its neck in a disgusting spray of blood.

Another shriek made CJ spin around.

The second earless king had seen the first one's demise and now it was zooming in toward CJ and her group.

"Oh, man . . ." Go-Go gasped.

This time the sight of the flying king dragon coming straight for them with its talons raised, its jaws bared and squealing its hideous attack-scream made even CJ

355

pause. It was coming in fast, way too fast to evade or avoid. Even her pistol would be useless. This was a sight no animal lived to remember.

Then CJ heard a deep *whump* from her left and suddenly a finger of smoke lanced out toward the incoming dragon, a finger of smoke that had come from the shoulder-mounted rocket launcher that Greg Johnson had extracted from his newly acquired case.

The rocket hit the dragon and an explosion flared out in the rainy night. One of the dragon's wings fell away from its body and its head lolled lifelessly, but due to its considerable inertia, it continued travelling straight for them.

"Move!" Johnson shouted. "It's going to hit!"

CJ took four bounding strides up the stone stairway, closely followed by Go-Go and Johnson.

Hamish, Syme and Wolfe all leapt *down* the stairs a bare second before the incoming dragon smashed against the stairway at phenomenal speed, turning a whole section of the steps to dust before it dropped to the platform below, broken and dead.

When the dust settled, CJ found they had a new problem.

A twenty-foot-wide void now existed in

the middle of the stone stairway, separating her group.

She, Johnson and Go-Go were on its upper side while Hamish, Syme and Wolfe were cut off below.

CJ locked eyes with Hamish as the rain came tumbling down.

"Get out of here, Cass!" he called. "We'll find another way up the mountain!"

She knew he was right — they had to go and they had to go now — but she didn't want to leave her brother.

"Hamish!" she yelled. "If we can't find each other, find a radio and do the call we did as kids: 20 at 20."

"20 at 20, got it!" he shouted back. "Now go —"

"Wait!" She tore off her watch and held it up. "Take off your watches! They're tracking us with them." She threw the watch down into the remains of the helicopter.

"But won't we lose our shields?" Syme called. "Then the dragons will be able to get us!"

"We trade one set of predators for another," CJ shouted. "And those dragons don't have tracking devices or guns."

Hamish unstrapped his watch and threw it away. "All right, now, go!"

"Be careful," CJ called.

"You, too," Hamish said seriously.

And so CJ ran up the stone stairs, followed by Johnson and Go-Go, drenched by the rain, separated from her brother and without the protective sonic shield of her watch. And without that, she was now exposed to attack from *all* the dragons in the Great Dragon Zoo of China.

A short way up the mountainside, CJ, Johnson and Go-Go came to a shallow cave. Inside it, artfully concealed from outside view, was a red-painted door embedded in a concrete wall. Emblazoned across the door was a sign in Mandarin and English: FIRE EXIT.

"This is the emergency exit from the mountain," Go-Go said. "If there's a fire in the restaurant or the cable car station, the fire stairs lead you here."

CJ cracked open the door to see a long corridor lit by dim lights. It stretched away for at least eighty yards.

"There are stairs at the other end of this tunnel?" Johnson asked.

"Yuh-huh."

"And they'll take us up the mountain?" Johnson said.

"Hope you're fit, Secret Agent Man."

"Let's hustle," CJ said.

They hurried down the concrete tunnel.

Back outside, Hamish Cameron was running hard through the rain, with Wolfe and Ambassador Syme close behind him.

They ran around the base of Dragon Mountain, following a muddy bush-lined trail, their eyes scanning the sky, searching for dragons.

"Hey," Syme said to Hamish as they ran. "What did your sister mean by 20 at 20?"

"It was something we did as kids," Hamish said. "Our dad was always taking us camping in national parks. If we ever got separated, Dad told us to find a ranger shack and get on the CB radio. We were to set the radio to channel 20 and send out a call at twenty minutes past the hour, every hour, until he answered. He would've set his own CB radio to channel 20 by then and be waiting for our call. Ergo, 20 at 20."

"Nice," Syme said. "Ever use it?"

"A couple of times."

"Looks like it's also handy when you're in a zoo filled with dragons that's gone to shit," Syme said.

"Yeah." Hamish looked behind them as they ran.

As they'd dashed from the site of the side-turned helicopter, he'd seen one of the red-bellied black princes spot them and now he could hear the braying of the dragon somewhere on the path behind them —

Whump!

A second prince landed right in front of him, claws and jaws bared!

Hamish dived right, off the trail, and suddenly he found himself sliding down a steep muddy slope. Wolfe and Syme must have done the same, because he heard them yelling behind him.

They were lucky they did. They slid much faster than they could have run and it gave them a lead on the two dragons. Hamish must have slid for about a hundred yards before he dropped off a ledge and slammed to a halt in a shallow muddy pool. Wolfe and Syme landed with twin splashes and a similar lack of grace behind him.

Hamish leapt to his feet and saw a high curving waterfall to his right, a lake in front of him and the ruined castle on the other side of the lake, all veiled in rain and lit by floodlights.

He knew where they were: they were on the western side of the valley, near the waterfall that their cable car had gone over earlier.

"Great, we're back where we started," he muttered.

"Not quite," Wolfe said, pointing to their right.

A small building stood on the near shore of the waterfall, with a dock extending out from it and a handful of riverboats tied to the dock.

A shriek from overhead made Hamish look up and he saw the two red-bellied princes fly across the rain-streaked sky.

"Get to that building!" he said, breaking into a run.

CJ panted as she bounded up the fire stairs inside Dragon Mountain. Johnson and Go-Go ascended the seemingly endless concrete stairwell behind her.

A hundred thoughts flashed through her mind: images of dragons and crocodiles, Chinese troops with guns and giant helicopters being pulled underwater.

But behind it all, there was something else.

Something about the earless dragons' attack that nagged at her. It was so coordinated, so deliberate, and yet . . .

These dragons were intelligent. But as Ben Patrick had said, theirs was an ancient reptilian intelligence and in her experience, a reptilian intelligence always had a *purpose*. Crocodiles and alligators were utterly single-minded in their thinking. They didn't do things by halves and the dragons' attack seemed to CJ to be somehow unfinished.

Unless it isn't over yet, she thought.

She replayed the various dragon attacks in her mind: first, assaulting the cable car, then using the cable car to storm the administration building and penetrate the waste management facility. Then, just recently, attacking the two helicopters, first in the swamp and then at the base of the mountain.

There *had* to be a purpose, but right now, she couldn't see what that purpose was.

After about eight minutes of hurried climbing, the three of them came to a landing at the top of the stairwell.

CJ doubled over, catching her breath.

A fire door branched off the landing. There was also an electrical junction box mounted on the concrete wall. It was open and stuck to the inside of its small steel access panel was a map of the zoo:

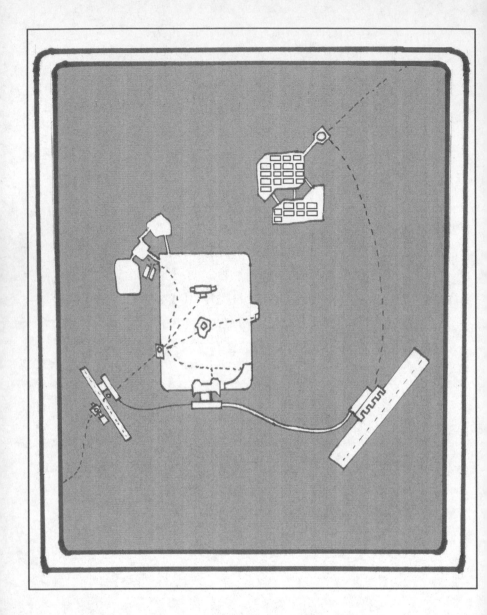

As she gazed at it, CJ realized that she'd seen this map before.

It was the map of the zoo's underground electrical cable network that she had seen inside the master control room earlier.

"CJ?" Johnson said, panting. "What's the matter? We gotta keep moving."

"Just wait a second —" CJ said, staring at the map.

Seeing it had made her think of two other maps of the zoo she'd seen since arriving here.

The first was the map she'd seen on the smartboard inside the Birthing Center, the one with the Xs written on it.

The second was the black digital map she had seen both in the master control room *and* on Colonel Bao's battlefield display unit in the hunting area, the one showing all the dragons as moving colored icons.

In her mind's eye, CJ recalled the first map, the one from the whiteboard in the Birthing Center:

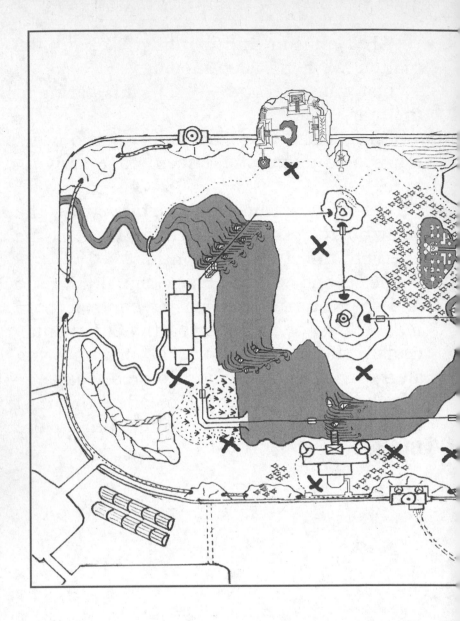

She remembered the series of Xs that had been splashed across the map, accompanied by the question: *Why are they digging?*

The Xs, she thought. *They were the spots where the dragons had been caught digging,*

but the person who marked the Xs on the map
— probably Ben Patrick — hadn't been able to
figure out why *the dragons had been digging*
in those places. They seemed so random.

CJ now looked more closely at the map stuck to the inside of the electrical junction box in front of her.

Her eyes zeroed in on the power lines inside the crater:

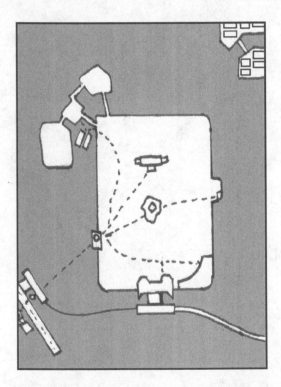

And suddenly she saw a connection.

"The power lines . . ." she said aloud.

"What?" Johnson said, perplexed. "What about them?"

CJ said, "The Xs on that smartboard map in the Birthing Center match the electrical power arteries of the zoo on this map. The dragons weren't digging randomly. They had a plan, a purpose."

Go-Go said, "What are you talking about?"

CJ said, "Your dragons have been planning for today for a while, Go-Go. Using their ampullae of Lorenzini, they can sense electrical energy. They've been sniffing out your power cables and digging along the power lines, tracing them back to the strongest power surge in the zoo, searching for the *source* of the zoo's electrical power. That search led them to" — she jabbed her finger on the map — "the administration building, the target of their first attack."

Johnson and Go-Go just stared at the map, astonished.

"But there has to be something more," CJ said. "I need to see . . ."

She tried to recall the black digital map from Bao's display unit on which the admin building had also featured, but then she realized she didn't need to remember it.

She had it with her.

Standing there on the landing, she pulled out the iPad-like battlefield display unit she had taken from the headless Chinese captain earlier. She looked at it now:

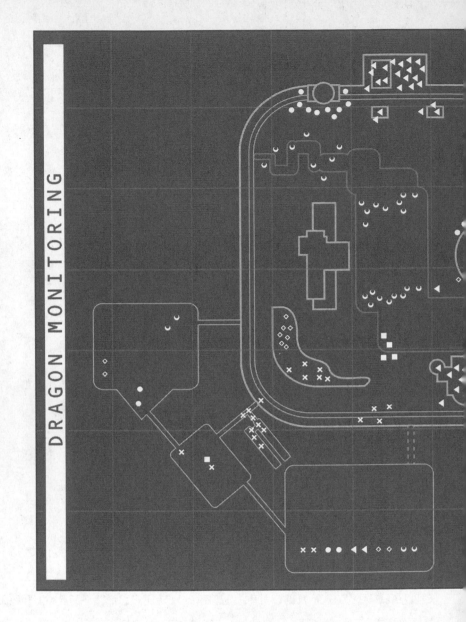

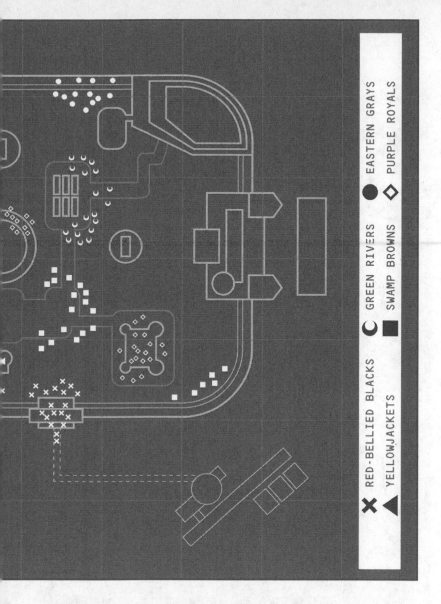

The cluster of red crosses — representing red-bellied black dragons — massing inside the administration building now screamed out at her.

CJ zoomed in on them.

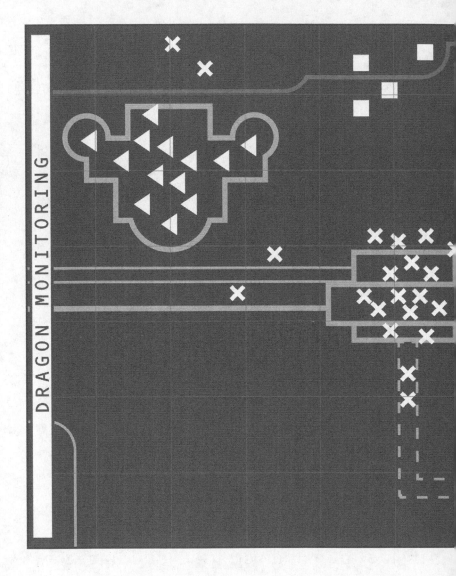

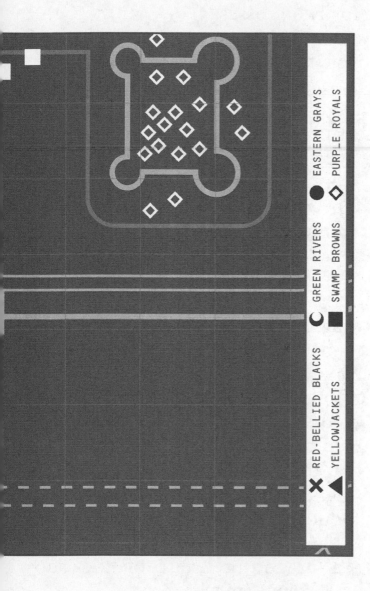

RED-BELLIED BLACKS ✕ GREEN RIVERS ☾ EASTERN GRAYS ●

YELLOWJACKETS ▲ SWAMP BROWNS ■ PURPLE ROYALS ◇

Most of the red crosses in there were unmoving: she guessed they represented dead dragons.

Except for two crosses.

That *were* still moving.

And those two crosses appeared to be fractionally *outside* the crater, inside a passageway of some sort. CJ recalled that the inner electromagnetic dome actually extended a little outside the valley, so the two dragons were contained. That said, they must have been at the absolute extremity of the inner dome.

Johnson said, "So let me get this straight. You're saying that the power cables led the dragons to the administration building. And then the dragons used the cable car and fuel trucks to smash open the admin building and get inside it."

"Yes," CJ said. "And judging from this image, two of them are still in there. Go-Go." She held up the BDU. "What's the passageway that those two crosses are in?"

Go-Go scanned the screen and shrugged. "It's a subducting tunnel for underground cabling."

"Could a dragon get out of the zoo through it? A prince, maybe?"

"No. Not even a person could get out through there. After about a hundred yards

374

or so that tunnel ends at a small hole in the wall through which the cables go. It's a conduit pipe only about a foot wide, so no dragon could fit inside it. That conduit pipe encases the . . . Oh, no . . ."

Go-Go paused, his face going ashen white.

"What?" Johnson asked. "What does it encase?"

CJ already knew the answer. "Some kind of main power cable, I'd guess."

Go-Go nodded. "*The* main power cable, the primary power cable that supplies the whole zoo with power. If you cut that cable, everything goes off, all the lights, all the antennas powering the sonic shields," he swallowed, "and the inner electromagnetic dome covering this valley."

"Surely this place has backup generators," Johnson said.

"It does," CJ said, "but they're offline. The dragons tore them up in the attack. I overheard Ben Patrick and the colonel talking about it."

Johnson and Go-Go exchanged worried glances.

CJ looked hard at them. "Gentlemen, the dragons at this zoo didn't just launch their attack today on a whim. It was a coordinated plan executed on a day when the staff at this zoo were nervous and off-balance.

These dragons don't want to kill us or just cause mayhem. They are executing a carefully prepared plan and the goal of that plan is *to get out of this zoo.* That's what they're doing. The inmates of the Great Dragon Zoo are busting out."

"Wait, wait," Go-Go said, "even if they do bring down the inner dome, there's still the second dome outside that one. They *can't* get out."

"Jesus, don't you get it yet? That's the whole problem with this place," CJ said. "You guys have underestimated these creatures from minute one. These dragons are unlike any other animal on this planet. They are smart and they are motivated and I'd be willing to bet they have a plan for bringing down the second dome, too."

The silver Range Rover sped around the northeastern corner of the Great Dragon Zoo of China, its wipers working furiously, its wheels kicking up spray.

Inside it were the two remaining visiting Politburo members, one of their wives and the little girl named Minnie.

After a time, their Range Rover was caught by a second silver Range Rover plus a pair of troop trucks filled with Chinese soldiers.

The second Range Rover contained the three most senior men at the Great Dragon Zoo: Hu Tang, Colonel Bao and Director Chow.

The four-car convoy now sped around the ring road, heading back to the main entrance building via the eastern wall of the valley.

Inside the second Range Rover, Hu Tang's mind was racing.

This was the worst mishap yet. First, there had been the incident in the river village, when a single adolescent dragon with a faulty pain chip had killed eight people before it had been taken down. Then the breakout last month, when the American expert, Bill Lynch, had needed to be liquidated: nineteen people had died in that one, plus Lynch. But this was bigger again. The cleanup alone, including rebuilding the administration building, would take at least a year.

This was an unmitigated disaster, for the zoo and for Hu Tang's career. Hu Tang began drafting in his mind the presentation he would have to give to the Politburo, explaining the delay and allocating the blame. He decided he would blame the foreign security consultants.

Just then, beside him, Colonel Bao touched his ear as a report came in.

"Well, they must be somewhere on Dragon Mountain, then!" Bao barked. "Send in Recon One. Tell them to find those Americans and kill them or I'll put *them* in front of a firing squad."

Bao turned to the others. "The Americans got away from our men in the swamp. We used the GPS chips in their watches to track them to the other side of the waterfall but then some dragons attacked; they destroyed another of our choppers and killed our men. The Americans got away and now we've lost their GPS signals. They must have taken off their watches."

Hu Tang said, "They cannot be allowed to get out of this valley. Too much is riding on this."

"I understand," Bao said.

He touched his earpiece again as another report came through. "In the administration building? Underneath it?" The colonel frowned. "If it's a dead end, then send Recon Two into the tunnel to kill them."

"What was that?" Hu Tang asked.

"It seems there are still two red-bellied black dragons inside the administration building. They're in an underground cable tunnel that branches off the waste management facility. The stupid animals must think it's a way out. They'll be dead soon. As will our American guests."

A few minutes later, a squad of twelve Chinese "reconnaissance" commandos arrived at the tunnel entrance to the waste management facility.

These men weren't regular infantry troops. They were special forces, which meant they didn't carry Chinese knockoffs of Russian-made assault rifles. They carried German-made Heckler & Koch MP-7 submachine guns with special compact M40 grenade launchers under the barrels.

The vast concrete hall looked like a war had been fought in it, which wasn't far from the truth. Dead bodies and debris lay everywhere; garbage trucks were overturned; there were even a few dead dragons in places around the hall.

The huge external gates on the western wall still stood resolutely closed. Slanting rain blew in through their massive bars. The gates had withstood the dragons' onslaught.

The commando team's leader spotted a nondescript door over in the far corner of the hall, to the left of the external gates.

It was an access door to a subducting tunnel. The tunnel, he'd been informed, was basically a passageway that contained bundles of electrical and communications cables; it allowed engineers to access the cables in the event of an overload or shutdown. About a hundred yards in, the tunnel ended abruptly. It just stopped at a pipe into which the cable bundles disappeared. A dead end. The two dragons inside it would be sitting ducks.

"Base, this is Recon Two, we have arrived at the waste management facility," he said into his throat mike. "Have spotted the sub-ducting tunnel. Preparing to make entry."

"Copy that, Recon Two," came the reply in his earpiece.

"Men. Ready your weapons."

One after the other, the team of crack Chinese commandos raised their MP-7s and fanned out across the waste manage-ment facility, heading for the subducting tunnel.

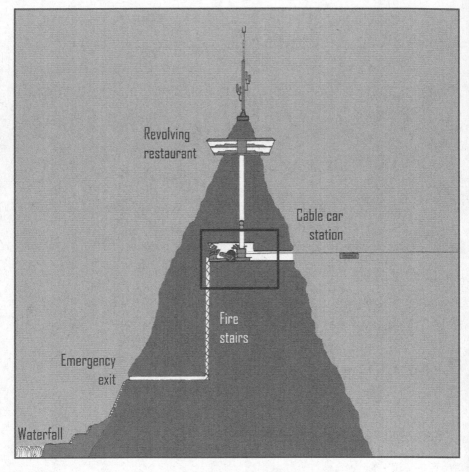

Revolving
restaurant

Cable car
station

Fire
stairs

Emergency
exit

Waterfall

DRAGON MOUNTAIN

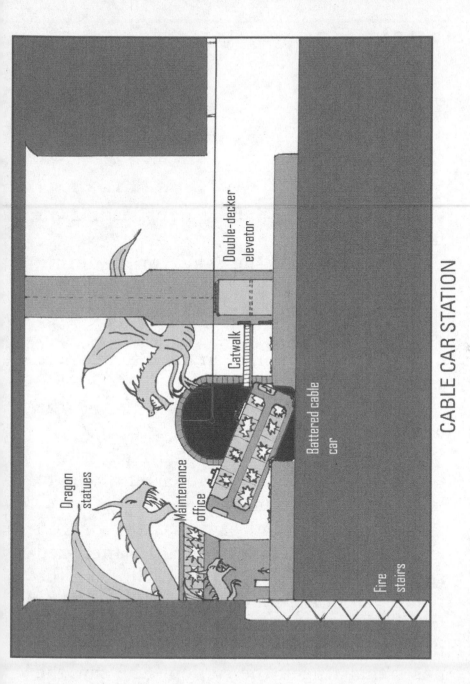

CABLE CAR STATION

CJ turned to face the fire door leading off the landing.

"Okay, Go-Go," she said, "on the other side of this door is . . . ?"

"The cable car station. We're halfway up the mountain."

"And there's an office in there somewhere with a phone or a computer?"

"Yes. The maintenance office. It's in the corner of the station."

"Okay, let's do this." CJ fell back with a shout, landing clumsily on her butt, only to hear Go-Go chuckling softly.

CJ looked up and saw that the dragon looming above her was in fact a life-sized stone carving of a king dragon cut from the rocky wall of the station.

She kicked herself. She'd forgotten about the giant carvings of dragons in dynamic poses that ringed the station. She saw the rest of them now, lunging from the walls in the strobing light.

She opened the door fully and beheld the wide, high space that was the cable car station. As she did so, Go-Go stopped chuckling.

There was carnage and wreckage everywhere.

What had until recently been a slick and modern area — with new concrete and shiny steel — was now the site of a grim bloodbath.

What little light there was flickered on and off. Only a few of the station's fluorescent lightbulbs were still working: the rest had all been smashed. Exposed wires sparked intermittently, giving off the strobing blue light that made the statues seem alive.

CJ recalled the team of electricians she'd seen here earlier, including the young one who had clumsily dropped his tools and clips.

Their dead bodies lay in pieces on the floor — heads, arms, torsos, legs. A huge double-decker cable car lay tilted at a crazy angle beside the platform, nose up, ass down. It looked like it had been savaged by dragons: all its windows were smashed and one of its walls was completely peeled away.

The station's platform kinked at a ninety-degree angle. It was here that the cable cars made their turn. The overhead steel cable disappeared down two concrete tunnels: it came in from the south and exited to the east. A chill wind whistled eerily as it swept through the long tunnels.

There was no movement.

No dragons.

"That's the maintenance office." Go-Go pointed at a two-storey glass-walled structure in the corner of the station. Its upper storey had slanted windows and nearly all of them had been smashed.

CJ hurried toward it.

The three of them raced through the maintenance office's lower door and hustled up some internal stairs before bursting through an open doorway.

The maintenance office had been ripped to shreds. Two dead Chinese technicians lay on the floor, their throats ripped out, their stomachs torn open. The main console had been wrenched apart. Naked wires sparked. Blood dripped off every surface.

And every computer screen was smashed.

Johnson tapped on some keys. "All these computers are useless."

CJ found a phone on the console. It had been cracked in two, broken beyond repair.

"We try the restaurant," she said.

A clunking noise from above made them

all look up.

A ceiling panel came free and CJ tensed . . . only to see a fearful young face appear from behind the panel, the face of the young Chinese electrician from before, the man named Li.

"Hello . . . ?" he said softly.

"Li?" CJ helped him down. "Are you okay?"

He nodded quickly.

"The dragons attacked your team?"

He nodded again. "Some red-bellied black princes and a king," he said in Mandarin. "They had no ears. We were working under the cable car here, relying on its sonic shield, so none of us was wearing our watches. But the cable car's shield was useless against them."

CJ glanced around nervously. She didn't like this place at all. There weren't enough exits. It was too easy to get trapped.

"We shouldn't linger here." She began to move. "We make for the restaurant —"

She cut herself off, glimpsing movement in her peripheral vision: she could have sworn one of the dragon statues outside had moved. No. It was just a trick of the flickering light. It was only a statue.

Then the statue really did move.

It turned its head to face the maintenance

office and looked CJ right in the eye.

It was a purple royal, king-sized, with high pointed ears.

With a roar it bounded forward, lunging at the maintenance office's upper windows.

"Look out!" Johnson pushed CJ sideways as the big dragon's foreclaws came rushing in through the shattered windows.

CJ fell one way, while Go-Go and Li dived the other way, but Johnson's reaction had put him in the middle and two of the dragon's razor-sharp talons slashed across the front of his body, drawing twin sprays of blood across his chest.

Johnson slumped instantly, dropped to the floor.

The dragon roared, its bellow shaking the little room.

CJ crab-crawled over to Johnson, ducking beneath the dragon's slavering jaws, threw his good arm over her own shoulder and hauled him away.

"Can you run?" she asked.

"Just," Johnson groaned.

With Johnson looped over her shoulder, CJ raced to the door leading downstairs, reaching it just in time to see two purple princes arrive at the base of the stairs below, spot her and roar.

"Shit . . ." she said.

"What the fuck do we do!" Go-Go yelled.

CJ slammed the door, locked it and turned just as the king's entire *head* came smashing into the maintenance office in a rain of glass.

Ducking below it, CJ saw the upturned cable car just outside the windows: the roof of its raised nose-end was level with the windows. The cable car's lower end lay over near the catwalk that led to the guest elevator.

"Go-Go, Li, follow me. Johnson, I need you to give me everything you've got!"

Without any further pause, she ran across the maintenance office, staying out of the reach of the king dragon. She skipped up on a chair and with Johnson beside her, leapt up onto the control console and then *out the shattered window,* past the dragon and onto the roof of the upturned cable car, where she slid down its length, dragging Johnson with her.

They slid wildly, past the king dragon, its head still thrust inside the maintenance office.

After they'd slid for about ninety feet, CJ threw out her left leg and caught the edge of the grated catwalk leading to the double-decker guest elevator. She and Johnson came to an abrupt halt.

Li and Go-Go slid to matching halts beside her.

CJ looped Johnson's arm over her shoulder again and made for the elevator. They got there with Go-Go and Li close behind them. CJ punched the call button.

A deafening roar answered her.

CJ turned.

The purple royal king was glaring right at her from the other side of the cable car platform. Its two princes were at its side, also staring at them, snarling.

Ping!

The elevator doors opened. CJ slipped inside it with the others.

The king growled, a deep resonating noise, and then it and the princes attacked.

As the elevator doors began to close with frustrating slowness, the king bounded across the void, kicking the double-decker cable car out of the way as if it weighed nothing, while the two princes took to the air and flew across the void at incredible speed. CJ willed the doors to close, because right now they were all that stood between her and certain death.

The doors joined, closed, just as — *wham!* — the whole elevator rocked as the king dragon rammed it from the outside.

But the elevator was away.

They were clear.

CJ breathed a sigh of relief.

Until a few moments later when the floor of her elevator began to get torn apart.

"Oh, you have got to be kidding me!" she said as she saw the claws of the two prince-sized purple royals appear through the floor of her double-decker elevator, tearing through the plush carpet, ripping it away with frenzied slashes.

They must have got into the lower level of the elevator before the doors had closed and now they were trying to claw their way through the floor separating the two decks.

"How long till we reach the restaurant?" CJ asked Go-Go quickly.

"Maybe thirty seconds, I don't know," Go-Go said, staring at the frenzied clawing of the two dragons.

The flooring of the elevator wasn't exactly a complex feat of engineering. It was just carpet over aluminium sheeting and beams. The two dragons punched up through the sheeting, cracking it.

"We're not gonna make it . . ." CJ said,

looking upward, as if she could see the approaching restaurant.

The two holes in the floor were growing larger by the second. Then one of the dragons managed to shove its head through the gap and snarled at CJ. She slid forward and kicked it squarely in the nose. The dragon squealed in pain and dropped back down to the lower level.

Then the second dragon squeezed its shoulders and one arm up through its hole. It was ready for CJ's kick: it batted her boot away with one of its foreclaws.

The dragon rose up out of the hole in the floor, first its head, then its chest. It bared its teeth —

Ping!

The elevator doors opened.

CJ lunged out of the elevator with Johnson on her shoulder and Li and Go-Go at her side. The dragon broke through the floor completely and bounded after them.

CJ flung Johnson across a table and dived over it after him as the beast spread its wings to cover the last few feet and —

Braaaaaack!

The dragon was pummeled with a spray of automatic gunfire and it dropped out of the air on the spot, collapsing in a tangle of spasming wings. It squealed until a final round slammed into its head and it flopped to the floor, dead.

CJ looked up to see a team of ten Chinese soldiers — dressed in black and brandishing better guns than any of the other Chinese soldiers she had seen — standing in a semicircle before her.

A Chinook helicopter — the biggest chopper she had seen so far — patrolled the air behind them, its spotlight blazing, illuminating the mountaintop restaurant with blinding white light.

The second dragon obviously didn't know of its comrade's fate, because it came screaming out of the elevator a second later, only to suffer a similar end. It was torn apart by a hail of gunfire from the waiting Chinese commandos.

Then all was silent, save for the rhythmic thumping of the helicopter outside.

CJ, Li and Go-Go stood and raised their hands. In CJ's case, she threw down her pistol. Johnson remained on the floor.

CJ glanced to her right and saw, behind the maître d's counter, an open doorway leading to an office: the restaurant manager's office. On a desk inside it, she saw a computer and a phone: the computer was on and the phone's lights blinked.

So near yet so far.

The ring of Chinese commandos closed in on them. They had saved their lives, sure, but only in the act of saving themselves from the two oncoming dragons.

That would be the last act of kindness they would show her, CJ thought, for as she looked at their hard faces, she realized that these commandos had been sent here to kill her.

At exactly the same time as this was happening, over in the waste management facility the other Chinese special forces team was in the process of entering the cable subducting tunnel.

They moved down it in single file, guns up. The concrete-walled tunnel was only a few feet wide, but it was well lit by overheard fluorescent bulbs.

As he moved along the tunnel looking down the barrel of his gun, Recon Two's point man glanced up at the many cables running along the roof and walls of the passageway. One extra-thick black cable ran directly down the center of the ceiling, dominating it: the primary main.

The point man rounded a bend and suddenly a monstrous apparition that was all claws and slashing teeth dropped from the ceiling above him and the man fell under the weight of a red-bellied black dragon.

His comrades opened fire and the tight concrete tunnel echoed with gunfire. The frenzied dragon managed to take down two more men before it was shot in the head and it dropped to the floor, dead.

The Chinese team stepped past its body, rounding the bend fully, their guns up, tensed for another attack. There was, after all, one more dragon down here.

They saw it.

The other earless red-bellied black prince was at the very end of the tunnel, but oddly, it had its back to them.

It was at the spot where all the overhead cables came together and disappeared into a small conduit pipe that led southwest.

The recon team's leader frowned. The dragon was tearing away with all its might at *all* the cables. It used its claws and its teeth. Sparks flew. Wires fell every which way.

"What the hell . . . ?" the leader breathed.

The dragon severed a final cable — the primary main — and immediately, one after the other, all the fluorescent lights in the ceiling went out and the tunnel was plunged into darkness.

Then the dragon rounded on the commando team and launched itself at them.

■ ■ ■ ■

All across the Great Dragon Zoo of China, electrical power was extinguished.

Every single light went out.

All the lights inside the main entrance building, in the administration building, in the casino hotel.

All the streetlights flanking the ring road.

All the floodlights mounted on the rim of the crater and atop Dragon Mountain.

And all the pilot lights on every single sonic shield–generating antenna on every wristwatch, car and building in the zoo.

Inside the master control room in the main entrance building, all the monitors winked out and the room went dark.

The head technician yelled, "What just happened!"

"Sir! Power's out across the zoo!"

"Switch to backup power."

"Generators are offline, sir. We do not have backup power. Repeat, we do not have backup power."

"What about the electromagnetic domes?"

"The inner dome is on the same grid as we are, sir. It's off . . ."

The head technician snatched up his desk

phone but he got no tone: all the phones were dead, too.

"Sir," one of his techs said. "The sonic antennas are all just receivers, as are all the watches. They have no power themselves. If the main power supply is gone, they're useless. Every building, vehicle and person in this zoo just lost their protection from the dragons."

The entire zoo was plunged into darkness.

In an instant, the Great Dragon Zoo of China was taken back to the Stone Age.

And with the coming of the darkness came the sound of beasts that had thrived in a more ancient time.

Dragon calls rang out across the valley, and with the calls came movement and suddenly the sky above the crater was filled with the gigantic creatures, all moving with purpose.

■ ■ ■ ■

SIXTH EVOLUTION

THE TIME OF THE DRAGON

■ ■ ■ ■

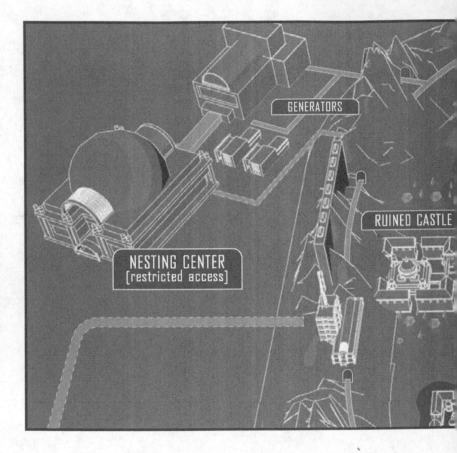

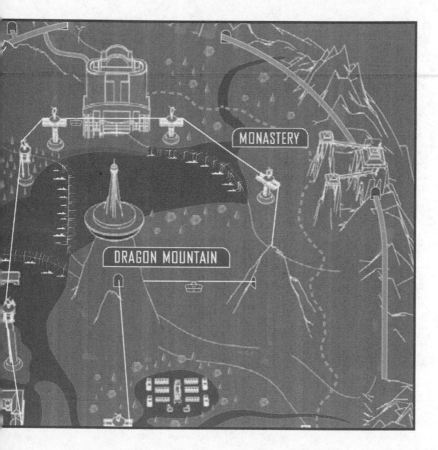

It does not do to leave a live dragon out of your calculations, if you live near him.
— J. R. R. Tolkien, *The Hobbit*
(George Allen & Unwin Ltd, London, 1937)

The two silver Range Rovers zoomed around the ring road with their two troop truck escorts.

They were speeding down the eastern side of the valley now, passing a high ravine cut into the eastern wall of the crater. The four vehicles shot through an awning-covered receiving area — it housed a turning bay which serviced an elevator that led up to the cliff-top monastery built in homage to the Purple Cloud Temple.

Sitting in the cab of the lead troop truck, Dr. Benjamin Patrick peered out into the night, concerned. Beside him, a Chinese sergeant drove.

Then, just as their four-vehicle convoy emerged from the receiving area, all the streetlights on the ring road blinked out.

The road went dark.

"We've lost power . . ." Ben Patrick said.

The driver said, "The backup generators will —"

"The generators were destroyed in the initial attack," Patrick said, looking quickly from the roadway to his own shield-generating watch.

The pilot light on it winked out.

"We have no protection anymore," he said ominously. "We're all exposed."

As he said this, something large and black swept past his truck. The rush of air that followed the flying beast was so great it made the eight-ton troop truck wobble.

"We're in trouble," Patrick said a split second before his truck was hit with incredible violence and his world flipped over and went black.

While CJ had been battling dragons inside the cable car station and fleeing to the revolving restaurant, Hamish, Syme and Seymour Wolfe had also been fleeing: in their case, to the small building they had spotted at the base of the waterfall.

They dived inside the little building and slammed the door. No sooner was the door shut than there was a loud bang from the other side, followed by furious screeches from the two earless red-bellied black princes that had been pursuing them.

Hamish took in the space around him.

They were in a very tastefully decorated café, with picture windows looking out at the curving waterfall and the ruined castle on the opposite shore of the lake. Six glass-roofed Great Dragon Zoo tour boats sat tied to the dock outside.

The café was dark. The only light came from the red glow of a Coca-Cola refrigerator and a cake display.

The dragons banged on the door for a time and then stalked around the side of the one-storey building, peering in through its windows.

Foiled for the moment, they retreated to the muddy tree line not far from the building — although Hamish had a feeling that they weren't far away. They might be watching the café, waiting for their prey to emerge again.

That had been fifteen minutes ago. He, Syme and Wolfe had stayed very still, below the windows, watching, waiting.

And then the twin glows of the refrigerator and the cake display went out and the café was plunged into total darkness.

Inside the revolving restaurant atop Dragon Mountain, CJ, Li and Go-Go stood before the ten Chinese commandos arrayed around

405

them with their hands raised. Johnson still lay on the floor.

CJ glanced at the restaurant around her. It had clearly not seen any fighting or attacks from the dragons: there was no wreckage or blood pools. The commandos, she guessed, must have landed on the roof and come in through a ceiling hatch or something.

The small lamps on each table glowed. The soft halogen bulbs in the ceiling gave off a dim light.

Then, abruptly, all the lamps and all the overhead lights winked out and the whole restaurant went dark.

CJ saw the computer screen in the adjoining office shrink to black.

And then she saw *every* source of illumination outside the restaurant — the floodlights encircling the valley, the streetlights on the ring road — extinguish.

The power was out across the zoo. The only light was that coming from the spotlight on the Chinook helicopter hovering outside.

The Chinese commandos aiming their guns at CJ instantly became a cluster of shadows.

It was then that CJ heard the shrieks. At first there were just a few of them, but then there came a chorus of replies.

Dragon calls.

The dragons were communicating.

The Chinese commandos looked about themselves, nervous, unsure.

With a loud *whoosh,* a large shape swept past the windows and CJ saw the underbelly of an emperor dragon rush by and, in a shockingly powerful move, collect the hovering Chinook helicopter as it did.

It simply snatched the helicopter out of the air — one second it was there, the next it wasn't. CJ didn't see the chopper hit the side of the mountain, but she heard the explosion and saw the sudden fiery glow.

She spun and, for the briefest of moments, locked eyes with the Chinese trooper in charge of the commandos. Hunter and prey, caught in the unfolding plan of an even more dangerous creature. Would he still execute her?

In answer to the unasked question, he clenched his teeth and raised his 9mm pistol, aiming it squarely at CJ's head —

— just as the entire wall of windows behind him shattered and an eight-ton Chinese Army troop truck came flying in through it.

CJ dived left, pulling the wounded Johnson with her as the troop truck smashed through the windows on the eastern side of the restaurant and bounced up its broad levels.

CJ glimpsed the red-bellied black emperor that had hurled the truck at the restaurant. It banked away before pulling up, its wings spread wide, and landing on the roof of the restaurant with a loud, floor-shaking thump.

The troop truck plowed through tables and chairs, sliding on its side *right through* the circle of commandos that had been threatening CJ. It ran right over the lead trooper and two other commandos before crushing two more when its side-turned grille smashed them against the wall.

While CJ had dived left, Li had dived right, only to have a section of the restaurant's ceiling come crashing down on top of him. The young electrician's shout was cut off as he was buried beneath the rubble.

The truck came to a halt and it was only when the noise of its spectacular entry had subsided that CJ heard the groans of the men *inside* it.

The dragon must have picked the truck up somewhere — with the troops inside it — and flung it at the restaurant.

Wind and rain whipped in through the gaping thirty-foot-wide hole in the eastern side of the restaurant. The open sky loomed beyond the opening. The valley floor yawned a thousand feet below it.

CJ lay on her belly beside Johnson inside the darkened restaurant, staring in disbelief at the side-turned troop truck.

There was a truck inside the restaurant. The mountaintop restaurant.

And then the other dragons came.

They came screaming in through the truck-sized opening in the side of the restaurant.

Red-bellied black princes, purple royal princes, even a couple of eastern gray princes: there must have been twenty of them.

CJ's eyes went wide.

It was a veritable *invasion* of dragons.

They launched themselves at the Chinese commandos, leaping astride them, ripping out their throats. A couple of the Chinese commandos managed to get off a few shots, only for the dragons to overwhelm them and throw them to the floor and start eating them alive. Screams filled the air.

And just when CJ didn't think it could get any crazier, *the whole southeastern section of the restaurant* was wrenched away.

The sound of rending steel drowned out the screams of the commandos and where only moments before there had been neatly laid tables and chairs and soft lamplight, now there was a gaping hole of loose wires and shredded floorboards and a hundred-foot-wide stretch of emptiness!

CJ saw an emperor dragon flying away with an entire section of the restaurant gripped in its claws. It dropped it, circled back and proceeded to stick its massive head in through the great hole it had created. Its roar sent wineglasses toppling and plates smashing to the floor.

Amid all this pandemonium, CJ shoved Johnson over a serving counter and into the kitchen. She dived over the counter after him just as a black prince snapped at her heels. Go-Go threw himself through the swinging kitchen door, the OUT door used by waiters and waitresses.

It was a standard industrial kitchen: there were five long island benches with gas stoves and hot plates, while one wall featured ten ovens. Pots and pans and cooking utensils hung from hooks in the ceiling.

CJ threw Johnson's arm over her shoulder and hurried away from the counter. She needed to find somewhere she could —

There!

She spied a dumbwaiter off to her right. Like everything else in the zoo, the boxlike miniature elevator was oversized; Johnson would fit inside it easily. It also had sturdy industrial doors. It would be a decent hiding place.

Johnson was weighing her down. She'd never outrun the dragons with him on her shoulder. If they were going to get out of this zoo alive, she was going to have to hide him somewhere safe and come back and get him later.

She hurled him into the open dumbwaiter and said, "Stay in here. I have to find a way to contact the outside world. I'll come back for you later, okay?"

"Okay. Hey," Johnson groaned. "Thanks."

CJ shrugged. "I'll probably be dead in five minutes, so don't get your hopes up. Mind you, given that we both might die soon . . ." She leaned forward and, surprising herself a little, gave him a quick impulsive kiss on the cheek.

411

Then CJ pulled the dumbwaiter's doors closed over Johnson's surprised face.

CJ stepped back into the kitchen proper to find Go-Go turning dials on all the ovens.

"What are you doing?" she called.

"They may be smart," Go-Go said, "but we're smarter. We unleash the gas, then we blow this place on our way out."

CJ could already smell the gas from the ovens. It wasn't the best plan ever but it wasn't a bad one either.

Go-Go moved down the line of ovens, stepping close to the serving counter CJ had dived over to get into the kitchen.

"Go-Go," she warned, "don't get too close to the —"

It happened so fast, CJ hardly even saw it.

A skeletal black claw reached over the counter, grabbed Go-Go by the arm and yanked him bodily out over it.

CJ saw Go-Go's face go slack as the dragon outside slammed him up against the counter. Life faded from his eyes as he slumped from CJ's view. He would be dead before he hit the ground.

CJ's eyes boggled. "Jesus . . ."

And then another prince pushed through the swinging door beside the counter.

Red Face.

Fresh blood dripped from his jaws. He

412

glared at CJ.

Beep-beep . . . beep-beep.

CJ ran.

Red Face sprang after her.

CJ slid over a benchtop just as the dragon dived at her and slid over it, too, sending pots and pans clattering to the floor.

But it was on its feet in a second, charging at her with a roar. CJ rolled as the dragon leapt astride her and lunged at her face with its mighty jaws — just as CJ snatched up a nearby frying pan and hit Red Face with it right on the snout.

The dragon screeched and recoiled and CJ took the opportunity to bolt for the other exit from the kitchen: the IN door.

CJ burst through the doorway — and immediately tripped on something and went sprawling to the floor, where she found herself staring into the blank, lifeless eyes of a dead Chinese commando who had no lower half to his body. He still gripped an MP-7 in one hand.

CJ snatched up the submachine gun and stood — and realized that she had emerged in a war zone.

The previously tranquil restaurant was now being pelted by wind and rain. A dozen princes feasted on dead commandos while two emperors yanked and tugged on the ceiling, trying, it seemed, to tear the place apart.

Beside her, a maintenance closet had been ripped open by the dragons. Its contents lay strewn all over the floor: mops, brooms, dusters, even a couple of backpack-mounted vacuum cleaners.

A roar from behind her made her spin.

Red Face stood in the doorway to the kitchen.

In the blink of an eye, CJ took in the situation.

Kitchen: no good.

The elevators: no good either; that meant running past a dozen dragons.

She glanced to her right and saw the torn-open section that was once the southern side of the restaurant. Tables that had sat cozily beside the windows now teetered at the edge of a precipice, lashed by rain.

She saw one of the vacuum cleaners by her feet. It was designed to be worn on someone's back and it had a long power cord, maybe ninety feet.

And she smelled the gas wafting out from the ovens in the kitchen.

Windows, precipice, power cord, she thought.

You're gonna die anyway . . .

"Screw it," CJ said to no one as she

grabbed the vacuum cleaner and bounded down the broad descending levels of the restaurant, dodging chairs and hurdling tables, heading for the open southern side of the structure.

Red Face gave chase, flinging tables out of its path.

CJ stopped at what had once been a wall of floor-to-ceiling windows. The world fell away before her: she was a thousand feet above the valley floor but about three hundred feet directly beneath her, a short way down the mountainside, she saw the cable car tunnel disappearing into the mountain —

Beep-beep . . . beep-beep.

She turned.

Red Face had her cornered. He crouched low, tensed, ready to leap.

Then the floor shook and CJ spun to see a gigantic emperor standing to her right, perched on the edge of the restaurant, grinning down at her. Girders moaned, straining under the weight of the beast.

CJ backed away, uncoiling the power cord of the vacuum cleaner as she did so.

The heels of her boots touched the edge of the precipice.

Nowhere else to go. It was now or never.

She had uncoiled the whole power cord

by now, so she looped it around the splintered frame of a floor-to-ceiling window and knotted it. Then she slipped the vacuum cleaner onto her back.

She sniffed the gas again and looked up at the dragons.

"You assholes can't breathe fire, can you? Try breathing this."

And she raised her MP-7 and fired it . . . not at the dragons, but at the doorway to the kitchen.

She only needed one round to spark off some metal, a spark that would —

One round sparked . . .

. . . and with an almighty *whoosh,* the gas-filled kitchen exploded.

A billowing cloud of flames burst forth from the kitchen, blowing the IN door off its hinges, sending tables and chairs and dragons flying.

And as all this happened, CJ jumped out the window.

CJ fell through the darkness.

She dropped away from the restaurant with the vacuum cleaner on her back, its long power cord trailing above her as a billowing fireball blasted out from every window of the circular restaurant.

If there was still glass in a window's frame, it shattered. If there wasn't, the fiery explosion just fanned out unimpeded.

Seen from afar, for a brief instant, Dragon Mountain looked like an ancient lighthouse, with a sudden flare of orange at its summit.

The dragons started crying out.

CJ kept falling.

And then her power cord went taut and her fall was arrested abruptly about ninety feet below the restaurant. CJ jolted to a halt. For a moment she just hung there, dead still, high above the world, about fifteen feet from the rocky flank of the mountain.

She rocked back and forth to build some

momentum and swing in toward the mountain. The force of her fall, however, had almost dislodged the cord from its socket in the vacuum cleaner. It had almost been torn clean off it. Now, as CJ swung, she felt that the cord was attached to the vacuum cleaner only by the barest of threads. Her first swing didn't bring her close enough to the mountainside. She swung back out again . . . and the cord stretched even more, almost to breaking point. CJ arced back toward the mountainside as — *snap!* — the cord broke and she fell —

— safely onto the rocky flank of Dragon Mountain. She'd made it, just.

"Sheesh," she breathed. "Talk about out of the frying pan."

She wriggled out of the vacuum cleaner's shoulder straps, discarded it and looked up to see flaming dragons flying out of the blazing restaurant, squealing. They burst out of the disc-shaped structure and made for the nearest lake.

CJ didn't have time to stop and watch. She started hurrying down the mountainside, heading for the cable car tunnel directly beneath her.

Rain pelted her as she stumbled and slid down the side of the mountain until at last she arrived at the opening to the concrete tunnel and dropped into it.

She landed on flat, clean cement. It was dry here. She was out of the rain.

CJ peered outside. She was still high above the world — the now-darkened world of the Great Dragon Zoo. Looking south, she could see the dark outline of the main entrance building and the high encircling wall of the crater.

She wondered where she could possibly go now and how she could possibly get there.

She couldn't steal a chopper. The dragons had been going after the choppers, presumably because they knew that the choppers were their jailers' best weapon against them.

She would have to get out of the zoo on f—

Something struck her. A sharp blow across the face sent CJ flying backwards as a dragon landed inside the tunnel in front of her.

Beep-beep . . . beep-beep.

Red Face.

A second and then a third red-bellied black prince joined him in the mouth of the tunnel: Melted Face and the fourth member of Red Face's gang.

CJ crawled desperately away from them, spittle and blood dripping from her mouth.

She felt dizzy from the blow and her vision was blurred. The tunnel around her was maybe eighty yards long. She could never outrun them, even if she could have got to her feet.

Spread-eagled on the floor, struggling to see, CJ slumped. She was officially fucked.

Red Face crept forward.

Beep-beep . . . beep-beep.

CJ shut her eyes and waited for the end.

Nothing happened.

It was only then that CJ heard a long, deep-throated growl.

She opened her eyes.

Red Face had stopped a few paces short of her and was standing frozen on the spot, staring daggers at CJ.

Actually, that wasn't true. Red Face was staring past her —

The growl had come *from behind* CJ.

CJ turned . . .

. . . and through blurred eyes, saw a yellowjacket prince standing in the concrete tunnel behind her.

But not just any yellowjacket prince. It had a black-and-yellow saddle on its back.

It was Lucky.

Lucky growled again and CJ saw that the dragon was not addressing her: it was growling at Red Face and the other two red-bellied black dragons.

She also noticed that Lucky's growls were not simple animalistic grunts: they were a mix of deep-chested coos, throaty vibrations and sharp squawks. It was like a —

With a startlingly quick swoop, Lucky took briefly to the air and landed in between CJ and the red-bellied blacks.

It was claiming CJ from the red-bellies. Or . . .

. . . CJ frowned . . .

. . . defending her.

Red Face snapped at Lucky with its jaws, only for the yellowjacket to lash out with a foreclaw and smack the red-bellied black prince on the snout.

Lucky backed up, grunting softly.

"What?" CJ said aloud. Barely able to stand, bleeding and exhausted, her mind reeling, it seemed as if the dragon was grunting at *her.*

Lucky grunted sharply again, but getting no response from CJ, the yellow dragon grabbed her with one foreclaw and pulled her backwards, thrusting her against the saddle on its back.

CJ slammed up against the saddle. Did it really want her to —

She dragged herself up into the saddle. Lucky wriggled slightly, assisting her, and suddenly CJ was sitting astride the dragon.

The three red dragons fanned out, edging forward.

There was a triple-point harness on the saddle's pommel.

"What the hell are you doing, Cassandra?" CJ said to herself as she fumbled with the harness, clipping it to her belt. She slid her feet into the stirrups.

Lucky backed further away from the three black princes.

Red Face and his buddies looked absolutely furious. They hissed and then . . .

. . . leapt forward, foreclaws raised and jaws bared, but Lucky was quicker, and the yellowjacket spun and took to the air and suddenly CJ found herself zooming at phenomenal speed back down the horizontal concrete tunnel!

The walls of the tunnel blurred with superfast motion as she shot through it on the back of the dragon.

Lucky flew like a missile. She pinned her ears back and streamlined her body for maximum speed. Her tail slithered behind her, long and sleek, guiding her like a rudder.

CJ glanced behind her and saw the three red-bellied black dragons in hot pursuit, wings flapping, bodies also extended.

Lucky shot through the darkened cable

car station in the heart of the mountain where she banked right, swooping over the smashed cable car and blasting into the eastern tunnel with the three red-bellied blacks right on her tail.

Again the tight walls of the tunnel became streaking blurs. Drawing on her experience riding horses, CJ leaned low and forward in the saddle, trying to diminish the drag effect she must have been having on Lucky's flight.

And then — *shoom* — they burst out into the night sky and rain slammed against her face and suddenly CJ found herself high above the world on the back of a dragon!

A wave of vertigo struck her as she beheld the landscape far below: the smaller pinnacle was directly ahead of her, a river town lay to her right, while the rim of the crater loomed level with her.

It was simply bizarre to be this high up and *not* be inside an airplane of some sort. CJ had paraglided once before but that was nothing compared to this.

This was rocket fast.

Lucky banked hard to the right and CJ felt her stomach lurch. The world tilted and she thought she was going to fall off, but the harness held her firmly in the saddle.

The three black princes were still close

behind them.

Lucky dived, down and around the pinnacle, but they stayed close. Then Lucky cut left, banking in an outrageously tight arc and CJ felt the G-forces assailing her body and she knew she was about to black out.

She did everything she could to keep her eyes open as Lucky brought them up toward the eastern wall of the crater and CJ suddenly saw the body of a yellowjacket emperor dragon rise up in front of her, filling her field of vision. It bellowed, and as CJ rushed under its batlike wings she spun around in her saddle and saw the emperor swipe at the three pursuing red-bellied black princes.

Red Face and his gang scattered at the sight of the much larger emperor and flew off into the rain-soaked night.

CJ sighed with relief and, leaning forward in her saddle, patted Lucky's neck.

"Thank you . . ." she breathed. "Thank you . . ."

Then she blacked out.

Hamish, Syme and Wolfe were still holed up in the café at the base of the curving waterfall.

They hadn't seen any movement from the tree line for twenty minutes now. All was still and quiet, save for the pattering of the rain.

Hamish peered out through one of the windows. As he did so, he said abruptly, "How do you become an ambassador for America?"

"I'm sorry, what?" Kirk Syme answered.

"I've always wanted to know. How does a guy become the U.S. Ambassador to China? Are you, like, buddies with the President or something?"

Wolfe said, "Close. He was a friend of the President's father."

"I was, yes." Syme half smiled. "I was a naval aviator. Flew with the President's father in Vietnam. After the war, I stayed in

426

Asia. Learned Mandarin, started a business in Hong Kong which I later sold for a fortune. When my buddy's son became President and it came time to appoint an ambassador to China, he wanted a real guy, not a party hack. He remembered me."

"And you said yes?" Hamish said. "If you've got all that money, why would you take up a job like that?"

"When the President asks you to do something, you'd be surprised how keen you are to oblige," Syme said.

The ambassador nodded outside. "You think they're still out there?"

"How about we find out?" Hamish grabbed a nearby dinner plate and brought it over to one of the windows facing the lake.

Holding the plate ready to throw, he cracked open the window. It made the tiniest squeak. With shocking suddenness a dragon head appeared in front of him, hanging upside down from the roof!

Hamish tumbled back in surprise.

The second red-bellied black prince appeared outside another window, also with its head upside down.

They must have flown up into the sky and then glided down in perfect silence, landing on the roof of the building so softly that

Hamish, Syme and Wolfe hadn't even heard them.

But then suddenly the two dragons at the windows turned and took off, abandoning the café without a second thought.

"What in God's name is going on?" Syme said.

"I don't think our Chinese friends have control of their zoo anymore," Hamish said, still staring out through the lakeside window.

And then he saw them. "Holy moly . . ."

Two red-bellied black emperors came swooping in over the broad lake, passing the ruined castle before banking around toward the café, and for a moment Hamish thought in horror that they were coming for him, but then they pulled to a halt *beneath* the rim of the waterfall. There the two gargantuan creatures crouched below the waterfall and waited, looking up expectantly at the cascading lip of the falls.

"What is this?" Wolfe said, leaning forward.

Hamish gasped. "It's a trap."

Right then, two red-bellied black princes came whipping over the lip of the waterfall from the north, flying low and very, very fast.

Orange tracer rounds went sizzling past

them, fired from —

— two Chinese Z-10 attack helicopters that came blasting over the rim of the waterfall, pursuing the princes at full speed.

The two emperors sprang up from their hiding place below the waterfall and clutched at the two skinny attack choppers.

Hamish could only imagine what it must have looked like to the choppers' pilots: one second you were sweeping over a waterfall, the next you were looking into the eyes of a brontosaurus-sized dragon!

The emperor on the right caught the first chopper in one of its mighty claws, crumpled it instantly and then tossed it away. The other emperor only managed to hit the second Z-10 with a glancing blow, but it was enough to dislodge the chopper's tail rotor, sending that chopper cartwheeling into the lake. It crashed into the water with a huge splash, toppling onto its side before going under.

A third Z-10 that had been trailing behind the first two saw the trap the dragons had sprung, so it powered away, banking hard — only to find itself assailed by three red-bellied black princes, all swooping in from different sides. They latched onto it and within seconds the attack chopper was covered in the things. The extra weight was far too much for it and it began to descend at an alarming angle toward the side of Dragon Mountain. It plunged toward the mountainside and a moment before impact, the dragons took flight, leaving the chopper to slam into Dragon Mountain and explode in a billowing fireball.

"They're taking out the choppers," Hamish said.

He recalled Go-Go saying that the Chinese had four of the Ż-10 choppers at the zoo, and he had just seen three of them get destroyed.

Go-Go had also said the Chinese had two Mi-17s — both of those had been taken out near the other waterfall — and a Chinook, which Hamish hadn't seen yet. He didn't know how many of the other helicopters at the zoo had been damaged or destroyed, but he had seen five of them taken out in the last hour.

"The dragons are knocking out all their aerial competitors," Syme said, realizing.

"That's right," Hamish said. "This place now has no electrical power and, by the look of it, no airpower either. The dragons just took control of this zoo."

Down on the ring road on the eastern side of the megavalley, inside the turning bay that gave access to the mountaintop monastery, lay the wreckage of two silver Range Rovers and one troop truck.

The second troop truck that had been part of the convoy speeding south — Ben Patrick's truck — was simply gone. The awning-like roof of the turning bay had been wrenched clean off.

The attack had been as ruthless as it had been swift.

As soon as the zoo's power had been cut and the roadway had gone dark, a gang of five red-bellied black dragons — two princes, two emperors and a king — had descended on the convoy.

The emperors had bowled over the two troop trucks, while the king had skittled the Range Rovers, flinging them into the walls of the turning bay.

The Range Rover containing Hu Tang, Colonel Bao and Director Chow slid wildly before it slammed hard into the wall beside the elevator that took visitors up to the monastery, while the second four-wheel drive containing the two Politburo members, one of their wives and the girl named Minnie, flipped entirely, landing heavily on its roof.

Hu and Bao crawled out of their car, bloodied and dazed. But Director Chow was trapped. The impact with the wall had caused his door to crumple against his leg and that leg — probably broken — was now firmly and hopelessly pinned. Chow tugged at it desperately but it wouldn't come clear.

As Hu Tang staggered to his feet, he looked at the turning bay around him.

It had become a slaughterhouse. The two prince dragons and the king were attacking the soldiers in the back of one of the troop trucks, tearing them to pieces, while one of the emperors just *flew off* with the other eight-ton troop truck gripped in its claws. The second emperor was stomping toward the upside-down Range Rover.

Inside the silver four-wheel drive, Hu saw one Politburo man and the little girl with the Minnie Mouse hat. They were both hanging upside down in their seats, held in place by their seat belts. Both were still, either dead or unconscious.

A shout from the other side of the Range Rover made Hu Tang turn.

It had come from the other Politburo member, who was trying to drag the bloodied and limp body of his wife out of the car. The woman was obviously dead, killed by the impact, but he was pulling her clear anyway, trying to get away from the incoming emperor.

The Politburo man's name was Sun Dianlong and he was the head of the Central Secretariat, the vast bureaucracy that controlled the Communist Party. It was a position that made him a very powerful man in Chinese internal politics.

Sun called to Hu Tang: "Comrade Hu! Help me!"

Hu Tang looked from Sun to the elevator near him. It wasn't the elevator that Hu wanted to use, it was the emergency exit door *inside* the elevator's shaft. That led outside the valley.

Colonel Bao was clearly doing the same thing: assessing whether he should help this very senior party official, or cut and run.

Hu and Bao swapped a glance . . . and then raced for the elevator.

Sun swore at them. "You dirty cowards!"

Bao flicked an emergency release switch up near the top of the elevator's doors and the doors came open easily. He and Hu slipped through them, both men stealing a final glance back at the turning bay behind them.

The three dragons that had been attacking the troop truck stepped away from it, their snouts smeared with blood. They had literally torn it to shreds.

Their hungry gazes turned to the two silver Range Rovers.

The dragons looked from Director Chow, still struggling in his car, to the other upside-down Range Rover, with the girl and the Politburo man still inside it, and Sun outside it.

As the dragons moved in on the two Range Rovers, Bao shut the elevator doors and coldly locked them.

"We can't help those people anymore," he said. "We must leave them to their fates."

Hu followed the colonel as Bao went over to a heavy steel door sunk into the rear wall of the elevator shaft. He inserted a high-tech laser-cut key into the lock and the door clanked open.

Bao pulled out a radio. "This is Colonel Bao. I need a helicopter at the east-side emergency exit in ten minutes."

A voice replied, *"I'm sorry, sir. But the beasts have knocked out all of our choppers."*

"Then send a fucking car!" Bao barked. "A jeep, a truck, anything! I have to get to the secondary command post at the airfield! Bao, out."

He clicked off. "Damn it. I can regain control of the zoo from the airfield, but it'll take us at least an hour to get there by car. *Fuck.*"

"Then let's go," Hu said, and the two of them took off down the long, dark concrete tunnel, one of the few tunnels that led out of the Great Dragon Zoo of China.

CJ dreamed.

Bizarre images flashed across her mind. She saw herself flying high above the world. Then she saw the face of a yellowjacket emperor dragon, impossibly huge, staring at her from very close range, opening its jaws —

CJ's eyes darted open.

To find a yellowjacket emperor dragon staring at her from *very* close range.

She started, but the dragon didn't attack. It was lying very casually in front of her, its chin resting on the ground, just watching her.

For a moment, CJ wondered if she was still dreaming.

Looking about herself, she was in what could only be described as another world: she lay on a wooden stage inside an ancient-looking monastery high up in some kind of chasm.

436

A wide wooden doorway opened before her, revealing a broad balcony that looked out at a second sky-temple mounted on the opposite side of the chasm.

It was still night and it was still raining. CJ didn't know how much time had passed since she had blacked out.

Completing the fantastical nature of the image were the dragons.

She was surrounded by a small group of yellowjackets, five of them, forming a tight ring around her — the emperor, two kings and two princes.

Like the emperor, all the others were staring very intently and curiously at CJ.

One of the princes stepped forward, easily distinguishable from the other dragons by virtue of the saddle on her back: Lucky.

As CJ looked at them all more closely, however, she began to see that each yellow-and-black dragon bore unique patterns on its face and neck. No two dragons had the same markings.

Lucky came up to CJ and, to CJ's great surprise, bowed her head.

CJ leaned back, confused.

Lucky brayed a series of low burring sounds from deep within her throat.

CJ looked from Lucky to the other yellowjacket dragons, unsure what was going on.

Lucky turned to the other dragons, apparently equally confused. She threw a meaningful look at one of the watching kings. The king growled deeply, a noise that sounded profoundly unimpressed.

Lucky turned back to CJ and repeated the sequence of low brays.

Lucky stepped up close to CJ so that her toothy snout was right in front of CJ's face.

CJ remained stock-still, not daring to move. The yellowjacket's fangs looked deadly.

And then Lucky nudged the earpiece in CJ's ear.

CJ frowned. The earpiece. The one she had taken from the body of Lucky's handler back in the waste management facility when she had rescued Lucky from Red Face's gang.

CJ touched the earpiece. "What are you trying to tell me . . . ?"

Then she saw the metal implant on the side of Lucky's head, the box-shaped one that had been painted yellow and black to camouflage it against the dragon's skin, the one trailing a small but distinct wire that disappeared into Lucky's skull.

"No way . . ." CJ breathed. "The Chinese

figured out a way to communicate with you . . ."

A flurry of thoughts and images came together in her mind:

Yim, the dragon handler, giving commands to Lucky and Red Face during the trick show.

Ben Patrick saying: "— *I have a database of over three hundred separate and identifiable vocalizations — Every squawk and screech you hear has meaning —*"

And the garbled electronic female voice CJ had heard through that earpiece after she had rescued Lucky from Red Face and his gang:

"— *Run . . . White head . . . Run —*"

And the male voice she'd heard before that: "— *black dragons attack —*" And the same voice she'd heard when Melted Face had shrieked at her: "— *Fear . . . me —*"

Even the way Lucky had growled and grunted at Red Face and his gang in the cable car tunnel. It had been communication, deliberate and articulate *communication.*

Holy shit . . .

During the crazy chase in the pickup truck, CJ had thought the strange voices coming through her earpiece had been crossed signals from other radios in the zoo;

439

the voices of workers panicking in the face of the attacks.

But now as CJ's gaze fell on the metallic box grafted onto the side of Lucky's head, she had a different idea.

The female voice had been Lucky.

The male voice: Melted Face.

Those metallic boxes on their heads were indeed implants of some sort — implants connected to the dragons' brains and larynxes, implants fitted with state-of-the-art data chips that somehow translated their grunts, squawks and coos into language. The Chinese had even had the sense to use separate male and female voices for the different dragons, a small but clever touch.

By the look of it, however, not all the dragons at the zoo had such implants. Only the performing ones: Lucky and Red Face and his gang. None of the other four yellowjackets surrounding CJ right now had implants on the sides of their heads.

CJ pulled out her earpiece and looked at it.

It was set to channel 4. CJ recalled switching it to that channel so she could speak with Hamish and Zhang in the garbage truck.

She tried to remember what channel it had been set to before then.

"22 . . ." she said aloud. She flicked the dial on the earpiece to 22.

She looked up at Lucky and — despite herself, despite thinking that this was absolutely crazy — she nodded.

Lucky cooed and mewled . . .

. . . and the electronic female voice once again came through CJ's earpiece, speaking in Mandarin.

It said, *"Hello . . . White Head . . . Me . . . Lucky."*

CJ almost fainted. Her mouth fell open in shock.

This was incredible.

She wasn't sure how the translation system worked, but it must have been extraordinarily complex.

She guessed a sensor was probably connected directly to Lucky's voice box; it detected the dragon's utterances, correlated them with Ben Patrick's database of known dragon sounds and then sent the translation via a computerized voice to CJ's earpiece. The implant in the dragon's brain must also reverse the process, so the dragon could understand people.

Such a device would have taken years to develop and refine; thousands of man-hours just to tabulate and interpret all the different dragon calls. But Ben Patrick, with the full resources of China behind him, had done just that.

It took CJ a moment to regather herself and reply.

"Er . . . hello, Lucky," she said in Mandarin.

Lucky reared back, eyes widening. Her pointy-eared head was surprisingly expressive. Her eyes were sharp and focused intently on CJ. Her ears folded backwards like a dog's: a very pleased expression.

The dragon, by all appearances, was delighted that progress had just been made.

Lucky squawked at the other dragons, turning specifically to the two kings — even though there was an emperor-sized dragon in the pack, they, it seemed, were its leaders. They grunted back with low growls.

Lucky faced CJ again and cooed.

The earpiece translated: *"Lucky say . . . White Head . . . good human."*

"White Head?" CJ frowned.

And then she realized: it was her hair, her blonde hair. In a world of black-haired Chinese, Lucky had given her a perfectly obvious name: White Head.

"Oh. Right." She ventured a complimentary reply, using the simplest Mandarin syntax she could think of: "White Head say . . . Lucky . . . good dragon."

Lucky's ears flew back again, her eyes positively beaming.

This is trippy, CJ thought. She was communicating with a dragon.

Lucky barked and mewled quickly. *"Red dragons want kill Lucky . . . White Head help Lucky . . . White Head good human . . ."*

"Ah-ha," CJ said, understanding.

Lucky may well have saved CJ just now, but CJ had saved Lucky first: from Red Face's gang inside the waste management facility. Lucky had been repaying a debt.

"Well, thanks anyway," she said.

Lucky cooed. *"Lucky no understand White Head."*

"Never mind," CJ said.

Now that she was talking with the dragon — and she was surprised how quickly she accepted this — CJ started to think about other things.

"Lucky, what is happening now?"

"Lucky no understand White Head."

CJ kicked herself. She needed to use simpler language, no what's, why's or now's, just simple nouns and verbs. She wondered if the translator might work with English — it *was* a translation program after all; also, given Ben Patrick's involvement in its development, she figured it was a distinct possibility. So she said in English: "Red dragons kill humans."

Lucky seemed to comprehend that, and

the electronic voice switched to English. *"Red dragons bad dragons . . . Like kill humans . . . Like kill dragons . . ."*

"And yellow dragons?"

"Yellow dragons good dragons . . . Yellow dragons like sleep . . . eat . . ."

"I'm beginning to like you yellow dragons," CJ said, smiling.

"Lucky no understand White Head."

"Never mind."

CJ asked, "Red dragons want fly away?"

"Red dragons want release red masters . . ."

"Red masters?" CJ said, frowning. She didn't know what that meant. "Red masters . . . emperors?"

Lucky said, *"No . . . Master dragon big big dragon . . . Two red masters . . . Two yellow masters . . . Two purple masters . . . Two gray masters . . . Two green masters . . . One master strong strong emperor . . . one master strong strong king. Black heads hold masters . . . in nest."*

CJ tried to process what she had just heard.

If she was White Head, then "black heads" must mean the Chinese. She also guessed that the repeated words "big big" and "strong strong" meant *extra* large and *extra* strong.

She didn't like the sound of this.

The notion of some kind of master dragon that was bigger and stronger than the other dragons wasn't that surprising: it was common in the animal kingdom, from queen bees to lions. If she was interpreting Lucky correctly, each variety of dragon had two of these master dragons, one supersized emperor and one supersized king.

More worrying, however, was the idea that the Chinese were keeping them captive in the "nest," which she translated as the Nesting Center.

The Chinese knew they were special and so had kept them there, separated from the other dragons.

CJ remembered the guards at the Nesting Center during the first attack: even in those extreme circumstances, they had flatly denied Zhang and her group entry.

This was why the Nesting Center had been strictly off-limits.

CJ also recalled the image of the Nesting Center she had seen earlier, with the pairs of dragons lined up neatly in a row: they must have been the master dragons.

But perhaps, she wondered, the Chinese had underestimated how special the master dragons were: it seemed the red-bellied black dragons now wanted to release their masters, perhaps even more than they wanted to escape from the zoo.

"Masters are very strong dragons?" CJ asked.

"Master dragons strong strong dragons . . . big big . . . spit fire . . ."

"Wait, what?" CJ said, shocked. "These dragons can breathe fire?"

"Master dragons spit fire . . . Fire help dig . . . Fire kill dragons."

"Oh my God."

"Lucky no understand White Head."

CJ didn't like the sound of this at all. She tried a different angle. "Dragons want . . . to kill? To fly? To be free?"

Lucky seemed to ponder this.

"Dragons want . . . open big big nest . . ."

CJ frowned. "Big big nest?"

Lucky brayed again. The earpiece translated: *"Two nests . . . Small nest, big nest . . . Dragons sleep long long time . . . Lucky nest small nest . . . Small nest open . . . Small nest dragons go big big nest . . . Open big big nest . . ."*

The blood drained from CJ's face.

"Are you telling me that there is *another* dragon nest in this area? A bigger one? And that the nest at this zoo is actually a small one?"

"Lucky no understand White Head."

CJ stepped out of the monastery building,

striding past the pack of yellowjacket dragons. She peered across the dark, rain-flecked megavalley in the direction of the Nesting Center.

Then she remembered something: the battlefield display unit in her thigh pocket.

She pulled it out and looked at it. It must have been connected to some external data system — perhaps a satellite or, more likely, the military airfield outside the valley — because it was still working despite the loss of power inside the zoo.

With the falling of the inner dome, however, it had changed completely.

Whereas before most of the red crosses had been clustered around the administration building, now they were converging on the Nesting Center. The red-bellied black dragons were going for their masters.

At the top-right-hand corner of the image, gray dragons were fleeing en masse from the valley, heading off to the northeast.

As she gazed in horror at the map, a question formed in CJ's mind.

The red-bellied black dragons had led the initial attacks. And now they were descending upon the Nesting Center. They were driving all this and they clearly weren't finished.

Stepping back into the monastery, she

said, "Lucky. Red dragons want . . . ?"

"Red dragons like red dragons . . . Kill other dragons . . . Like rule . . ."

"And if they release their masters," CJ said to herself, "they become the only dragons with fire-breathers. They become the most powerful dragons."

She turned to face Lucky. "Lucky help White Head?"

"Lucky like White Head . . ."

"Lucky help White Head fight red dragons?" CJ pointed at the Nesting Center. "Lucky fly White Head to nest?"

Lucky looked off in the direction of the Nesting Center, peering into the rainy night. The dragon seemed to be considering the question very seriously.

If anything, she seemed apprehensive about the idea, fearful even.

She pivoted and coo-barked at one of the two yellowjacket kings. The king dragon looked at CJ hard, as if evaluating her. Then it grunted at Lucky permissively.

Lucky turned back to CJ. *"Lucky . . . White Head . . . fight red dragons."*

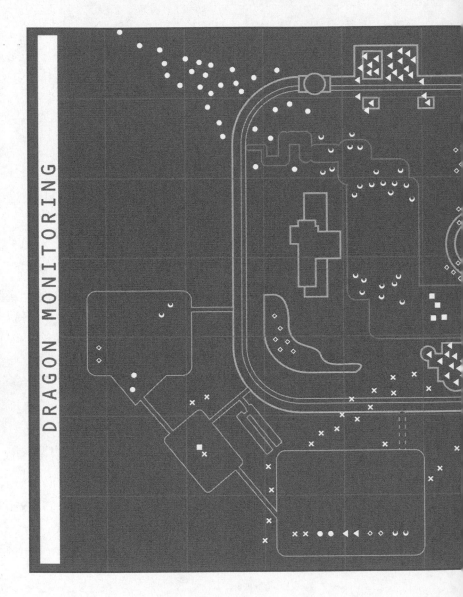

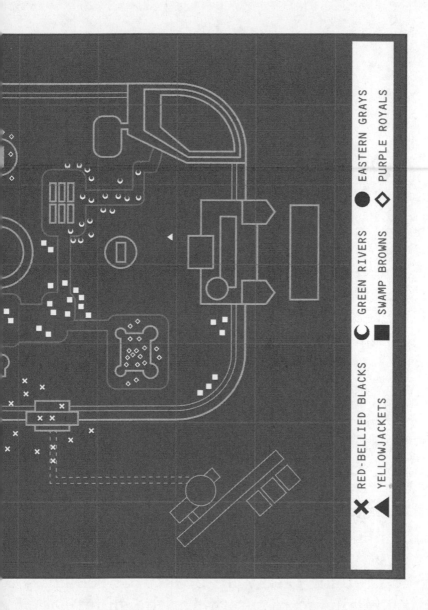

RED-BELLIED BLACKS ✖
YELLOWJACKETS ▲

GREEN RIVERS ☾
SWAMP BROWNS ■

EASTERN GRAYS ●
PURPLE ROYALS ◇

With CJ on her back, Lucky soared over the blacked-out zoo.

CJ gazed at the landscape below her: the rain had lessened to a weak drizzle now and she could see the whole megavalley. Without any man-made light, it seemed as if the valley had lost all its color; it was now a world of blacks and grays.

She eyed the distant western rim of the crater. She could see many dragons making their way there, gliding across the sky. She hadn't seen the inside of the Nesting Center before and she was nervous about what she might encounter there, not least a super-sized "master" dragon.

She had, however, one stop she wanted to make on the way.

She brought Lucky in toward the remains of the revolving restaurant at the summit of Dragon Mountain.

The disc-shaped structure had literally

been torn apart in the dragons' attack and the later gas explosion. It looked like a tuna can that'd had its lid peeled back. Half of its roof was simply gone, wrenched away. On its entire southern side, its four broad descending levels lay open to the sky. The Chinese troop truck still lay inside it, turned on its side, nose pressed up against the central elevator bay. The corpses of Chinese troops and commandos lay all over the place, in various states of dismemberment, guns on the floor beside them.

Lucky landed lightly on an open-air part of the restaurant.

CJ dismounted quickly and hurried toward the kitchen, racing for the dumbwaiter in which she had left Greg Johnson. She hoped it had withstood the gas explosion. She pulled its heavy steel doors apart.

Johnson wasn't in it.

Swipes of blood slicked the walls of the boxlike elevator.

"Damn it," CJ breathed.

The CIA agent was gone.

CJ emerged from the kitchen to find Lucky poking her nose under a section of fallen ceiling.

"What have you found there?" CJ said, coming over.

Lucky pushed the section of plasterboard away, revealing the body of Li, the young electrician CJ had met twice before.

Li groaned, waking, only to shout in terror when he saw Lucky staring at him from so close.

CJ stepped in hastily. "It's okay, it's okay. She's with me."

Li blanched in surprise.

For her part, Lucky seemed a little, well, offended by the man's terror. She hadn't been threatening him in any way. She snorted huffily.

Kneeling beside Li, CJ switched to Mandarin: "Are you all right? Can you move?"

Li grimaced in pain. "I think . . . I dislocated my shoulder when the roof fell on it."

CJ examined his shoulder. It was indeed out of position. "We gotta get that baby back in. Here, lean forward and stay still."

"Are you a doctor?" Li said.

"I'm better than that. I'm a vet. Vets do everything: brain surgery, heart surgery, lab analysis, dislocations —"

Whack. She shoved his shoulder back into the socket. Li yelped but then immediately began to breathe easier. His shoulder was in place again.

"What is happening?" he asked in slow English, taking in the scale of the destruction around him and the darkened zoo outside.

"The dragons cut the power. They've brought down the inner dome —"

A groan made them both spin.

Lucky turned, too, and growled.

It had come from the cabin of the side-turned troop truck.

CJ approached it cautiously. Another section of fallen ceiling covered the top of the truck's cabin, concealing it from view.

She scooped up an MP-7 machine pistol from the floor and aimed it at the cabin. The windshield of the truck had popped halfway out of its frame. CJ yanked it clear and, expecting to see a dragon come bursting out of it, quickly aimed her gun —

— only to see Dr. Ben Patrick lying inside the cabin, his forehead covered in blood, his glasses askew.

CJ lowered her gun.

A few minutes later, Patrick sat patiently while CJ wrapped his forehead with bandages.

He kept glancing at Lucky, who watched curiously.

"White Head . . . help . . . Big Eyes . . ."
Lucky's voice said in her ear.

CJ half-laughed. Big Eyes. What else

would a dragon call someone with glasses?

"Yes," she replied. "Humans help humans."

Patrick watched the exchange. "I see you've discovered Lucky's translation chip," he said.

"Found it while I was looking for a radio. It's pretty amazing," CJ said. "But it only works for her and the four red-bellies from the trick show, right?"

"That's correct. That implant grafted onto the side of her head connects directly to her larynx, giving us precise readings of her utterings. The unit then compares her utterances with the hundreds of vocalizations that have been collated in my database of dragon calls and, voilà, you hear what she says," Patrick said proudly.

He added, "Lucky must like you. She's very choosy. She doesn't speak with just anybody. In fact, she's always favored women."

"I helped Lucky out of a nasty situation earlier," CJ said. "She has an admirable sense of gratitude." She turned to the dragon: "White Head like Lucky."

The dragon's ears twitched backwards again. *"Lucky like White Head."*

CJ said to Patrick: "We're on our way to the Nesting Center. The dragons cut the power, knocking out the inner dome. Now the red-bellied black ones are gathering at the Nesting Center. They want to release some kind of bigger dragons from there, something called masters."

Patrick's eyes went wide. "They're going after the masters? Shit, if they get out . . ."

CJ showed him the battlefield display unit, with all the red crosses converging on the Nesting Center.

"Tell me about these master dragons," she said, "and how I can stop them."

"You can't."

"I can try," CJ said.

"No. *You can't,*" Patrick said. "If those masters get out, it'll make what's happened so far look like child's play."

"Humor me," CJ said.

Patrick sighed, then said, "Out of the original 88 eggs, there were two master dragons born to each clan: one super-emperor and one superking. They are kept in the Nesting Center, bound, with their snouts held firmly shut. The reason is that these master dragons have a unique set of glands at the back of their throats that release a kind of incendiary acid. Alone among the dragons at this facility, they can project liquid fire."

"So what we were told on the tour about

there being no fire-breathing dragons at the zoo was a lie," CJ said.

"You were never supposed to see the masters, so think of it as a half-truth," Patrick said.

"Seems to me that this place is filled with half-truths," CJ said. "I repeat: how do I stop them?"

"Let me be clear, CJ. It's not just fire that they breathe. It's a liquid acid-based fire. If that acid-fire touches your skin, it'll turn your entire body to mush. It's not a pretty sight. I've seen it."

"For the third time, Ben, *how can I stop them?*" CJ said.

Patrick said, "There are two protocols in place in the event that we lose control of this zoo. The primary protocol for use in the event of a *total* security breakdown involves the detonation of several thermo-baric bombs at strategic locations around the zoo. A thermobaric bomb creates an oxygen vacuum that will kill every living thing within a very wide radius. That is the last-resort plan."

CJ didn't feel the need to tell Patrick that she was already aware of the three thermo-baric bombs held somewhere at the zoo.

Patrick went on. "There is a secondary protocol, however, that doesn't go as far as that. It involves the implants in the dragons' heads, the chips in their brains that emit an electric shock if a dragon comes into contact with one of the electromagnetic domes.

"When we train the dragons, we use what we call 'training units' to trigger those implants. Pain is a swift teacher."

CJ recalled the trick show and the moment during it when Red Face had balked at doing a trick. The trainer Yim had held up a yellow handheld remote and Red Face had performed. Yim had been threatening the dragon with a shock. CJ also now knew why Red Face had smashed that same remote to pieces when Yim had reached for it in the waste management facility moments before her death.

"Lucky's trainer had a yellow remote," CJ said. "Is that one of these training units?"

"Yes. As you will have seen, each dragon has an alphanumeric ID code branded onto its left thigh. You enter a dragon's code into the training unit and then you can shock that individual dragon."

"How many of these training units are there and where can I get one?"

"There aren't many, maybe five or six, kept in the Birthing and Nesting centers, since that's where we train the young dragons."

"Shocking them is a temporary measure, Ben. How about killing them?"

"Let me finish," Patrick said. "Those implants in each of the dragons' heads were equipped with a *second* capability for use in the event that a dragon or dragons got excessively violent or out of control."

"Yes . . ."

"Each implant contains two grams of the plastic explosive PVV-5A inside it; not a lot, but enough to blow a dragon's head apart from the inside."

"Now you're talking," CJ said. "So how do we detonate these implants?"

Patrick said, "A regular training unit can't detonate those chips. It requires a special detonator unit. And there are only two detonator units in the whole zoo. They look exactly like the training units, only they are red, not yellow. For obvious reasons, both of these detonator units are kept inside high-security safes, the combinations for which are known only to a few senior people."

"Who?"

"Director Chow, Colonel Bao . . . and me."

"Why you?"

"Because Chow is just an administrator and Bao is simply muscle," Patrick said

460

dismissively. "By virtue of my research, I know more about these dragons than anyone else at this zoo; more than anyone else alive, for that matter."

"So where are the safes?" CJ said.

"The first is at the military airfield to the southwest of the zoo. That airfield is basically the zoo's second command center; you could run the whole place from there. I imagine that's where Colonel Bao has gone, if he's still alive."

"That'll be tough to get to. And the second detonator unit?"

"It's inside the Nesting Center."

"Of course it is," CJ said. "Where exactly?"

"Bao has an office there, inside the observation booth overlooking the main chamber of the Nesting Center. The main chamber houses the master dragons and the opening to the dragons' original nest."

"What's the combination to the safe?" CJ asked.

"9199," Patrick said.

CJ nodded, memorizing the code. She started walking around the side-turned truck, peering at some objects on the floor near it.

As she did so, she said, "Ben, they knocked out the *inner* dome by trashing the genera-

461

tors and cutting the main power cable. If they go after the *outer* dome, how will they go about bringing it down?"

Patrick said, "The inner dome only had one set of laser-emitting emplacements. Since it's a backup barrier, the outer dome has two sets. The first set of emplacements is at the airfield. The second set is over by the worker city to the northeast, on the opposite side. Both sets of emplacements are fed by separate main power lines, so if one set of emplacements is cut, the other set still maintains the dome."

"Tell me more," CJ said from behind the truck. "Describe them for me, so I know them when I see them."

Patrick shrugged. "There are fifteen emplacements in each set. They project the outer dome both into the sky and into the ground, forming a diamond-like shield around the zoo. Each emplacement is made of nine-foot-thick concrete. They are each about the size of a house but they look like World War II pillboxes."

"Is there, like, a central pillbox?"

"Yes. Of the fifteen laser emplacements, one is paramount: the middle one. It alone is connected to the external main power line — it then sends power on to the other emplacements. If that central emplacement is destroyed, *all* the emplacements on that side of the zoo will lose power."

CJ reappeared from behind the truck, carrying a helmet, some weapons and a roll of duct tape.

"These dragons can sense electrical impulses," she said. "They'll be able to spot the large amounts of electrical energy entering those central emplacements. They'll go for them."

She put on the helmet. Taken from the body of a Chinese commando, it was a lightweight model with a flashlight mounted on one side and a flip-down visor. CJ tore off the arms of her special UV glasses and duct-taped the glasses onto the fold-down visor.

She also held a Russian-made ROKS-5 flamethrower. She wriggled the flame unit's propane tank onto her back while she gripped its gunlike nozzle in her left hand. She taped an M79 pump-action grenade launcher to her MP-7 and slid the combined weapon into a thigh holster. Finally, she used the duct tape to crudely affix her battlefield display unit to the left forearm of her leather jacket.

It was an ad hoc uniform to say the very least, but CJ Cameron suddenly looked ready for battle.

Patrick said, "A flamethrower? You ever used one before?"

"No. How hard can it be? You aim it and pull the trigger. Hell, I made my own earlier," CJ said. "And since I can't talk to the dragons in the Nesting Center, I thought fire might be a language they understand."

"You're not seriously going into the Nesting Center *right now*?" Patrick said.

"Somebody has to. And I'm going to need help."

"You want me to go with you? Are you out of your fucking mind? There must be forty red-bellied black dragons in there! Plus the masters! We won't last ten seconds. I won't go —"

"I will go," a soft voice said.

CJ turned to see the young electrician, Li, stepping forward.

"I will go with you," he said in English.

"Thank you, Li," CJ said. "Grab yourself a gun, a helmet and a flashlight."

She stepped over to Lucky and placed a foot in one stirrup.

Patrick said, "Don't do this, CJ. You'll be dead inside half an hour."

"Then at least I won't be scared anymore," CJ said.

Li returned wearing a flashlight-mounted helmet and carrying an MP-7. CJ pulled him up onto Lucky behind her. "Hold on tight. This is gonna feel weird."

Li wrapped his arms around her waist like a motorcycle passenger riding pillion.

CJ leaned close to Lucky's ear. "Lucky. Go nest."

Lucky keened and the electronic voice replied: *"Lucky . . . go nest."* Then she turned slightly and grunted something else. *"Lucky . . . no like . . . Big Eyes. Big Eyes . . . bad human."*

"What's she saying?" Patrick asked.

CJ looked over at Patrick, standing there in his broken glasses and dirty lab coat.

"She's saying she doesn't want to go to the nest either, but she'll go anyway," CJ lied.

"Good luck, CJ. You're gonna need it."

Lucky took to the sky from the smashed-open restaurant with CJ and Li on her back. She soared out over the zoo, wings spread wide, gliding.

As Lucky banked westward, CJ saw the shadows of the last few red-bellied black dragons ahead of them: all flying west, out over the rim of the crater toward the Nesting Center.

Staying high, Lucky swept over the rim and the Nesting Center came into view.

CJ caught her breath at the sight that met her.

The Nesting Center was covered in dragons.

Red-bellied black dragons of all sizes — princes, kings and emperors — crawled all over it, a writhing mass of leathery bodies and batlike wings.

The Nesting Center was no small structure either. It was perhaps the size of four airplane hangars, square in shape but with a circular cagelike structure on its roof, a hemispherical steel-barred dome.

As they came closer to the Nesting Center — but not too close — CJ saw six emperors attacking the steel dome from the outside, tearing it apart. The squeal of rending steel cut the air as the immense dragons, working together, wrenched the girders away, creating a huge ragged opening in the great metal dome.

When the opening they'd created was wide enough, prince-sized red-bellies slithered into the Nesting Center. When it became wider still, the kings entered, and then finally the emperors dived in as well, tails slinking behind them.

CJ swallowed hard. She couldn't believe she was doing this, literally going into the dragons' den.

Okay, she thought. *How do I get in there?*

She gazed off to the right and saw the Birthing Center, and she recalled that there was a tunnel that connected it to the Nesting Center. That was the way in and hopefully an entrance that the multitude of red-bellied black dragons wouldn't be watching. She checked her battlefield display unit, but it was hard to tell if the dragons shown on it were *inside* the Birthing Center or above it. She had to take the chance.

She guided Lucky down to the right, toward the ring road and the entrance to the Birthing Center.

The Birthing Center was deserted.

CJ and Li entered it on foot. Li held his MP-7 raised, while CJ led with her flamethrower. Lucky loped along behind them, eyeing their rear.

CJ saw the smartboard with the map on it again and the dead bodies. The female crocodiles down in the water pit still bellowed and groaned. Looking down into the pit, CJ saw the corpse of the red-bellied black dragon she had encountered before — it was in the process of being eaten by the olive-colored swamp dragon that had attacked it. The swamp dragon glanced up at CJ and Li, growled, then continued its feast.

CJ saw a glass cabinet attached to the wall. It had been smashed and battered. On the floor beneath it were the shattered remains of five yellow training units. The dragons, keenly aware of the shocks the remotes gave, had taken care of them when they'd come through here.

"Clever things," CJ said.

She approached the doorway in the far

left-hand corner, moving silently and cautiously.

The door was open.

A corridor stretched away beyond it. From the end of the corridor, she could hear dragon calls and roars. It sounded like a gladiatorial arena.

With great trepidation, CJ edged down the corridor, leading with her weapons. Li and Lucky crept down it behind her.

At the far end of the corridor was a door. It dangled off its hinges. It had been smashed open at some point. A large dark space was beyond it.

CJ came to the end of the corridor just as a deafening chorus of dragon roars echoed out from within the Nesting Center and, to her horror, a great, hundred-foot-high column of yellow flame extended into the sky, lighting up her corridor.

She slammed herself against the wall.

Then, holding her breath, she peered around the doorframe.

"Mother of Mercy . . ." she gasped.

If she somehow managed to survive this, the sight CJ beheld inside the Nesting Center would be one she would remember for the rest of her life.

Her doorway was positioned three storeys above the floor of the main chamber, so she had a good view of it. To her immediate left was a small building with glass windows, also three storeys tall. It was the only man-made structure in the chamber and it overlooked the space: it must've been the observation booth Ben Patrick had mentioned.

The floor of the chamber was a broad expanse of concrete, like the floor of an airplane hangar, except that in the exact center of it was an extraordinarily wide circular hole that was at least forty feet in diameter.

The hole looked like a monstrous well and it bored down into the earth.

The dragons' original tunnel, CJ realized. *The tunnel they dug themselves and through which they'd emerged from their nest deep within the Earth.*

This was where the Chinese had built their trap to capture each dragon as it had emerged from the nest two miles underground.

But it was the terrifying scene *around* the great hole in the center of the chamber that had made her gasp in shock.

It looked like Hell itself — fiery light, prisoners bound in chains, squawking dragons surrounding them like a crowd of demonic spectators, roaring and beating their wings in approval of what was going on.

And what was going on was not pleasant at all.

CJ saw nine "master" dragons lying in a long row, but they were not lying there by choice.

Each was bound by thick steel bands that were bolted to the concrete floor. The sturdy bands held down the animals' necks, bodies, wings and walking limbs, keeping them rigidly immobile. Special metal sheaths kept their snouts tightly shut.

And they were, quite simply, enormous.

There was one king and one emperor of

471

each type: two yellowjackets, two purple royals, two green river dragons, two eastern grays. There were no olive-colored swamp dragon masters: CJ guessed that was because they were a new species created by the Chinese using the crocodile-breeding program. Each master was slightly bigger than the regular kings and emperors.

There were also two red-bellied black master dragons, but only one of them, the superemperor, still lay on the floor. The other, the superking, stood free, released from its bonds, bellowing at the sky. It blew a blazing column of fire up into the night.

As it raged, three red-bellied king dragons attacked the steel bands restraining the still-bound superemperor. Suddenly, the bonds broke and the superemperor reared onto its hind legs and it, too, roared at the sky, releasing a towering burst of liquid fire.

The assembled crowd of red-bellied black dragons shrieked in delight.

Their two masters were free.

CJ watched in awe as the mass of red-bellied blacks fawned before their masters.

Like queen bees in a hive, the two masters were visibly superior to the other dragons. Their crests were higher, their necks longer, their chests broader, their wingspans wider, and of course, they could breathe fire.

The superemperor was beyond enormous. It towered above the chamber looking like something from another world. Every time it sprayed the air with a column of fire, its minions roared appreciatively.

The superking struck CJ in a different way.

Not only was it slightly larger than the other king dragons, it was also somehow more sinister. It had a sharpness to its eyes, suggesting an extra level of intelligence that sent a chill through CJ. It surveyed the chamber with cool calculation.

Its gaze fell on the other captive masters and it screamed a furious, ear-piercing shriek.

All the watching dragons fell silent. An eerie stillness fell over the chamber.

The two red-bellied masters stomped over to the two yellowjacket masters bound to the floor. The yellowjackets were utterly immobile. They could not even open their snouts. They were totally defenseless.

Without so much as a pause, the red-bellied superking lowered its head, opened its jaws and vomited forth a horizontal column of blazing liquid fire.

The superemperor did the same.

The twin streams of fire enveloped the yellowjacket masters and the two pinned-down beasts immediately caught fire.

They squealed and writhed in their bonds as their hides ignited. The chamber echoed with their cries as the two creatures were burned alive.

The crowd of spectating dragons erupted in roars of demented joy.

"Oh, God . . ." CJ breathed.

Behind her, Li stood with his mouth open.

Lucky whimpered softly at the sight of her own master dragons being killed so cruelly.

The two yellowjacket masters were now covered in flames. They tore at their bonds, twisting with all their might, but they were held fast to the floor. They could do nothing but burn, and burn they did.

The two red-bellied masters stepped along the line of captive superdragons and stopped in front of the next pair, the two gray masters. Another tongue of liquid fire enveloped these two.

They're eliminating the competition, CJ thought. *One pair at a time.*

She stood. She didn't have to watch this and, indeed, while the crowd of dragons was distracted by the grotesque spectacle, it might give her the opening she needed to get to the observation booth unnoticed.

"Lucky, stay," she said. "Li, come with me."

As the two gray masters writhed in flames,

CJ and Li hurried toward the observation booth.

Moving low and fast, they scurried unseen across an exposed catwalk and clambered up some steel stairs, entering the booth.

No sooner were they inside it than the world outside lit up again and there were more roars and CJ peered out the booth's viewing windows to see the next pair of masters — the purple ones — come alight. The yellowjacket masters now lay still, their corpses smoking.

Then the last pair of defenseless masters, the green river dragons, were set alight by more sprays of fire, and now the whole Nesting Center really resembled Hell: squeals of pain, flaming bound creatures being tortured, roars of sneering delight from the crowd of dragons, all of it ruled over by the two merciless red master dragons.

"We need to find the detonator unit," CJ said to Li as she began searching. "It's in a safe somewhere in here."

The booth looked like a mine office. It contained desks with computers and printers, plus cupboards and lockers. Several Taser units of different lengths and sizes dangled from hooks; the smallest ones were handheld, the biggest ones were the size of cattle prods. Helmets hung off coat hooks beside four thick industrial-yellow heat suits — they were made of a bulky fireproof material and had hoods with Lexan glass faceplates. Each looked like a cross between a HAZMAT suit and the blast suit that a bomb-disposal specialist wears.

CJ flung open the cupboards. Li did the same.

No dice.

There were a couple of offices adjoining the observation booth. CJ disappeared into one of them.

Inside it, she found a shelf on which sat a compact yellow remote identical to the one she had seen Yim holding during the trick show: it was one of the training units that could give a shock to any of the dragons. She grabbed it.

But still no safe.

She came to another office. It had a wide mahogany desk, nice carpet and an open window overlooking the main chamber. The office of a senior person like Colonel Bao. CJ could hear the roars and the whooshing of flames outside, frighteningly close.

Then she spotted it, under the mahogany desk.

A little safe.

It had a small battery-powered digital

screen and a ten-digit keypad. Inside it — hopefully — was one of the red detonation units.

CJ crouched in front of it and punched in the code Ben Patrick had given her: 9199.

The safe beeped angrily: INCORRECT CODE ENTERED.

"What . . . ?" CJ frowned.

She punched in the code again.

INCORRECT CODE ENTERED.

CJ's brow furrowed. Had she punched in the wrong code? Or had Patrick got it wrong? Or was this perhaps the wrong safe —

At that moment a different kind of scream from outside interrupted CJ's thoughts.

The scream of a little girl.

CJ snapped up and looked out the window.

There on the floor of the main chamber, surrounded by the horde of snarling dragons, were four captive human beings: Director Chow, two of the senior Communist Party officials — still wearing their outdoorsman clothing — and the little girl named Minnie.

"It's a feeding ritual," CJ whispered as she stared out at the scene.

A gang of four princes pushed the human captives forward, toward the two master dragons.

It was indeed a feeding ritual, like the one CJ had witnessed earlier on the ring road, when the red-bellied black princes had offered the Chinese workmen to their king. These junior dragons were presenting their superiors with a food offering.

The two master dragons peered imperiously down at the four quivering people in front of them.

The superemperor lunged forward and took Director Chow in its mouth, and the zoo's director disappeared in an instant, taken in one swallow.

The superking took more time. It lowered its head to examine the two Communist Party men and cocked it to the side. The two men shook with fear. The dragon grunted, then it snorted with its nostrils and both men were knocked to the ground by the rush of air.

They tried to get back to their feet but the superking just scooped them up in its jaws and gulped them down with a jerking movement of its chin.

And suddenly all that remained before the two dragons was the little girl, Minnie.

She stood before the pair of giant beasts, impossibly small, sobbing, still wearing her Disney mouse ears cap.

The crowd of dragons hissed and snarled. It was a child's ultimate nightmare become real.

The superemperor lowered its mighty head. Minnie shook before its gigantic slavering jaws, quivering and crying.

It opened its jaws.

Strings of saliva extended from the upper fangs to the lower ones.

Then a stream of horizontal fire suddenly extended *between* the dragon and the girl, cutting *across* them, and the superemperor recoiled, startled.

Indeed, every dragon arrayed around the wide chamber reared in surprise as a human on the back of a yellowjacket prince appeared in the middle of the space and stood defiantly before the two red-bellied black masters.

CJ Cameron and Lucky.

CJ looked like a knight on a stallion, only instead of a lance she held a flamethrower, and instead of armor she wore an industrial-yellow heat suit with the hood flung back.

As soon as she'd seen Minnie, CJ had moved, abandoning her difficulties with the safe.

She wasn't concerned for Director Chow or the Communist Party big shots. They had known the risks of this place when they'd come here.

But Minnie was different. She was innocent. She didn't deserve to die this way: abandoned, alone and in total fear.

And so CJ had dashed out of the office, grabbing the yellow training remote on the way and snatching a heat suit off a wall hook.

She'd slid into it, then mounted Lucky and swooped down to the floor of the chamber and fired her flamethrower across the face of the superemperor.

Now, she sat astride Lucky, in front of the two enormous master dragons. The bulky heat suit made her look like the Michelin Man and with the hood flung back, her helmeted head was exposed.

The two master dragons glared down at her, their eyes furious.

CJ leapt off Lucky's back and placed herself squarely between them and Minnie.

"Get back!" she yelled.

The masters growled.

The army of surrounding dragons began to hiss ominously . . . and slowly move in.

Maintaining eye contact with the super-king, CJ loosed another spray from her flamethrower.

The masters arched back. CJ hoped they figured that any other fire-breathing animal was to be respected. The ring of dragons paused, wary of the flames.

She pushed Minnie toward Lucky.

"Hi, Minnie," she said. "Get on."

The little girl's face was streaked with tears, but she nodded. She edged toward Lucky —

— when suddenly the superking raised its head to the heavens and sent a geyser of fire shooting up into the sky.

Then the big animal swung its head down so that it stared directly at CJ . . .

. . . and it opened its jaws . . .

. . . and CJ's eyes boggled as she saw the dragon's giant mouth yawn wide, saw its many teeth, its pink tongue and the depths of its throat — and rising from those depths, a surging ball of flames.

The next second, the dragon sent a horizontal pillar of fire spraying right at CJ and Minnie.

CJ flipped her hood over her helmet and pushed Minnie hard toward Lucky before she herself spun on the spot, turning her back to the dragon.

Superhot flames slammed into her, lashed around her. It was unbelievably hot, unbearably hot. The flames totally consumed her body.

Then the inferno stopped and in the smoke haze that followed it . . . CJ remained standing.

The master dragons reared back in surprise, stunned that CJ could possibly still be alive. Clearly, no animal had ever survived such a blast.

"Still here, motherfuckers," CJ said.

As she said this, CJ saw the superking's left thigh, saw the brand on it: R-02.

She quickly pulled the yellow training unit from her suit and punched its touchscreen display with a gloved hand: R-02 then

SHOCK.

The superking immediately squealed in agony and clutched at its head, causing all the dragons ringing the confrontation to look at one another in confusion.

CJ dashed over to Minnie and threw her onto Lucky's back. "We can't stay here."

No sooner was CJ in the saddle than Lucky sprang into the air — a nanosecond before a horizontal tongue of fire lanced out from the superking's mouth and liquefied the floor where Lucky had been standing.

CJ didn't care where Lucky went so long as it was somewhere else, but with dragons flanking them on every side, it turned out there was only one direction Lucky could go: down.

Lucky dived into the vertical tunnel and shot down it at rocket speed.

With Minnie seated between her thighs, CJ quickly clipped herself in. She also attached a clip to Minnie's belt, but as she did so, she lost her grip on the training unit and it went tumbling away into the tunnel.

"Shit!" CJ reached after it, but it fell into the darkness, never to be seen again.

CJ spun in her saddle to see three red-bellied black princes sweep into the tunnel behind them in hot pursuit.

The two masters, she noted, didn't follow.

The walls of the circular tunnel swept by at phenomenal speed. There were dim orange lights spaced along its length: aging military-grade glow sticks.

At first the tunnel was dizzyingly vertical, then it bent at a forty-five-degree angle. CJ held on to Minnie while Lucky streamlined her body to get maximum speed.

CJ flung back the hood of her heat suit, revealing her commando helmet. She flicked on the flashlight mounted on its side.

Then, without warning, the walls of the tunnel simply disappeared and CJ found herself flying out in wide open space above a vast underground cavern.

Hundreds of glow sticks illuminated the cave in a faint orange glow. Mainly used by the military and by cave explorers, glow sticks were a clever choice of light source by the Chinese: powered by a mild chemical reaction, they required no external power or cabling and, importantly, they made no noise, so they would never have disturbed the dragon eggs. These glow sticks, however, were at the end of their chemical lives and many had gone out. The ones that still worked gave off a sickly orange glow.

The cavern itself was shaped like a gigantic funnel, wide at the top, narrow at the bottom. Sweeping down its flanks in a wide spiral was an irregular shelflike path on which sat dozens and dozens of oversized leathery eggs. At the very base of the funnel CJ saw a small steaming pool of water, a natural spring of some sort that had kept the cavern moist for millennia.

The dragons' original nest, CJ thought.

The eggs, she noticed even in her haste, were of different sizes: the larger ones, she assumed, were for the emperors and kings, the smaller ones for the princes.

All were hatched, open.

A small demountable booth had been erected at the top of the cavern beside the exit tunnel, but it looked long abandoned, covered in dust and dirt. Once all the dragons had hatched, it had lost its usefulness and, like the glow sticks, the Chinese must have simply left it here.

With three whooshes, the three pursuing red-bellied black princes sped into the cave. Two covered the exit tunnel, while the third hovered in the air and bellowed a roar of the utmost fury at CJ, Lucky and Minnie.

CJ recognized the dragon instantly.

It was Red Face.

"Not you again," she said.

Lucky landed on the spiraling path on the

side of the cave and said, *"White Head . . . off . . ."*

CJ hesitantly obeyed. "What are you doing?"

"Lucky . . . fight . . . red princes . . . Lucky help White Head . . ."

Before CJ could protest, Lucky took to the air and, hovering in front of CJ and Minnie, she roared back at the red-bellied black princes, a terrifyingly fierce shriek that CJ had not thought her capable of.

The electronic voice in CJ's ear said: *". . . Begin challenge . . ."*

CJ stared at the scene in amazement: there was Lucky, hovering on one side of the cavern, while high up on the other side, guarding the exit tunnel, were the three red-bellied black princes, also hovering.

Red Face snarled at Lucky, then nodded at one of his companions and it flew forward.

It was another red-bellied black prince that CJ knew. She recognized its hideously melted snout. It was Melted Face. She had to hand it to the dragon: he was a survivor.

Melted Face shot down toward Lucky.

Lucky answered the roar and flew up at Melted Face.

The two dragons raced toward each other and CJ realized that she was seeing what

Zhang had called a "joust."

The two prince-sized dragons raced at each other at shocking speed and as they passed they lashed out with their claws.

There was a cry of pain — CJ couldn't tell if it had come from Lucky or Melted Face — and then suddenly they were past each other and hovering again, ready for another pass.

They sped toward each other again, faster this time. Lucky streamlined her body, beat her wings. Melted Face flexed his claws.

And they clashed again . . . only this time Lucky rolled at the moment of impact . . . and again there was a shriek of pain . . . and once again they both kept on flying . . . only this time, Melted Face did not pull up into a hover. He just went careering into the opposite wall, smashing into it — lifeless, dead — before his body dropped down the length of the cavern and splashed into the little pool at its base.

CJ snapped round to look at Lucky.

Lucky held a ragged chunk of flesh in her right foreclaw. She had landed a killer blow on the second pass.

Red Face squealed and flew into a jousting position.

Lucky readied herself for battle again.

But then the third red-bellied black

dragon took up a position beside Red Face.

CJ looked on in horror. It was two against one.

"Lucky!" she called.

The dragon turned.

"White Head and Lucky fight!" she yelled.

In answer, Lucky swooped around in a tight circle and allowed CJ to leap onto her back before resuming her face-off with the two red-bellies.

CJ felt her heart beating loudly in her head. She reached inside her heat suit and pulled out her MP-7. She couldn't believe she was doing this.

She was partaking in a dragon joust . . .

The three dragons sprang forward, racing toward each other, two against one.

CJ had never felt Lucky accelerate so quickly. She saw the two red-bellied black princes speeding toward her across the massive cavern. They were going to pass by on either side of Lucky and double-team her.

Then she saw Lucky extend her left foreclaw — Red Face was coming at them from that side, so CJ levelled her gun at the dragon on the right. It wasn't exactly a lance but in this aerial joust, it was the next best thing.

They all came together in a blur of claws and roars — Lucky shooting in between the two oncoming dragons — and CJ loosed a burst of fire from her MP-7, aiming as best she could at the right-hand dragon's head.

She saw blood spurts erupt from its snout, mouth and eyes — while on the other side, Lucky and Red Face extended their claws and slashed at each other and then — *swoosh!* — the two red-bellies rocketed past.

The right-hand dragon, hit in both eyes by CJ's gunfire, crashed at full speed into the far wall in a starburst of rocks, breaking its neck with the impact.

Red Face squealed as he banked away and CJ saw a trail of blood dripping from his rib cage and he landed on an egg shelf, whimpering and wounded. He cried to the heavens, a squeal of agony.

Lucky continued flying, wings beating powerfully —

— before she jerked unexpectedly, faltering, and lost speed.

Worried, CJ looked down to see that Lucky's entire left flank was slicked with blood.

"Oh, no . . ." she gasped.

Lucky may have wounded Red Face, but Red Face had also landed a serious blow on her.

CJ tried to figure out what to do now.

Then it hit her: the infirmary in the Birthing Center. If she could get Lucky there, maybe she could patch her up. But that would mean getting past all the dragons upstairs.

CJ rolled back the sleeve of her heat suit and looked at the battlefield display unit duct-taped to her left forearm, to check on the dragons up in the Nesting Center.

What she saw surprised her:

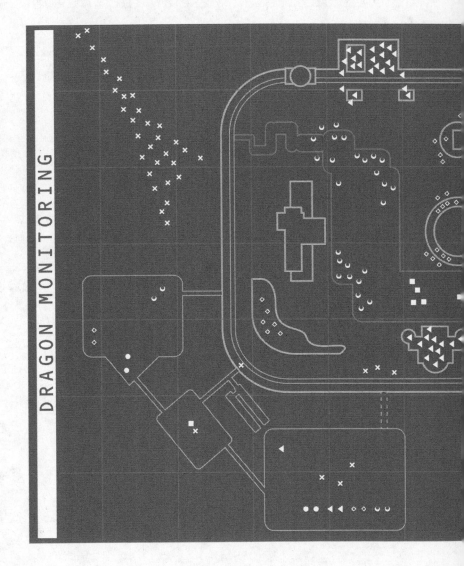

DRAGON MONITORING

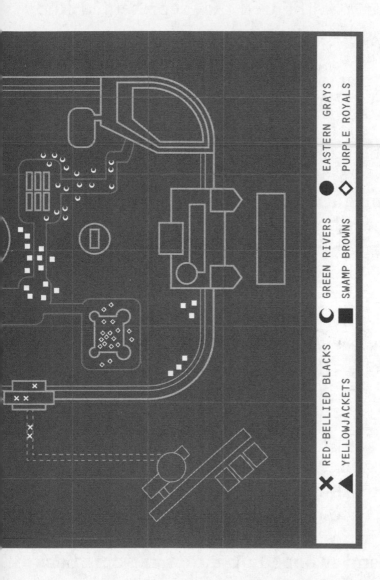

RED-BELLIED BLACKS
YELLOWJACKETS
GREEN RIVERS
SWAMP BROWNS
EASTERN GRAYS
PURPLE ROYALS

The crowd of red crosses was no longer massing around the Nesting Center. There were now only three red icons at the Nesting Center. CJ figured they represented Red Face and his two buddies.

The rest of the red-bellies were flying like a coordinated flock to the northeast, in the direction of the worker city.

Their plan was now clear to CJ: having freed their masters, they were heading for the first of the two sources of the outer electromagnetic dome, the worker city.

This was bad. This was very bad.

CJ turned back to Lucky.

"Lucky hurt?" she asked.

"Yes . . ."

"Lucky fly?"

"Lucky . . . fly . . ."

CJ said, "If Lucky fly now, White Head help Lucky later . . ."

In response, the wounded yellowjacket beat its wings with extra strength.

CJ brought Lucky around to where they had left Minnie and scooped her up. Then as Red Face remained on the egg-path licking his wounds, they flew over to the exit tunnel and swooped up into it, heading back to the surface.

After a short time, the mouth of the tunnel

came into view.

CJ slowed Lucky. She was cautious even though the BDU said there were few or no dragons still here.

Rising to the rim of the tunnel, CJ peered out.

The Nesting Center was deserted.

Apart from the smouldering remains of the eight dead master dragons, their wretched charred corpses still fastened to the floor, there was not a single dragon to be seen.

A shout made CJ turn and she saw Li running from the stairs near the observation booth.

CJ landed Lucky on the floor near him.

"They all took off as soon as you flew down into the nest!" Li said.

CJ gazed off into the distance. "They freed their masters and now they're going after the outer dome. They're heading for the emplacements at the worker city."

Lucky groaned painfully and CJ looked back at her, concerned. She saw the wound on Lucky's side: a gaping bloody gash.

"We have to stop them bringing down the outer dome," she said to Li as she dismounted. "But first I have to mend this brave dragon. Come on."

In the café at the base of the curving waterfall, Hamish Cameron stood. "We're no good to anyone just sitting around here. We've got to find a radio and get in touch with CJ."

"If she's still alive," Seymour Wolfe said sourly.

"My sister's a tough nut, Mr. Wolfe," Hamish said, "and surprisingly hard to kill. Ask the bull alligator that tried."

"We also have to be out of this valley by the time the Chinese regain control of it," Ambassador Syme said. "If we're not, they'll just hunt us down and kill us."

Hamish peered out through the window beside him, gazing westward across the lake. He saw the ruins of the administration building beyond the castle on the opposite shore.

"There was an exit in that waste management facility," he said, thinking aloud.

"That's our way out. We cross this lake and make for the waste management facility."

"And how exactly do we cross this lake?" Wolfe asked.

Hamish nodded at one of the six wide-beamed, glass-roofed boats tied to the dock near the café. "On one of those."

"Won't that make us an instant target for any dragon that's watching?" Wolfe said.

Hamish said, "It will. But I have a plan for that. Let's move."

Five minutes later, the three of them dashed out of the café, running across the dock toward the six parked boats.

No dragons pounced.

Each man powered up two boats, untied them and set them off from their moorings. Then they all jumped aboard the last boat and sped away from the dock.

The six boats fanned out from the café, heading onto the lake in a starlike pattern.

Still no dragons attacked.

From the controls of his boat, Hamish scanned the dark sky. It was entirely empty of dragons.

The boat they'd jumped on was specially designed for sightseeing cruises. Not only did it have a broad glass-domed roof to allow for easy viewing of the dragons, it also, he now saw, had a glass bottom. Running up the middle of the boat's hull was a long glass trough about eight feet deep. It had curved glass walls and clear plastic seats on which visitors could sit and look out at the underwater world of the lake.

Right now, in the deep of the night, that world was inky black.

Hamish kept looking up at the sky. "Where have they all gone?"

"Maybe they got out?" Syme asked.

"Fine with me," Hamish said. "If they're not here, it'll give us a clear run across this lake."

As he said this, one of the five other boats puttering along beside his one suddenly cracked in the middle, folded into a V-shape, and was violently pulled under the surface by some unseen force. It shattered, spraying glass, before disappearing into the lake.

"Shit!" Syme yelled.

Hamish's face went pale. "They're not above us, they're below us."

He searched his control panel for a switch, found the one he was looking for — UNDER-WATER FLOODLIGHTS — and hit it.

Instantly, the eerie underwater world outside the boat's glass hull came alive and Hamish saw the enormous head of a green-skinned emperor dragon not far away, gripping the boat that had just been yanked under the surface and looking back at Hamish like a child who has been spotted with a stolen candy bar.

It was crouched on the bottom of the lake, wings flat on its back, tail curled. A king-sized green dragon lay beside it — also looking right at Hamish's lights — while three green princes slithered through the underwater haze like oversized lizards, their four walking limbs hanging beside their bodies while their tails propelled them powerfully through the water.

Then the emperor moved.

It opened its jaws and Hamish saw two rows of terrifying teeth, and then the animal heaved upward, pushing off the lakebed, and Hamish's stomach lurched sickeningly as the surge of water created by the beast's movement lifted his boat high into the air.

The massive green emperor dragon rose out of the lake in all its terrifying glory.

Framed by the beautiful curving waterfall behind it, the colossal creature rose to its full height, standing two hundred feet tall and spreading its wings. As it did this, it sent a huge wave of water flowing outward from its body, a wave that pushed Hamish's boat — infinitesimally small compared to the mighty dragon — away from the animal, toward the ruined castle on the western shore.

Hamish held on tight as his boat sped away from the dragon like a surfer on a wave. The dragon, unaware that it had aided Hamish's escape with its sudden movement, spun where it stood, snatched up the nearest decoy boat in one of its foreclaws and crushed the entire boat in an instant.

It roared as it flung the boat away.

Then the rest of the pack of green dragons — river dragons, Hamish guessed — started attacking the other boats. Princes boarded them. Kings smashed them. The emperor rampaged among them, standing waist-deep in the lake.

Hamish's boat powered westward and as the force of the wave behind it diminished, Hamish turned off the underwater flood-lights and hit the gas.

The shore was only fifty yards away.

"Faster! Faster!" Wolfe urged.

Hamish was peering forward when one of the decoy boats landed with a splash right in front of his boat, missing the bow by yards, thrown by the furious emperor.

He banked around it.

"Faster, man!" Wolfe yelled.

"We're going as fast as we can!" Hamish

said. "This thing isn't built for speed!"

They were twenty yards from the shore when the boat simply stopped moving. Hamish pushed the throttle all the way forward. The boat revved loudly, but it didn't respond.

"Why aren't we — ?" Syme shouted, turning.

He cut himself off when he saw the answer: the emperor stood behind them, gripping their stern.

"Jump!" Hamish yelled, pushing open one of the forward windows and diving out through it.

Syme and Wolfe did the same and they all leapt clear as the boat was pulled wholly out of the water. They landed with matching splashes as the emperor lifted the boat seventy feet into the air and shook it like a broken toy. It peered inside it, looking for them.

Hamish swam for the shore. So did Syme.

Wolfe swam for a jetty off to their right. He arrived at it, reached up and began hauling himself onto its wooden slats when something grabbed his leg and wrenched him downward. Wolfe was pulled so forcefully, his head smacked against the edge of the jetty.

Hamish saw Wolfe's neck snap as his head

struck the jetty, the blow killing him in-stantly. It was a horrible way to die, but still better than being eaten alive by a dragon.

Hamish swam harder. He wasn't ashore yet.

With every stroke, he waited for the talons of a dragon to clasp around one of his legs and yank him backwards, but then he hit the shore, scrambled to his feet and ran for the tree line beside the ruined castle. Syme also made it and joined him in the trees.

They both looked back as a prince-sized green river dragon threw Wolfe's lifeless body onto the jetty with a thump and began eating it with foul bone-cracking bites.

Beyond that grisly image, the huge green emperor sank back into the lake, slowly slid-ing under the surface until all that remained were a few sets of ripples. Not one of the six boats they had launched from the café could be seen.

Every one of them had been destroyed.

CJ led Lucky, Li and Minnie through the tunnel that connected the Nesting Center to the Birthing Center.

They emerged inside the Birthing Center to find it empty — except of course for the crocs down in the pit and the olive swamp dragon. Having finished eating the red-bellied black prince it'd killed earlier, it had wrenched open one of the cages and was now halfway through devouring a crocodile.

A digital clock on the wall read 3:30 a.m.

Is it that late? CJ thought. She felt desperately tired but pure adrenaline was keeping her going.

She found a medical examination room. It had a stainless steel exam table with gutters and a drain plus a few carts filled with surgical equipment. It reminded CJ of her veterinary clinic back at the San Francisco Zoo, only it was bigger in every respect, dragon-sized.

She got Lucky to lie down on the exam table, left side up. In the light of her helmet flashlight's beam, she peered at the wound on the dragon's torso.

It looked terrible: it was a hideous slash, ragged at the edges, at least two feet long. Blood and puss oozed over exposed flesh.

CJ threw on a pair of rubber gloves and some anti-spray goggles and then grabbed a suture kit from one of the supply carts. She set about cleaning the wound. Li found a flashlight in a nearby cupboard, switched it on and held it over CJ's shoulder, providing more much-needed light.

Minnie watched. "Are you a doctor?"

"I'm an animal doctor, yes," CJ said as she found an ampoule of local anesthetic in one of the cupboards and injected it near the gaping wound.

She frowned. She had to close the wound. But the gash was so wide and Lucky's hide so thick, simple stitches wouldn't be strong enough: she would have to use staples.

Which would hurt, despite the anesthetic.

"Lucky. White Head sorry . . . big big pain . . ." she said before, *shwack,* she punched in the first staple.

Lucky howled.

Twenty-four staples later, the wound was secure and Lucky lay with her head pressed on its side against the steel table, panting, exhausted.

CJ stroked the dragon's brow. Lucky looked up at her plaintively.

"This'll make you feel a little better." CJ gave her a jab of Xylazine, a muscle relaxant, and the dragon sighed and visibly relaxed.

CJ ran her fingers over the small box attached to the left side of Lucky's skull. She gazed at the wires that ran from it into her brain.

It got her thinking.

Lucky's implant was special. It allowed for communication between her and humans.

But like all the other dragons, when she'd been an infant, Lucky would have had the other standard chip inserted into her brain, the one that sent an electric charge into the pain center when she touched the domes and which also contained a small wad of plastic explosive. CJ recalled the X-ray images of a dragon skull she had seen during the tour, showing the chip behind the dragon's left eye.

She leaned close to Lucky's side-turned head, peered at her left eye.

Lucky's eye was the size of a softball, a huge aqueous orb with a splotchy iris and a

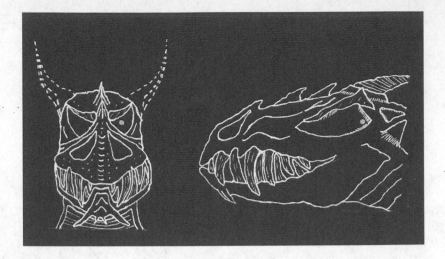

slit pupil.

CJ's gaze moved from the dragon's eye to its yellow-and-black skull. With her spiky crest and osteoderms, Lucky's head was heavily armored even before you got to the skull. Getting a chip inside it would've been difficult.

"Unless they went through the eye socket . . ." CJ said aloud.

She snatched up another ampoule of local anesthetic and jabbed it near Lucky's eyebrow. Then she grabbed a pair of scissorlike reverse-pincers and a curved silver surgical instrument.

Lucky saw it and grunted in panic. *"White Head . . . hurt Lucky?"*

"White Head like Lucky. White Head help Lucky. Lucky trust White Head," CJ said.

The dragon didn't reply. CJ wasn't sure the word "trust" was in its vocabulary. But Lucky did relax, gruffly exhaling as she tilted her head slightly lower, allowing CJ to work.

Trusting her.

CJ used the pincers to hold open Lucky's eyelid, before she reached in with the curved instrument and . . .

. . . gently popped Lucky's eyeball out of its socket!

Li gasped.

Minnie clutched her mouth to stop herself from throwing up.

The eyeball dangled from the optic nerve, still connected. CJ laid the huge eyeball carefully on Lucky's snout and not even noticing the indescribable grossness of what she had just done, grabbed a penlight and peered in through the exposed eye socket *into Lucky's skull.*

"There you are . . ." she said.

She could see it on the front of Lucky's brain, directly behind the eye socket: a small metal chip the size of a quarter. It looked like a spider, with eight wires stretching out from it, latching onto the brain.

Beyond that, it was quite crude. It had some circuitry on it plus a tiny silver cylinder that CJ guessed was the plastic explosive.

CJ grabbed a pair of long-armed surgical scissors.

"Stay still," she said to Lucky as, leading with the scissors, she reached *inside* the dragon's eye socket.

Her hand fitted easily, the socket was so wide, and with a few deft snips, she cut the eight wires. Then she reached in with some forceps and, looking more like a bomb defuser than a vet, ever-so-gently removed the chip.

It came out of the eye socket.

CJ placed it gently on a bench top on the far side of the examination room.

Then she returned to Lucky's side and carefully reinserted the dragon's eyeball, maneuvering the optic nerve gently back into the skull first. The huge eyeball slotted back into place, rolling around in the socket before Lucky blinked a few times and it was back in place.

"You, my yellow friend," CJ said, "are no longer susceptible to any electromagnetic domes. Nor can those Chinese bastards blow your head off anymore."

Lucky just exhaled loudly, braying like a weary horse.

As she removed her rubber gloves, CJ

turned to Li. "Now. Li. I need a lesson in main power lines."

While Lucky recovered in the infirmary, CJ and Li sat down in a nearby office.

It was 4:15 a.m.

Working by the light of their two flashlights, Li grabbed a sheet of paper and drew a quick sketch of the zoo and its surrounds . . . to which he added some prominent dotted lines.

"Here is the zoo," he said in Mandarin, "with the military airfield at the bottom left and the worker city at the top right. The two dotted lines entering the map from the corners are the main power lines."

"Got it," CJ said, also in Mandarin. "What I want to know is: if the dragons cut a main power cable, *can it be repaired?*"

Li said, "In theory, yes, if you have some replacement high-voltage cable *and* an insulation-repair kit. You see, it's not really the cable that is difficult to fix, it's the insulation layer around it."

"How so?" CJ asked.

"Main power cables are not regular cables; you don't just solder them back together. They are heavy-gauge HVDC — high-voltage direct-current — cables with a thick insulating layer of cross-linked polyethylene.

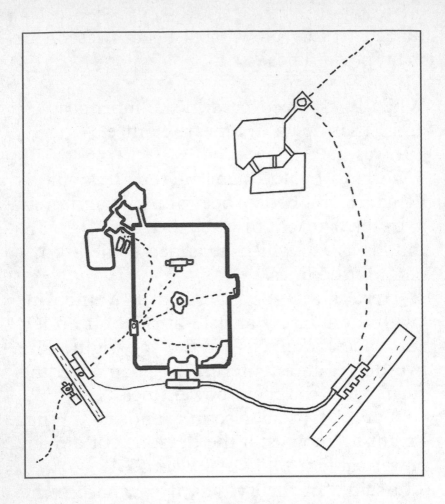

Because of the voltage flowing through them, they get very hot, which is why you need an insulation layer around them.

"It's the insulation layer that must be repaired correctly, without any air pockets or impurities. That's why you need the insulation-repair kit: it lays down a new insulation layer around the HVDC cable without any imperfections. If you don't get that right, you get no power."

"Do you guys keep any high-voltage cable and insulation-repair kits here at the zoo?"

"Not inside the zoo, no," Li said. "As you can imagine, cuts in the main are rare, almost unheard of. But we have fully equipped cable repair trucks at both *outer* power junctions, at the worker city and at the airfield. Those trucks have spools of HVDC cable and insulation-repair kits."

"Okay, right." CJ thought for a moment. "Damn it, I need more people . . ."

As if on cue, there came a crackling sound from a nearby battery-operated CB radio, hanging from a hook.

"Chipmunk, this is Bear. Do you read me? This is the 20 at 20 call. I tried at 3:20 but got no answer. Do you copy?"

It was Hamish.

CJ snatched up the radio. "Bear, I'm here!"

The voice at the other end lit up. *"Chipmunk! You're alive!"*

"Only just. Where are you?"

"I'm in the waste management facility. Syme is still with me but we lost Wolfe. We had a couple of close calls and our escapes weren't exactly works of art, but you know what Dad used to say, you've got to fail a few times before you succeed."

CJ blinked suddenly at his words.

"You've got to fail before you succeed . . ." she said absently.

An idea began to form in her mind.

She snapped out of it. "You called at just the right time, Bear. The dragons are about to bring down the outer dome and we have to stop them."

"How about we just leave this clusterfuck of a zoo to the punks who built it and get the hell out of here? I don't particularly like the idea of

saving their asses while they're trying to kill me."

"There's another nest, Hamish. A bigger one," CJ said.

There was silence at the other end of the line.

CJ added, "The Chinese only found a *small* nest. If the dragons get out, they'll go and wake the other nest and then there'll be a *whole* lot more dragons. The entire populations of any towns or cities near here will be slaughtered. Then the dragons will fly away and open *more* nests and it'll be an exponential expansion, a plague of dragons. We can't let that happen."

Over in the waste management facility, Hamish swallowed hard.

"Okay. What do you need me to do?" he said.

"Can you get to the military airfield?"

Hamish was standing near the huge barred external gates of the waste management facility. Through them he could see the many lights of the military airfield a few miles away across a flat plain.

He turned back to face the waste management hall, searching for a vehicle he could use . . . and he found one.

"I think we can do that, yes," he said with a grin.

"I need you to get to that airfield and protect the emplacements there. There'll be about fifteen of them and apparently they look like concrete pillboxes. You won't be able to hold the dragons out forever, but I need you to hold that dome up for as long as you can."

"What about you? What are you doing?"

"I'm going to the worker city," CJ said. *"Oh, and Hamish?"*

"Yeah?"

"There are two new dragons and they, well, breathe fire," CJ said.

"Of course they do," Hamish said wryly. "CJ. How do you know about this bigger nest and all that?"

"I've been talking to a dragon," CJ said simply. *"Gotta fly now. Out."*

CJ clicked off, thinking. "Sometimes you have to fail before you succeed . . ." she said.

She pursed her lips in thought. Then she turned to Li. "You," she said.

"Me?"

"I need you and one of those cable repair trucks. And I need you to come with me to the worker city. You up for it?"

Li thought for a moment. "You really

think the dragons will grow in number if they get out of here? That they will open other nests?"

"Yes," CJ said. "And then the dragons *they* release will open more nests. The numbers will get very big, very fast."

Li nodded. "Then I will come with you to the worker city."

CJ turned to Minnie. "As for you, little one, we have to keep you out of harm's way till this is over." She took the little girl's hand and led her to a barred cage in the corner. "You'll be safe here. Just do not leave this cell until I come back to get you, okay?"

"Yes, CJ," Minnie said.

CJ grabbed another flashlight, some food and some water from a nearby office and gave it to Minnie before she closed the barred door over her face.

Then CJ returned to Lucky in the exam room.

The dragon was standing now, testing the staples and stretching its wings. When expanded, the great leathery things almost filled the room.

"Lucky good?" CJ asked.

Lucky mewed. *"Lucky strong . . . White Head good human . . ."*

"Lucky . . . fight?"

515

The dragon turned to face CJ, a look of steely determination on her expressive face. *"Lucky . . . White Head . . . fight."*

■ ■ ■ ■

SEVENTH EVOLUTION

THE BATTLE FOR THE OUTER DOME

■ ■ ■ ■

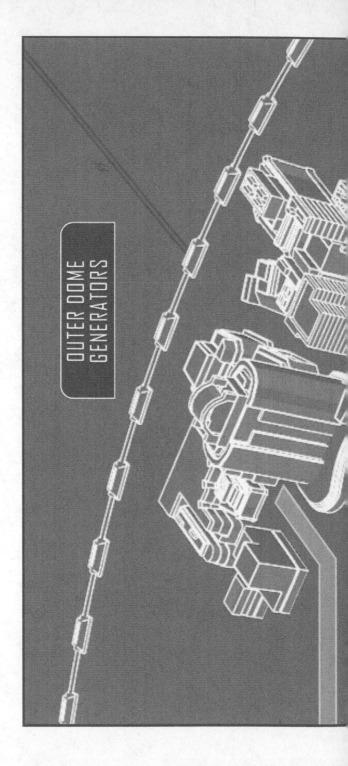

OUTER DOME
GENERATORS

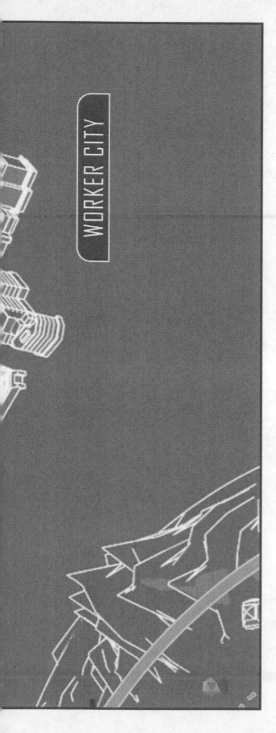

THE WORKER CITY

Come not between the dragon and his wrath.

— William Shakespeare
King Lear

Lucky soared high above the rectangular valley that contained the Great Dragon Zoo of China with CJ and Li on her back. It was almost five in the morning — an hour till dawn — and deprived of any kind of electrical power, the zoo was now just a shadowy collection of blackened landforms and buildings. The rain had stopped and the storm clouds had passed, leaving a beautiful star-filled sky and a glorious full moon above it all.

After about ten minutes of flying, CJ spotted a cluster of man-made structures a few miles beyond the northeastern corner of the zoo.

The worker city.

Seen from the air, it appeared to jut up from the plain: a few blocks of apartment buildings and office towers, warehouses and parks, and, snaking its way through them, a winding river. A couple of bridges spanned the river.

It was, to CJ, yet another example of China's amazing ability to simply build whatever it needed. The Chinese needed a miniature city here, so they'd just built one.

Several buildings were still under construction. Hammerhead cranes towered above them while the exposed levels of unfinished towers lay open to the elements.

There was only one problem.

The city was on fire.

Fires blazed all over it: from the upper storeys of buildings, to the shops at street level and overturned cars and buses.

The master dragons had been through here.

Unlike the zoo, the worker city still had power thanks to its external main power line. Amid the many fires, building lights glimmered and the streetlights were on.

Staying high, CJ peered into the urban chasms.

It was strange to see city streets so deserted and empty. Car alarms wailed, calling for owners who would never return. There were no people in sight.

The worker city was now a ghost city.

And then she saw the first dragon.

A huge gray emperor lumbered up onto the tallest building of the worker city and perched itself on the summit. There in the orange firelight, it raised its snout to the heavens and roared.

Twenty other gray dragons — kings and princes — swarmed up the other buildings, clambering up their sides, and joined their emperor roaring into the night.

"Gray dragons smell Lucky . . . smell White Head . . ." Lucky's electronic voice said in CJ's ear. *"Gray dragons . . . mean dragons . . ."*

"They're warning us off, but also . . ." CJ cut herself off.

They were not *all* looking in CJ's direction. Some of the grays were facing away from her, looking to the northeast.

CJ listened more closely, and with her trained ears, she detected something extra in their bellowing. There was a plaintive tone to it, a kind of keening. The keening of a dragon population that had laid claim to a territory . . . only to be pushed out by a bigger fish.

At that moment, two sudden flares of flame caught CJ's eye off to the right, at the extreme northern edge of the ghost city: two billowing extensions of fire that lit up the night.

Her gaze fell on an industrial complex over that way: it looked like a power substation, with a transformer farm and high steel fences. On its outer side, it was ringed by a curving arc of fifteen evenly spaced black concrete emplacements that looked like a miniature Maginot Line.

The small army of red-bellied black dragons from the Nesting Center — their red-and-black bodies were clearly discernible in the firelight — was gathered just beyond the power station. There were perhaps forty of them and they were led by their two masters, the superking and the super-emperor.

The two bursts of fire that CJ had seen had been fire-blasts from the two master dragons.

They were blowing fire at the concrete emplacements, in particular, the very middle one.

"No wonder the gray dragons are upset," CJ said. "The red-bellies barged into their city and took over."

Soaring high above the scene, careful to avoid being spotted by the two packs of dragons, CJ peered at the emplacements: the laser-emitting base stations that supported the outer dome.

Illuminated by the fires and the ghostly streetlights, they did indeed look like war-time pillboxes, solid, low and sturdy.

CJ flipped down her helmet's visor — stuck to which were her oversized UV glasses — and beheld the dazzling red grid of the outer electromagnetic dome. It slanted into the sky from the fifteen emplacements.

She flipped up the visor and looked more closely at the middle emplacement that was the object of the red-bellies' assault.

Alone among the fifteen emplacements, it was accessed by a service road coming in from the north. That road ran alongside a ditch in which she could see a reinforced concrete pipe: the high-voltage main power cable.

The dragons were going directly for the source of the dome's power.

"Li!" she called above the wind. "Where is the cable repair truck kept?"

Gripping her waist, Li replied, "In a loading shed inside that substation! What are you planning to do?"

"Right now, nothing," CJ said.

"Nothing? I don't understand," Li said.

"What I mean," CJ said, "is that in order for us to succeed in this battle, we first need to fail."

CJ brought Lucky into a landing on a small hill overlooking the emplacements and from there, she, Lucky and Li watched the red-bellied black dragons assault the middle one.

The dragons worked together with almost frightening efficiency.

The masters blew acid-fire at the emplacement — or more precisely, at the soil under it, liquefying the soil. Then some king dragons stepped in and raked out the melted soil with their huge claws. Princes positioned behind them cleared that soil even further. Then the masters would return and blow more fire, creating more melted soil, which would then be cleared away again. It was a digging operation.

The dragons had got a good head start. They had already created a substantial hole in front of the middle emplacement. It must have been four storeys, or forty feet, deep.

After a little more digging, the emplacement's foundations were exposed: a thick wall of gray concrete. The master dragons turned their fire on the foundations.

The two masters blew matching tongues of fire at the concrete foundations, softening them, before four red-bellied emperors did their part by flying in and flinging some buses and trucks *right at* the exposed foundations.

The vehicles slammed into the concrete

foundations, chipping away at them, cracking them.

Then the masters blew more fire and the circuit continued until, on the fourth go-around, with a screech of rending rebars and the crunch of cracking concrete, the foundations of the middle emplacement could resist no more.

They crumpled.

And like a slow-falling tree, the emplacement toppled into the huge hole the dragons had created in front of it, tearing itself free of its power source.

Sparks flew. Electricity flared.

And where the middle emplacement had been there was now a huge void with a thick high-voltage cable and some other minor wires sticking out from it.

The damage was done.

CJ flipped down her special glasses.

The dome was still there, only now it was not nearly as dazzling as it had been earlier. Now it was only half as bright as it had appeared before, since it was now being emitted only by the emplacements over at the airfield.

The two masters squealed in triumph and immediately took to the air.

They swept away to the southwest. Their army of red-bellied black dragons launched into the sky after them, heading in the direction of the airfield on the far side of the zoo: now the only thing standing between them and freedom.

From her vantage point on the hill, CJ watched them fly off.

She pulled out her radio. "Bear, this is Chipmunk. The dragons are coming to you. I need you to hold them out for as long as you can."

"Copy that, Chipmunk," Hamish's voice replied. *"We're almost at the airfield."*

"Try to stay alive, little brother." CJ clicked off and turned to Li. "Okay. Time for us to go in."

They leapt onto Lucky's back and zoomed down toward the worker city.

Hamish Cameron was driving like a maniac down the road that connected the waste management facility to the military airfield, at the wheel of an absolute beast of a vehicle.

Amid all the wreckage and debris inside the waste management facility, one truck had remained largely unscathed by the mayhem that had occurred there.

A fire truck.

It was one of the two superlong ladder trucks that had been parked in the cavernous hall when Hamish had first arrived there.

Now, driven by Hamish with Kirk Syme beside him, the huge semitrailer-sized rig thundered across the plain between the zoo's crater and the airfield. The extendable ladder on its roof bounced with every bump as the big truck boomed through the night.

The airfield loomed before it.

It was lit up like a Christmas tree: eighty floodlights blazed with white artificial light, illuminating cargo planes and fighter jets, storage hangars, an air traffic control tower, some support buildings and . . .

. . . about thirty Chinese Army jeeps and trucks arrayed in a defensive line in front of the airfield, with over a hundred Chinese soldiers manning them, their rifles and RPGs pointed at the very road Hamish was now racing along. There were even four Type-99 tanks in the defensive line.

"What are we driving into?" Syme breathed.

Hamish leaned out his window and looked up into the night sky behind him.

A swarm of black shadows, perhaps forty of them, blotted out the stars, dark aerial wraiths.

It was the flock of red-bellied black dragons and they were coming for the airfield.

"I'll tell you what we're driving into," Hamish said. "The last stand."

With booming thruster-blasts, four small Chinese fighters took off from the airfield, screaming into the sky, shooting out over the plain toward the incoming dragons.

They opened fire, sending tracer rounds lancing into the dragon pack.

Three dragons dropped instantly, squealing. The rest of the pack scattered and the fighters shot through their midst.

But then a few dragons, led by the superking, banked and gave chase and suddenly it was fighter jets versus dragons — while the rest of the dragon force, thirty-plus dragons led by the superemperor, descended upon the airfield.

Hamish looked up at the incoming swarm of dragons. With their huge batlike silhouettes, they looked positively fearsome.

But then he spotted something else about them, something odd.

All of the larger dragons — the kings and the emperors — were carrying objects in their claws.

Hamish squinted to see what the objects were and when he finally saw them, he gasped, "Oh, this is gonna be messy."

In their claws, the king dragons were holding Great Dragon Zoo cars and vans. The emperors, however, were carrying much larger objects: garbage trucks, whole pieces of the revolving restaurant, a section of the concrete ring road; one emperor even carried the smashed remains of the control tower that had once stood atop the administration building.

The dragons swooped over Hamish's fire truck — still half a mile from the airfield — and the battle began.

The Chinese launched their defensive measures.

RPGs shot into the sky. Gunfire rang out. The massive 125mm cannons on the four tanks boomed as they launched fragmentation rounds at the incoming creatures.

In the face of this fire, the dragons squealed, roared, wheeled and exploded. But they kept on coming.

Five dragons fell while the rest blasted through the wave of fire and, flying fast and low, the big ones released their improvised bombs.

Suddenly it was raining cars, vans and garbage trucks. They sailed down out of the sky and *slammed* into the ranks of Chinese military vehicles, crushing soldiers in an instant, bowling their vehicles over. The heavier garbage trucks caused the most damage. They were simply lethal.

Then came the larger objects.

The piece of the revolving restaurant's roof flattened a troop truck as it landed. The section of the ring road hit the ground with a colossal boom and tumble-rolled over two tanks and three troop trucks, crushing all of them. The control tower slammed into a hangar and took down all four of its walls before the roof caved in and the whole thing was levelled.

And then, having expended their aerial weapons, the dragons themselves entered the battle zone . . .

. . . and what followed was a bloodbath.

The lead superemperor landed on a tank, crushing it with its talons before the great beast let loose with a tremendous tongue of fire that incinerated three Chinese jeeps and two troop trucks.

Chinese soldiers fell to the ground, their skin melting before their eyes.

King dragons grabbed jeeps and hurled them away. Emperors picked up the tanks and flung them down the runway, tumbling end over end.

Up in the sky, the fighter jets returned, guns blazing, only this time three dragons — the superking, one emperor and one regular king — came streaking out of the air from the side, their bodies elongated, their wings pinned back.

They flew at phenomenal speed and on a

perfect intercepting course.

As the three big dragons intersected with the fighters, the superking spewed fire at two of them, lashing their cockpits, melting the pilots in an instant. The two fighters exploded in midair.

The emperor lashed out with a claw and tore another fighter's right wing clear off and that fighter went screaming into the ground, crashing at full speed in a billowing explosion.

The regular king simply collided with the last fighter and latched itself onto it, and to the pilot's horror, the fighter lost all its aerodynamics and began spiralling toward the ground. A hundred feet off the ground, the king released it and the fighter crashed into the side of the zoo's crater while the dragon just flew off, rejoining the other two as they headed for the battle at the airfield.

Watching all of this from the safety of a bunker just outside the electromagnetic dome were Hu Tang and Colonel Bao. They had arrived there by car only fifteen minutes earlier.

Their reinforced concrete bunker — a superstrong double-storey command post — sat just behind the line of fifteen emplacements that emitted the dome.

There was movement everywhere in the bunker: technicians at consoles, soldiers on radios, officers peering through binoculars at the disaster unfolding outside. Monitors and plasma screens showed various views of the dragons' onslaught.

A technician turned to Bao. "Colonel! Telemetry is confirmed: the outer electromagnetic dome is operating at half-strength. The dragons somehow disabled the emplacements at the worker city. If they knock out the emplacements on this side, the outer dome will fall."

Hu Tang stared incredulously at the scene in front of him. He hadn't thought this could get any worse, but it had.

He turned to Bao, panicked. "Did you hear that? They disabled the emplacements on the other side! Do something!"

"Be quiet, *sir*," Bao said calmly. "We still have options." He turned to an officer behind him. "Major. Prepare the thermobaric bombs: airfield, worker city and at the Halfway Hut."

"Yes, sir."

Hu Tang's eyes went wide. "You're going to destroy everything?"

Bao turned to face him, his eyes hard. "We have kept other eggs elsewhere, Minister. We have all the elements required to build another dragon zoo. What we cannot rebuild is our nation's reputation."

"Will *we* be safe?" Hu asked.

"Of course we'll be safe, you fool," Bao growled. "This command bunker stretches ten storeys belowground. It's strong enough to withstand a thermobaric blast on its doorstep while everything outside it will suffocate in the ensuing vacuum. Minister, hear me well: the moment those dragons bring down that outer dome, I will detonate all three thermobaric devices and destroy every living thing in and around this zoo."

The Chinese military airfield was crumbling under the dragons' attack. It was mayhem, pandemonium; a maelstrom of fire, explosions, carnage and death.

And it was into this that Hamish Cameron drove his ladder truck.

Hamish gripped the wide steering wheel with white knuckles. Syme sat by his side holding a pistol he'd found in the waste management facility. Given the circumstances, it seemed pretty puny and useless but he clutched it grimly anyway.

The entire airstrip in front of them was bathed in fire. The charred remains of Chinese Army vehicles lay alongside sections of the revolving restaurant's roof, the concrete ring road and the smashed control tower. *All* the Chinese jeeps, trucks and tanks were either overturned or smashed.

In the flickering orange light of the many

infernos, the dragons looked like monsters from the underworld: with their fierce red bellies, black skeletal hides, slavering jaws and howling cries, they were the embodiment of the word *terrifying.*

"Feels like we're driving into Mordor," Hamish muttered.

"What's Mordor?" Syme asked.

"Never mind."

Hamish floored it.

The big red truck reached the edge of the runway and banked wildly as it sped around a crushed tank and, with its immense weight, smashed right through the remains of a burning troop truck.

Hamish pointed forward. "They're going for the emplacements supporting the dome!"

Indeed they were. Having dealt with the defensive human force, the dragons were gathering at the line of emplacements behind the airstrip and its hangars.

Hamish saw the flare of the superking's fire-breath.

"Whoa, baby!" he exclaimed. "Here, take the wheel!" he called to Syme.

The U.S. Ambassador slid into the driver's seat as Hamish kicked open the door and leaned out.

"Where are you going?!" Syme yelled

above the inrushing wind.

"CJ told me to hold off those dragons for as long as I could, so that's what I'm going to do," Hamish said. "I'll be on the back. Get us to those emplacements, Mr. Syme!"

With those words, Hamish swept out of the truck's cabin, slamming the door shut behind him.

The fire truck wended its way through the fiery airfield. It sped past the wreckage of troop trucks, jeeps and cargo planes.

As the long-bodied truck swept through the battlefield, the small figure of Hamish Cameron could be seen on its back, slowly making his way along its length before he arrived at the hose station at the very rear of the superlong truck.

The hose station looked like a gun turret: an open-air revolving cannon, only instead of firing bullets, this cannon fired water.

Hamish dropped into the revolving chair of the hose station, found a switch marked INITIATE PUMP and looked up just as two prince-sized red-bellies landed on his truck right in front of him and roared angrily.

Hamish swung the water cannon around and jammed down on the trigger and a powerful column of compressed water came blasting forth, slamming into both dragons, knocking them off the fire truck!

"Take that, you reptile motherfuckers!" Hamish yelled.

But then, with a great *whump,* an emperor dragon landed right in the path of the fire truck.

In the driver's cabin, Syme yanked on the steering wheel and the truck swung right, disappearing inside a hangar.

The fire truck whipped past the shattered remains of a couple of planes and Syme ducked as the truck blasted through the rear wall of the hangar.

Syme raised his head again to see the line of emplacements now right in front of him.

"Not exactly the route I meant to take, but we got here," he said to himself.

The dragons were already there.

The two masters were blowing fire at the ground in front of the middle emplacement while other dragons dug.

Syme saw them and had an idea. He searched the switches on the console above him and found the one he was looking for.

The fire truck's lights lit up the area with strobing red rays while its siren wailed.

Blaring away with light and sound, the fire truck swept in among the gathered dragons and they all turned, surprised at the arrival of this loud, large beast.

The truck swept in front of the super-emperor just as the huge animal reared back, readying itself to blow liquid fire — at the exact instant that Hamish appeared in front of it and let fly with a blast from his water cannon!

The superemperor's fire was extinguished in its throat. It whimpered, confused, as Hamish brought his cannon around and blasted the superking in the face as well.

Then Syme was speeding away again and at a squeal from the masters, the red-bellied black princes leapt into the air and chased the troublesome fire truck.

While Hamish was racing around the airfield in his fire engine, CJ was speeding along in a different kind of truck.

After seeing the pack of red-bellied black dragons disable the emplacements on the perimeter of the worker city and then depart, she, Lucky and Li had flown down from their vantage point on the hill.

They headed straight for the electricity substation just inside the arc of emplacements.

The substation was deserted, its walls streaked with blood.

Lucky landed in front of a large warehouse and CJ and Li dismounted. Li threw open a sliding door to reveal several electrical repair trucks parked inside.

He went straight to the largest of them, an oversized white truck. This vehicle had a regular cabin but a specialized rear section which was filled with electrical spare parts.

"This is the worker city's main cable repair truck," Li said. He threw open one of its compartments to reveal a spool of thick copper cable, black insulation rubber and a very high-tech-looking silver box that was covered in digital displays. "High-voltage cable and an insulation-repair unit," he said.

CJ gazed at the parts.

"These dragons are smart," she said. "Smart enough to bring down the domes. But what they don't realize is that while they can destroy things, *we* can rebuild them. *We can fix the outer dome.* Repair it. I needed the dragons to succeed at this end and then head off to the airfield. Now, while they're attacking the airfield, we're going to repair the emplacements at this end. We needed to fail before we could succeed."

"Provided the others can hold the airfield long enough . . ." Li said.

"That's right. Which means we don't have much time. Here, you drive." CJ held open the driver's door for Li. "We've got to get to that middle emplacement."

They zoomed out of the shed.

It was a short drive to the middle emplacement, barely a mile, but the movement of the cable repair truck in the streets of the otherwise deserted city caught the attention of the eastern gray dragons.

They swooped from their perches atop some nearby apartment buildings, dive-bombing the truck.

A prince landed on top of the speeding truck, leaned over the front edge and smashed the windshield with a gray fist but, amid the hail of glass that washed over him, Li swerved, bringing the truck under a concrete overpass and the dragon hit the underside of the ramp and, with a screech of metal, was swept off the roof.

Emerging from the underpass, the truck turned onto the final stretch of road leading to the emplacement — just as a second gray prince came roaring in, only to be crash-tackled by Lucky, zooming in from above, and the gray prince thrashed in pain as it hit the road, its intestines spilling from its belly.

Only fifty yards to the emplacements.

Li risked a smile. "We're gonna make it . . ."

As he said it, the repair truck was hit with *ferocious* force by a gray emperor that CJ hadn't seen coming and which Lucky would never have been able to stop.

The immense dragon came roaring out of the sky and it lashed out at the truck, swiping it with one of its foreclaws.

544

The truck was lifted clear off the road and fell onto its side before it went sliding — on that side — at speed, down the road.

Both CJ and Li were wearing their seat belts so they were held in their seats as their world turned sideways.

CJ lay against her window, with the road speeding by only inches from her face.

They slid for some time — as they did so, their truck actually spun laterally — so when at last it began to slow, they were facing *back* toward the worker city.

With a lurch, the side-turned truck came to a stop.

Still fastened in her seat, CJ found herself looking through her truck's smashed windshield back down the road on which they had come.

Boom.

Four huge claws landed right in front of her: the giant forelimbs of the gray emperor.

Then the impossibly huge head of the emperor appeared outside the windshield, two feet away from CJ's face. It opened its massive jaws and growled. Saliva stretched between its fangs.

"We almost made it," CJ said. "Almost . . ."

She closed her eyes in exhaustion and waited for the end.

But for some reason the emperor didn't attack. It bellowed with rage at CJ's face.

CJ opened her eyes.

It was *right there.* It had them, but why wasn't it —

CJ flipped down her visor and saw some dazzling red laser grid-lines separating her from the dragon. Her truck's slide had ended just outside the electromagnetic dome, *inches* outside it.

CJ released the breath she'd been holding. "Now that's what I call close."

Beside her truck stood Lucky, also on the safe side of the dome. Since the yellowjacket no longer had the pain chip in her head, she had been able to pass through the dome unhurt.

CJ unbuckled her seat belt. "Come on, Li, let's get this truck upright again and do our thing."

■ ■ ■ ■

It took a little help from Lucky to right the truck, but soon CJ and Li were driving it up to the outer edge of the gigantic hole in the ground nearby, the hole into which the middle emplacement had fallen.

Frayed cables stuck out of the hole on three sides: first, the main power cable coming in from the north; and second, the two lesser cables branching off to each side, connecting that incoming cable to the other emplacements.

Thanks to the emplacements over at the airfield, the pulsing laser dome cut across the hole, separating CJ and Li from the pack of gray dragons now watching them from the other side.

Li backed the truck up to the edge of the void and got to work.

CJ helped as much as she could, unspooling replacement cable and holding insulation rubber while Li did the technical stuff.

As Li had said, reattaching the copper cabling wasn't that hard. It was insulating the new joints that was time-consuming. If the new connections weren't perfectly insulated, with no bubbles or imperfections, the new cabling wouldn't transmit enough power.

That was the function of the high-tech silver box: it was the insulation-repair unit that sealed the thick rubber layer around the new joints. But it worked slowly and they had three reconnections to make.

As Li worked, CJ kept an eye on the pack of gray dragons on the inner side of the dome. They looked like a flock of giant vultures, peering at their prey.

There were perhaps twenty of them, of all sizes, and they just glared balefully at the two humans working at the cabling not ten feet away.

"Okay," Li said. "The first reconnection is done."

"Only the first?" CJ said. "Can't you work any faster?"

"I'm trying to . . ." Li said, moving around the edge of the hole.

As she glanced worriedly at the gray dragons, CJ wondered what was happening over at the airfield. If the emplacements at the airfield fell before she and Li reconnected the cables here, not only would all the dragons at the Great Zoo be free, these gray dragons would pounce on Li and her in a heartbeat.

It was a race now, pure and simple.

Either she and Li succeeded or they died.

She keyed her radio earpiece. "Bear? You copy? How's it going over there?"

The radio squawked. Hamish's voice came in over the sounds of roars and explosions.

"Hey, Chipmunk! It's a clusterfuck of monumental proportions over here! They're trying to bring down the middle emplacement! We're harassing them but we won't be able to hold 'em out much longer. You?"

"Working as fast as we can. Out."

CJ spooled more cable to Li as he commenced the second reconnection. This required him to stand even closer to the gray dragons and they growled at him ominously. But the young Chinese electrician kept his cool as he worked barely three feet away from their drooling jaws. He waited patiently for the insulation unit to join this connection. It beeped.

"Second connection is done . . ." he said.

Li moved over to the other side of the hole to begin the final reconnection.

"Miss Cameron," he said, "stand by the truck, please. Once this last cable is connected, we will be ready to restart the power. To do that, you must first disconnect the truck from the main power cable: that is the switch marked DISENGAGE EXT SOURCE. Then you must throw the big blue switch labelled OPEN LINE.

CJ saw both switches on a nearby panel. "Got it."

Li kept working. He rejoined the cable. Then he stepped in with the insulation unit.

"Almost done . . ." he said.

CJ looked from Li to the dragons. "Come on . . . come on . . ." she whispered.

Over at the airfield, surrounded by fire and chased by dragons, Hamish's fire truck whooshed past an outlying hangar.

Consumed by their battle with the dragons, neither Hamish at the water cannon nor Syme in the driver's seat saw a panel in the floor of the hangar slide aside and a platform rise up out of the ground.

On that platform was a 6.5-ton fine aluminium/ethylene oxide thermobaric bomb.

It was about twenty feet long with a pointed nose and tailfins.

Second in power only to a nuclear warhead, it was the most powerful conventional weapon in existence. Its blast would vaporize *all* things within a three-hundred-yard radius while the ensuing shock wave would suck the very oxygen from the air, asphyxiating any living thing within a ten-mile radius.

At the same time, two other thermobaric

devices emerged from underground chambers around the Great Dragon Zoo, powered by independent emergency reserves: the first appeared inside the electrical substation in the worker city while the second rose up from a concrete chamber buried three hundred feet beneath the Halfway Hut, the watchtower-like cable car station situated halfway between Dragon Mountain and the main entrance building.

This device was lifted on a hydraulic elevator that rose within the struts of the hut until it came to a clunking halt just below the cable car station, the height from which it could do maximum damage.

Inside the Chinese bunker behind the airfield, a technician reported: "Colonel Bao, the three thermobaric devices are in place and ready for detonation."

Bao stood. "All personnel are to retreat to the alternate command center on the lowest level of this bunker."

The colonel and his staff, along with Hu Tang, caught a secure elevator to the alternate command center, ten levels belowground.

There, a series of display screens showed Bao real-time images of the airfield above: the dragons, the speeding fire truck, the flaming hangars. Those images were overlayed with an ultraviolet filter so that he could also see the red laser grid of the electromagnetic dome still in place.

He inserted a key into a console. Three red buttons shielded by clear-plastic safety latches illuminated.

Bao flicked open the three safety latches.

Then, as he watched the dome outside, he held his finger poised over the buttons that detonated the thermobaric bombs.

Kirk Syme brought the fire truck round for another pass at the dragons gathered around the middle emplacement. The big red fire engine came rushing in, sirens wailing, lights flashing.

The dragons had excavated a substantial hole by now, so large that the foundations of the emplacement were exposed.

Hamish had his water cannon ready to go, but then something unexpected happened.

The emplacement toppled into the hole.

Sparks sprayed outward as the emplacement tore away from its cabling and fell into the hole created by the dragons.

"No!" Hamish swore. "No . . . !"

He keyed his radio. "Chipmunk! We're cactus! The dragons just wrecked the main emplacement here!"

■ ■ ■ ■

Inside the underground bunker, Hu Tang
saw the red grid of the dome wink out . . .

. . . and then, to his absolute horror, he
saw the superking and two emperor dragons
swoop out over the line of emplacements.

The dome was down.

The dragons were out.

"God help us all," Hu Tang breathed.

Beside him, Colonel Bao reached for the
first red button.

FINAL EVOLUTION

THE LAST CONFRONTATION

THE LARGER NEST

A zoo is a place for animals to study the behavior of human beings.

— Unknown

Thirty seconds earlier, as Li performed the final reconnection, CJ flipped down her visor.

She saw the thin red grid of the dome separating the Chinese electrician from the pack of gray dragons on the other side.

And then the grid vanished.

Just blinked out.

Gone.

The dragons rose, their wings spreading, their jaws opening.

Li's head was bent over his work. He was oblivious to what had just happened.

"Last reconnection is . . . *done*!" he shouted. "Hit the switches!"

CJ flicked the first switch, disconnecting their truck from the main power line. Then she slammed down on the big blue switch labelled OPEN LINE.

A gray king roared at Li from a distance of three feet and readied itself to pounce at him when — *whack* — the dazzling red grid sprang back into place between them, and the dragon lunged into it only to fall instantly, like a boxer punched square in the face.

"Whoa," CJ gasped.

Over at the airfield, Colonel Bao's finger was mere inches away from pressing the first detonation button when a technician shouted, "Look! The dome! It's back up!"

Bao snapped up to see, on a screen, a fleeing dragon hit the dome and drop out of the air. The dome was indeed back in place.

"It's been restarted from over in the worker city!" another tech called.

"How many dragons got out?" Bao demanded.

"I counted three," someone said.

"I did, too," Hu Tang agreed. "One of the fire-breathers and two emperors. All red-bellied blacks."

"Only three," Bao said. "We can handle that."

Then he was up and moving: "Initiate the tracking chips for the three escaped dragons and send some gunships from Guilin to kill them! Get the internal power reconnected! I want somebody to tell me how the hell that dome got back online! And I want some fucking training units found so we can stun all the remaining dragons into fucking submission and drag them back into the valley! It's time to reclaim our zoo."

CJ keyed her radio. "Bear, this is Chipmunk. We got the dome back up."

"We could tell. But some of the dragons got out in the few seconds that the dome was down. A fire-breather and a couple of emperors."

"One of the fire-breathers . . . shit," CJ said.

"And who knows where they'll go."

"I know where they'll go," CJ said flatly. "They'll go to the larger nest and open it."

"Where is that?"

"I have an idea. And I have to get there fast to stop them, or else the whole world is going to have an unstoppable dragon problem."

Twenty minutes later, CJ found herself flying alone with Lucky over the spectacular moss-covered landforms of southern China.

She still wore her heat suit with the hood thrown back plus her lightweight helmet. She also still had her flamethrower slung over her shoulder, its liquid propane canister on her back underneath the heat suit, and her MP-7 with the grenade launcher duct-taped to it.

Dawn was coming.

The eastern horizon glowed pink. The beautiful landscape — lush, green and wet — glistened in the early morning light. A low-lying mist ran between the sheer-sided buttes and the steep mountains like a river. The near impenetrable rainforests of these parts meant there were few villages here.

CJ had left Li back at the worker city with instructions to get to the airfield. She suggested he drive there the long way, in a wide circle staying outside the dome — and, if he could, repair the main emplacement there. She even said he should inform his Chinese superiors that it was he who had fixed the emplacements at the worker city; but he needn't tell them he did it at CJ's urging or with her help.

After a few minutes' flying over this lush terrain, CJ beheld a singular landform: a wide meteor crater. It was perfectly round, like Meteor Crater in Arizona, only smaller. Over thousands of millennia, its vertical walls had crumbled in places and a lake had formed in its middle. A small forest had grown at its fringes, around the base of its inner wall.

The low-lying mist surrounded the crater, a soup of thick gray cloud.

CJ heard Na's voice in her head, from when she'd been talking to Seymour Wolfe about this very land formation yesterday:

"Crater Lake was created by a nickel meteorite that hit here about 300 million years ago."

And Zhang's voice from the tour:

"Our dragons — our archosaurs — survived the Alvarez Meteor 65 million years ago by hibernating deep beneath the surface of the Earth underneath dense nickel and zinc deposits."

And Hu Tang's comment about the nickel

deposit underneath the Nesting Center:

"Our zoo is built on top of the second-largest nickel deposit in these parts; the largest is over at Crater Lake about fifteen miles to the northwest."

The largest nickel deposit . . .

CJ figured that the bigger the nickel deposit, the bigger the dragon nest —

A blaze of orange light flared up from the inner wall of the crater and CJ saw a round hole at the base of the crater there. It looked like a tunnel.

Two red-bellied emperor dragons peered down into the tunnel, their backs to CJ.

Then another blaze of light flared out from within the tunnel and the black superking emerged from it. The two emperors immediately slithered into the tunnel and large chunks of melted soil — soil that had accumulated in the dragons' tunnel over the years — began to be flung out from within it.

"Shit," CJ said aloud. "They've already started digging for the nest." She hoped she wasn't too late.

Abruptly, the two emperors reappeared, barked something to their superking and the superking dashed inside the tunnel. The emperors then took up positions by the entrance, facing outward, standing guard.

"What are they doing?" she said aloud.

"Master . . . warm eggs . . ." Lucky's voice said. *"Wake nest . . ."*

"We have to get in there and stop it —"

A mighty roar cut CJ off.

The two emperor dragons were staring directly up at her and Lucky. They had spotted them.

One of the emperors took to the air with a great beating of its wings and charged right at them, roaring with rage.

CJ looked left and right for options, and saw something. She pulled Lucky into a steep dive and the chase began.

With its larger wings, the red-bellied black emperor was much faster than Lucky, but the yellowjacket prince was more maneuverable and as she and CJ shot down toward the fog layer, Lucky made a sharp turn that took the emperor by surprise and it overshot them by three hundred yards.

But then it banked around like an airplane and kept on chasing.

"Lucky! Down!" CJ called and with the emperor closing in behind them, they dropped into the mist.

From CJ's point of view, it was like being on a superfast roller coaster without any tracks and with only ten yards of visibility.

The walls of buttes and cliffs emerged

from the soupy haze with frightening suddenness and Lucky banked and bent superbly.

Crouched low over Lucky's neck like a jockey, CJ risked a glance over her shoulder —

— and found herself looking right into the jaws of the pursuing emperor! It was only a foot behind the tip of Lucky's tail!

CJ snapped to look forward and saw it.

"Lucky! Up! Now!" she yelled, pulling on the reins, and Lucky went vertical, avoiding a cliff-face shrouded in mist right in front of them.

The red-bellied black emperor, bigger and less agile, didn't.

It slammed into the cliff-face at full speed, headfirst. An almighty crash could be heard and a spray of rocks went flying out from the cliff-face and CJ heard a sickening *crack*.

The emperor didn't emerge from the fog.

CJ swung Lucky around and they risked a peek down at the base of the cliff. There they saw the body of the emperor, curled in a ball, neck twisted at an impossible angle. Dead.

"One down," CJ said. "Two to go."

CJ and Lucky looped around and returned to Crater Lake.

Lucky landed halfway up the rim of the crater, a few hundred yards from the second emperor standing guard at the tunnel's mouth.

CJ was trying to figure out what to do when Lucky's voice spoke in her ear.

"Lucky fight red dragon . . . White Head fight red master . . ."

CJ frowned. "What?"

"Lucky fight red dragon . . . White Head fight red master . . ." the dragon repeated. *"Lucky . . . challenge . . . red dragon . . ."*

CJ wasn't sure she understood until Lucky bucked gently, suggesting she get off.

CJ dismounted.

And immediately Lucky flew off, zipping out into the open, positioning herself *right in front of* the red-bellied black emperor.

Lucky pulled into a hover, lowered her head and barked fiercely: an invitation to joust.

The emperor snorted with contempt before issuing a low growl of pure anger.

With a lazy beat of its wings, it rose into a hover of its own and lowered its own head menacingly.

Challenge accepted.

CJ was torn. She didn't like Lucky's chances at all against the emperor, but she knew what Lucky was doing: Lucky was drawing the emperor away from the tunnel so that CJ could run to it and get inside . . . even if it meant an almost certainly suicidal joust with an emperor.

So CJ ran, dashing through the forest toward the tunnel's yawning entrance.

As she ran, the two hovering dragons glared at each other, sizing each other up.

CJ was almost at the tunnel when, with a bloodcurdling shriek, the emperor charged at Lucky.

Lucky launched herself forward in response.

Dragon rushed at dragon: the huge red-and-black emperor against the tiny yellow-jacket prince.

The emperor flexed its massive keratin claws.

Lucky streamlined herself as she sped forward.

CJ came to the tunnel entrance and looked up just as the two hurtling dragons came together.

Lucky rolled. The emperor lashed out. There was a slash of claws and an explosion of blood and . . .

. . . to CJ's horror . . .

. . . Lucky went peeling off to the left, her body lifeless, her wings and tail unmoving. Her body flew downward toward the edge

of the lake before it slammed into the shallows in a spray of water.

"No . . ." CJ breathed.

A far louder smashing noise made CJ snap around to look in the other direction.

The emperor, also wounded, went crashing into the hillside not far from her. It crunched through trees, turning their trunks to splinters before it, too, came to a crashing halt.

It moaned painfully, deep and loud. It wasn't dead, but it wasn't doing very well either. It tried to get up but instead it dropped back to the ground with a heavy *boom,* unable to lift itself.

CJ risked a glance around a tree trunk and saw that the great beast had a ragged gash running right up the length of its belly. Its huge intestines were pouring from the wound.

Lucky had completely eviscerated the emperor.

But at great cost. CJ turned to see the gutsy yellowjacket lying in the shallows of the lake, also still. She couldn't believe Lucky's courage. She had done this to give CJ a chance to stop the superking and CJ wasn't going to let Lucky's sacrifice be in vain.

Suddenly the emperor moaned again and CJ jumped in fright, but then the great beast slumped and, with a final sighing exhalation, went completely still.

CJ turned and gazed at the tunnel's yawning mouth.

It was just her and the superking now.

She hurried into the tunnel on foot.

The tunnel stretched downward at a steep angle, in a dead-straight line, cutting through the nickel.

CJ flicked on her helmet flashlight and hastened down it.

As she ran, she noticed the occasional flare of fiery orange light illuminating the lower end of the tunnel.

When she arrived at the base of the tunnel, she saw the reason for those flares.

CJ stood on a ledge high above an enormous — *enormous* — underground cavern. Like the nest back at the zoo, it was funnel-shaped — wide at the top, narrow at the bottom — with a single curving ledge running in a spiral all the way down its nickel-sided walls.

And lined up neatly on that spiral were dragon eggs: hundreds and hundreds of them.

CJ gasped. The nest at the zoo had held 88 eggs. *There must be over 2,000 of them here.*

In the middle of it all was the red-bellied superking, blowing gentle bursts of liquid fire around the cavern, warming it, creating the right conditions for the eggs to . . .

. . . an egg not far from CJ cracked. CJ saw a tiny snout pecking at the shell from within.

The egg was hatching.

Consumed with its task, the superking hadn't seen CJ arrive.

"Okay, genius," CJ said to herself. "What are you going to do now? How do you stop a ten-ton fire-breathing dragon?"

She checked her weapons: the MP-7 with its taped-on grenade launcher and the flamethrower with its liquid propane tank.

She looked out at the superking as it blew another tongue of fire.

That was its greatest strength — the ability to breathe fire — but perhaps it was also its greatest . . .

"Go hard or go home, Cameron," CJ said

572

aloud. "Win or die trying."

And so she laid her trap. It took her three minutes.

Then she sprayed fire from her flamethrower out into the cavern and called, "Hey! Fire-breather! Are you looking for me!"

The red-bellied superking turned at her shout.

CJ was standing in the mouth of the tunnel at the top of the enormous cavern, waving. She loosed another burst from her flamethrower.

The superking accepted the challenge and rocketed up at her.

CJ immediately turned and hurried back up the tunnel, making it about twenty yards by the time the superking appeared in the tunnel's entrance, filling it.

It roared, a deafening sound in the confined space.

CJ froze, as any normal prey would do.

The superking responded by doing what any normal predator would do: it folded its wings, stomped up the tunnel, reared its head and blew a great extended blast of fire right at CJ.

At which point, two things occurred that most certainly did *not* happen in the usual predator–prey dynamic.

First, CJ flipped on the hood of her heat suit, so that now her whole body was protected, just as the wave of fire rushed over her.

Second, the dragon's great tongue of fire ignited the pool of liquid propane that CJ had poured onto the tunnel's floor from her flamethrower's tank . . . a pool that extended out from where CJ stood down to the spot where the superking raged.

The propane pool immediately lit up in a curtain of blazing fire and suddenly the superking itself was engulfed in flames!

The dragon shrieked as its wings and skin caught alight. It bucked and thrashed against the walls of the tunnel.

Then its head was consumed by fire and the hideous flaming thing turned and locked eyes with CJ — to find her holding her MP-7 aimed directly at its face.

Braaaaaaaack!

CJ loosed a burst on full auto and the rounds slammed into the superking's eyes and forehead, ripping its skull apart. Its eyes exploded, shredded by bullets.

And the superking dragon fell.

It hit the floor of the tunnel with a monumental thump, its body still on fire. Its muscles twitched and then it went completely still.

The superking was dead.

CJ exhaled, utterly spent.

But she wasn't done.

Without hesitating, she strode past the burning body of the superking and headed into the cavern, still holding her MP-7.

Then, standing at the mouth of the tunnel above the massive cave, she fired off nearly every grenade she had in her grenade launcher.

Explosions rocked the cavern. Eggs blasted out in sprays of albumen before they caught fire and burned. The squeals of dying infant dragons cut through the air.

Then CJ aimed her grenade launcher at the ceiling of the cavern and fired off more grenades.

Under the weight of those explosions, the cavern's ceiling crumbled, dropping great boulders of nickel down on the eggs, smashing them, crushing them, while the curved spiralling ledge containing the eggs just fell away from the cavern's walls.

Eggs and nickel dropped down into the giant funnel-shaped cavern. Owing to the shape of the cavern, they all fell into the narrow base, where they were more easily crushed by the falling rocks.

In a final move, CJ stepped back up the tunnel, moving past the remains of the dead superking, and fired off her last few grenades there, causing the tunnel's roof to collapse and cave in.

The roof came down, flattening the corpse of the superking and blocking the exit, and leaving CJ Cameron standing there, breathing hard, her face blackened with soot and dust but her victory achieved.

Her ammunition spent, CJ tossed her MP-7 to the ground and began the long trudge back up the tunnel.

CJ emerged from the tunnel to see the first rays of sunlight peeking over the crater wall to the east.

She had survived the night.

No sooner was she out of the tunnel, however, than she dashed for the lake. She splashed to her knees beside Lucky.

The yellowjacket lay on her side in the shallows, moaning painfully.

She jerked suddenly at CJ's arrival — probably assuming CJ was the other dragon coming to finish her off — but then she relaxed when CJ began stroking her forehead.

"Easy, girl. Easy."

CJ saw a large gash running down Lucky's right hind leg: a terrible wound. She embraced the dragon, resting her head against Lucky's huge cheek.

Lucky sighed, a pained braying noise.

"White Head . . . fight master . . . ?"

"Yes," CJ said. "White Head fight master. White Head kill master."

Lucky grunted, still lying on her side. *"Lucky like White Head . . ."*

And for a short while the two of them just lay there together in the shallows of Crater Lake as the sun crept over the horizon.

After a time, CJ rose and took a look at Lucky's laceration.

It was an awful wound — right across the top of her thigh — but CJ figured if she could stitch it up, it would only affect Lucky's ability to walk. She should still be able to fly.

"This is not going to be pretty and not very hygienic either," CJ said as she fashioned a needle out of a sharpened stick and used her own bootlaces as thread. "And it's going to hurt like hell."

It hurt, all right.

Lucky howled in agony throughout the operation but eventually CJ stitched up the wound, drawing the skin firmly together.

Lucky panted quickly.

"Lucky stand?" CJ asked.

The dragon tentatively rose to her feet . . . and promptly fell down as the leg failed to bear her weight. But she tried again, favoring her other legs, and managed to hold herself upright.

CJ grinned. "You are one tough chick, you know that, Lucky?"

"Lucky no understand White Head . . ."

"White Head like Lucky."

The dragon nuzzled CJ. *"Lucky like White Head . . ."*

CJ then got Lucky to test her wings and the dragon proved able to fly. Not exactly powerfully; it was more gliding than flying, but it was enough.

And so, soon after, they were soaring over the forests and rock formations of southern China, heading back toward the zoo.

The sun had risen fully by the time CJ and Lucky beheld the vast rectangular crater containing the Great Dragon Zoo of China.

In the harsh light of day, the amount of damage that the dragons had done to the zoo was simply astonishing. Columns of black smoke rose from numerous sites around the megavalley, from smashed helicopters and destroyed buildings. The revolving restaurant at the top of Dragon Mountain had literally been ripped apart. Its two levels yawned open to the elements.

At 6:20 a.m., CJ keyed her radio to channel 20. "Bear? You out there? Bear, come in?"

Static . . . then: *"I hear you, Chipmunk."*

"Are you good?"

"Lying low after a shitstorm of a battle but not in enemy hands yet. Whatever you did, sis, it worked. The dragons are contained. The outer dome is working. I'm gonna guess that

whatever you got up to was character building?"

"You better fucking believe it," CJ said. "What about the Chinese? What are they doing now?"

"They suffered heavy casualties, but those who are left are on the move. Saw a fleet of jeeps zoom in toward the zoo ten minutes ago. What do we do now, Chipmunk?"

CJ was thinking the same thing. "Now we have to find a way out of this place —"

"CJ?" Another voice came on the line. A male voice, speaking in English. *"CJ, is that you? It's Ben Patrick."*

Patrick, CJ thought. She'd last seen him in the revolving restaurant, when he'd said she was crazy to be going into the Nesting Center.

"Ben? Where are you?" she said.

"I'm at the main entrance building. On the roof. I came over on a maintenance cable car. I can't believe you're still alive."

"Only just."

"CJ, the zoo is under control again, which means the Chinese are about to go into serious damage control," Patrick said. *"They'll kill all of us now to keep this disaster a secret. It's time to get the hell out of here and I know a way out. If you're still riding your yellow friend, meet me on the roof of the main*

581

entrance building as soon as you can."

CJ thought about that. "Okay. We'll be there as soon as we can. Bear?"

"Yeah?" Hamish's voice replied.

"I'll contact you shortly."

CJ and Lucky made two stops on their way to the main entrance building: the first was at the Birthing Center, where they picked up Minnie. CJ grabbed a portable surgical kit from the infirmary there: scalpels, stitches, anesthetic, cleaning alcohol. She also took the opportunity to clean and re-stitch Lucky's new wound with a sterilized needle and proper thread. She finished by giving the dragon a shot of epinephrine to make sure her heart rate and blood pressure stayed up.

Then, with Minnie riding pillion, they took off.

Their second pause was a quick stopover at the mountainside monastery on the eastern side of the zoo where Lucky's pack of yellowjackets lived.

CJ, Minnie and Lucky arrived to find Lucky's family very agitated by recent events, but after a short series of barked communications between Lucky and her pack, CJ performed a quick surgical operation on each of the four other yellowjacket dragons: on their left eyes.

Then CJ and Lucky, with Minnie, took to the air again and headed for the main entrance building.

The colossal main entrance building still stood at the southern end of the valley, but it was not looking its best.

The huge white building had been assaulted at some point by the rampaging dragons: many of its windows were shattered. The large eyelike circular window of the master control room had been smashed and the control room now lay empty, trashed and blood-smeared.

Suddenly, lights began to wink on all over the building . . . and all over the zoo. The Chinese must have driven the airfield's cable repair truck to the waste management facility and reconnected the internal main there.

As she soared in toward the main entrance building from high above, CJ saw the broad sunken amphitheater on its roof, the same amphitheater in which she had first seen Lucky.

And there, standing on the amphitheater's wide central stage, was a figure.

Ben Patrick, and he was waving.

■ ■ ■ ■

Lucky landed on the stage a short distance from Patrick. CJ and Minnie dismounted.

A light breeze blew. The vast valley stretched northward behind CJ. It would have been a postcard shot, gorgeous in the early-morning light, had it not been for all the fires and wreckage.

CJ began to walk toward Patrick — when suddenly Lucky nudged her and grunted.

"Lucky . . . no like . . . Big Eyes. Big Eyes mean human . . ."

CJ paused, glancing from the dragon to her old colleague, and for a brief instant she wondered if she had made a huge mist—

"CJ," Patrick said. "Thanks for coming. I'm so sorry."

CJ frowned. "You're sorry? Why — ?"

The answer stepped out from a door beside the stage: Colonel Bao, Hu Tang and three Chinese soldiers brandishing assault rifles.

Before CJ could react, Ben Patrick whipped out a Taser unit — like the ones she had seen in the observation booth in the Nesting Center — and jammed it against Lucky's flank. Sparks flew and Lucky dropped to her knees, squealing in agony.

CJ slid to the dragon's side, staring daggers up at Patrick.

She suddenly recalled the code he had given her to open the safe in the Nesting Center . . . and how it *hadn't* worked.

"You gave me the wrong code for the safe in Bao's office, didn't you?" she said. Beside her, Lucky moaned. Minnie huddled behind her.

Patrick shrugged. "To be honest, I didn't think you'd get that far. But I couldn't have you getting your hands on a detonator unit. There's too much riding on this place. For China and for me. This zoo will make me the most famous scientist in the world, CJ.

I couldn't have you succeed in killing the dragons. No matter what damage is sustained here, we *cannot* lose the dragons. Too much time and effort has gone into raising them. Buildings can be rebuilt, but those dragons are priceless. And they can always be retrained, no matter how harshly. The Chinese will rebuild this zoo, we will reintroduce the surviving dragons with new and better safety measures, and it will be like nothing ever happened."

Colonel Bao and Hu Tang stepped up beside Patrick.

Hu Tang said, "And we will bring new journalists here to marvel at it."

Bao nodded at CJ. "Dr. Cameron. You are a survivor, I will grant you that. But now it is time for us to restore control. A battalion of troops is on its way here from Chongqing in helicopter gunships. That force will arrive in a few hours and it will bring the remaining dragons into line."

With those words, Bao calmly drew his pistol. "You, however, will go no further."

CJ threw a horrified look at Minnie. "You're gonna kill this little girl, too?"

Hu Tang strolled toward the edge of the stage, gazed out at the magnificent sight. A few dragons could be seen flying across the valley, specks against the sky. CJ got the distinct impression he was looking away so he would not have to see the executions that were about to take place.

"She will tell someone eventually," Hu said, "and we cannot have that. This zoo is bigger than a few individuals, even a child. It will rise again and it will be the glory of the world."

He nodded at Bao. "Kill them both and take the dragon away for reeducation."

"You callous motherfuc—" CJ breathed.

She cut herself off when she heard it.

Beep-beep . . . beep-beep.

She didn't even have time to react.

The next moment something red and black leapt up from below the roofline and took a slashing bite at Hu Tang's face, and the front of the Communist Party man's head spewed blood and suddenly Hu Tang turned and CJ saw that *he no longer had a face.*

The dragon had bitten off his fucking face!

From forehead to jaw, Hu Tang's face was now a mess of pulp and exposed bone. It was perhaps the most hideous thing CJ had ever seen.

Hu's body collapsed to the stage, convulsing, not dead but not quite alive either, and standing there in his place was the one dragon who had pursued CJ since all this

587

had begun: the prince-sized red-bellied black dragon she had christened Red Face.

Bao and his troops didn't know or care for CJ's history with Red Face and they immediately opened fire on the dragon. In the face of their fire, Red Face took flight, disappearing as quickly as he had arrived.

Colonel Bao looked impassively down at the still-shuddering body of his old boss, Hu Tang. "How unfortunate." He fired a bullet into the faceless head and the body went still.

Then he turned his pistol on CJ and Minnie.

"You know something, Dr. Cameron? Just before your mentor, Dr. Lynch, died, he said something to me about you."

"You were there when Bill Lynch died?" CJ said.

"I was the one who let a dragon tear him apart," Bao said. "He said you were tougher than he ever was. This may indeed be so, but in the end, you will die just as he did. It is time for you to make peace with your god, Dr. Cameron, because you have nothing else to call on."

"She might have this, Colonel," a voice said abruptly over their radio earpieces.

A man's voice.
Greg Johnson's voice.

Bao spun, searching for the source of the voice. CJ did, too, but she couldn't see Johnson anywhere. She'd been kneeling beside Lucky. Now she stood, searching for the CIA agent.

"Down here," Johnson's voice said. *"In the Halfway Hut."*

CJ and Bao both looked out at the watch-tower positioned midway between the main entrance building and Dragon Mountain.

A tiny figure could be seen inside its struts, standing on a platform just below the Hut's cable car station, beside a large device the size of a small car.

"Dr. Cameron may not have anything to call on, Bao, but I do. I have your thermobaric bomb."

Bao's eyes went as wide as saucers.

"I've reset the detonation sequence," Johnson said. *"It's mine now. I have to destroy this*

place and everything in it."

"You would kill yourself to destroy this zoo?" Bao said.

"Yes."

"You're bluffing."

"I'm wounded, I'm pissed off, and I have absolutely nothing to lose," Johnson said. *"You can't control these animals, Bao. I'll blow us all to kingdom come to protect the world from these monsters. And if you think I'm bluffing . . ."*

Down at the Halfway Hut, Johnson held his radio close to the thermobaric bomb and flicked a switch on its detonation panel. A timer came alive, beeping with each tick:

10:00 . . . 9:59 . . . 9:58.

". . . think again. You have ten minutes to make peace with *your* god, asshole."

As this exchange took place, CJ edged over to the lectern on the stage. Unseen by her captors, she flicked on its control panel.

Bao raged. "This is insanity!"

CJ saw the button on the lectern that she was looking for, one she had seen hit during the trick show. With the power back on in the zoo, she hoped it still worked. She slammed her finger down on it.

Immediately, the pyrotechnic flamedischargers arrayed around the stage launched tongues of fire into the air. White smoke enveloped the stage.

And then everything happened at once.

CJ took two bounding steps and hurled herself into Ben Patrick, knocking him off the stage into the front row of seats and sending the Taser unit flying from his hands.

The two closest Chinese soldiers raised their guns at her only to be swept off their feet by a whip-cracking yellow dragon's tail. Lucky, groaning and weakened, had risen to her elbows and lashed out with her powerful tail, sending the pair of Chinese soldiers flying off their feet.

The third and last Chinese soldier opened fire at Lucky, but Lucky sprang at him and, with a fearsome swipe of her foreclaw, slashed his throat. Blood spurted and the man hit the ground, killed instantly.

Minnie screamed.

In the haze of smoke, CJ now dived at Bao, crash-tackling the colonel, punching his gun hand, sending his pistol skittering away.

They went sprawling toward the vertiginous northern edge of the stage.

Bao's legs dangled off the rim, four hundred feet above the world, while his chest still lay on the stage, his hands desperately gripping onto the lapels of CJ's heat suit, the only thing he could cling to.

But Bao was much heavier than CJ. His weight was slowly pulling her closer to the edge as well.

"At least we die together!" the Chinese colonel spat as their combined death-slide continued.

CJ struggled desperately but she could do nothing to release Bao's grip on her.

The edge came closer.

Then with a lurch, Bao's body dropped completely off the rim, and CJ — still held by him — found herself perched precariously on the edge, her head and shoulders overhanging it, staring down at the four-hundred-foot drop!

She searched for a weapon of some sort, something she could use to undo Bao's grip, but she found nothing. Not even Lucky could help; she was on the other side of the stage, too far away.

"Let's fly to our doom . . ." Bao said.

"Not . . . today . . ." CJ said grimly as she grabbed the one thing she could think to use: the saltwater crocodile's tooth attached to the leather cord around her neck. She reached inside her protective suit, yanked on the tooth, snapping its cord, and held the big sharp tooth tightly in one fist.

"Bill Lynch gave this to me," she said. "This is from him to you!"

Gripping the tooth like a knife, CJ brought it down on Bao's fists, stabbing them repeatedly.

Bao roared in pain and he released his grip on CJ's heat suit and the Chinese colonel dropped —

— only to snatch hold of CJ's sleeve on the way down and she went flailing over the edge with him!

As she went over the rim, CJ threw her hands out and caught the very edge of the stage with her fingertips.

Bao lost his grip on her sleeve as they fell, but he caught her heat suit's right leg and so now he hung from CJ while CJ hung from the edge.

CJ's fingers strained at the extra weight, her arms fully extended. She wouldn't be able to hold on for more than a few seconds.

"Like I said, we die together!" Bao called.

CJ's left hand lost its grip.

She hung one-handed above the deadly drop, with Bao dangling from her right leg.

And then she started wriggling, squirming strangely, releasing her free left arm from the suit and then using that hand to unzip the front of the suit. Then she reached up with that hand and regripped the edge with it.

Now she wriggled her *right* arm out of the suit and it suddenly came free —

— and the suit slipped off CJ entirely —

— leaving her hanging there while Bao fell away from her with the heat suit still gripped in his hand, the look on his face one of thunderstruck surprise.

And so while CJ dangled from the edge of the stage, now without her heat suit, Bao fell four hundred feet down the face of the main entrance building. About eight seconds later, he hit the ground with a sickening thud. He screamed all the way down.

Gasping for breath, drawing on her very last reserves of strength, CJ hauled her elbows over the edge, her feet still swaying above the dizzying drop.

The body of one of the Chinese soldiers lay right in front of her.

Beep-beep . . . beep-beep.

A dragon's head rose up from behind the dead body, staring right into CJ's eyes: the red earless face of her old nemesis, Red Face.

Lucky was too far away to help: she was

over by the front of the stage.

Half-hanging off the edge of the stage, CJ was defenseless.

And then she saw the weapons belt on the dead Chinese soldier between her and Red Face.

Hanging from it were a couple of —

"You want to eat something?" she said. "Eat this."

With those words, CJ reached out with her right hand, grabbed one of the hand grenades on the soldier's weapons belt, popped the pin and threw it directly into Red Face's open jaws.

The dragon gulped once, confused and shocked, as CJ called, *"Lucky!"* and released her grip on the edge of the stage, dropping away from Red Face an instant before the cruel dragon's head exploded.

CJ fell down the face of the main entrance building as, above her, the grenade blast blew apart the edge of the stage, sending a cloud of smoke and rubble billowing outwards.

She didn't see Red Face's head burst apart, didn't see his decapitated body convulse for a few seconds, blood pouring from its headless neck.

She hoped Lucky had heard her.

She fell fast, frighteningly fast. The windows of the building flashed by in front of her.

Then suddenly Lucky was there, flying vertically beside her, with her body elongated and her wings pinned back!

Lucky caught up with CJ and when they were flying/falling at the same speed, CJ reached out and grabbed Lucky's saddle and hauled herself into it just as Lucky swooped away from the ground with maybe thirty feet to spare.

CJ swallowed. "Now *that* was character building."

CJ and Lucky returned to the amphitheater to get Minnie.

They landed on the stage. Covered in smoke, bodies and blood, it looked ghastly.

CJ dismounted and ran to collect Minnie, cowering in the front row of seats. She scooped her up and was turning to hurry back to Lucky when someone stepped into their path.

It was Ben Patrick, standing on the stage. He was holding a pistol in his hand, aimed directly at her.

"Ben —" CJ said a split second before Patrick was bent almost in half, struck violently from behind. An awful *crack* echoed out: the sound of Patrick's back breaking, so powerful was the blow.

It had been a kick from Lucky, with one of her hind legs.

Ben Patrick dropped to his knees before he fell to the ground in front of CJ, landing with a perfect face plant. He moaned, but did not move. The kick had snapped several vertebrae. However long he had to live, Ben Patrick would never walk again.

CJ shook her head. "You chose your side, Ben. Sorry, but we've got to go."

She threw Minnie up onto Lucky's saddle and climbed up after her.

"Hang on, kid," she said. "We gotta fly fast. Lucky, *go*!"

Lucky zoomed away from the main entrance building, her wings spread wide, diving toward the Halfway Hut.

She came to a halt at the platform just below the Hut's cable car station, her claws clinging to the lattice of metal struts.

Greg Johnson sat there, bloody, wounded and pale. He sat with his back pressed up against the thermobaric bomb and he smiled grimly when CJ arrived.

"Well, look at you," he said. "Riding a goddamn dragon."

"I thought you were dead," CJ said. "I went back to the restaurant but the dumb-waiter was empty."

Johnson said, "I couldn't stay there. I had to keep moving. I went down to the cable car station and found a diesel-powered maintenance cable car. It brought me here." He nodded at the thermobaric bomb. "Then, about an hour ago I saw this baby rise up out of the ground. I finally found one of the bombs I've been tracking."

CJ looked at the bomb.

Its digital timer read: 5:02 . . . 5:01 . . . 5:00 . . .

"*Were* you bluffing? Can you stop it?"

"No," Johnson said. "I disabled the disarm sequence, in case they sent someone to kill me. This thing is going off whether we like it or not. It can't be stopped."

"Then we have five minutes to get away." CJ looped Johnson's good arm over her shoulder and brought him over to Lucky.

"Hamish?" she said into her radio.

"Yeah," came the reply.

"You got anything over at that airfield with wings and a working engine?"

"Not a thing, sister," Hamish said. *"This place is cactus."*

She thought a little more. "Wait, what about a car or a jeep?"

"Yeah . . ."

"Get into it and get it out onto the runway. We're on our way and we'll be coming in fast."

Lucky soared over the megavalley, weighed down by the three humans on her back. As she did so, she squawked a shrill call and a minute later, she was joined by her pack of four yellowjackets: the emperor, the two kings and the prince.

They descended on the airfield's runway, where Hamish and Kirk Syme were waving from a captured open-top jeep.

The timer on the bomb hit: 1:00 . . . 0:59 . . . 0:58 . . .

Lucky landed first, depositing Johnson and Minnie into the jeep a bare second before — *whoosh!* — the yellowjacket emperor picked up the entire jeep in its mighty talons and swept it up into the air.

Led by Lucky, with CJ on her back, the pack of yellow dragons then sped south as fast as they could, trying to put as much distance between them and the Great Dragon Zoo as possible.

0:30 . . . 0:29 . . . 0:28 . . .

The dragons flapped their wings powerfully, flying hard.

Buffeted by the wind, Hamish and Syme looked down from their jeep at the landscape far below. The huge body of the emperor carrying their jeep blotted out the sky above.

0:20 . . . 0:19 . . . 0:18 . . .

As she flew, CJ peered back at the rectangular crater that housed the zoo, the huge landform now a distant speck on the horizon.

0:10 . . . 0:09 . . . 0:08 . . .
CJ patted Lucky on the neck.
"Fly, Lucky. Fly," she whispered.
The timer ticked downward.
0:02 . . . 0:01 . . . 0:00 . . .
Detonation.

A flare of blinding white light flashed out from the Halfway Hut.

The lateral outrush of white-hot fire that followed immediately after it incinerated everything in the vicinity of the hut.

Then came the shock wave.

Terrible destruction radiated outward: trees toppled, cable car towers were thrown to the ground, the beautiful white castle blew apart, the roller coaster in the amusement park splintered into a thousand flying struts. The main entrance building's entire facade just fell away, ripped clean off it.

All the trees on the lower reaches of Dragon Mountain were flattened by the shock wave but the great mountain withstood it, the ravenous surge of energy racing around it like a river around a rock.

The blast wave fanned out in every direction. It shot northward, blowing out the windows of the casino hotel. Eastward and westward, it simply ran up and over the slanted crater walls, felling trees and flinging boulders.

And as the blast wave expanded, it sucked all the oxygen from the air. Any dragons in the air just dropped from the sky, instantly asphyxiated. Any on the ground just collapsed where they stood, the life in them extinguished in a single moment. The blast wave extended all the way to the worker city in the northeast and the airfield to the southwest, where it suffocated all the dragons gathered in those places as well. Any Chinese troops still in or near the valley were also killed.

It was the same for Ben Patrick.

His back broken, his body immobile, Patrick got to see the main entrance building's facade fall away from him. It would have been better to fall with it and die that way.

For it was then that the vacuum blast hit him . . . and sucked his lungs clean out through his mouth. Patrick's last sensation was vomiting up the two fleshy sacks that were his own lungs and seeing them right in front of his eyes. Only then did he black out and see no more.

The thermobaric device had done exactly what it had been designed to do: kill every dragon in and around the valley but retain most of the landforms and the basic infrastructure of the zoo.

As she flew away from the megavalley, having seen the distant flash of the blast, CJ sighed.

It was over.

The Great Dragon Zoo of China was no more.

Former Naval Station Magellan
Mindanao Province, the Philippines
20 March (Two days later)

When Mount Pinatubo erupted in 1991 it generated a massive ash plume that covered much of the Philippines. The local monsoonal rains had since mixed with that ash, overlaying many of the Philippines' more remote islands with a foul black sludge that made them all but uninhabitable.

Among those islands were several old U.S. military bases, most of which had lain abandoned since World War II.

One of the smallest and most remote of these was Naval Station Magellan. It lay ninety miles west of Basilan Island in the far south of the Philippines.

Assaulted for six months of the year by torrential rain and by stifling humidity for the other six months, it had little to recommend it. Its old airfield was potholed and overgrown with weeds. The mush from the Pinatubo eruption had caked the hills, making them useless for any kind of farming.

Which was why not a single human being noticed when five strange yellow beasts landed on the island's weed-strewn runway.

It had taken them two whole days of island-hopping to get here from southern China. The dragons had needed a lot of reassuring from CJ — speaking through Lucky — that there would be land on the other side of each stretch of dreaded salt water, but they had trusted her and braved each leg of the journey.

It had required multiple stops to cross the South China Sea, with the dragons needing to rest after each long glide. At times, the yellowjacket emperor had had to carry Lucky and the other prince on its enormous back, while it carried the jeep, since its colossal wingspan allowed it to glide for far greater distances than the smaller dragons. The emperor and the two kings could also, it appeared, fly quite a bit further than the few miles the Chinese had given them credit for. It was a tough, gruelling journey but in the end they made it.

Six hours before they'd arrived at Magellan, the yellowjacket emperor had deposited the open-top jeep — containing Hamish,

Johnson, Syme and Minnie — at the tip of another island containing an active U.S. supply base. They would walk from there, make contact with the personnel at the base and arrange to get home.

Only one member of the group continued on with the five yellowjackets and remained with them at Naval Station Magellan: CJ.

A month and a half later, a small Cessna "Caravan" seaplane with no transponder landed at the remote island. Its pilot was Kirk Syme, U.S. Ambassador to China and former naval aviator.

After it pulled to a halt, three men stepped out of it: Hamish Cameron, Greg Johnson and Syme. All were dressed in casual clothes. Johnson's left arm was in a sling.

Standing beside one of the old base's rusty buildings, waiting for them, were CJ and Lucky.

Hamish said, "So, how's the new home?"

CJ smiled. "It's got everything the modern dragon needs: fresh water flowing down from the hills and lots of big fat fish in the lagoons. Lucky and her family are doing just fine."

609

Three of the other four dragons peered out from the surrounding trees, watching cautiously. The emperor lay in the nearby freshwater lagoon, only its massive snout protruding above the waterline.

"They don't want to be found," CJ said.

"And we're happy to keep it that way," Syme said.

Johnson said, "I checked the intelligence logs: this base isn't even considered U.S. property anymore. And local Filipinos steer clear of the area. It's off the radar. Might as well be off the map."

"What happened with the zoo?" CJ asked.

Syme said, "We listened in on the cleanup. All the animals were killed in the blast, either incinerated or asphyxiated. The Chinese government issued a bullshit story about Wolfe and Perry dying in a car crash on a mountain road, their bodies sadly burned beyond recognition. They planted some DNA on the scene and the media bought it."

"What did you do about that?" CJ asked.

"What could I do?" Syme said. "What could I say? That they died after the Chinese government found, nurtured and put on display two hundred dragons and then lost control of them? I made a special report to the President — a verbal report — alone with him in the Oval Office. Your efforts, and those of your brother, were specifically mentioned. It'd be the end of my career if I put anything about this in writing. Either way, the Great Dragon Zoo of China is history."

"What about Minnie?"

"We returned her to her parents in Nanjing," Johnson said. "Since all the key players at the zoo are now dead, she should be safe."

Johnson changed the subject. "This island may have everything a dragon needs, but how is it for the modern woman?"

CJ smiled. "An old infantry tent isn't exactly the Ritz but it's okay. And I'm learning to love fish cooked on an open fire. There's some wild fowl on the island; they're scared shitless of the dragons. They taste like chicken."

She nodded at Lucky. "But then I'm not here for the lifestyle. I'm here for the company."

Hamish hefted a couple of containers from the back of the plane. "We brought you a few home comforts and some tools. Figured we might help you fix up one of these old buildings."

Hamish opened the containers to reveal a little diesel generator, jerry cans of fuel, some lightbulbs, a toolbox, power drill, screws and nails, a portable stove, some gas canisters and packet after packet of vegetable seeds. He also presented her with a satellite phone, a medical kit and batteries for her earpiece, which had run out of power a couple of weeks earlier.

"Thanks, Hamish," CJ said, "that's very thoughtful of you, but much as I'd like to, I can't stay here permanently. I don't think dragons and people were designed to live together. I've spoken to Lucky and she understands. I told her that she and her family must avoid humans. They've dug a deep den under the hill and they'll go there if any people arrive, however unlikely that may be. They just want to live in peace."

She stroked Lucky affectionately on the snout. The dragon purred.

"That said, I'd like to come by here every now and then to visit my friend, and having a solid roof over my head would be nice."

"How would you get here?" Syme asked.

CJ said, "Thought I might take a job in Darwin, down in Australia. Lot of crocodile jobs there and it's only a few hours' flight time to here. Figured I could take up flying lessons and, well, if I could somehow get my hands on a plane . . ."

"You know," Syme said, "the President

told me very specifically that a reward of some kind was in order for your efforts, Dr. Cameron. I think I might be able to find some spare funds in my budget to help you purchase a decent plane. After all, there's got to be *some* reward for saving the life of the U.S. Ambassador to China and preventing a global outbreak of dragons. In fact, if you ever need *any* money for *anything,* you just give me a call, okay?"

CJ smiled. "Thanks. I will."

The four of them spent the rest of the day rebuilding one of the base's shacks, flanked and followed by the family of yellowjacket dragons.

At one point in the course of the day, Greg Johnson said to CJ, "I was wondering if, you know, we ever found ourselves on the same side of the world, you'd like to grab a coffee sometime?"

CJ looped a stray strand of hair over her ear. "Are you asking me out on a date, Agent Johnson? I don't get asked out on many dates."

"I might be."

"I'd like that," she said, smiling.

When the day was over, they all returned to the seaplane. It was time to go.

CJ stepped to one side with Lucky and

gave the dragon a huge hug. Tears welled in her eyes.

"White Head like Lucky," she said.

Lucky mewed. *"Lucky . . . like like . . . White Head . . . Lucky sad . . ."*

"White Head sad, too." CJ gave the yellow dragon a kiss on the snout. "But White Head will return."

And with those words, she walked off to the seaplane.

A month later, CJ Cameron resigned from her position at the San Francisco Zoo and took up a senior role at Kakadu National Park in northern Australia, outside Darwin, observing and studying the large saltwater crocodile population there.

Many of her students commented on how fearlessly she treated the big crocs. CJ would just shrug and say, "I've seen bigger."

And her colleagues gently ribbed her about the handsome American gentleman with the salt-and-pepper hair who would swing by every few months to meet with her.

She also took up flying lessons.

Soon she was flying solo in a compact Pilatus PC-12 that she'd bought secondhand from the Australian Flying Doctor Service. A small plane, the PC-12 was known for its considerable range. It became common for her to fly off alone in her plane, "Just to spend some time on my own for a few days," she would say.

None of her colleagues noticed that the plane always flew north from Darwin, out over East Timor and Indonesia, toward the remote southern islands of the Philippines.

They did notice, however, that she always returned from these trips with a faraway but very contented smile on her face.

ABOUT THE AUTHOR

Matthew Reilly is the international best-selling author of numerous novels, including *The Five Greatest Warriors, The Six Sacred Stones, Seven Deadly Wonders, Ice Station, Temple, Contest, Area 7, Scarecrow,* the children's book *Hover Car Racer,* and one novella, *Hell Island.* His books are published in more than twenty languages in twenty countries, and he has sold more than 7 million copies worldwide.